WRAITH LORDS OF ZEIGLON

WAR OF STAFFS TRILOGY: BOOK TWO

STEVE STEPHENSON & K.M. TEDRICK

BLACK ROSE writing™

ISBN: 978-1-61296-905-3
PUBLISHED BY BLACK ROSE WRITING
www.blackrosewriting.com

Printed in the United States of America
Suggested Retail Price (SRP) $19.95

Wraith Lords of Zeiglon is printed in Garamond Premier Pro

"To my Mom, who passed away last February 2016.
Her support and belief in my writing will always be with me.
–Kathryn M. Tedrick

"Thank you to my family and my mother who always believed."
–Steve Stephenson

Praise for the *War of the Staffs* Series

Hard-core fantasy and sci-fi fans will become enraptured with this book from the opening chapter. The authorial duo's sequel to *War of the Staffs* delivers a fast punch in genre fiction and follows up with a stunning series of breathtaking events that will keep readers enthralled from start to finish.

In the magical world of Muiria, the vampire lord Taza continues to weave intense dark spells in a demonic attempt to find the missing piece of the Staff of Adois that will restore full power to the relic and bring the world under his exclusive control for evil purposes. Taza uses a dark warlock named Melgor to find and destroy Taza's nemesis, the great wizard Celedant, who accompanies Prince Tarquin, the prophesied savior of the world, on a dangerous quest to find the missing Staff piece, encountering horrific attacks by earthly and inhuman bands of assailants.

Freedom and existence itself is at stake for all Muiria dwellers, and the adventurers who are desperately seeking the lost Staff piece successfully bring together supporters that include elves, dwarves, humans, and other races who join forces against Taza's dark magic to save their beloved world and peaceful way of life. Against the backdrop of the raging conflict that flares in unspeakably violent battles destroying life and limb, tender romance begins to blossom between pure-hearted souls who find each other in the midst of a war-torn landscape and mythical quest. Loyalties are tested and lives are lost in the classic battle between good and evil.

Admirable heroes, humorous sidekicks, knowledgeable healers, and powerful rulers vie for survival and ultimate control in this epic battle of good vs. evil. This is a book that readers will never forget. The authors have crafted a work of art that deserves a place of honor in contemporary fantasy / sci-fi fiction.

~ Roman A. Littlefield, author of *Say What You Really Mean*

Wraith Lords of Zeiglon

CHAPTER ONE

Taza relaxed on his black onyx throne, drinking a goblet of deep red wine laced with blood, as he mused over the loss of the dwarvan city of Brackus and the other schemes he had devised that had not gone the way he had hoped they would. Even though the city had suffered considerable damage and vast numbers of enemies were dead, his attacks against Celedant, Dragon Isle, and the dwarves had been miserable failures. Obviously, the beasts he had summoned from the void to attack his enemies were not powerful enough, which meant he would have to spend more time within that desolate dark nothingness to find others who would be.

He was also less than pleased with the minions he had to work with on this planet. With the exception of Melgor and Sellis, the Warlocks' Council was reluctant to become involved in global warfare, preferring to sit back on their magical backsides and observe. Well, Taza had news for them. Once his army of vampires held complete dominance over the races of the continent, the council would either play by his rules or join the ranks of his underlings under the subjugation of the Illanni, the first – a race of dark elves – to accept his offer of undead life. Only then would the world be safe.

Taza rested his head against the back of his throne. All this plotting, planning, and fuming had given him a headache. It was late. Tomorrow was another day. Closing his eyes against the pain, the vampire decided to retire as he thought fondly of his darkened bedchamber and the comfortable bed waiting for him.

However, as he stood to leave, the Staff of Adois began vibrating, gently at first, but then harder and harder. Puzzled, Taza exerted his will to control the staff, but found it impossible, even with his vampiric strength. A moment later, his vision blurred and his stomach churned as something ripped him from this reality and threw him into another. When his vision returned, he found himself standing in a vast, unknown hall.

The room was unadorned expect for row upon row of polished black marble columns. Taza estimated the room to be over a hundred paces long. As his gaze fastened on the distant wall, he saw an elaborate, white marble throne with carvings and shot through with veins in three shades of brown. Precious jewels were set into the eyes of mystical beasts, including vampires, chimera, basilisks, ogres, orcs, and numerous other dark creatures. A luxurious deep-red carpet six feet wide stretched the length of the room to a magnificent throne. Seated upon a pure white cushion made from unicorn hide was a beautiful woman who beckoned him to come closer. Curious, he moved toward her, the staff making no noise as it struck the carpeted floor. The silence was complete until he reached his destination and drew in a breath. Without knowing how, he realized that the woman motioning to him was the Goddess Adois.

As Adois reclined, she nibbled on a slice of juicy orange fruit. She wore a low-cut, white-silk gown that accentuated the curves of her shapely body. Taza smiled. His fangs were visible as he strutted up to her, the Staff of Adois firmly clutched in his right hand. This was the goddess who had rescued him from the Void, brought him to Muiria, and set him upon his present task. If anyone could help him defeat the races of light, it was she. The undead warlock, however, was suffering from delusions of grandeur. He did not see Adois as his mistress but as an equal, and he did not bow to his patroness as he came to a stop before her. Goddess or not, she was female, and after being betrayed and imprisoned by his own mother, Taza had little respect for the fairer sex.

The deep black, cat-like eyes of Adois stared at the proud vampire. She could read the contempt in his mind. His aloofness was obvious in every cell of his body. Never before had another being, other than a fellow deity, approached her thus. Adois had expected the meeting to be tense, but Taza was proving to be tougher to handle than she had anticipated. Finishing the fruit, the goddess licked her fingers and then tucked her long black tresses behind her ears. Smoothing her clinging silk dress with a motion of her hand, she struggled to regain control of her temper. Otherwise, she would have struck him dead on the spot, and that would not do, not if she wanted Muiria back in her control.

Taza bowed his head in the briefest nod. "Madam Adois, I am here as you requested."

Adois' hands tightened on the arms of her throne as she thought, *This is what I chose to be my champion?* That statement echoed in her mind, fueling a fire that burned in the pit of her stomach. Her voice was honey sweet, but as she spoke, it filled with granite determination.

"I plucked you from the Void and gave you life and the means to conquer a planet, yet you address me as Madam?"

"I mean no disrespect," Taza replied, but the sneer on his face revealed otherwise.

"I did not ask you to come. I commanded. You may wish to believe the little fairy tales you spin for the Illanni, but I assure you, you are nothing compared to me!"

Taza jauntily leaned against the staff. "The Staff and I have bonded, and we are one. You poured your magical abilities into its creation, but now it is mine to use as I wish." His smile was wide, prominently displaying fangs still stained from the blood-laced wine he had drunk earlier.

Adois became calm, chastising herself for reacting to the words of such an insignificant worm. She leaned back, hidden mockery in her voice as she responded. "Such is true, Lord Taza. I have summoned you to discuss what progress you have made in my brother's world."

Taza waved away the question. "There have been a few unforeseen but not insurmountable difficulties. It is hard to judge how races will evolve or react. Still, things are progressing, thanks to a number of grasping fools, greedy to share in the spoils. Yet, I must deal with powerful enemies that seek your brother's staff. Even if they find it, they will not be able to master it. Then I will have both rods of power, and Muiria will be mine."

Adois shook her head like a mother about to scold a young child. "Fool! My brother's staff is an artifact of light made by his hands, unlike mine, which was crafted by a warlock I highly favored. But I should expect such words from a pawn like you." Her tone and response raised Taza's ire. "Let me assure you. Regardless of if they find my brother's staff or not, I expect results, and my patience wears thin."

"We have more than enough time to see to our goals," Taza answered, ignoring the dangerous tone that had crept into her voice. Realizing he would get no help from her, he recklessly plunged ahead. "Don't worry your pretty little head. I will handle everything."

Adois' eyes narrowed. She had had enough. It was time to put this petty vampire in his place. Standing, she moved to within five steps of him and stopped. He watched with a bemused expression until she began to transform. Taza's arrogance disintegrated into the most gut-wrenching fear he had ever experienced as the beautiful creature before him morphed into the most monstrous thing he had ever seen.

The lovely silk dress and lithe figure became a muscular, hideous beast with skin resembling the tough hide of a rhinoceros, clothed in a heavy robe the color of blood. Her face lost its delicate features as it broadened, giving her a protruding flat brow with heavy eyebrows. Large yellow eyes with slits like a snake's and two holes where her nostrils should had been completed the distorted face. Her hair was no longer the long silken tresses it had been. It became a short cap of bristly white fur. Her hands and feet stretched into cruel claws with long fingers and toes that ended in six-inch nails capable of slitting a person open as efficiently as the sharpest blade, and wicked curving horns protruded from her head. Her smile turned Taza's insides to water. She opened her mouth and roared her displeasure, which sent his robes flapping; her vampiric fangs gleamed wickedly, as did all the razor-sharp teeth in between. "You foul, insignificant little worm," she sneered in a voice that had lost its honey sweetness to become deep and guttural. "Your small mind cannot begin to comprehend that vampires were created from a higher being and are thus accountable to me. Look upon the visage of your goddess!"

She pointed to the staff and using the tiniest portion of her power, sent a surge of energy through it, cramping and twisting every muscle in his body. An unbearable agony tortured Taza, making all the others he had experienced seem like a scratched finger. His neck constricted so tightly that choking sounds emerged from his lips as his eyes grew larger, and the bones of his body bent and broke one by one, driving the once-proud vampire to his knees.

"You will do *my* bidding," Adois growled, "or suffer the tortures of the damned for eternity! And no one will dare rescue you this time."

Taza blacked out from the pain, and when he regained consciousness, he found himself lying in a fetal position on the stone floor of his tower, surrounded by four of his personal guards. Unable to speak for the moment, the guards took their stricken lord to his chamber and settled him into bed with a drug-laced goblet of wine.

The next morning when Taza awoke, his bones were once again whole, thanks to the vampire's ability to heal quickly. The fear that he had experienced at the hands of his goddess, however, still lingered around the edges of his psyche. When young, he had wondered how the first vampire had come into being, but since no one knew, he had let the matter slide from consciousness. Now that he knew who she was, there was no doubt in his mind that if he did not succeed in conquering this world and turning it from a place of light to one of darkness, the centuries he had spent in the void would seem like a pleasant interval compared to what Adois would do to him.

Rising, he ordered his guards to bring two victims to his chambers, and he drained them to restore his strength, motioning the guards to remove their corpses. A new determination formed in his mind. He would find a way to beat the races of light and drive them into a subservient existence under his rule. He would destroy Celedant and Tarquin along with anyone else who dared to resist him, even if he had to bring forth every dark creature that lurked in the void to do it.

CHAPTER TWO

When Morganna joined Tarquin, Celedant, and the dwarves in their quest for the last piece of the Staff of Adaman, she added to the unusualness of such a mixed group. Celedant befriended the solemn, formerly dark elf and often took her into his confidence. When introducing her to the others, Tarquin had assured them that had she not appeared when she did during the battle, her vampire cousin, Despres, would have killed him. From birth, Morganna's natural coloring had always been more like a Wood Elf with long, dark tresses and deep olive green eyes, unlike her Illanni family with their platinum hair and deep black eyes. After she had accepted her quest from the dwarvan god, Dolgar, her transformation, both physically and mentally, was completed. Although Morganna had been born Illanni and lived as such for hundreds of years, she was now a true Wood Elf.

With the rebuilding of Brackus well underway and the fortifications to the underworld improved, constantly manned by vigilant dwarves, General Grimilzor proclaimed that the city proper was safe and ready for habitation. At first, while the army celebrated victory and mourned their dead, no one but the civilians that had followed the army had access to the city.

Grimilzor proclaimed a distant removed relative of the long-dead Lord Brackus as regent of the city. The new Lord of Brackus commanded a force of 5,000 dwarves and 2,500 human Parthian lancers to defend the city. Even though the dwarvan command believed that the horrible losses suffered by the local orcan tribes made the area reasonably safe, they wanted to assure a long and peaceful stay for the dwarves and settlers heading north to repopulate the city.

After the new regent took command, General Grimilzor ordered the rest of the army to ready themselves for the long march home. It would be a slow, careful march back to the dwarvan capital of Nars. Soldiers headed south while long lines of heavily loaded wagons meandered north, clogging the roads. The prospect of working the long lost mines and new territory prompted many adventuresome dwarves and Parthians to undertake the trip to the Brackus to seek their fortunes and a new start in life.

After escaping their harrowing experience in the tunnels, Donli and Count Eldahir, Commander of the elven army in the south and son of Celedant's long-time friend, General Orthorion, finally reached Brackus and began looking for the wizard. The tall, handsome Wood Elf had received orders from his father and Queen Elornith to help the wizard in his quest, while making certain that the Staff of Adaman did not fall into the wrong hands.

The wizard and the company occupied a suite of rooms above the entrance hall, and Eldahir had no trouble finding Celedant's chamber. Diffused morning light filtered through deep shafts cut into the mountain, illuminating the hall and room above through a broken stone lattice where the wizard and his companions had fought their desperate battle to open the city's gates. He crossed the hall, noticing the scattered remains of orcish occupation and the darker stains of blood that marred the floor.

Soon he found himself striding along a carved hallway, which contained an etched and painted mural that had once been quite beautiful. He was dismayed that the orcs had defaced such a work of art with their crude carvings. Even his olive-green, elven eyes could appreciate the master artisanship of the dwarvan masons and painters. However, it had always been the orc's innate nature to despise all objects of beauty both animate and inanimate. Beauty was a head on a spike to that ill-bred race.

Halfway down the corridor, a solitary dwarf stood guard at what Eldahir saw had once been a secret door in the defaced mural. At this time, the doorway stood open, guarded by the small wary dwarf with a black beard, wearing the gray uniform of the Borderers.

The elf stopped in front of the dwarf. "I'm in search of Master Celedant. Is this where he is staying?"

The dwarf looked suspiciously at him and nodded. "Who wants to see him, might I ask?"

The elf smiled. "Tell him, Lord Eldahir of the Elven Court."

The dwarf eyed him suspiciously before slipping into the inner chamber, leaving Eldahir in the room to examine the remaining latticework that had survived the awesome power that only a wizard of Dragon Isle could possess.

Before long, a white-robed man with deep blue eyes, looking far younger than he ought to for a human his age, appeared and bowed to the elf. "Count Eldahir, please forgive my friend, Botreg. He is one of the most suspicious dwarves I have ever known. Yet, his alertness saved us many times, during our trip through the underworld."

Celedant led the elf into the next chamber where Eldahir noticed the bedding along the walls.

"The Borderers that journeyed through the underworld with me use this room as a barracks. Come sit by the fire. It would seem that winter is approaching fast and these halls can get very cold. Please feel free to warm yourself." They seated themselves on low benches near the hearth where the wizard had brewed water for tea. He handed a cup to the elf. "What brings you to see me, Lord Eldahir?"

"Please, can we drop the formalities between us?" Eldahir replied sipping the strong brew and smiling in appreciation. "My father told me of your quest and asked that I seek you out. I would like to offer my services to get a better idea of what is happening, so I can keep him and our new Queen apprised of the situation. Though I must admit, from what I have seen thus far, I feel certain my people will want to participate in the coming battle."

"That is good news indeed." Celedant chuckled. "I learned recently of the murder of your king and queen, a heartbreaking and cowardly act to be sure. Please send my condolences and well wishes to the young queen."

"Thank you. I will."

"Orthorion was chomping at the bit to accompany me on this mission. Since he could not, the old dog has sent his son instead. I fear he will forever plague my footsteps. But in all seriousness, I welcome your assistance and agree that what we face affects all races."

The elf stared into the fire's dancing flames and sipped his tea. "I believe you know about the creatures in the tunnels." When the wizard nodded, he continued. "Although initially I was sent to be an observer, I found I could not sit idly by and watch. With Captain Donli as my guide, I went into the tunnels seeking you and your company."

"You are your father's son," Celedant replied.

"Needless to say, we were attacked, and as I was about to kill one of the Illanni undead; he spoke to me. No, more correctly, he pleaded with me to save the dark elves, and he advised me to seek you out."

"Curious indeed," Celedant said, wrinkling his forehead. "Why would an enemy ask you to seek me out?"

"Whatever the reason behind the plea, the Illanni vampire knew you may be the key to the destruction of the evil that has taken control of his people," Eldahir told him. "Even more disturbing, he realized that he was a distant relative of mine, and as he died, that kinship or bond between our two races overcame the evil that had corrupted its body. That was why he begged me for help. I believe there is a link between what we face and the cause of the defilement of the Illanni."

"I agree. I have recently learned that several Illanni have formed an underground movement to fight the vampires. One of their leaders saved Tarquin's life and has joined my quest."

"Is that wise?"

"Yes, indeed. Just wait until you meet her." Celedant then related the story of Morganna's transformation from Illanni to wood elf.

"That is an interesting story. It will be good to meet her, but tell me. Do you know where these brethren came from?" Eldahir asked. "Never in our long history have I heard of such creatures."

"The one responsible is named Taza, a vampire that was brought through the void by the goddess, Adois." Celedant related the story of Taza that Morganna had told him. When he finished, the wizard cleared his throat and whispered. "If you wish to accompany me, I will be leaving within seven days along with a few trustworthy companions. We are approaching a critical time for the races of light, and the journey will be dark and fraught with danger. Yet the rewards may save this world from the evil that has risen to such power." He eyed the elf and continued. "In the morning, I will explain to those who accompany me the dangers we will face. Meet us at the mouth of the valley at sunrise a week from now, and I will unveil our quest."

The elf stood. "I shall be there."

The morning the wizard had designated ultimately came, Donli and Eldahir joined Celedant and the surviving members of Tarquin's squad at the head of the valley. The wizard gathered them all together and explained that they were seeking an item that could end the spread of evil in their lands and the abomination that had been brought through the void, Taza.

The party headed for Nars on horseback down a secondary trail, where they would meet up with Hortus, an Abbot to the dwarvan god Thierry, to examine some maps of the ruins of Zeiglon, where rumors proclaimed the remaining piece of the staff was located. Winter was once more upon them, and the journey would take two weeks. Although Celedant felt the need for urgency, he decided not to push the horses too hard.

One night after the evening meal when everyone was asleep but Eldahir, who had taken the first watch, Celedant felt a familiar tug on his mind. Rising from his bedroll, he slipped through the trees, carefully picking his way across a thick carpet of dead leaves and twigs covered with a light dusting of new-fallen snow. After walking three hundred paces, he reached a large clearing, filled with the presence of Azimuth, a magnificent, one-hundred-fifty foot, golden dragon.

"What a wonderful surprise," Celedant exclaimed as he approached his dearest friend and the dragon he had bonded with upon entering the Wizard Academy on Dragon Isle so many centuries ago. "What brings you?"

Azimuth lowered his head to allow the wizard to rub his neck ridges. His rumble of pleasure sounded like a deep purr in the otherwise silent forest.

"My mate and I were relaxing in the aviary, surrounded by our dragonets when for some reason, I felt guilty."

"Really? Why is that?" Celedant replied with a knowing smile as he brushed a few errant flakes of snow from his shoulder-length, chestnut-brown hair. "I thought about you out here, risking your life on a quest for an ancient artifact that could change the course of the war, while I relaxed among my family and fellow dragons. So I decided to join you."

Celedant chuckled. "What you really mean is that the dragonets were driving you crazy so you decided this would be the perfect excuse to get away for a while."

Azimuth gave him a wolfish, draconic grin. "Exactly."

"I would like nothing better than to have you along, but are the dragons ready to reveal themselves to the world at large?"

"I fear that with the coming war, we may have no choice. Wouldn't you agree, Lord Eldahir?"

Startled, Celedant turned to find the elf entering the glade next to him. "I wish I knew how to move as silently as an elf. It would be a great benefit at times."

"I did not mean to intrude," Eldahir apologized. "But when you left camp and did not return, I thought it best to make sure some mishap hadn't befallen you."

"I appreciate your concern," Celedant replied honestly.

"When I sensed his approach, I thought it best to include Lord Eldahir in our conversation," Azimuth explained.

"Thank you," Eldahir said with a bow of respect. "It has been many years since I have had the honor of speaking to a dragon, let alone to the esteemed leader of all dragons. To answer your question: I share your concerns. Although elves, wizards, and sorceresses have known and interacted with the true dragons for centuries, the rest of the world has always believed that fire drakes are dragons."

"Those puny little pretenders are an embarrassment to my kind," Azimuth grumbled. "But for the safety of all concerned, we have always felt it better to keep the knowledge of our existence from the others."

"Considering how immense dragons are, compared to fire drakes, I have always believed that decision to be a wise one," Eldahir agreed. "But with the kind of evil the world is now facing, I don't think the dragons can sit back and watch from the safety of Dragon Isle."

"And I agree. For the past week, my fellow dragons and I have been in council to discuss the situation, and we came to the same conclusion." Turning to Celedant, Azimuth continued. "Even though as their leader, I could have commanded it, I decided that all should have a say on whether or not to enter the fight. You will be happy to know that we all agreed that our presence was crucial. In fact, I had to draw the line and restrict the younger dragons under the age of two hundred. They will remain on Dragon Isle to care for the dragonet's, in case... If the rest of us were wiped out, their existence would insure the continuation of dragon kind."

Celedant patted his friend reassuringly. "That's not going to happen. So what's your plan?"

"From now on, we will assist in all major battles. In the meantime, I have sent several spies to infiltrate the major cities and governments."

Celedant and Eldahir looked so surprised that it was Azimuth's turn to chuckle.

"How is this possible?" Eldahir asked. "Your immense size would make it..."

"Impossible? Yes, it would, but we don't plan to appear as dragons."

This announcement left his audience dumbstruck.

"But how?" Celedant asked.

"Like this," Azimuth chuckled.

The dragon's immense body disappeared in a whirling mass of confusion, and a moment later, the figure of a tall, handsome, High Elf, complete with long, golden blond hair tied back in a ponytail and deep lavender eyes stood before them. Azimuth spoke his next words naturally in a smooth, baritone voice.

"I am sorry we had to keep this ability secret from everyone. But it was decided long ago that we would not reveal our tri-nature until it was necessary."

"Tri-nature?" Celedant and Eldahir both said at once.

"You mean...there's more?" the wizard asked.

"Yes and the ability should prove quite fortuitous on our journey. I'm too large and noticeable to travel with you as a dragon, and since you don't have a spare horse for me, whenever we're on the move, I will travel in my third form."

As he finished speaking, the elf became a large, muscular golden wolf and his voice once more filled their minds. "When in this form, I will need to communicate telepathically, since neither my wolf nor dragon vocal cords are capable of human, elven, or dwarvan speech." Changing back to an elf, he continued. "The rest of your party will need to be told of my ability to become a wolf, since it would be impossible to hide. However, I think for now, we should keep my true draconic nature to ourselves. At least until a situation arises where returning to my dragon form would be more beneficial."

"Agreed," Celedant said, shaking his head in continued amazement. "What else are you keeping secret?"

Azimuth smiled wickedly. "That, my bonded friend, remains to be seen."

"We had best get back to camp before the others awake and come looking for us," Eldahir said. "I will leave the explanation of Azimuth's sudden appearance to you, Celedant."

The wizard nodded in agreement. As they headed back to camp, Celedant has to ask, "Why a High Elf?"

Azimuth chuckled. "No offense, Celedant. Appearing as an elf makes perfect sense. As the guardians of the world, the dragons have infiltrated human, elven, and dwarvan cities for centuries. No one has ever realized that we weren't true elves. If we looked human, it would be extremely difficult to explain our long lives.

Some of our dragons spend centuries in the same city."

"That makes sense," Celedant agreed.

"As for my looking like a High Elf, our appearance is regulated by our draconic coloring. Since I am gold, my hair would naturally be blond. The lavender eyes just came with it to complete the disguise. Berlundi my mate being a red dragon has red hair and brown eyes, so she looks like a Wood Elf.

"Fascinating," Eldahir marveled. "I wonder how many elves I know are really dragons?"

"Maybe someday, I'll enlighten you," Azimuth said with a chuckle.

CHAPTER THREE

Sellis the teleporter was a vain man with straight black hair and light brown eyes. He knew his love of money and good living had badly affected his mastery of magic over the years and could be his downfall. Nevertheless, he had spent those years with one goal in mind, and that was to make certain that when he retired, it would be in the lap of luxury.

Things went sour when Melgor, Taza's chief henchman, sent Sellis to the abandoned dwarvan city of Brackus to retrieve the rhodium crystal, belonging to the Staff of Adaman. Before Sellis could find the crystal, he came face-to-face with his old nemesis, the Wizard Celedant.

The warlock struck first. Pointing his slender staff, the words of a spell left his mouth and streaked toward the wizard, enveloping his magically constructed shield.

Then Celedant launched his own attack, pointing his index finger at Sellis. "Electriskt Kastasig."

Sellis spun his staff before him, and the beam struck the spinning staff.

Although the wizard was stronger, the warlock drew substantial energy from the dark forces that lent him additional power. Celedant drew more power from his staff Forestae and as Sellis weakened, green energy engulfed the warlock, and Sellis blinked.

Taza or no Taza, I've got to get out of here, or I am sunk! Using Nashmeol, his ring of teleportation, he disappeared in a blink of the eye, reappearing inside a hidden treasure vault he had discovered by accident many years earlier. The warlock had already looted it rather nicely, taking the treasure to his home hidden in the myriad of city-states.

He gathered up the last of it and fled through the ethereal plains, reappearing in the mansion he had built for his retirement. The grand estate was equal to any aristocrat's, consisting of twenty-five elaborately decorated and furnished rooms and sitting on two hundred acres of fertile land with ancient oaks that lined both sides of the main road. His nearest neighbors were wealthy members of the city-states, including a Duchess' youngest brother.

Working as fast as possible, Sellis began transporting the rest of the treasure to his new home and was about to teleport with the last of his belongings when he felt a slight tug at his mind. The room swam before his eyes, and his muscles cramped, wracking his body with pain. He dropped the remaining sacks of gold. This was one of the strongest spells ever cast upon him.

"Celedant, no!" He screamed. Should the wizard succeed in pulling him back to the scene of battle, punishment or death awaited him, his dreams of a wealthy retirement gone forever.

Although he fought it with every ounce of magic he possessed, the little warlock soon lost all control and blacked out.

He awoke on a filthy stone floor in total darkness. Confused, he listened for any sounds and searched for a source of light, but came up empty. The warlock gingerly sat up, drawing his legs beneath him and touching his eyes to be certain he was not blind. Reassured, he felt the index finger of his right hand for the Ring of Nashmeol, a teleportation device he had depended upon for years, and he smiled when he realized he was still wearing it. Picturing his estate, the warlock tried to teleport there, but nothing happened. Sellis then tried casting a simple spell to produce light, but as he spoke the words, the spell dissolved like sparks from a dying fire, swallowed by the suffocating blackness that surrounded him.

This is bad, he thought. *Really bad.*

The warlock stood up and extended his hands over his head, in case the ceiling was low. Encountering nothing but air, he cautiously explored his prison, sliding one foot in front of the other in case of holes or drop-offs. When he had gone about ten feet, his hand touched a damp, cold, rocky wall, which he followed by touching it with his fingers as he slid his feet onward. At some point, Sellis bumped into a stone staircase, which he climbed, finding a solid wooden door at the top. No matter what he tried, however, he could not open it. In frustration, he sat on the relatively clean top step and used his handkerchief to clean the dust and muck from his exquisite boots.

Now what?

The warlock had never been in a situation where his magic was useless. He tried to calculate how long he had been in darkness, but had no way of determining if it was day or night outside. Such gloom could be deceiving, but he was certain that the darkness came from a spell, one that limited his vision and dampened his magic as well.

As he sat and contemplated, he accepted the fact that he was a prisoner and his jailor was Celedant. *Maybe not,* he thought. *This feels too dark to be the work of the puritanical wizard. In that case, who is my jailor? Is it Melgor or Taza?* Sellis cleared his thoughts, allowing his conscious mind to flow into a deep meditative state to conserve his strength.

After what seemed like forever, he fell asleep, curled up on the top two steps. The magical battle with Celedant had left him so exhausted that he never heard the tiny click of the lock or the well-oiled hinges as the door to his prison opened outward. He did not feel the gag or the coarse bag pulled over his head, until it was too late. Jerking awake, he tried to fight his captor until rough hands seized him and forced him to face the wall.

Chapter Four

Still shaken by his encounter with Adois, Taza was furious. So far, an ancient wizard and a human man-child had overcome his underlings and their traps. This was unacceptable. Then there was Melgor. What was to be done with him? He contemplated the warlock, who was formable in his own right. Melgor, however, was his most valuable asset in this endeavor. He was Taza's eyes and ears in the world of light, and he alone could be trusted to tell the truth and face the consequences of his failures.

"What to do? What to do?" he muttered softly to the cavernous room.

Taza had dispatched a monstrous flying creature that morning and used a spell to inform Melgor where he was to rendezvous with the beast. The trip would be a three-day journey for Melgor, giving Taza a brief moment of wicked glee. He had searched the Void for hours until he found the right mount. He chose a chimera, a dangerous, formidable beast, whose unpredictable nature was sure to strike terror in Melgor's heart. Extremely rare on Muiria, the Staff of Adois had plucked this one from its home world, and it towered above most species living on the planet, except for the dragons, of course.

The undead warlock moved to the outer wall and stared through an open space, a simple crenellation five feet wide and seven feet deep. There were ten such openings evenly spaced about his tower room. Taza was a vampire, but the staff of Adois had brought about changes in his physical and mental awareness, allowing him limited exposure to the sun's deadly yellow rays. Unable to tolerate the light any longer, he drew the heavy black draperies across the opening and turned, emitting a dry scream of frustration that echoed through the nearby mountains as he contemplated the dwarves and the Parthians, who, in his mind, were a symbiotic pairing from the lesser hells.

Even now, their ambassadors rode from place to place, reminding allies of an accord signed centuries ago and persuading them to honor it. One of Taza's spies had stolen a copy, and the treaty read that if the eastern territories were threatened, the elves and other races would give military aid to the Dwarves and Parthians and vice versa. Moving across the not quite barren room, Taza dropped onto his onyx throne. Despite his meddling, he was certain that most of the allied nations would gather troops against him to honor that agreement. Did they not understand that he was offering a peaceful world to all the denizens of Muiria?

After consulting with his font, the outcome for the battle for the dwarvan city of Southgard was uncertain. Still, if the dwarvan city did not fall, it would bleed the East dry of defenders and resources. Melgor could be trusted to do that much at least, but his right-hand warlock had warned him of possible discord in the giant-led army, thanks to Sellis's murder of the former giant king several months earlier.

Regardless, many would die pushing these behemoths back into the hills. Taza did not trust humans and considered transforming them into zombies. Although the approaching armies would cause many human villages and wild tribes that had not pledged support to him to evacuate. His vampire captains would see to the slow transformation of those foolish enough to stay behind.

While he contemplated his woes, the captain of his guard waited discreetly with a scroll. Looking up, Taza motioned the vampire closer. He unfolded the piece of parchment and read then reread the missive again, dropping his hands onto his black-robed lap while allowing the letter to flutter to the floor. Another frustrated scream echoed through the tower as Taza slumped, cupping his head in his hands.

The dragons had pledged their support to Celedant and Tarquin. The silly prince, leading the quest, was no longer a child. He had become a skilled warrior. On top of that, the Wood Elves had also agreed to honor their pledge, although the High Elves had offered no support as of yet.

Taza's enemies could summon the best of their races against him. What did he have in response? The warlock's overly cautious council, orcs, wild humans, mercenaries, and an incompetent group of giants so stupid, they would be next to useless in any situation that required even the simplest kind of strategy. He had struck at the dragons with an elemental creature summoned from the void, and although they had been vulnerable, their superior forces and age-old magic had won the day. Now it was time for a strike against the High Elves that would cause them to stay home and defend their precious forest. A single fire elemental could be overthrown without trouble, but if he gathered thousands of such creatures, the elves would never be able to stop the elementals in time. Their homes and forest would go up in flames.

It was a grand idea, and he relished the thought of striking at those aloof dullards. The best part of this plan was that he and the Staff of Adois would not have to venture into the void to enlist the aid of the fire elementals. They already existed on this planet in the form of fireflies, and the ageless warlock could exert his power to summon an even larger elemental from the bowels of the earth to negotiate for the use of an army.

Taza stood at the black onyx font near his throne and spoke the words of a spell that would summon the most powerful fire elemental on Muiria. The font's water swirled and boiled as ominous smoke drifted from its surface. When the water finally calmed and flattened out like a sheet of dark glass.

Then, a white-hot face appeared with red and yellow flames flowing off it.

"Who dares to summon me?" a deep, crackling voice asked.

"I require aid. In return, I will bestow upon you that which you most desire," Taza replied, unfazed by the creature's ire.

"What could you possibly offer that would interest us, vampire?"

The warlock wanted to destroy the arrogant being, but he needed its cooperation. He decided to be politic. "I offer you an entire mountain range, where you can create the perfect haven for your kind. Imagine a chain of mountains that you could mold with your lava instead of being trapped underground with limited air to keep your flames alive."

The elemental eyed him thoughtfully. "That would indeed be grand. However, I am wary. When could this be arranged?"

The warlock kept his face neutral. "Within the next two years."

The elemental creature laughed, shooting white-hot flames from its mouth. "Two years is nothing to us. We have existed for millennia, and we will continue to do so unto the planet's dying days. Speak your desire."

Taza smiled. "Nothing elaborate; just a few thousand fireflies banded together to feed upon some prime elven forest."

"They would enjoy that and will be at your command when you require them," the elemental said. "But I warn you, do not back out of your end of the bargain. No matter where you live, I can find and destroy you."

Taza gave the elemental a cold stare. "I have no intention of backing out." *You, however, will never receive your reward, and there is nothing you can do about it.*

Chapter Five

The next morning Celedant introduced Azimuth to the others, as the company began to ready their mounts for the long trek to Nars. Count Eldahir penned an urgent message carefully worded and written in old elven script to his father and Queen Elornith. If it fell into enemy hands, it would be undecipherable to most. In essence, the letter spoke of the victory at Brackus, and the unspeakable horrors that had been unleashed in the northern mountains. The letter went on to say:

These attacks are the direct result of a vampire named Taza, who is in possession of the artifact we spoke of during our last meeting. Celedant has learned that this monster is not natural to our planet. The vampire is turning the Illanni into creatures of its own making. I have also learned, through personal experience, that these so-called anointed ones' feed off the blood of the living. In addition, they retain their living magic making them powerful foes. Rest assured, I am unharmed, but our people need to know that the only way to kill such demons is with fire or by cutting off their heads, which causes them to explode into dust. All other injuries, no matter how serious, heal within moments.

Celedant believes that the danger will not be isolated to the dwarvan kingdom. Moreover, I agree with his assessment. I urge you, my Queen, to open negotiations with the dwarves and form an alliance between our two nations in order to combat this evil. As I write this letter, I have learned that ambassadors from Nars and Parthia are journeying to every nation on the continent in an effort to renew the alliances formed centuries ago when the world battled the evil of Zeiglon.

As you requested, Father, I have joined Celedant's quest and will investigate the matter further, sending more reports whenever the opportunity presents itself. From what I have learned thus far, I believe the prophecy to be true, and the evil we face is indeed worse than that of the Zeiglon Empire.

On a final note, after extensive meetings, I have also learned that Azimuth and all of dragon kind are prepared to help in this endeavor, even though it will expose their existence to the rest of the world. Even now, they are infiltrating the enemy, but for the moment, I am not at liberty to explain further. I can promise, however, that at the appropriate time, the dragons promise to reveal all.

May the gods have mercy on us and send their aid. For I fear that without it, we are doomed.

Count Eldahir

As soon as they reached Nars, Eldahir would send the missive off with a courier. His official duties accomplished, the elf felt certain he could help with the quest, while looking after his people's best interests. Nevertheless, he decided to be honest with Celedant. A straightforward elf, he favored opening relationships with other races. Keeping secrets from the wizard did not sit well with him. It smacked of his father's intrigues, a trait of the Elven Court he had despised since childhood. It was the main reason for their disagreement that sent him south to fight the orc incursions in the great swamp.

After breakfast, the group broke camp and prepared to continue their journey to Nars. Tarquin saddled his horse and approached Azimuth.

"I'm afraid we don't have an extra mount, but you are welcome to ride with me. My horse is sturdy and won't mind the extra weight."

"Thank you for your kind offer," Azimuth said. "But there is no need. I am quite capable of keeping up on my own and have decided to scout ahead with Ronli and Ralav." He laughed when he saw Tarquin's and the other's expressions. Azimuth was too tall to ride a dwarvan pony.

"Do you plan to run?" Morganna asked. Being an elf, she knew how swiftly her kind could move, but she sincerely doubted that even he could keep up with a galloping horse.

"Yes, but not as you see me."

As the others looked on in confusion, Azimuth's elven image swirled into a cloudy mass. When it dissipated, the elf was gone. Before them stood a large golden wolf, larger than the dwarves' ponies. His transformation startled everyone but Celedant and Eldahir.

"Azimuth has a rare ability that allows him to change into a wolf. He finds it easier to travel long distances that way. To my sorrow, most wizards are incapable of this type of magic," Celedant told them. "It's a pity, really. I can think of numerous occasions when transforming into an animal would be quite useful."

"What I wouldna give to be able to do that," Botreg said, his voice filled with envy. "Can ye imagine what an assassin with that ability could accomplish?"

"Yes, and it's just as well, ye canna do it," Aegir interjected. "Dolgar forbid what roads such a thing could have led ye down."

His words brought smiles to the others as they mounted their horses.

"Azimuth, Ralav, and Ronli, if you would be so kind," Celedant said, "please take the lead."

Azimuth took off, followed by the dwarvan scouts, who had to gallop their horses to keep up with his mile-eating pace. Occasionally, the wolf would return and trot next to Celedant's horse while updating the wizard telepathically. Afterward, he ran ahead once more. After one such incident, Tarquin moved his horse up next to Celedant.

"Does Azimuth see anything troubling ahead?"

"No, it would appear we have a clear path all the way to Nars. Fortunately, those heading north to Brackus are keeping to the main road instead of this trail, which is why we have seen so few travelers on our journey," Celedant responded.

"I hope King Braveslayer is fortifying the tunnels near the dwarvan cities."

"A point I plan to bring up when I meet with him in Nars. The enemy's loss of Brackus will fuel the flames of war. This Taza does not strike me as one to give up. I am afraid that the level of evil I felt in our brief contact will cause him to step-up his attacks. Things are going to get much worse."

A week later, they arrived in Nars. While Celedant, Azimuth, Eldahir, and Morganna met with King Braveslayer, Tarquin and the dwarves went to the Borderers' headquarters to report to Commander Thormon Bravehunter. Although he understood the importance of the quest, the Commander was less than enthusiastic about losing one of his best squads.

"Although ye signed the contract of yer own free will, ye are a Parthian Prince and the lad mentioned in the prophecy. If Master Celedant wants ye on his quest, I canna stand in yer way, especially since it was his suggestion that ye join the Borderers in the first place."

"Thank you," Tarquin replied. "I wouldn't have gotten this far if I hadn't trained with the Borderers. I am grateful for your friendship and all I have learned. I know it will stand me in good stead."

"Nevertheless, I'm afraid I canna be so generous with the rest of ye," the Commander continued. "If ye choose to accompany yer Lieutenant and the wizard, ye will have broken yer contract and will be considered deserters subject to prosecution. However, with things being as they are, ye need not worry about the authorities sendin' someone after ye. They just canna spare the manpower."

"If yer quest is successful, and we win this war, Master Celedant may be able to convince the King to pardon the lot of ye," Thormon confided. "To be truthful, I wish ye were stayin' on. Rumor has it that after the losses we suffered retakin' Brackus, we will need all the soldiers we can get."

"Trust me," Tarquin said, "the success of this quest is vital to the final outcome. If we fail, the combined armies of all the nations will be incapable of winning this war."

After dropping off their uniforms and gathering the rest of their gear together, Tarquin and the dwarves went shopping for sturdy traveling clothes, meeting up with Celedant and the others afterward for supper at the Dancing Lamb, owned by Captain Donli's uncle.

"I approve of your choice of clothing," Celedant told the six former Borderers as he examined the woolen tunics, coats, linen shirts, leather breeches, and heavy woolen cloaks they had purchased.

As a Borderer, Ronli was used to wearing a uniform, so she had opted for the same type of clothing, believing that a dress would get in the way during a fight and would not keep her as warm. The only variance was in the colors. Tarquin and Botreg had chosen black, Donli green, Ralav and Aegir brown, and Ronli a deep blue. The party enjoyed a hearty dinner of roast lamb with seasoned potatoes and vegetables, and thick chunks of bread, followed by apple pasties, and washed down with an excellent dwarvan ale for Tarquin and the dwarves, and a red elven wine for the others as they discussed the journey ahead.

"After we finish eating, I have a meeting with Hortus, a Theirrian Abbot and an old friend to look over some maps of the region around Zeiglon that his monks have dug up," Celedant said. "By the way, the meal is on me."

That brought a cheer from all and another round of drinks.

"We leave at dawn, so enjoy the evening, but don't imbibe too much," Celedant advised.

A short while later, the wizard enjoyed a mug of ale while he spoke with his friend, Hortus. The monk took a sip, spilling a drop or two on his brown robes as he nodded to Celedant.

"The maps we found were disappointin' to say the least. I sent me right-hand cleric, Baldo, with an armed party of me most proven warriors to the peninsula two weeks ago to locate the Clorian archives. To tell the truth, we are uncertain if the records exist. Worse yet, there is some doubt as to whether their archivist is still alive."

"This is disappointing news," Celedant said, shaking his head. "However, I don't believe we have a choice but to pursue every avenue. The more I know about the area we are heading into; the better chance we will have. The tales coming out of the region surrounding Zeiglon have given many brave warriors nightmares."

"Aye, that they have," the ancient cleric agreed, shaking his bald head sadly. He stroked his long grey beard. "That's why I thought it important to pursue the Clorian angle. After the upheaval and downfall of Zeiglon, those misbegotten excuses for clerics explored that region for a number of years. Sadly, most of them were never seen again, but the few that lived returned with extensive knowledge of the area and the horrors residing there."

"Then that knowledge is our best hope," Celedant said. "Have you received any news from your brothers yet?"

"Nothin' of import. Baldo has located a single Clorian in Southgard, living alone on the exposed side of a mountain that houses the city. He has a small cave, no more than an overhang, where he lives on a pile of rotted furs. The cleric told Baldo to head east and once they had left the valley; they were to follow the river. There he would find a trail leading to the domain of the Clorians."

The dwarf took a long drink. "They traveled for miles on nothing more than a goat trail until it opened into a barren valley with a small domed hill in the distance. Although Baldo said it looked more like a slagheap made from the dross of some ancient dwarvan furnace. There in the valley amid the tumble of boulders, they discovered what the Clorians called their 'Mountain of Enlightenment.' This is where the Clorian clerics live out their lives in small hollowed out holes or shallow caves."

Celedant smiled. "I know of the Clorians, but I'm afraid I've never heard anything nice about them. Most people can't abide their smell."

Hortus nodded. "Aye. Of all the dwarvan gods, Clor is the strangest. Most folks have chosen to forget him because of his clerics' outlandish ways and love of dirt and garbage. Anyway, the last I heard, Baldo was still tryin' to speak to their Abbot, who had apparently sealed himself in a cave for the past two hundred years. He receives food and water through a small window, issuing orders to the other monks through written messages."

Celedant paused and thought a moment. "I wonder if our presence might help the situation along faster."

"I suppose it's possible that a fellow Abbot and a wizard might be able to encourage the Clorians to be more helpful."

"Am I to assume that you will be joining our party?" Celedant asked with a smile.

The monk solemnly nodded.

"Thierry be blessed. After remaining in your monastery for the past three hundred years, I find myself speechless that you would undertake such a dangerous quest."

Hortus laughed. "The trip to Nars from the monastery has invigorated me. So when are ye plannin' on leavin'?"

"At dawn, but I could make it later in deference to your age," Celedant said with a wink.

"Just be ready to go. I havena slept through a dawn since I was a lad," Hortus replied indignantly. "Besides, ye are far older than I."

"Then I had best be finding my own bed," Celedant said, standing up. "I'll send one of the lads to pick you up in the morning. Good night, my friend; pray that Thierry blesses our endeavor and guides our way. This quest must succeed or none but the wicked will be able to live with the consequences."

The following morning, the journey began without incident. They traveled south for several days. On the fifth, they heard a loud boom that ripped the fabric of their world apart and left a dark hole across the trail, followed by a loud clicking sound. Then out of the hole crawled three monstrosities: orange hued insect-like creatures with huge triangular shaped shields growing from each of their six legs. Upon sighting the company, one of the creatures reared and emitted a screeching call. Two large segmented pincher topped arms flailed the air, displaying the terrible weapons hidden behind the shields. Four appendages, that could draw prey to the monster's mouth and row upon row of inward pointing teeth.

The company's horses reared and screamed in fear, making their riders fight for control or risk becoming unseated. Azimuth, who was still in his wolf form, bared his teeth. He charged the creature, fastening his teeth around one of its arms. Although he had a fierce grip, the monster was too powerful. It flung him into a tree fifty paces away as easily as a child might toss a toy. When his head smashed against the broad trunk, he lost consciousness. Protecting the unconscious wolf, Tarquin charged the creature, his sword ringing off the shielded arm.

Celedant could spare his friend but a moment's glance. He fervently hoped the dragon was not seriously hurt. Lowering his staff, he called forth the power of the earth through Forestae, casting a spell that sent a green-hued beam of raw energy shooting toward the monster. The bolt sliced through one of its shields, striking the beast in the side. It reared up screaming in pain before rushing toward the wizard. Eldahir used his bow, shooting arrow after arrow into the head of the monster. Morganna followed suit, her arrows striking the softer tissue behind the shield, whenever it was exposed.

The arrows that struck the shields broke upon impact, causing no damage, while the others drove deep into the monsters' flesh. One mandible-like arm arced toward Tarquin, hoping to pin him to the ground. The prince controlled his horse and swung his sword, Dragon Bolt, at the coming terror. Burning red with magical fire, it struck the mandible, cleanly severing it in two.

The other members of the company centered their attention on another of the monsters. After dismounting, the dwarves approached it in a semi-circle, their swords and axes clanging as they struck the natural shields of the Void creature. With each attack, their weapons chipped away at the animal's armor, forcing it back. Seeing an opening, Vannor the Northman dodged under one of the shields and came up instantly, striking out at the legs of the creature. The sword struck deep into the unprotected leg, severing it neatly in two and causing the monster to screech in agony as viscous orange liquid oozed from its wounded leg. Botreg dodged between Ronli and Aegir, sinking his sword deep into its neck.

Meanwhile, Eldahir, Morganna, and Celedant kept up their attack, backing up Tarquin, whose sword rose and fell, cutting through the creature's shields whenever he could land a blow, while dancing away from its remaining arms. Eldahir shot arrows into the monster's maw because he did not see anything that resembled eyes.

Tarquin made quick work of the four grasping arms that surrounded the creature's mouth, cutting each of them neatly in two. When it was clear that the others could finish it off, Celedant turned his attention to the remaining animal. He lowered his staff and drew upon the Earth's energy to fire a bolt of pure power at the beast. The ray flew from his staff, striking a powerful blow to one of its shield-like arms, and blasting through the protective barrier, tossing the strange looking arm high into the air spraying bright orange blood.

Dodging in and under the shields, and striking at the body of the creature, Vannor and the dwarves' attack brought the desired results. The creature's attacks slowed as it swayed back and forth like a drunken sailor. They pushed the monster on its side and continued bludgeoning it with their axes and swords.

Tarquin attacked the base of the monster's mouth. He swung repeatedly, savaging the tooth-ridden maw as orange fluid spewed out, covering him as he swung. Having used the last of his arrows, Eldahir slung his bow over his shoulder and charged to Tarquin's aid.

As the attack continued, Azimuth regained consciousness. Getting to his feet, he transformed into his Elven shape, knowing that as a wolf, he was useless against this creature. He wanted to return to his dragon form, certain that he could dispatch the monster in no time, but he was not yet ready to reveal his true form to the others.

As the battle continued, the sharp edges of their attacker's shielded arm struck out, knocking Tarquin to the ground with a bloody blow to his forehead.

Aegir rushed to his side and dragging the prince away from the battle, began administering aid. The wound was bloody but not very deep. The cleric used his powers to heal the wound. As soon as the monsters were dispatched, a third much larger creature emerged from the ripped opening to the Void.

It was exactly like the first, except it was twice as large. It used its armored triangular shaped shields almost like wings, fluttering back and forth like a bumblebee settling onto a flower. The defenders fell back from the monster, unable to reach it due to the speed of the shields. Azimuth joined Celedant, Morganna, and Eldahir, and as they prepared their spells, he used his powerful dragon magic and pummeled it with mighty blows that ate into its carapace like acid.

"Acidium." Azimuth's voice was low, but rumbled with an intensity that bespoke his true dragon nature.

Celedant's spell was next. "Electriskt Kastasig!" he shouted sending a jagged bolt of lightning that struck against one of the shielded arms, causing the arm and its shield to explode in a mist of orange haze.

By then, Eldahir completed his spell and small bolts of pure energy shot forth, striking the monster first in its shielded arms and then into its body. The energy bolts struck where the shield, which Celedant had destroyed, had recently been, penetrating the oversized body.

"Avfrya Kastasig." Morganna released her spell, a great ball of fire that rolled outward from her hand to engulf the monster. As large as it was, the creature amazingly rolled, trying to escape the ever-persistent fire. As it tried to douse the flames, the other members of the group fired arrows into the exposed flesh. Hortus waded in using his war hammer to great effect.

The huge monster's thrashing shield arms squealed like metal on metal. The shields gave off sparks as they scraped against each other, while arrows burrowed deep into its exposed side. Celedant readied another spell and began the casting. Channeling energy through Forestae, he sent a huge blast of lightning that shook the air in a massive green-and-white flair of power that exploded from the end of his staff. It ballooned out to engulf the enemy. The creature screamed in agony, forcing the members of the party to clap their hands over their ears. Then, as the flesh burned, the monster lay still. As it died, the hole between this world and the Void snapped shut and disappeared.

Spooked by the monsters, it took some time to find their horses. The steeds were scattered in all directions. Celedant, whose horse had returned, and Azimuth remained behind, studying the insect-like creatures and especially the area where the rift had occurred. After finding their horses, Tarquin and Eldahir joined them, looking on in silence as they examined the area.

Celedant turned and with a look of amazement said, "There's power beyond imagination at work here."

"What we just saw was an actual rift ripped between our world and the Void," Azimuth said. "The power required to do this was immense. Yet neither of us could locate the source of it nearby. This has either been done from a distance or from the Void itself."

"I know few beings in this world capable of that kind of power," Celedant agreed. "There is but one thing that can achieve such power, Taza and the Staff of Adois. We must be extra careful from here on out. We are dealing with the unknown, and there is no way of telling what else that vampire might send against us."

"It is hard to be wary of something that can strike from such a distance," Eldahir said. His expression showed that he was clearly worried.

"You speak of a Void, and I see these monsters," Tarquin said. "But what do you mean?"

Celedant nodded sagely and looked at the company. "The hole, we have just witnessed, was the nothingness that exists between our world and the different planes of existence. Anyone powerful enough can travel through the Void, visiting the different worlds. In the past, no one but the dragons and the gods themselves could do so. It appears that we now face an enemy capable of this. This Taza is truly a powerful being. We must remain on guard so that he does not catch us unaware again."

CHAPTER SIX

Melgor was worried. Several days earlier, Taza had told him to go to an isolated field in the middle of nowhere to await transportation. The warlock had figured that his master would make him wait, a least for a while. The vampire took great delight in lording it over his underlings, but Melgor was running low on food. Luckily, he had stumbled upon a rabbit warren and with the deft use of his staff, trapped and cooked several, storing a few in a sack for the upcoming trip after using a preserving spell to keep the meat fresh. Feeling content and sated after his meal, he put aside whatever fate awaited him in Taza's city of Dormin. It was early afternoon, and with his belly full, he dozed off until the sound of huge flapping wings, coming from beyond the western trees, caused him to jerk awake and jump to his feet.

Above the tall trees appeared a flying, three-headed monster, the likes of which the warlock had never seen but had read about as a young wizard studying at Edain, the wizard university. The rear of her body looked like a dragon with a serpent's tail. The center was a goat with massive wings, and the front was that of a lion. The three heads included a lion, a goat, and a dragon. Its demeanor was sinister, and Melgor detected the magical power of its evil aura. Unbeknown to the warlock, Lord Taza was planning to send dravens for the Shadow Lords of Zeiglon to ride, once he convinced them to join his cause, but the mounts he had picked out for them would be like worms next to the creature heading for Melgor. The chimera was capable of breathing fire from all three heads and would be a deadly foe to anyone who got in its way.

Melgor put all of these thoughts aside and closely studied the creature.

Perched behind her wings was a high saddle. As the massive beast landed, she dug her sharp claws into the earth and waited, focusing three pairs of eyes on the warlock. The chimera frightened him, and his first instinct was to disappear and find a place of safety. However, reason soon overcame his fear. The beast would be under Taza's influence, exerted before bringing it through the void. The chimera would be a formidable foe against any dragon or firedrake, but it would not hurt Melgor.

The warlock's scrutiny of the creature abruptly halted when a great force snatched him around the ribs and levitated him into the high seat. He felt like his bones would crack under the immense pressure, but there was no escape. He dared not use a spell on the creature since it obviously possessed its own magic. As he wheezed and gasped for what he thought was his final breath, the force dropped Melgor into the well-made leather saddle with footholds that comfortably covered his legs.

The saddle was soft and supple with a rather complicated harness, but Melgor was no novice. As a wizard growing up on Dragon Isle, he had ridden dragons, but the magnificent creature he had bonded with so long ago had forsaken him when he began practicing dark incantations. No dragon would abide dark magic, and any warlock that used it, soon lost his bond mate to a new apprentice and was exiled from the Isle.

Melgor slipped on the harness and tightened the buckles. The next moment, he was aloft as the creature winged its way skyward. Feeling the arctic air whipping past, the warlock cast a warming spell around himself to keep from freezing to death. In spite of the saddle's comforts, for the next three days, Melgor's nonstop ride was dismal. Just before reaching the foothills of the mountains, the creature flew through a thunderstorm, and although the warming spell kept him dry, the lightning came dangerously close to turning the chimera's passenger into a skeleton. They emerged from the storm, his steed flying well above the high peaks of the Sargorian Mountains, and as they pulled away from the clouds, he could see the citadel in the distance. A bright shelter perched in the dangerous western mountains.

The chimera closed the distance, circling the massive structure so fast that Melgor's stomach revolted, and he came close to losing what little he had eaten for the past three days. They headed closer to an open crenellated roof, located between several towers. The warlock braced himself for a rough landing, but amazingly, the chimera back-winged to drop on the roof as smoothly as any dragon.

Melgor's legs were wobbly after so long in flight, but he hurriedly composed himself as he gingerly dismounted and crossed the roof. This was one of Lord Taza's personal towers, and his undead master waited at the bottom of the winding staircase. Holding onto the tower's stonework, the warlock descended, passing several closed and locked doors. Melgor sensed numerous secret panels hidden within the masonry as he continued downward. When the stairs ended, he found himself in front of his master Taza the undead warlock.

"Come, my child, stand before me."

Melgor, his cloak and clothes travel-worn and smelling of sweat, moved towards the throne and stood ramrod straight in front of his master. A black robe with a hood hid Taza's dark shape and deep red eyes. Taza had placed his hand on the arm of the chair, his bone white fingers drumming a slow beat. In the crook of his left arm, the Staff of Adois gleamed malevolently.

The dark lord leaned closer, and a sniff came from the darkness of the cowl. "You need a bath, my friend."

Melgor was astonished. After learning of Sellis' fate, the warlock had assumed that his master would punish him as well. He was unprepared for the meeting to begin in such a way.

"I apologize for my appearance. The...ah...trip was long, my lord," he stammered. "We passed through some foul weather along the way."

"Nicely put," Taza laughed. "You can observe the upcoming battles from the unique vantage point on the Chimera's back. She will also serve as an ominous reminder of the power I can summon at will."

"Thank you, my lord," Melgor said, hesitantly. "I did not expect this sort of interview upon my arrival."

A sharp hissing laugh issued from the vampire's cowl, which was shaking with mirth. "How refreshing to have someone speak his mind. I have lived so long and held such power that my underlings bow before me in fear, seldom daring to speak directly or to the point. It has gotten so bad I thought I had lost the art of conversation. You believed I would punish or kill you when you arrived?"

Melgor nodded. "That thought had crossed my mind."

Taza chuckled again. "Why would I sever my right arm? What purpose would it serve? You are the vessel through which my power flows across the world. You are my eyes and ears. For the time being, I cannot leave this citadel, so your service to me is vital. That does not give you immunity from my wrath," Taza continued, when it appeared that Melgor would not speak. "I can still kill you in an instant, should you displease me. It would be as easy as stomping on a cockroach."

Melgor insides cringed as he fought to restrain his anger. How dare he speak to him like that? The anger fueled his growing desire to kill the undead thing before him. That, however, would have to wait for a better opportunity.

"But that is not why I brought you here. This...prince and Celedant appear rather difficult to kill, but I am not blind. I realize you have done all that can be expected. Actually, I thought the lich would finish off that meddlesome wizard, but he is stronger than I perceived. Over the years, I have seen so many things go awry."

The dark lord's words calmed the warlock. "Thank you, my lord. I had limited resources in place to send after one as powerful as Celedant."

"Yes," Taza agreed. "I have sent several powerful beasts and demons after him, but to no avail. My spies in Nars tell me that the wizard and the prince now travel with a large party of fighters, including a rebel Illanni, whose meddlesome interference prevented my agent from killing Tarquin in Brackus. I had hoped to recapture her and turn her into my servant, but her actions have angered me, and now I would see her dead. I'll pay 1,000 pieces of gold to anyone who brings me her heart."

"That's quite a generous sum, my lord," Melgor replied. "Too bad Sellis is languishing in prison. He would relish the idea of adding such largess to his horde."

"Sellis is an incompetent fool. I doubt he would have any more luck killing the elf than he did the other two. Morganna is a highly competent warrior and a self-taught sorceress of considerable power. Were she on my side, I believe she would be a serious threat, even to Celedant. Somehow, she has managed to change her very nature from Illanni to Wood Elf. I suspect she had some powerful help. Yet every time I try to see who is helping her, my spell is blocked."

"Whoever it is must be very powerful indeed, if they could block your spell."

"Yeeesss...powerful indeed," Taza said, his eyes narrowing in thought. "Possibly even a god. I wonder which one."

Melgor's eyes flew open in shock. "A god?"

"Why not? After all, Adois has given me her staff. My goals and hers are the same."

"Then you suspect her brother Adaman," Melgor stated.

"I did at first, but now I think not. If Adaman had entered the picture, he would have retrieved the remaining piece of the staff and given it to Celedant, or at least, shown him the exact location where it rests. Yet this does not appear to be the case. No, it isn't Adaman. I do not know why he is not intervening to stop his twin sister. Whoever is helping her wants to keep his or her interference a secret."

"Why not ask Adois if she knows?"

Taza turned on Melgor in sudden, violent anger. "I will decide what is important enough to bother my goddess with. She does not appreciate incompetence any more than I do."

"I am sorry, my lord. I meant no disrespect," Melgor humbly apologized. Mentally, he suspected that Adois might already have voiced her displeasure with Taza's progress, and it took every ounce of discipline he possesses not to secretly smile at the vampire's discomfort.

"At any rate, I am working on new ways to eliminate Celedant and the Prince. I have several ideas in mind and plan to travel through the void in search of new and greater creatures to pit against them. I have also decided to contact the Shadow Lords."

"The Shadow Lords? My lord, they are bickering idiots trapped within the confines of Zeiglon. No doubt they can be useful once the wizard and his party enter their territory, but...."

"I know what perverted power holds them in sway. Once I have their loyalty, I can destroy it." Taza chuckled. "No doubt they will be willing to do anything I ask to win their freedom from that dismal prison."

Little realizing they will simply be trading one master for another, Melgor thought.

"Nevertheless, let's get to the point of your summons. King Herroth's replacement as king of the giants is moving too slowly. The envoy I sent to him has never returned, and I have yet to receive a response to my inquiry. I suspect that after Sellis' treachery, my currier may be dead, but I cannot be certain. I have no sense of what is happening in that place."

"I fear I underestimated Sellis' incompetence," Melgor interrupted.

"You may have," agreed the dark lord before he continued. "I am sending you to sort things out. Your magic and the chimera should be able to keep you from harm. In the meantime, take the rest of the day off and go home. Bathe, rest, and have a decent meal. After which my lovely pet chimera will fly you to the abandoned city of Zigar-shan and the giant king."

Melgor bowed. "One way or another, I will motivate the giants and their minions to act."

Taza extended his hand with a medallion dangling from it. "If Herroth proves difficult, use this pendant to alert me. If I have to, I will use the Staff of Adois and punish the pompous fool until either he agrees, or we find a new king." Taza slumped in his throne. "Go now and rest. I tire of being congenial."

Sellis gagged, bound, and hooded was dragged from his cell by two sets of hands that took each of his arms and dragged him up a set of stairs. They moved so fast his feet kept banging off the stairs as they ascended level after level. When they crossed a flat area and into a tower, he could tell by his captors' steps that they were going upwards. Taza would be awaiting him. Sellis was certain. His captors were certainly two of his vampire guards, considering the ease with which they carried him. Sellis tried to use the ring of Nashmeol but it remained unresponsive.

They arrived at a door, heard it open, and then they ripped off his hood, causing him to blink to get his vision back. He saw the torch-lit top of Taza's tower. The red drapes were closed the darkness of the chamber sent shivers up and down his spine. Sellis knew that in the next few minutes, Taza would decide his fate. After dragging him up the stairway, the vampires hurled the warlock across the slick marble floor. He stopped when he struck Taza's throne. Seated above him was the vampire warlock, wickedly staring at the forlorn man below him. Taza could not help smiling, showing his long teeth as Sellis struggled to stand. As he stood up, the prisoner tried to look as noble as he could be despite being bound and gagged with stagnate mud and water soaking his clothes.

"You have been quite the troubling man," Taza began. "Killing the giant king was rash, but that can be excused. Yet, it is the number of times you have used your position for your own betterment that disturbs me most. That cannot be overlooked."

Drool leaked out of Sellis's gagged mouth as he tied to speak with Taza, but the vampire would have nothing of it. Spittle came out of his mouth as he screamed, "Your failure at Brackus is inexcusable and coming back alive was abdominal! Moreover, you stole from me. The gold used to build your mansion was mine!"

As Taza spoke, Sellis desperately tried to command his ring to teleport him anywhere but in this tower. The warlock wizard laughed, "Your little ring will not do you any favors here."

Then with a snap of Taza's fingers, Sellis' bindings and gag disappeared. As he engaged the ring, the last thing he saw was Taza give a simple wave of the Staff of Adois.

When Sellis awakened, it was to the utter darkness of the dungeon, and he broke down and sobbed like a young child, knowing his dreams were gone and his life would end in despair.

Melgor took the medallion and went to his home, located nearby in the surrounding city of Dormin. There, he enjoyed a leisurely bath and a hot meal, allowing it to ease his anger at Taza. Afterward, he fell asleep in the comfort of his own bed. It felt like he had just placed his head on the pillow when his servant woke him.

"One of Lord Taza's initiates is waiting in the parlor with a message, sir," his thin, elderly housekeeper told him.

The wizard dressed and left his room. When he entered the parlor, the Illanni servant gave him a sealed scroll and a folded note. Then without saying a word, he turned and left. Melgor waited until he was alone before breaking the wax seal on the paper. A second sealed scroll was inside it. It was short and to the point:

"Present this scroll to King Herroth, answer his questions as you see fit, and summon me if he gives you any problems."

Melgor stuck the scroll in a pocket of his robe, felt the medallion that hung around his neck to reassure himself that the summoning stone was still there, and sighed with relief. Contemplating the impossible tasks Taza always gave him, he ate breakfast, packed a bag with fresh clothes, and a few personal things. The he headed back through the corridors to Taza's tower and the roof, where the chimera waited.

After visiting the kitchen for bread, dried meat, and fruit for the trip, he walked up to the beast, followed by three muscular servants, carrying heavy buckets of raw mutton. The warlock tossed several large chunks to each of the three heads until the meat was gone. "There's a good girl. I expect you know where to take me."

The chimera rumbled happily and bobbed her heads up and down as she elevated the warlock into the saddle, sending the kitchen drudges scrambling inside to the safety of the tower.

"I think they're frightened of you, my pet," Melgor laughed. During the time they had been together, man and beast had become good friends.

The beast made a rumbling noise and as soon as Melgor fastened his bag in place and finished tightening the flying harnesses, the chimera leapt off the tower and into the morning air. All three heads sent a jet of fire skyward, as if to prove that the servants had good reason to be frightened. The flight would be a relatively short jaunt over the mountains and then south to the occupied city. The shortness of the trip made Melgor happy, yet oddly enough, he was getting used to riding the beast. Another heat spell kept him warm until they left the mountains, supplemented by the warmth of the morning sun.

As the light of the new day settled on the snow-covered land west of the Sargorian Mountains, Melgor and his mount began a slow, circular dive to the southwest. The warlock reached down, patted the beast's side. "I would like a closer look at the city. Could you make a few circuits before landing? Besides, it will make a good impression on the inhabitants."

The warlock's flying companion gave the deep rumbling noise that Melgor associated with consent, and they were soon circling lazily above the city. A few years earlier when he had visited King Herroth, it had been at the giant's palace outside Dormin. Melgor had never been to Zigar-shan, which the giants now occupied, thanks to a little underhanded interference on his part. He wanted to get a feel for the lay of the land.

Sellis had reported that the main part of the city consisted of ruins. However, the giants had built defenses to protect the new inhabitants and were constructing a massive wall from the rubble. It was shoddy workmanship but large enough for a giant to defend. In the middle of the old dwarvan city, he saw an area where they had removed the rubble. Massive wooden houses and a variety of other buildings now filled the space.

The chimera flew lower. It didn't take long before he was seen by the inhabitants, who ran helter-skelter, creating an amusing scene that made Melgor chuckle. By their actions, it looked as though someone had kicked over an anthill as giants spilled into the streets and thousands of smaller, orcan shapes poured out of a dark cleft in the mountain. Throughout the city, orcs rang the huge bells. Their hands and arms pulled up and down as the bells swung from side-to-side, making a terrible din. The warlock found it quite amusing as he watched his supposed allies dissolve into utter chaos, running hither and yon as they stared at the sky like frightened children.

After another circuit, he watched as a much calmer giant emerge from the largest of the buildings. Melgor had already picked out the structure as a landing site, figuring it to be the logical place for the new king to set up headquarters. The warlock hoped the chimera would help dissuade the giants from trying to kill him, but he was fully prepared to use the medallion to bring Taza's full wrath upon them if they tried.

CHAPTER SEVEN

Celedant and his party rose before the dawn. After breaking their fast with boiled eggs, ham, coarse black bread, and strong tea, they set out heading southeast. The company traveled swiftly, arriving at the Theirrian clerics' camp several days later. The temperature in the south was mild, and everyone was happy to get away from the snow and bitter cold that they had endured for the first few weeks of their journey. While the other members of the quest watered and fed their horses, Hortus, Tarquin, and Celedant met with the dwarvan priest Baldo.

"Abbot, Master Celedant, Prince Tarquin, what brings ye to our humble camp?" Baldo asked in greeting.

"Since ye were not havin' much luck with the Clorian Abbot, I figured we might have a better chance," Hortus replied. "Have ye made contact with him yet?"

"It's glad I am to have ye," Baldo said, earnestly. "I dared not approach their enclave directly, because so little is known about this order. I didna want to offend them by inadvertently committing some transgression. Should I be involved in the slightest mishap or venture a misspoken word, me journey would have been in vain. Therefore, we set up camp here at the head of the valley and waited. Three days later, a decrepit hermit approached, wearing nothing more than a stained and tattered loincloth. His hair and beard were badly matted with twigs, dead leaves, and other bits of questionable matter, and the smell was so overpowering, none of us could guess the last time he had bathed."

"Do they have the records we seek?" Celedant asked worriedly.

"I don't know yet," Baldo replied with a frustrated shake of his head. "After days of writin' back and forth in the dirt, tryin' to get through to him, the cleric, if that's what he really is, volunteered this morning to take written messages to someone named Hority Beamingrot. I wrote our questions out for the Abbot, and when I finished, the cleric snatched the page from me hands and hurried down the path, disappearing behind a hill down in the valley. Unfortunately, he hasna returned yet."

"Then we must wait for him to bring us an answer," Hortus said. "In the meantime, I am hungry enough to eat a bear."

"I'm afraid we havena much to offer ye, Abbot," Baldo said, sadly. "Game has been scarce. It's all we can do to snare an occasional rabbit or two."

"Not to worry," Celedant said with a laugh when he saw Azimuth, Eldahir, and Morganna approach, dragging the carcass of a dead buck. "Our friends did a little hunting before we arrived."

Baldo's eyes lit with delight as Celedant introduced the three newcomers. "This will be a welcome feast. If ye would drag the deer over to the side of camp, I'll clean it and fix a nice venison stew with the last of our vegetables."

Azimuth and Morganna helped the dwarf butcher the meat and that night, everyone enjoyed a hearty meal. The remainder of the meat was cooked, preserved with a spell, and divided among the various members of the group. The clerics from Baldo's group volunteered to stand watch that night, so that Celedant and his party could get the first full night's sleep they had had since leaving Nars.

The next day as the sun crested over the eastern edge of the valley, two small figures approached. One was the Clorian that Baldo had already met. The other was dressed in a loose fitting robe that at one time might had been grey, but was now the mottled color of the dry valley floor, stained from years of wear and covered with countless patches. His hair was the color of newly ripened wheat, streaked with gray. The dwarf's face was as rugged as the region, wrinkled and scoured by time and weather. Twigs and leaves stuck out of the tangles in his hair. The strange dwarf advanced, carrying a staff that looked more a long branch topped by a misshapen lump of pumice that must have come from a dormant volcano.

Celedant and the others watched their approach as they sat around their small campfire. The monk hitched up his robes and sat next to Baldo, exposing thin, dirty legs. He gazed at each member of the group before locking eyes with Hortus.

At that point, the Clorian smiled happily. "I see ye wear the medallion of an Abbot," the Clorian said, referring to a large gold pendant with a black pearl at its center. "Welcome to the Valley of Clor. I am Hority, caretaker of the valley and me order. Ye must be Baldo of Thierry. I can sense the power that ye wield and through it, a great sense of urgency."

"That's Baldo sittin' over there next to ye," the Abbot said, pointing to his cleric. "I am Hortus, the Abbot of Thierry. Baldo sent word with yer brother monk that we needed to speak with yer Abbot about a matter of great urgency."

"I must apologize for the misunderstanding," Hority laughed. "Xor isna a cleric and hasna a clue as to what goes on in this world. Therefore, ye can imagine me surprise when he found me last night. Years ago, he came to us a scholar. His goal was to chronicle the various dwarvan religions and their practices. Unfortunately, a band of orcs that assailed the valley captured him. The orcs tortured the poor lad mercilessly, until I rescued him. Since that time, he has been unable to speak and has remained as ye see him, a simple fellow, who is a bit addled."

"But he wrote quite legibly in the dirt and readily took me message for yer master," Baldo said, puzzled.

A bemused look crossed the grizzled dwarf's face. "I can merely speculate that our deity may have intervened on yer behalf. I was miles away, yet he found me. It is an event that bears thinkin'."

"If Xor gave ye the message, then do ye understand our quest?" Baldo asked.

"Aye," Hority replied. "I have the message. Now that I have seen and taken me measure of ye, I will deliver it to our Abbot, but I canna offer any reassurance that he will grant yer request. Wait another day, and we shall see. The valley is in grave danger, and the Abbot has been seeking divine assistance for some time. In the meantime, I have been searching for a worldlier means to solving our predicament."

Hority got to his feet. Taking a handful of dirt, he sprinkled it in the fire and rubbed the rest in his hair. Then he turned and disappeared.

"Hority seems a decent chap...a bit odd, but decent," Hortus ventured. "I wonder what is troublin' their valley. Has anything attacked ye since yer arrival?"

"No, everything has been quiet," Baldo replied, scratching his head.

A couple hours later, Hority returned and sat beside the fire, motioning Hortus to sit opposite him." Unconcerned with the smoking fire, he took a handful of ashes, rubbed it in his robe and let the smoke waft about his head.

"I have spoken with the head of me order. Well more to the point, I have corresponded with him. Our esteemed Abbot has forsaken the world and everything it holds, including speech. If it weren't for me takin' him food every day, he would have become a martyr to Clor a long time ago. The Abbot believes that ye have been sent to aid in our deliverance."

"Deliverance from what?" Celedant asked as he joined them at the fire.

"We rely on provisions donated by the Bonecrusher Clan, but as I mentioned earlier, our valley is beset with danger."

The dwarves about the campfire knew that the Bonecrushers were members of the Confederation of Clans. In the southern Mordolwyn Range, as many as thirty dwarvan clans lived in the high valleys and deep places common to the mountains. The clans more or less came under the control of King Braveslayer and regularly supplied soldiers to the dwarvan army. Nevertheless, Imperial rule might or might not apply. Each clan ruled their own territory and defended it against transgressions be they orc, dwarf, human, or otherwise.

"I donna know how to ask this of ye," Hority said, "but a dragon has settled in a cave that sits next to the trail leading to Bonecrusher land. It is our only supply route and with that beast menacing everyone that comes anywhere near the cave, we canna get our supplies. Without them, our order will cease to exist. Me Abbot feels that ye are the answer to his prayers, and that Thierry, the renowned warrior god, has sent ye here to battle the beast and save us. I have been tryin' to come up with a different solution, but ye are our best chance. If ye can kill or at least drive the beastie off, the Abbot has promised to allow ye access to our archives. What do ye say?"

"It would seem that our arrival is fortuitous," Hortus replied. "The young clerics I sent with Baldo are trained and hardened for combat, but I'm afraid that facing a dragon is beyond their abilities."

"However, I and those who travel with me will have no trouble taking on the animal," Celedant assured him. "We'll be happy to rid you of it." As he finished speaking, he glanced up at Azimuth and spoke to him telepathically. *Do you know of any dragons in the area?*

None, it is probably just a firedrake, Azimuth thought back.

Hority smiled at Celedant, displaying a few gaps between yellowed teeth. "When I first met ye, I knew ye could be counted on to help. Never fear, I will accompany ye. I have protected this valley for years. Ye will find that I am quite skilled with me branch." He waved his staff back and forth, "and Clor will aid me as well. The dragon's lair is but a day's travel. Gather what ye need for a two-day journey. I will inform the Abbot and wait for ye at the base of the mountain." The bedraggled dwarf grinned and started down the path at a run.

Hority seemed a nice enough dwarf, but truth be told, Celedant and the others were dreading the thought of spending a lot of time in his company. The cleric smelled terrible.

"If I have to travel very far with that dwarf, I swear I'm goin' to throw him in the nearest river or lake and scrub him down with the biggest bar of soap I can find," Botreg grumbled.

"And we'll help ye," the other dwarves chimed in laughing.

"There's no reason for everyone to go after this firedrake," Azimuth interrupted. "Celedant, Eldahir, Tarquin, and I should be able to handle it with no trouble."

Celedant turned to Azimuth and spoke telepathically. *Are you planning to take dragon form?*

If need be. A firedrake is no match for a dragon. Azimuth replied.

True. You would make short work of it. However, I think the risk of exposure is too great. I would rather you kept your dragon persona secret for a while longer.

Very well, Azimuth agreed. *We will do it the old-fashioned way.*

Aloud, Celedant said, "Yes, I believe the four of us can take care of the problem."

Tarquin, Celedant, Azimuth, and Eldahir gathered their weapons and a few provisions and set off after Hority, arriving at the rendezvous point within an hour. Hority greeted them with a toothy grin and motioned for them to follow. As the path meandered around the mountain, it split and the five of them took the left fork that led up the valley's side along a trickling streambed. Hority set a steady pace and before long, they crested the valley rim, going deeper into the interior of the Mordolwyn Mountains. Their guide was not very talkative and as night approached, and when the path came to a broad flat plain, he stopped. Hority removed his rucksack and began setting up camp. After a moment, the others followed suit.

"I'm afraid I'm not much of a talker," Hority said, when he realized he had not told them they were stopping for the night. "I'm used to being alone. Come, we will set up camp and get a good night's sleep. The dragon lies just ahead."

"Not a problem, we're used to traveling in silence," Tarquin assured him, "usually because we don't want to alert the enemy to our presence."

An hour later, the five of them sat around a small campfire and talked. Celedant placed wards around the camp to alert them should anything approach.

"It is good to be able to talk with someone again. The Bonecrushers tend to be closed-mouthed and suspicious. In addition, the converts Clor sends to the valley seem a bit touched in the head. Ye canna carry on a decent conversation with them." Hority shook his head, sadly. "The ways of the gods are strange. I found it easier to just collect me share of filth and keep to me self."

Despite their location in the south, it was far enough along in the season that the night grew chilly. Hority chose a spot away from the others on the opposite side of the campfire and huddled in his threadbare blanket.

In the morning, they awoke to find him bent over the fire, cooking some of the leftover venison. A kettle of tea bubbled merrily next to it. The five of them filled their bellies, and when they finished, Hority stood, wiped his greasy hands on his robe, and with a jerk of his head, bade the others to follow. They crossed the rock shelf where the path descended into yet another valley. The beast's lair was but a few miles away as the crow flies, and the party followed a path up and down the mountainous region that ran alongside a rapid stream flowing east. As they walked along its banks, the terrain came to life with plants and trees, and about a mile further, the stream merged with several others, becoming a swift-flowing river.

At one point, they crossed a muddy creek bed that led to the river, and an excited Hority began jumping up and down. "Oh, Clor, a miracle!"

"What is the matter, friend?" Celedant asked.

The monk dove into the muck and started rolling around. A moment later, Hority's head popped out of the mud. "Come, brothers, it is rare to find such a wonderful sight. Clor will be pleased if ye partake of his blessings."

Celedant and Eldahir wrinkled their noses in distaste, but Azimuth had to hold himself back. As a dragon, rolling in the mud was a grand way to cool off in the heat of the day and a great way to rid oneself of annoying insects. Nevertheless, in his present elven form, there was no need. Besides, mud wallowing was something most dragons were careful not to share with their two-legged friends. It would seem too undignified.

"Barren lands often have hidden wonders, waiting to be found," Azimuth concurred. "Since we are not dwarves, I don't believe Clor would want us to disturb your...ah...worship. Feel free to enjoy yourself."

"Okay, but ye don't know what yer missin'," Hority replied.

Much later, the party continued their journey and came to the end of the valley where the river dropped off the cliff, creating a massive waterfall. The path switched back and forth, as it descended beside the falls. The five of them admired the view of snow-capped mountains and mile after mile of untamed forestland.

Hority raised a cautionary hand. "This is where the dragon lives." He pointed to an outcropping of rock in the middle of a great pool that the waterfall had created over the past millennium. "See? That is where it lies. From that rock, it has already waylaid two caravans bound for the valley. We have to kill it or drive it away."

As the dwarf finished speaking, a massive firedrake left the shadows and shot a blast of flame at Celedant and the others. Its size was half as large as a dragon, and if Azimuth could have changed back to his original form, he would have made short work of the beast. Since he did not want to expose his true form to the cleric, at least not yet, he and the others would have a fight on their hands.

CHAPTER EIGHT

Ress Logdan sat astride her roan horse, allowing it to forage in the meadow. Thoughts of self-pity, the same ones that had plagued her for the past five years, rebounded through her mind. Rather than succumb to them, she had dedicated herself to revenge.

From birth, the young woman had been destined for a better life. Long, naturally curly red hair that fell to her waist, lively brown eyes, and delicate features turned many male heads. Catching the eye of a young royal at court was once a definite possibility. Then one fateful day, a single instant destroyed all of the possibilities before her.

On the day she turned sixteen, Ress prepared a small feast for her father and herself in celebration. Setting out for the market, she planned to buy the foodstuffs to make a grand meal. She made her purchases and headed home. As Ress neared her house, she spotted her drunken father sitting slack-eyed in the rocking chair. She sighed, determined not to let it spoil her special day when a scaled monster unexpectedly descended from the sky and belched a gout of flame, instantly burning her home and father to ash before turning and heading down the trail toward the village.

Shocked and paralyzed with fear, Ress ducked behind the trunk of a large tree. The monster was a firedrake, but before she could turn and run, it was upon her. At this point, her memory faded. When she regained consciousness, her vision was blurry and after a few moments, she realized she had no feeling in the left side of her face.

The village healer patted her right shoulder. "Ress dear, do not worry. Your other eye is fine, tis just swollen. I have wrapped your wounds and applied my best healing salves. Rest easy, I will take good care of you. Unfortunately, I fear the numbness will fade before long, and pain will come. There are so many wounded, I have little enough to go around. But I will do what I can to ease your discomfort."

The left side of Ress's head, arm, and shoulder were swathed in bandages for several weeks as the poultice worked its curative powers. A month later, the healer and two apprentices stood by the girl's cot and removed the bandages. They could not hide the worry in their eyes, and when the last of the wrappings came off, the two aides turned to hide the pitying looks on their faces.

"What's wrong?" Ress asked, alarmed.

"Thank the gods there is no sign of infection," the healer replied with a haunted look in her eyes. "But...I'm afraid the scarring is...."

"Let me see."

"I don't think you should. Not yet."

"Let me have a mirror," Ress insisted. "If I am disfigured, then the sooner I come to terms with it, the better."

Sighing, the healer retrieved a small mirror from the other room and handed it to the girl. Ress took a deep breath, gathered her courage, and looked. A combination of feelings ran through her mind as she examined her face and saw the hideous scarring. The firedrake had obviously struck her with its flame, but apparently, the tree had shielded most of her body. Ress panted as tears flowed down her cheeks. She had to escape the horror that stared at her. Jumping up, she hurriedly pulled on a dress and ran to the door, stopping in horror when she saw the destruction the beast had done to her village.

"We lost half the villagers, including your father," the healer said as she moved up behind her. "I'm sorry, Ress."

For the next five years, Ress ran from that hated day, herself, and others' pity she could not bear. Bent on revenge, she roamed the countryside in search of firedrakes, hunting down her nightmares and killing each one she found, but their deaths brought no relief. Her hair grew back to its original length, and she used it to cover the left half of her face. For the most part, her scars were not obvious.

Earlier that day after killing her latest firedrake and saving a group of dwarves headed for Brackus, an elderly dwarf with a long white beard who appeared unaffected by her hideous face approached her.

"Why do ye seek yer death in this pointless endeavor?" he asked gently.

"Excuse me? I just saved your lives," Ress answered. She was somewhat bewildered and annoyed.

"Aye, and we are grateful. By the way ye handled yerself, I can tell ye have been doin' this for some time. Might I ask why?"

"I have my reasons," Ress replied. She was not about to explain. The last thing she wanted was his pity.

"And I'm guessin' they're painful ones, but I ask ye to consider one thing. I dunna think this is the life yer meant to have. No one knows what the gods have in mind for us. I canna tell the future, but yer aura makes me think ye have somethin' a lot more important awaitin' ye. Just promise ye will be open to it when it comes."

Ress eyed the dwarf curiously, as she thought about how empty her life had been the last five years. "If something more important comes along, I promise, I will keep an open mind."

CHAPTER NINE

"Careful," Azimuth warned. "It's female, which means she's staked out new territory and will defend it violently."

The firedrake perched on a great boulder that parted the flowing river, creating a small islet a hundred feet wide. The beast's length was forty feet from snout to the tip of its tail, with scales that looked as hard as diamonds and glistened like silver in the watery spray. Her massive head had a small crest with four wickedly curving horns, and a fifth, smaller horn on the top of her muzzle, perfect for goring prey.

Before leaping off the stone to take flight, the drake drew back her lips and displayed a mouthful of dagger-like teeth. She then took off and emitted a roar so loud that it shook the nearby trees.

"Give ground!" Hority shouted.

The little group scattered, skidding to a halt fifty paces from the edge of the cliff where the firedrake landed. The impact was enormous and the ground buckled, making the five of them stagger and fight to remain upright. The cliff's edge crumbled beneath the beast's weight, but her claws dug into the rock to keep from falling.

"It's now or never," Celedant said as he began a shield spell to protect them from the next blast.

The beast roared again, and Hority ran at her just as she loosed a stream of molten fire. Protected behind the shield the wizard had raised, Celedant, Azimuth,

Tarquin, and Eldahir were unharmed, but Hority was ten feet away. Quick as a rabbit he changed directions, running faster than a dwarf should be able to as he dodged out of the fire's way and continued toward the beast. His image was a blur as he ran. Hority's actions distracted the firedrake, giving the others time to attack. Tarquin, Azimuth, and Eldahir drew their swords as Celedant hurled blasts of power at it, but the little dwarf was already in place, his branch whirling as he rained blows upon the scaled body while dodging claws, teeth, and tail. His figure moved out of harm's way an instant before the creature struck.

"Electriskt Kastasig!"

Celedant hit the monster with a powerful lightning bolt, hoping the blow would break the creature's vertebrae. The blast hit her scaled neck, knocking her back several feet almost to the edge of the cliff and damaging numerous scales, but little else. A few dangled precariously before falling to the ground. Hority continued attacking with his staff. As Eldahir neared the firedrake, he swung mightily with his sword, damaging several more scales and leaving the beast roaring in pain. Hority's attacks increased in intensity as the monster's clawed feet attacked the little dwarf, who looked like he was dancing a jig.

Meanwhile the firedrake's head snapped at Azimuth with its mouth agape. Sidestepping the mighty dragon-turned-elf brought his sword up to meet the drake, delivering a fierce backhanded blow to the lower side of her jaw. Bone broke and several glittering teeth snapped off, flying through the air. Even as he struck, Azimuth jumped out of the way, as the firedrake claws scoured deep marks in the earth where he had just stood. Celedant's next blast struck the creature's chest near her front leg. Weakened by Hority's blows, the scales held for a second longer before cracking and falling to the ground, allowing Tarquin's sword to penetrate, sinking up to the hilt.

The firedrake roared in agony, and one of her forelegs folded under her body. As she collapsed, the other leg struck Tarquin a solid blow, then using her head as a weapon, she slammed into Tarquin's side, sending him tumbling head over heels. His body came to a rest forty feet away, gasping for breath and dazed by the blow. Hority darted off and danced about the firedrake's head, bashing it repeatedly with his stone-tipped branch, which should have broken the first time he used it.

Realizing the dwarf was using magic, Celedant and the others watched in amazement. The Clorian monk moved so fast, their eyes could hardly focus on him. The firedrake grew confused as Hority hit her with lightning-quick attacks, and the lump of pumas that adorned the branch's tip dripped blood. The firedrake had lost her left eye and one of her horns had been broken from the repetitive strikes. Nevertheless, she had not given up the battle yet. She lashed her tail, scoring a lucky blow that sent the cleric flying through the air to land in a heap near the edge of the river.

With the dwarf unconscious, Azimuth decided it was time to finish it. "Stand back," he ordered as he morphed into dragon form and attacked.

The surprised firedrake shook its head in confusion as the massive dragon charged, blasting a steady stream of molten death. The smaller beast panicked, extended its wings, and took to the air, but it never stood a chance against a full-sized dragon. Azimuth launched upward and using teeth and claws attacked the smaller animal. Allowing it to escape, he roared a warning, knowing she would never return to this region.

Celedant turned to an opened-mouthed Tarquin and said, "Not a word or question. I will explain later."

Azimuth returned to his friends and joined the others who were examining the still-unconscious dwarf. The Clorian looked badly injured. The firedrake's tail had opened a vicious wound to the scalp and jaw, and blood flowed over the dwarf's face and down the front of his robe.

"*Leave this to me*," Azimuth said telepathically.

Lowering his massive head, the dragon breathed a mist upon the dwarf's wounds, healing his injuries. Then before the monk awoke, he changed back to his elven form.

"What of the firedrake?" Celedant asked.

"I scared her away. Believe me when I say that she will never return here."

The wizard smiled and raised an eyebrow.

"What?" Azimuth asked him. His demeanor was still gruff.

"You old softy," Celedant laughed.

Azimuth's shoulders relaxed and a small smile brushed his face. "I wasn't about to kill her for doing what comes naturally. It's not her fault she picked the wrong territory to settle on." His expression turned serious. "I will not kill for naught."

Celedant patted his friend's back. "That's one of many things I like about you."

Hority awoke moments later and looked questioningly at everyone.

"Where's the beast?"

"Somewhere licking her wounds," Celedant replied. "Azimuth used his special magic to send a message it won't soon forget."

"Ye did well, Azimuth. Ye saved the valley."

Azimuth smiled. "No, we did it. You fought bravely, my friend."

Rising to his feet, the dwarf retrieved several firedrake's scales from the ground, shouting, "Amour at last. Clor shines on me this day. Oh, massive one, I will use these in yer memory as I smite me foes."

His words made Azimuth chuckle. If the little dwarf thought the firedrake was massive, he wondered what the cleric would think when he got his first look at a real dragon.

"I think we had best get back to the valley," Celedant said. "We've a long trek ahead of us."

The other man nodded. "Once we're back, I will meet with the Abbot and arrange for ye to view our writings. Afterward, I'll be heading off to the Bonecrusher Clan to arrange for more supplies."

"Your words to the Abbot will be appreciated," Celedant replied.

"Assured that yer mission won't have an evil effect on our valley, the Abbot will surely allow ye access to our library."

It was very late when they arrived back at camp. Hority would approach the Abbot in the morning with Baldo, and he left the others to bed down for the night.

Shortly after sunrise, as the members of the quest sat around a campfire eating their morning meal, Hority and Baldo returned looking somewhat crestfallen.

"Why do ye look so sad, Hority?" Hortus asked alarmed. "Has the Abbot denied our entry into the archives?"

The dwarf sat down with a puff of fine sand, dispelled by his habit. "Sadly, the Abbot wanted proof and took two of me firedrake scales. He was most concerned with the relationship between Clor and Thierry. Unfortunately, I canna paint a true picture. Neither Baldo nor I know anythin' about their relationship. Yet, realizing we had to persuade him, I focused on both gods and our pantheon's common goals."

Baldo took up the story. "Just when we thought we were making headway, the Abbot asked our order's opinion on lice and their stance between thick mud and runny mud. I had to come up with a response before he would entertain me inquiry about the records. Yet, as I began to despair, a final note arrived from the Abbot saying, "Ye are beneath consideration and a waste of time. Seek out Wersa. She can aid ye."

"And where can we find this Wersa?" Hortus asked.

"To the East; we can go there as soon as yer ready," Hority replied.

An hour later, the company and their guide neared the mountain, and Hority stopped the group to explain a few things.

"The Abbot is concerned that Clor is a much-forgotten deity. I think the other gods simply find him a great bore. Anyway, ye have the Abbot's approval. Wersa is the librarian. I cannot join ye as I havena received permission to go to her cave at the end of the valley. Just follow the trail. I must be on me way to the Bonecrusher Clan."

Hority wished them well and left while the others continued onward. As the valley narrowed, the track they followed began to rise, ending at a small cave with a thick hide covering the low entrance.

Hortus called out: "Wersa! We've been sent by the Abbot."

Several moments passed, but nothing happened. When she still did not respond to either Baldo or Celedant, the four hefted their weapons, lit their torches, and pulled aside the heavy hide. The passage beyond was low, and they had to crawl until the party came to another thick hide. Hortus called out again before tentatively pulling it aside. Piled on the floor of the cave were stacks of books and parchment. The cavern opened into a high vaulted ceiling and stretched far into the underground mountain stone. The Clorians' archives were a disheveled mess.

Hortus and his companions carefully treaded around the mounds of written material in search of the caretaker. When they reached the rear of the chamber, Celedant stared into the gloomy darkness lit by slender white tapers and said softly,

"Here is Wersa."

She had been the keeper of the Clorian Archives for as long as anyone could remember, but had obviously died long ago without anyone realizing it. Her mummified corpse rested peacefully on a bed of manuscripts. Around her on makeshift shelving were stacks of scrolls and manuals.

Baldo's head sagged. "Now what are we going to do? Should we intrude on her resting place? Did the Abbot's permission to use the library mean siftin' through everything it contains? And what should we do with the body?"

"I don't see where we have a choice," Hortus reasoned. "We'll have to sort everything to find what we need. We'll bury poor Wersa close by."

Several days passed as they worked. Once the cave was clean and aired, the Theirrian monks, aided by Celedant and his party, started going through the records. They preserved every scrap of paper, whether the Clorians wanted them to or not. Hortus instructed the workers to sort carefully, but they were to concentrate on anything containing information about their mission.

"Once we find what we need, I'll leave the rest of the monks behind to archive the Clorians' mess," Hortus said. "But I want Baldo to accompany us. It won't hurt to have another warrior along on this quest."

For the next several days, they scanned every scroll, book, and document for information about the history of the staff. Many of the writings were useless. The Clorian archives included a gripping treatise on how lice could bring an ordinary dwarf closer to his god. They had produced numerous studies of this type, baffling the Theirrian monks.

"Truly, Clor should be commended on the knowledge his monks gathered on filth and odoriferous smells," Baldo said late one afternoon after an exhaustive search through hundreds of such texts. "The subject reminds me of the Abbot's questioning."

It was exhausting work, but there also were many interesting writings hidden in the Clorian enclave that Hortus wanted cataloged and sent to the Royal Librarian in Nars, not the least of which was a dwarvan adventurer's journal of an attempt to locate the fallen capital of Zeiglon.

With a glint in his eye, the Abbot handed the journal over to Celedant.

After scanning the tale, Celedant smiled. "I believe I may have discovered the resting place of the final piece of Adaman's staff." He held up a small leather-bound book for the others to see before continuing. "This journal talks about a dwarf who traveled with twelve companions to the foot of the escarpment and found the lost capital of Zeiglon. It contains details about the area surrounding the city. Unfortunately, once the dwarf found it, the narrative ends. We will never know what happened to him or his companions. Yet somehow, his journal ended up in the Clorians' hands - and now in ours."

Hortus took the book from Celedant, and the others gathered around him. He opened its age-worn cover, and continued the narrative as he leafed through the pages. "This is a journal of a dwarvan warrior named Kreeg. It begins in the coastal city of Bau's Port in the Eastern Confederation. Kreeg describes a wizard that traveled with them and an old map of the city of Zeiglon. I think they must have overlaid it on a modern map and concluded that the city would be located along the southern edge of the great desert, by the coast. Kreeg hired a small boat to take them south past the Mordolwyn Peninsula to where the edge of the great desert meets the ocean. Past the mountains, the group skirted the coast for many leagues. The captain of the ship grew nervous as they neared the escarpment, yet the ruins of the capital never revealed themselves."

"Understandable," Azimuth said. "As you are all aware, the escarpment was formed by the great quakes that caused the earth to shift and lay waste to the region known as the Zeiglon Empire, turning the Kingdom of Partha into a desert. The southern portion of the land mass buckled and lifted upward, leaving the escarpment. It is reportedly a mile high in some places. This phenomenon of nature now separates the northern portion of the continent from the southern."

The listeners uttered words of interest.

"Traders of the City-states and the Brae often ply the southern waters to trade with foreign kingdoms located many leagues to the south," Azimuth continued. "Yet, there are still unexplored lands between the escarpment and a high mountain range that cuts the southern continent in two. The desert has kept all but the hardiest adventurers from braving the heights to seek information about what lies above. Few have attempted it and lived."

Celedant took up the story. "According to legend, many became lost in the desert and were taken as slaves by the nomads. Others were found wandering around, crazed and incoherent. As far as I know, even in the South, the land above these mountains is taboo. The tribes that border the mountain range believe that their dead enter the mountains to await rebirth."

Hortus nodded and continued. "Kreeg's company wanted to go to the escarpment, but the captain of the ship would not venture beneath its forbidding heights and dropped the adventurers off at the ocean's edge many miles away. They traveled on foot the rest of the way. At the time, the unnamed wizard was certain that the ruins lay just over the top of the escarpment. They had arranged to meet the ship in four weeks, leaving ample time to explore, but the adventurers spent the next several days at the base of the wall, searching for a way up."

"By Kreeg's calculations, the escarpment is over a mile high but appeared to angle downward as it proceeded into the desert." Hortus looked up, his brow furrowed.

"Did they find a way in?" Tarquin asked.

Hortus nodded and continued reading. "Kreeg decided to march into the Great Desert along the base of the wall, looking for favorable places to scale the cliff. Days passed as they moved further into the desert, until they chanced upon a portion that had fallen into the wasteland. As he and the others searched the rubble, they found bits and pieces of broken ruins and a small narrow stairway leading upward."

Sighing, Hortus gently closed the old journal. "The tale ends there. I do not know Kreeg's fate, but his daily entries stop. After his last entry, a different hand penned a sentence claiming, 'We were right. Zeiglon still thrives.'"

As Hortus ceased his narrative, Celedant stood up and stretched.

"An intriguing tale; it renews my hope that we will find the lost city of Zeiglon and complete our mission. Nevertheless, it also raises many questions. What will we encounter at the escarpment and beyond? If the area is still inhabited, who or what lives there? Unfortunately, I believe that as we travel further south, the danger will increase."

They sat up late that night, deciding what course of action would be best and discussing what little they knew about the land beyond the great desert. Celedant insisted they follow Krieg's example by hiring a ship to take them south. The desert, he argued, would be too exacting a challenge if they chanced a crossing. Tarquin and his remaining Borderers agreed and told the others of the intense heat they had endured during their desert training. That night, after everyone else had fallen asleep, Azimuth and Celedant spoke softly a short distance away.

"The heat won't bother me, even in this form," Azimuth said. "But it will become unbearable for the rest of you."

"Somehow I think the heat is going to be the least of our problems," Celedant said as he smoked his pipe. "Have you heard tales of the Shadow Lords of Zeiglon?"

"I'm afraid they're all true, but we will have to survive the other dangers lying in wait first," Azimuth warned. "It won't be easy."

"I know, my friend. However, I see little choice. The Staff of Adaman is the sole way to defeat Taza and the Staff of Adois."

"Maybe I should enlist the aid of my fellow dragons."

"Not yet," Celedant said as he knocked the remaining tobacco from his pipe. "I'm reluctant to expose you to the rest of the world until it is absolutely necessary. Nevertheless, I will not hesitate to call the dragons into battle should the need arise."

CHAPTER TEN

Taza had been traveling the Void for what seemed like weeks, but he knew that very few hours would have passed in his world. The denizens he recruited or had taken from their worlds assured him that Celedant and Tarquin would die sooner than later.

Circling the dark planet one last time, chilled to the bone from his experience in the limitless Void between worlds, Taza had come upon this place merely by happenstance. It was so dark that he almost missed it, but the staff's pull alerted him of its existence. Traveling through deep umber clouds, he came upon a mountainous world of crags and twisted slag.

He used the staff of Adois to seek out the most dangerous denizens there. Taza allowed the power of the staff to direct him deep into the mountainous world, which was devoid of the type of ground normally associated with a planet. Enormous mountains and slag rose up, creating deep trenches filled with fog. It was to one of these trenches that the Staff of Adois guided him. The fog chilled him to the bone. Without the aid of the staff, he could hardly see his hand before his eyes. Without the staff's guidance, he would have slammed into the enormous peaks.

Deep within the trench, the staff slowed his descent. He instantly felt the presence of dark evil nearby. Casting a spell of protection around himself, he spoke another enchantment, driving back the fog and revealing the monster. It looked similar to a dragon coiled on an up-thrust piece of rock, but on closer examination, he saw that it was more like a snake coiled to strike. It was dark and invisible in the fog, a waiting predator.

As Taza hovered in midair admiring the creature, the light attracted its attention. He saw the head move and then the body uncoiled as the monster struck upward toward him. Taza had little time to react as the creature's long fangs stopped a few feet from him. Using the staff, Taza pushed the monster away. It hung in midair for seconds before falling downward into the abyss. However, it did not disappear. It latched its tail to the rocky ledge and swung itself up to coil once more on the rock.

It sat there, head swaying back and forth, eyeing the warlock.

"Clever girl," Taza said. Using the staff, he opened a rift back to his adopted world, and soon located the prey he sought. The undead warlock felt the power of Celedant, and with one swift motion, he sent the monster through the rift with images of Celedant and Tarquin firmly imprinted on its mind.

Sitting around a fire pit the company was eating their dinner when Tarquin brought up the question that was on everyone's mind. "How are we going to get to the escarpment?"

Celedant said. "I know a ship's captain in the coastal city of Bau's Port who may be willing to take on our mission."

Everyone agreed that an early start was in order. Their knowledge of the land to which they were traveling was extremely vague, based for the most part on old myths about the escarpment being unsalable or even cursed. Of those willing to scale it, few souls ever returned. Those who did told of unspeakable horrors, but they were uncertain of what those horrors were except that it was a land of monsters, gods, and/or the dead. The common thread in the tales was that evil ruled over the escarpment and the land beyond.

In a fog-filled morning, the company, with Aegir and Vannor leading two over-burdened mules, left the Clorian's enclave and took the road east. The group had traveled about a hundred paces when Hority, dressed in threadbare robes, stood in the middle of the crossroad before them, his hands holding the reins of a swaybacked donkey.

"Hoy, Brother Baldo."

Baldo reined in his small horse and cried, "By Thierry, Hority, I thought ye were headed to the Bonecrusher Clan."

"I was, but last night I had a vision of Clor, and he directed me to join yer quest. So I sent another brother to notify the Bonecrushers that the way was open again and to send supplies," Hority said as he mounted his donkey. The poor animal looked ready to topple over from exhaustion. "I am tired of defending the valley, and while they catalog the library, yer brothers look to be more than a match for any stray orc. Besides, the Abbot asked that I follow ye. Clor might be a forgotten god by most, but our Abbot believes I might help our deity gain some respectability among the dwarvan pantheon of gods."

Baldo laughed. "We welcome ye. Yer a great warrior, but Celedant leads."

Celedant urged his horse closer to the little monk. "Hority of the Clorians, since I have already witnessed your bravery and efficiency in battle, you are welcome."

Hority almost blushed. "'Tis nothin'. I simply follow Clor's bidding." He swatted the donkey's flank and raced ahead, calling back, "Adventure awaits!"

Baldo rode after him, catching the reins of the donkey. "Come Hority, we go east - not south."

The company turned and followed Celedant, many secretively smiling at the newest member of their group. Nevertheless, several were concerned about the smell that hovered around the Clorian monk like a fog bank.

The wooded road followed a mountainous path past the Valley of New Partha. Snow-capped peaks surrounded them, leveling off by late afternoon. As night began to fall, they reached the area where the road climbed steeply until it crested and spread out before them with foothills stretching to the horizon. The road turned right and zigzagged with wide curves as it made its way into the foothills. That night they camped on the crest of the road, which had a majestic view of the stars as they twinkled to life in the nighttime sky.

The company had just crested a hill when they heard a crackling, popping sound and before them, a rift opened once more. It was as though the very fabric of their world was torn open, and a deep blackness stared back at them. They watched in horror as a long dark, sinewy creature emerged. The monster was gigantic, its girth as big around as an ancient tree trunk, its length as long as 100 paces. Black scales glistened in sunlight as its head swung toward the party, and its body undulated in their direction.

The company did not wait, recognizing a dangerous threat. Celedant,

Morganna, Eldahir, and Azimuth began casting spells as the others drew their weapons. The four spell casters released their power at the same time. Lightning and energy beams slammed into the snakelike creature. Wherever the spells struck, scales flew into the air, revealing darkened raw flesh.

The arrows and crossbow bolts struck true, but the projectiles bounced off the scales, attracting no notice from the creature as it continued toward the attackers, drawing ever closer. Spells and weapons failed to impede its progress. When it was close enough, the huge misshapen head struck at them. They pulled their horses away from the gaping maw, but the creature's bulk threw them aside like matchsticks. As it slithered closer, Tarquin drew his sword and struck at the creature's side.

His sword, Dragon Bolt, flamed red hot as it sliced through scales, penetrating deep into the monster's hide. The snake turned back on itself and struck again, sending Tarquin's horse bolting away after disposing of its rider. The prince had no time to get to his feet, and he rolled from side to side as it struck repeatedly. He could not keep this up for long. The snake was too fast and as it rose up for the deathblow, Tarquin raised his sword and prayed his blade could stop the deadly fangs from impaling him.

The majority of defenders had dismounted and with weapons raised, they rushed to help Tarquin, which distracted his attacker and allowed the prince to escape. Focusing through dark, lidless eyes, the creature glanced at the now-empty ground where its prey had been. Then it swung swiftly around to this new threat and advanced. Its tail whipped, slamming into Azimuth's head and knocking him backward into a gulley. Ralav and Botreg ducked, but it got them as it swung back, knocking them tumbling away.

Rattled, Azimuth regained consciousness at the bottom of a rocky dry steam bed. He knew what he had to do. Jumping to his feet, he left the gulley and morphed into his dragon body, flying upward. Concentrating on the monster, his comrades never saw the transformation.

The golden dragon flew straight up into the air, turning fast and diving at the snakelike creature. Talons outstretched, Azimuth roared a warning, sending the others scrambling out of the way. Then he breathed white-hot fire that seared the monster's armor and as it rose up in fury, the dragon struck, digging his claws into the newly-exposed skin and grappling with it. The monster rolled and turned repeatedly in an attempt to dislodge Azimuth, but the dragon held on tightly, his claws ripping out great chunks of flesh. Enraged, the snake tried to sink its fangs into the dragon's flesh, but dragon scales are tough and other than a few scratches, did little damage. Working his way to the head of the monster, Azimuth struck again, spewing tongues of flame that engulfed its head. Pain caused the monster to rear upward and scream.

Falling over, it pinned Azimuth to the hard ground. The snake's great weight came close to breaking the dragon's back. Using heroic strength, he used his powerful wings to flip the monster over as the beast was still trying to bite him. With its eyes burned to a crisp, it was blind - but that mattered little coming from the pitch darkness of its native planet. Azimuth curved his head this way and that, avoiding attacks. Then, when he was in the right position, he buried a mouth full of gleaming white teeth into the snakelike creature's neck just behind the head.

Azimuth rode the flailing monster, digging his claws deeper into its sides, viciously biting the creature's charred flesh. But the dragon's luck ran out. The monster struck backward, latching onto a forelimb with its mouth and flinging its attacker roughly away. Azimuth's leg stung as he crashed to the ground, sending debris flying as the monster pulled away sharply to escape its pain.

Then several powerful spells struck it near the tail, severing it from the body. It hit the ground and flopped around like a fish out of water. Azimuth recovered, took to the air, and dove toward the head of the monster, breathing flames that baked its head and body until its death throes slowed. In a desperate attempt to escape, the snakelike creature rose into the air, but it could go no further. Doubling over, it spewed black blood from its mouth and collapsed to the ground.

Azimuth struck one final time, his flames rolling over the beast and his claws digging deep rents. Adding their firepower to the battle, Celedant and the others continued riddling the creature with arrows and causing great wounds from their powerful spells.

The creature convulsed one last time and lay dead on the battlefield. The party stared dumbfounded at the monster.

"We are safe!" Celedant counted their number and called out to Azimuth as he crawled from the dry stream bed, clothes torn with ragged rents in his flesh from the thick thorns of the briar patch.

As the battle ended, the golden dragon had dived toward the thicket, changing form back to an elf before striking the ground, assured that he had remained hidden from the eyes of the company. His arm bitten and broken, he used his dragon ability to heal every wound except for minor cuts and bruises he had received from the thorns.

Tarquin jumped down into the small ravine to help him out of the thorns.

When they reached the top, Aegir healed the small wounds scattered across

Azimuth's body.

At the beginning of the battle, the horses had fled in fear and were nowhere in sight. Even if they had found them that day, the animals would have been too frightened to ride. Celedant and the others camped well away from the creature's corpse, knowing that the smell of death would bring bloodthirsty scavengers.

The next day Ralav, Ronli and Morganna tracked the horses, which took most of the morning. When they returned to camp, everyone mounted up and headed south.

CHAPTER ELEVEN

The giant that joined the throng assembling in front of the great building was impressive. With his appearance, the crowd quieted, looking to him for orders. He was taller and broader in the shoulder than most of his race, and he wore plate mail and a full-face helmet, which he carried under his arm and that glinted in the sunlight. Melgor noted smooth blond hair cut short and a rugged, pockmarked face as the giant scanned the sky and issued orders. Moments later, the crowd made room for an army of orcs wheeling an enormous ballista that they aimed skyward. Though a semblance of order had settled over the inhabitants, the warlock saw that the streets were filling up as orcs poured from caves scattered across the mountainside.

"The peaked roof of that large building, if you please," Melgor called to his mount.

The chimera responded and headed for the building, settling on the roof and turning so the warlock could see the crowd below. The ballista with its large, spear-like projectile followed Melgor's path. He was not pleased that his perch had placed him in the direct line of fire, but there was nowhere else suitable to land. Therefore, the warlock and his many-headed steed stood on the roof as the sun set behind the mountain, casting its last rays magically on the pair. Melgor remembered Sellis' description of Herroth the Great, and the blond-headed giant that patiently waited for Melgor to speak was definitely not Herroth.

"I bring tidings of peace and friendship from the Warlocks' Council of

Dorian," the warlock began after magically magnifying his voice. "I am Melgor, Lord Taza's personal representative."

"You bring nothing but trouble. Last messenger poison great Herroth," the armored giant responded coldly.

Murmurings from the crowd caused the warlock to pause before answering. "My master was not responsible for this betrayal, which has been accounted to Sellis," Melgor replied. "Rest assured that upon discovering this deception, the council apprehended the scoundrel. He died during the most painful torture our experts could devise."

There was no reason for the giant to know the exact nature of Sellis's condition. He hoped the added bit about torture would appease the new King's lust for revenge. "May I approach?"

The giant bowed. "Me King Jordic."

The giants surrounding him beat their weapons against their shields and shouted, "Long live Jordic, conqueror."

As the chimera took to the air, a large area in front of the King cleared for her to land.

Jordic smiled at the warlock, motioning for him to come down from his beast and walk with him.

Melgor dismounted.

"Your master powerful. Maybe good ally," the giant stated. "He summon mighty creatures."

As the chimera returned to the roof, the warlock noted that the walls were made of whole tree trunks caulked with mud. Inside the door, four giants in chainmail bowed their heads as Jordic passed. The King led Melgor into a dining hall of immense proportions that contained a central fire pit running the length of the room with long rows of rough-hewn wooden tables that ran parallel to the pit. Jordic passed these, taking the warlock to the far end of the hall and his throne, carved from solid black rock and padded with several cushions. The giant snapped his fingers, and a smaller giantess brought forth a human-sized chair set on extra high legs with rungs for Melgor to climb up. The warlock had never seen a female giant and, although she was not as tall as Jordic, she looked equally formidable.

Once the warlock settled into his chair, the giant leaned toward him with a glint in his eye and asked, "Who is warlock's master? Why he want help?"

Melgor cleared his throat but before he could speak, the giant held up a hand. "Me not expect your visit. We drink first."

The same giantess brought a huge pitcher and tankard for Jordic and a smaller mug for the warlock. Although the King appeared hospitable, the warlock could not help wondering if this was to be the last drink for a condemned man, but after Jordic gulped down half his mug, he smiled and nodded his thanks, and took a sip of the cooled ale before beginning.

"My master's existence is shrouded in mystery. Legend says he was here at the formation of the planet. That might be an exaggeration told by those who fear him, but he has lived a very long life, much like the ageless elves. May the gods devour them."

The giant drained his mug. "Me agree; elves rot."

Resting his cup on the arm of his chair, the warlock continued. "My master offers conquest and riches. He will aid you and your hosts in marching on Southgard and later, the city-states. You and your minions can plunder the great wealth of the dwarves. Lord Taza has magic that can summon creatures from unknown places. You have seen my steed. He can provide creatures that will crush the walls of the strongest dwarvan fortresses."

Jordic sat back in his chair and rubbed his short beard. "How this help Taza? Me like gold, gems, shiny things, but what your master get?"

Melgor mouth formed a sly smile. "The dwarves and their allies have interfered with the task my master is trying to complete. Lord Taza has no need for worldly wealth. He seeks deeper, darker secrets of the arcane along with an ally he can trust – an ally who will be rewarded beyond what is taken during the invasion."

"Me not trust offers of plenty," Jordic replied, narrowing his eyes at the warlock. "Warlocks offer Herrick gold. Got dead instead."

"King Jordic, I understand how you feel and do not expect a quick answer," Melgor readily agreed. "Ponder this proposal, but know this. My master needs your army to march within the month." Melgor realized belatedly that he might have pushed the giant too far, but Taza had been specific about the timetable he wanted for the invasion. The warlock saw the giant's face developing a reddening frown and calmly addressed him. "I have been given the authority to summon creatures to aid your conquest."

"You show Jordic creatures in morning. Rest now."

Thinking he would have to sleep on the floor as the giant's beds were too high for him, Melgor was pleasantly surprised when they provided him with a child's bed, roomy for a giant child and perfect for a human.

The next morning Melgor rose, washed, and shaved in the small basin they had provided. He was just finishing when a loud thud sounded against his door. The warlock deactivated the perimeter spells so when the giant's head poked through the crack, it would not explode.

The giant motioned to the warlock, simply saying, "You come."

As they exited the main hall, the sun was cresting over the horizon, driving away dense clouds that enshrouded the hills and mountains. Jordic stood in the center of the fortress grounds, waiting for him.

Melgor scanned the area without moving his head and saw that over fifty giants had assembled and several dozen orcs, some of who appeared to be chiefs. He drew a deep breath. They were armed and glared at him as he casually walked across the courtyard. Mentally, he grasped the pendant that hung around his neck and called *Taza*. As he approached Jordic, a calm soothing voice entered his mind: *Do not be afraid, my faithful minion. Use your staff and summon the creatures. They have no name, but they will come.*

"A fine morning, is it not, your highness?" Melgor remarked as he reached the King of the giants.

Jordic sneered and with an evil grin snarled, "Show me power or die."

Melgor laughed inwardly. "If that were to happen, I would release a curse and the fortress, along with any living beings in it, would be destroyed, long before I drew my last breath." He bowed, showing no fear. "Nevertheless, I will do as you wish, your highness."

Melgor walked a few paces to the center of the yard and looked haughtily at the assembly. He thrust his oaken staff into the ground. The onlookers could detect nothing as the warlock sent out a call using the power of his staff to multiply his magical abilities. Seconds passed. Even though his concentration was on the spell he wove, he could see that the crowd was becoming restless. In the periphery of his mind, the idea that in their impatience they could still kill him spurred him on.

Magic flowed into his body through the staff, making the soil ripple outward, and the onlookers took several steps back while others fell to their knees as ground waves made them stumble and lose their footing. The spell reached its zenith as three-foot waves of dirt and rock radiated from where Melgor stood motionless, causing one section of the ill-fitted rubble wall that surrounded the fortress to teeter, collapse into shambles, and fall into the moat below.

In several places, the hard-packed dirt boiled and out of this vortex of minerals, a bleached white maw appeared. The front of the creature had row upon row of broad, square teeth, which it used to grind rocks to pebbles before swallowing. A few feet from the mouth, a boney raised brow protected the small humanoid-like creatures seated behind it. In their hands were small rods used to control their monstrous beasts that measured thirty paces in length with a tapering whip-like tail that rose fifteen feet into the air.

As they emerged, Melgor counted three creatures covered with small rows of stiff bristles that wound about the animal. Using an undulating movement, they propelled the beast toward its destination. Once all three creatures were uncovered, one of the handlers climbed down, using these protrusions like a ladder. What approached Melgor looked like a segmented insect or its equivalent; its knee pointed backward so it walked with a hopping gait. The creature raised a claw, palm outward, implying, the warlock hoped, that it came in peace. Then in a shrill voice almost too high to comprehend, it spoke.

"We have been promised much rock to grind and eat and were told to seek a warlock named Melgor. We know not this term, but you have summoned us and thus to you, we speak."

"Yes, I summoned you. However, let me introduce you to the one who will be your master while you reside on this planet. He will lead you to places where you can devour as much rock as you desire."

Jordic moved closer, towering over the three-foot high creature. "You help Jordic. Me like. Give you plenty rock to eat."

The insect creature clicked and chirped, nodding its head. "We will follow you, tall one, and graze to test the rocks of this place, devouring that which you point out."

Jordic raised his arms shouting, "Raise army. We fight with new allies. Warlock promise much treasure. Blow battle horns."

The army's assembly was miraculously fast. Melgor thought that the orcs with their myriad of commanders might take months; however, Jordic had a quick answer to every complaint. He would simply grab the malcontent, bite off its head, and toss the body to his soldiers to snack on. The questioning commander's second-in-command would then assume leadership, knowing better than to complain.

Once assembled, the warlock climbed the steps of the rough-hewn tower to get a better view of the army. What stretched out before him was a sea of terror that made even him shudder inside. In the courtyard below, the strange creatures disappeared beneath the ground, leaving small craters. As the giants assembled, Melgor counted seventy-five heavily armored behemoths waiting to transport the giants to Southgard. Each beast was capable of carrying two giants and had two pairs of swirled horns that topped a massive bull-like head and body. He recognized the beasts as wandering creatures that roamed the plains subsisting on grass. Melgor turned his gaze from the castle's courtyard to the surrounding hills that were literally swarming with orcs carrying a thousand different banners, marking their individual clans.

Melgor exited to the roof, climbed upon his steed, and soared into the air. Below, the ground seemed alive and flowing as the army advanced like a colossal wave rolling up a beach. There had to be tens of thousands. No, he reconsidered. With an untold number of orcs still hidden behind hills or in forests, the total number that marched with the giants had to be closer to a hundred thousand. As his steed circled the army, he nudged it westward, flying over the army as he headed for the dwarvan territories.

The trip took many days. Melgor and his beast flew ahead first over the ocean and then passed over the unpopulated southern shore to where many tribes of wild humans, orcs, and other creatures eked out a paltry existence in the wilderness of forest and caves. The foothills grew larger. He entered the low mountains, where he located the nearest border fort that was the first line of defense, protecting the dwarves from the chaos of the west. This, however, was not the one he wanted. The warlock continued searching for the middle fortress, Ruger, which held reinforcements and supplied the needs of the other dwarvan forts.

He followed the smaller fortresses and after an hour, Melgor found the one he wanted. This outlying post was the largest, standing several hundred feet high and set on a low plateau that overlooked several main trails that wound through the mountains. It featured a strong outer bailey with squat towers standing evenly along the wall. If overwhelmed, the keep had an excellent killing zone within and on the outer walls. An enemy would have but one sure path to the inner courtyard, and that was the main gate. Unless the besieging army tore down the walls around the keep, there would be no easy way to attack, and Melgor was convinced that Southgard would send a relief column there before that occurred.

The warlock flew high over the surrounding mountains, looking for a vantage point where he could watch the oncoming battle. Spotting a likely perch on a cliff overlooking the fortress, he brought his steed to rest on a small outcrop of rock that offered an excellent view. Melgor dismissed the chimera so it could hunt and feed while he settled in. He then moved rocks and large boulders using levitation spells and formed a rough wall of stone along the edge of the outcrop. Melgor wanted to be certain he did not accidentally fall over the edge during the night.

When he finished, the warlock sat with his back against one of the larger boulders and searched through his pack for a small, yellow drawstring bag. When he found it, he untied the strings, pulled it open, and plunged his hand inside, bringing forth a few pieces of dry firewood, a small kettle, tea leaves, and a joint of meat.

All the items were larger than the small sack. *This Bag of Holding was worth the death of its former owner*, he thought with a smile as he cooked his meal. After he had eaten, the chimera returned from consuming its own supper, and Melgor sat with his back to the beast's side for a nap. The army would march day and night until it reached the dwarvan outpost. Then the battle would begin.

CHAPTER TWELVE

The eastern lands were comprised of loosely allied city-states, called by other nations the Confederation. The inland and coastal cities vied against each other for trade but rarely fought openly. Each city relied on border raids, capturing a small section of territory and then forcing one of the larger cities to negotiate a peace settlement. After receiving their reward, the invaders returned the land to its original owners.

Aside from petty squabbles, the cities would band together in the face of peril, most often to repel encroachments from the abundant tribes of orcs or other monsters residing in the southern portion of the Mordolwyn Mountains. Although the Confederation was orderly, the lands between cities were lawless and dangerous, with borders frequently shifting during the course of a year. It was across this land of continual flux that Celedant and his party now rode.

The last dwarvan way station was a solidly fortified fort, twenty-five leagues into the foothills. The nearest city, Omsford, was forty leagues to the southeast, and its control extended twenty leagues beyond its walls. This was the last secure place for traders or travelers, going or coming to the Dwarvan Empire, to stay. The grandfather of a dwarf named Hemlit had inherited the station from a close friend. Hemlit's Station was originally a small fort on the summit of the hill. The dwarves had established the station to provide protection for their caravans heading into the Confederation for trade. Over the years, a small town had grown up around it, and the proprietor of the station became its mayor.

Hemlit currently had a population of just over a thousand and was growing each year. The dwarvan army stationed troops there to guard the trade route, and the border town was becoming an asset to the Empire. The inhabitants of this small frontier city were a mixed group of races and included brigands and adventurers. It was the gateway to the Mordolwyn Mountains and for a few, a sure path to glory, but for most, their reward was deprivation and death.

Two days after they left the Clorian compound, Ralav rode past the town's gate, turned, and waved back at the company hidden at the edge of the forest. He was sent ahead to determine how closely the guards queried travelers. Ralav rode at an easy pace, and the guards allowed him to pass the rough-hewed timbered walls of Hemlit without questioning.

Evening was fast approaching as Tarquin and the others entered the border town. Celedant was aware that with the coming of nightfall, the town transformed into a riotous and dangerous place. Town folk and adventurers packed the inns, and the noise from their interiors spilled into the street. The wizard assumed the lead from Ralav, following a meandering path through the crowded roads. He had traveled through this town many times over the years and had frequented a number of Hemlit's inns, both the richly appointed and the seedy ones.

He felt that Roules was the best inn for meeting their needs on this trip, which was located against the southeastern wall of the town. It would offer both security and a quick escape if needed. Seedy might have been too nice a term to describe Roules' establishment, or Roule himself for that matter. The inn was three stories high and listed gently to the right. The outside had once been painted brick red, but that was long ago. The paint had been peeling off for years.

As Celedant and the others dismounted in the yard, a raggedly dressed, pox-scarred man in dung-smeared leather leggings and a loose cotton shirt took charge of their horses. He led their mounts to a ram-shackle stable located across the courtyard. Celedant spoke softly to the stable hand before ascending the warped wooden steps to enter the inn.

As the wizard opened the door, he turned his head and spoke in a low voice. "We should be safe here. Roule is a friend of mine. You will treat him as such."

As he finished, the wizard noticed Hority standing beside his donkey, frozen like a statue in the yard. The dwarf stared wide-eyed at the inn.

Celedant left the front steps and went to him. "Is something wrong?"

Hority shook his head. "I've never seen the like of these buildings. Clor doesna allow me to sleep in such places."

Understanding, the wizard nodded. "What about the stable? It is much like a cave. Dwarvan sheepherders use caves in the winter to shelter their flocks. What do you think Clor would say to that? Besides," he said with a wink, "you're bound to find lots of filth inside to examine."

Hority looked at the stable skeptically while scratching the nits in his beard. "If that's the case, aye, that would be acceptable."

Secretly relieved, Celedant slapped him on the back, knowing the smelly dwarf's presence inside the inn would not be welcome. "We'll send food and drink out to you. You may guard our horses so that no one harms them."

That appeased the reluctant dwarf, and he led his donkey to the stable as the others entered Roules Inn. The inn's atmosphere ignited Tarquin's imagination, and a smile spread across his face. Meanwhile Eldahir, Azimuth, and Morganna arched their eyebrows in disapproval at the scene before them. The tables and chairs were mishmash and like the exterior of the building, paint was peeling from the walls. The lighting was so poor; it cast the common room in perpetual gloom, while a thick cloud of smoke clung to the rafters like fog, making it an ideal setting for dark conspiracies and devious plotting.

The patrons were just as diverse and dark. Heading toward a back corner of the room, Celedant and the others shoved three tables together and sat around them. Three serving girls descended upon them, and although they tried to appear attractive, their looks and low-cut dresses could not hide the wrinkles on their grimy skin. After ordering ale and wine, Celedant asked one of the girls to send Roule over to the table.

Sitting across from Celedant, Ralav looked casually about the room until he spotted an enormous human hybrid waddling toward their table. The grizzled dwarf could not decide if he should draw his sword and alert the others or wait. Seeing the dwarf's puzzled expression, Celedant smiled. Roule's appearance often elicited that kind of reaction. The wizard stood and turned, coming face-to-face with the most hideous man he had ever known. They stared at one another a moment before Celedant found himself enfolded in two monstrous, hairy arms.

"Tis good to see you again, Master Celedant," Roule declared in a booming voice. "What may I do for you?"

Celedant motioned for him to take a seat at the table. "My friends and I need a place to spend the night."

Roule slid back an old chair and eased his bulk into it. The chair creaked under the stress of his weight but held together. The innkeeper's extreme weight, however, was only one of his problems. He was half-Minotaur. Raped during a raid, his human mother gave birth to him nine months later. Roule retained most of his mother's traits, having human hands and feet, but his father's blood showed in startling ways. He was extremely hairy, almost furred, and he had the head of bull, disguising the fact that Roule was probably one of the wisest individuals in the city. To make things worse, fangs extended from his lower and upper jaw, disappearing within his bushy beard and mustache.

His appearance might have been monstrous, but within seconds, he and Celedant were laughing like old friends as they swapped recent tales. Roule had most of the party chuckling before he had to leave to tend to the bar. The company enjoyed surprisingly good venison meat pies for supper before heading upstairs to their rooms. As Tarquin moved toward the steps, Botreg grabbed his arm and steered him back to the bar.

"Tarquin, let's stay awhile longer," Botreg whispered. "I swear I've seen one of the patrons before."

Tarquin called to Roule for two more ales. "Who would that be?" he asked as he handed a mug to the dwarf.

Botreg climbed onto a barstool. "Sneak a glance at the small table by the stairs. See the bald man with a patch over his left eye? I canna be certain if I know him or have just seen him around before. Nevertheless, he has avoided me eye every time I look in that direction. He might be searching for us as a group, or he might be an assassin lookin' to claim the price on me head."

"What makes you think he's after you? Celedant and I both have prices on our heads as well."

"Let's just call it a gut feelin'."

Tarquin nursed his ale and scanned the room, getting a good look at the man who had his friend concerned. He could understand why Botreg was worried. The man was muscular and well armed. Clean-shaven, he was dressed in close-fitting black leather armor, and his bald pate had a livid scar running horizontally above his left ear. Alone with an empty mug in front of him, their suspicions were further aroused because he did not order a refill.

Tarquin asked, "What do you want to do?"

Botreg shrugged. "I suppose we can follow when he leaves and see where he goes. Who knows? It might prove to be an exciting night."

His human friend snorted. "Ha, or our curiosity might get us killed," he replied sarcastically.

Botreg nodded. "This is to get ye back for always volunteering me in the Borderers."

Two mugs of ale later, the man, who never refilled his mug, got to his feet, tossed a coin on the table, and walked to the door. He passed within a few feet of Tarquin, animosity emanating from every pore. For just a moment, the prince felt like the man was about to bury a dirk in his back.

As the stranger exited the inn, Botreg reached up and slapped his friend on the shoulder. "Let's go."

When they reached the street, they saw the bald man heading north up the busy road. A full moon rode high in the sky, offering plenty of light to follow their target as they made their way through the crowd of people. Botreg dodged through them, moving folks out of the way and pulling his Lieutenant along as Tarquin kept a close eye on their prey. The man did not appear to be going anywhere in particular and seemed to be wandering through the milling people without a specific destination. He strolled down the street as if he did not have a care in the world. It was clear to both friends that the man was purposely leading them on because whenever he got too far ahead, he would slow down and allow them to catch up.

When the bald man disappeared around a corner, Tarquin was certain they were heading into a trap. Botreg stopped in the middle of the road, looking around, while Tarquin ran to a carter's shop and vaulted on top a barrel. Even from this vantage point, he could not see where the man had gone.

Botreg anxiously joined him, but Tarquin jumped down. "We lost him."

The dwarf cursed and stomped his booted foot. "I coulda sworn he was leadin' us into a trap."

"Me too, but apparently he just wanted to keep us in sight until he could give us the slip," Tarquin said in dismay.

Two hands firmly grabbed them by the arm and pulled them back.

"Quickly, this way," Morganna said in a hushed voice. She guided them to a dark alley hidden in shadow next to the carter's shop. "The man you were following headed down the alley just as you turned the corner," she whispered.

"How do you know?" Tarquin blurted.

The Illanni silenced him. "I noticed him watching us a bit too keenly. When I realized that Botreg was also interested in him, I slipped out of an upstairs window and waited in the shadows nearby. Come on, he shouldn't be far."

Botreg chuckled. "Never thought I would like having a dark one on me side."

The Illanni paused and blandly said, "Times change. I have thought the same thing about dwarves, humans, and wizards many times of late."

Morganna led them deeper into the shadows of an alley five feet wide, hemmed in by two- and three-story buildings on both sides. However, the moonlight that illuminated the street so brightly was unable to penetrate the darkness here. They walked cautiously, avoiding the trash that littered the ground, careful not to make any sound that might alert the man to their presence. Morganna drew her sword and bent low to follow their quarry's tracks through the alley's gloom. After years of honing her tracking skills in the darkness of the underworld, she found the faint traces of his passing easy to follow. Behind her, Tarquin drew a dagger while Botreg kept his hand on the hilt of his sword as he glanced back the way they had come. A moment later, they heard a door ahead of them quietly open and close.

"He apparently thinks he lost us," Morganna whispered. "Who do you think he is?"

"Botreg believes he's out to get us. The Assassin's Guild placed a hefty reward on his head when he quit and joined the Borderers. Then again, he might be after me or Celedant, or maybe he was sent to keep us from going after the remaining piece of the staff."

Morganna shook her head. Even in the underworld, the Assassin's Guild was a power to be reckoned with. She pondered, not for the first time, what sort of people she had chosen to join. This company was already facing a powerful enemy. Now she learned that assassins might be stalking them as well. She slowed as the tracks came to a halt at a blank wall made of ill-fitting boards, but they saw no sign of a door.

Tarquin slipped in front of her and scanned the gloomy alley to see where it led, while Morganna approached the wall without making a sound. The Illanni's dark hair seemed lustrous in the near pitch-blackness of the confined space as she stood in front of the wall and studied every aspect of its surface. Her left hand moved, and she whispered a spell in her native language that revealed the faint outline of a secret door glowing with amber light.

Morganna waved to the others. "It is safe to open, but I sense that somewhere beyond this portal, dark magic is at work. That is the one spell I will use for now. If this is a trap, I don't want to alert those inside."

She reached out to toggle a hidden latch that opened the wall inward and stepped into the darkness. Botreg and Tarquin followed into what appeared to be a dense, neglected garden filled with dead vegetation. Prickly bushes planted throughout the plot turned the area into an obstacle course. Then in the moonlight, they spotted a small trail leading deeper into the gloom of the garden.

Morganna again took the lead, a mere shadow in the darkness. After a few feet, they realized that the trail led to the rear of a large, shuttered, two-story brick house – an abandoned mansion when compared to Hemlit's typical buildings. They followed the trail to the back door.

Morganna and Botreg listened at the portal, while Tarquin, who had exchanged the dagger for his sword, stood guard, his blade emitting a slight glow in the night air, warning of danger. The dwarf pushed the door open. Inside was an old kitchen covered with a heavy layer of dust, broken by a set of slushy footprints covered in the grime of the alleyway. They followed the trail to a large dining room that contained a broken table and overturned chairs collapsed into a heap of rotted wood, but nothing else.

The windows were boarded over, and Morganna led the way through the house, following the wet footprints into a foyer and up a marble staircase. They slowed their pace as they mounted the steps, and as the three of them neared the upper floor, they heard a hushed conversation coming from one of the rooms along the hallway. The marble steps were cracked and threatened to collapse at any moment, but their quarry had left an obvious trail through the dust up to the second floor. Morganna eased onto the landing on the second floor and saw a bright light coming from under a door down a short-carpeted hallway.

As they neared the room, they heard a voice. "Come, Lord Taza. Hear me." The unknown voice held an edge of urgency as he spoke.

For a moment, silence followed the man's plea. Then a harsh, inhuman voice that sounded like it was coming from far away, answered. "I am here. This had better be pleasant news."

"Lord Taza," the first voice said. "Celedant and the crystal have left the dwarvan kingdom."

There was a distant curse before the eerie voice of the unseen Taza answered. "Idiot! I already know that! My staff is in harmony with the crystal and shows me its general location. Where are they headed?"

"At the moment, Celedant and his party are at Hemlit's. They travel east into the Confederation. The Theirrian Abbot Hortus travels with them."

Lord Taza's grim voice asked, "What are your plans?"

"I have long waited for this day," the man laughed, "and have alerted Melgor of the situation. Before daylight, Celedant and his little band will be dead, and your minions will be headed your way with the crystal."

Once again silence filled the room before the disembodied voice of Taza said, "If you fail me, there will be nowhere you can hide that I won't find you."

They heard a whistling sound and the light extinguished, followed by a sigh as the man uttered, "Demon spawn! I must have been out of my mind when I accepted this task."

Everyone gathered at the door realized that the fire had been a conduit to the man's master, Taza. Tarquin kicked the door open and the three rushed inside the room. The man at the fire acted without hesitation; using his hand, he cast a quick spell with fire encompassing his fingers and flicked it at the charging warriors. A barrier of fire sprung up from the floor, but because of the hasty way it was formed, it did not slow the companions as they ran through the magical wall of fire, their clothes smoldering and their skin reddening as they raced toward him.

The warlock that they had been following bolted toward another door. As he did, he sent small fireballs at his pursuers. Morganna was barely able to put up a shield as one came close to striking her. Their enemy was near the door when one of Botreg's daggers struck him in the shoulder. The pain lanced through the attacker, and his hand had just reached the door when Tarquin was upon him. Despite his wounded shoulder, the man pulled out two short swords and raised them defensively as they clashed against Dragon Bolt.

The man knew his master Taza would kill him if he was captured. So he kicked the door open, drawing his attackers after him. He fought his way across an old ballroom, the ancient parquet floor cracking under his weight. As he attempted to gain a solid stance, something heavy landed on his shoulders. He looked to his left and saw the visage of the smiling dwarf. Trapped, he turned his sword, the point drawing blood at his sternum, and fell on his face. Botreg was lucky. He flipped off the man's shoulders just in time, or he might have been skewered as well.

With the knowledge they had come for, Morganna led the group's return at a run. They paused briefly to scan for enemies before exiting the house. Running down the half-deserted streets of Hemlit, they headed back to Roules' Inn. There, Tarquin led Botreg and Morganna up the stairs at an easy, unhurried pace. They dared not alert anyone who might be watching. The company shared four bedrooms with a meeting room between, while the wizard had a private chamber down the hall. Tarquin waved the other two toward their friends' rooms before heading for Celedant, who answered his urgent knock. When he saw the concern on his young friend's face, he waved him in.

"What's wrong?" the wizard asked.

"Botreg, Morganna, and I just overheard one of Taza's minions speaking to him. They plan to attack tonight, kill us, and steal the crystal."

"Ah, I was expecting such a move. No doubt you spotted the man in the corner, who seemed a bit too interested in us."

"Yes, well, no," Tarquin admitted, embarrassed. "Botreg and Morganna did, so we followed him to an abandoned house where he contacted his master."

"It is good we have more watchful eyes than yours," Celedant said, his eyes crinkling with humor to soften the reproach he had just delivered.

"You're right. I should have noticed," Tarquin admitted.

"Best be on your toes at all times, my boy. I need not tell you how serious that creature is about killing us to get the Staff of Adaman for himself. If he ever gets his hands on it, more than just our cause will be doomed."

"I know, and I'm sorry. I'll not let my guard down again," Tarquin promised.

"Good. Now, wake the others. We must be ready to give our attackers a surprise of our own."

CHAPTER THIRTEEN

Melgor had just finishing drinking the last of his wine when the giant and orc army appeared, swarming across the horizon like a great plague of locus and flowing into the valleys surrounding Fort Ruger. For the next hour, the warlock watched the garrison soldiers run across the top of the outer walls, setting up defensive weapons. He grinned as the dwarves labored to position the ballistae and trebuchets. Those weapons would be useless against the giants.

Once they were in position, the orcs shot massive arrow barrages to keep the dwarves' heads down. The defenders returned fire, but the ballistae and trebuchets hardly made an impact on the besieging army. Huge boulders rolled through the orcs, crushing and throwing their twisted bodies aside like dried cornstalks, but the dead were merely a pittance to such a large army. Iron spears shot by the ballistae hardly made a dent in the tens of thousands of orcs, but caused considerable damage to the behemoths ridden by the giants. The giant's steeds were enormous six-legged monstrosities with ivory horns sprouting from their heads. Melgor mounted the chimera and flew overhead, watching the massive army surge ahead.

As the warlock continued his vigil, he saw the first signs of the insectoid creatures burrowing through rock and soil toward the dwarvan fortress. Their tunnels tossed the orcs left and right. The massive moving trails headed for their destination and promptly disappeared. As the siege continued, Melgor cast a spell, allowing him to see the area beneath the walls. He smiled as wide, jagged cracks formed in the rock base of the fortress, splitting the walls all the way to the top. A huge wave of orcs pressed onward in anticipation of the coming slaughter. Before long, the cracks had widened enough, making the structures sway. Along the top of the wall, dwarves ran like drunken soldiers toward the safety of the corner towers.

When the stone wall broke away from its foundation, it leaned outward before collapsing onto the besieging orcs. It was a small price to pay as thousands more poured into the fortress, and the massacre began. Afterward, the strange rock-eating creatures were gone. Melgor nodded in satisfaction as he thought about this same scenario occurring at each of the six dwarvan border forts.

Sleeping quarters for General Grimilzor and his aide Sergeant Dargan were situated several minutes' walk from the King's council room. When they arrived, the room was overflowing. Judging from those present, the general figured that the latest messenger had brought even worse news than the rumors suggested. Ambassadors from Partha, the Court of the Wood Elves, the Eastern Confederation of City-States, the Southern Dwarvan Confederation, and the Dwarfs of Lothian mingled with several leading clerics of different holy orders as well as all of the senior military officers that could arrange to be there.

The noisy crowd speculated about the reason for the conference, and as they waited, the King's servers walked through the mass of milling bodies, bearing trays laden with warm beverages. Dargan was ill at ease as he took his place behind Grimilzor's chair at the table, the same table where the dwarves had eagerly planned their recent campaign to retake Brackus. Now a more ominous tension settled on the occupants of the room as the king's herald pounded his ornate staff against the floor.

"All rise! King Braveslayer is in attendance."

Those seated stood until the King of the Dwarves took his chair at the center of the table. He looked young despite his advancing years and the sprinkling of white in his black hair. His face was lined with new creases of concern, and prominent dark bags under his eyes portended bad news.

The King waved the others to silence as he took his seat. When he spoke, anger colored his voice. "I have evil news. Five days ago, an army from the west seized the southern border forts, using powerful creatures never before seen in our world. Orcs swarm the countryside like ants. They are led by an upstart giant, who recently claimed the throne after the murder of the former giant king by a rogue warlock."

A moment of shocked whispering spread among those present.

The king allowed the whispering to die down before adding, "To make matters worse, the giant's army is based in the lost dwarvan city of Zigar-shan."

Several dwarves slammed their fists against the tabletop in anger, and more than one called down the wrath of their gods.

Dwarvan clerics shouted, "Blasphemy!"

"This is an affront to the gods and our people," one of the more vehement clerics added.

The gathered diplomats and soldiers added loud cries of concern, punctuated with shouted questions and curses. It took three loud raps of the herald's staff to quiet the room so that King Braveslayer could continue.

"My eldest son Prince Dunrow has sent a brief message that a huge army is marching east following the paths and trails of the hill country. There was no advance warning. The prince and his advisors suspect sorcery. Reports of the fighting indicate that mighty beasts, also unknown to us, roam the western territories, beasts that were called forth from the seven hells."

He let those words sink in before continuing. "Crown Prince Dunrow's last message indicated that he was leading his forces back to Southgard. He vows to hold the enemy there and fight to the last dwarf." Braveslayer looked into the eyes of those present. "A time of unprecedented crisis has arisen. We are fightin' a mighty host that threatens not just the Dwarvan Empire, but the Dwarves of the Confederation and the City-States as well. The prince has an additional ten to fifteen thousand soldiers at Southgard, if ye count the citizen levies, but he estimates that at least one hundred thousand enemy soldiers have crossed our borders."

The King grew quiet and allowed this news to sink in while he gauged the mood of the council. Individuals spoke in lowered voices to one another. The Elven Ambassador, Ithrenion's slender features and angular face shape gave the elf an appearance of wary calm, despite the alarming events they were discussing.

"It is indeed a tragedy," he said, calmly. "These are dark times, and I am sure the advisors to my Queen will urge her to send aid. However, and I believe I am voicing the opinion of many in this room, we must urgently request help from leaders of every nation. As a member of this council, I speak plainly when I say that I am concerned about the time that will be wasted arranging for assistance, be it military force or supplies."

Dargan and some of the others understood the elf's point. They did not like it, but saw his wisdom. However, not all shared Ithrenion's view, and there were a few angry whispers and stares. The old Sergeant touched Grimilzor on the shoulder. The general glanced briefly at Dargan and nodded, knowing what needed to be done.

Grimilzor stood up, pushing his chair back with a screech. "Sire, I can be ready to march in the morning with twenty-five thousand veterans of the siege of Brackus. We have numerous wagons filled with supplies confiscated from the enemy that will serve our needs for at least a month."

King Braveslayer looked his son in the eye. "Ye've just come from a bloody siege that have vastly weakened our forces and cost many of our most renowned leaders and warriors their lives. Yet, ye propose to march to the aid of yer brother?"

Grimilzor nodded. "Additional forces capable of assessing the situation will reach Southgard in smaller contingents. We can fortify the northern hills and wait for our troops to increase. The enemy will find it difficult to breach the gates of the city, which will give us time to prepare."

Beaming with pride, King Braveslayer slammed his fist on the table. "Then so be it. Ye are all aware of what we face. I trust each member of the council to notify yer respective countries of the current crisis. Any help will be appreciated. Now, if ye will excuse me. The military and me personal council must plan for the coming battle. Again, I solemnly thank everyone who can come to our aid. Please relay me gratitude to yer leaders."

Grimilzor dismissed Dargan to draft marching orders for the army. They would leave in the morning. The general's plan was to have his army occupy the territory along Hywel's Way, while the battalion commanders joined the general at Brule's, a fortified way station twenty miles to the south. By necessity, many units were camped some miles away from Nars. Therefore, the road seemed to be the best place to begin aligning the troops for the march.

After Dargan left, the Confederation commanders and the King's closest advisors remained in the cleared conference room. For a brief moment, King Braveslayer allowed his head to sag and the others could see that he was worried.

Raising his head, the King gave the council a puzzled look. "Why now?"

"Because we are at a disadvantage," Grimilzor said. "After bleeding us in the north, it is a perfect time for the enemy to strike in the south. Thanks to Lieutenant Tarquin and his Borderers, we know that the Illanni were supplying the orcs at Brackus, and Celedant is certain this undead warlock, Taza, is behind it and has decided to bring his full strength against us."

"If the Illanni are involved in this latest incursion, we can expect additional pressure from the underworld," General Falsoof Veinhunter grimly added.

"If you're correct, it reduces the number of troops we can send to Prince Dunrow's aid," Este Axesharpener, Braveslayer's oldest advisor, stated.

The King sighed. "I wish Celedant and Abbot Hortus were here to add their wisdom, but they are necessarily occupied elsewhere. We must fend for ourselves. I am sorry, son, but for now, I canna spare ye or yer brother much in the way of extra troops. I dare not risk leaving the city undefended. Who knows what surprises are in store for us here? Once I have a better idea of the enemy's troop movements, I will be able to determine how many soldiers I can ship south."

"That's all right, Father," Grimilzor said to reassure the king. "The ambassadors will be sendin' word by carrier pigeon or fast riders, reinforcin' the messengers we sent to the various nations. Their response will soon show our true allies."

The King nodded. "It will be a month before help arrives from our allies. By that time, we should have a better feel for what we will need to defend the city. Try to hold your position until help shows up, son. Once the extra soldiers arrive, ye can mount an attack and relieve yer brother at Southgard."

He raised a glass and toasted. "May the gods walk with us."

The assembled dwarves drained their mugs and slammed them down on the table, leaving the room in a somber mood. Braveslayer called his son over and the two left together. The King was silent as they wound their way through the royal chambers. Servants bowed as father and son walked past, but the two dwarves hardly noticed. Braveslayer and Grimilzor were making their way to a private meeting room when all the torches went dark.

The dwarves were instantly alert and drew their weapons. In the gloom, their night vision took over and as creatures used to living in the dark, they were able to see clearly. They heard someone speak the words of a spell and an even deeper darkness descended over the corridor, blinding them so that their eyesight could not penetrate the inky blackness. Father and son stood back-to-back, waiting for what was to come. Unable to see the attackers, their ears strained to hear the smallest sign of movement.

Then, Grimilzor heard a footpad, and he struck out into the darkness with his ax. His weapon whistled in the stillness of the passage. He had intended to cut his opponent in twain. Instead, he felt a sharp pain in his shoulder. He brought his weapon to bear, striking the hilt of his attacker's sword, breaking several fingers. He thrust his ax point straight out, catching the shadowy figure with the sharp point of his weapon. With a grunt, the attacker dropped back several feet.

His father faced the same predicament of the ever-closing darkness. To fend off his potential attacker, the king held his sword and dagger before him to impede an attack. He circled the points of those blades, reaching out for the enemy, until he felt the blade of another sword slide against his long sword. Braveslayer thrust his sword and threw his dagger where the attacker should have been. The dagger struck stone as his long sword met resistance, its point penetrating his attacker.

The darkness rose and in the shadowy hallway, the two dwarves saw that their attackers were Illanni assassins. Grimilzor lashed out at his assailant, swinging his ax overhead, but the Illanni stepped back, and the ax head clanged as it hit the stone floor, sending sparks into the air. The dwarf was quick in blocking the sword of the Illanni. He neatly reversed the ax stroke, cleaving into the Illanni's arm and penetrating the light chain mail, cutting deep into the muscle.

The Illanni grabbed his arm, turned, and ran. Grimilzor drew another dagger from his belt and threw it after him. The dagger took the dark elf in the fleshy part of the back. He fell writhing in pain on the floor. The dwarf chased him, calling for the household guards. By the time he reached the Illanni, the assassin was already dead. His brow furrowed as he examined the wounds, wondering how the dark elf had died. None of his wounds had been lethal.

Meanwhile, his father fought his opponent, both dueling with long swords and driving each other back and forth down the small passage. Braveslayer used all his strength to trap the dark elf's sword against the wall and hold it there. Then the dwarf struck out with his left fist, landing a mighty blow to the elf's face. The Illanni felt bones break from the blow, and he dropped backward onto the stone of the passage, blood gushing from his nose and mouth. He gave up and turned to run, but the guards came from the other direction while Braveslayer stalked him from behind. Knowing his master would not allow him to live after his defeat, the dark elf drew a dagger and, with all his strength, plunged the blade deep into his own heart.

Panting from his exertions, Braveslayer called to the guards. "Search the entire city. There may be more Illanni lurking, and reinforce the guard to the lower levels."

He turned to see that his son leaning against the wall holding his shoulder and called to the nearest guard. "Get a healer here, now."

The King ran to his son. Fortunately, the wound was not serious, and the cleric was soon by their side attending to the wound. Afterward, father and son continued up the hallway to Braveslayer's private meeting room, where they found Queen Aladear in an adjoining sitting room, staring at a map of the mountain kingdom. She sat on a cushioned chair with a massive wheel connected to each side. Aladear had lost the use of her legs ten years earlier while hunting wild boar with her husband. Her knowledge and keen sense of strategy, however, were still a valuable commodity to her husband and sons.

Ignorant of the attack, she looked up and smiled as her youngest son entered. "Grimilzor! It seems we always see each other when yer about to leave."

Grimilzor smiled and gave his mother a warm hug. "I'm sorry, Mother. I hurried to disband me army, so I could spend more time with ye, but now...."

She patted his arm. "I know, son. Everyone must make sacrifices to win this war."

Braveslayer and Grimilzor pulled up chairs as servants brought the evening meal and pot after pot of strong black tea. The three talked about the current situation until the wee hours of the morning. Outside in the city and countryside, a bewildered army prepared for the march south.

Two days later, Dargan weaved his way through the crowded common room of Brule's way station. He spotted many familiar faces among the army commanders, as well as a few newly promoted officers that the old retainer did not yet know. Grimilzor sat at a long table with Major Freeland Rohaus of Partha, Captain Ruger Zander, Commander of the Borderers, Duke Joher Swordsticker, the new leader of the Contingent of Southern Dwarves, and Willum Faithmaker, Cleric of Halsbod and leader of the clerics that would handle the army's spiritual and healing needs. They did not have long to wait for the rest of the commanders to arrive. Dargan forged ahead and signaled to the prince that everyone was present.

The assembled warriors quieted as Grimilzor gazed at the faces he had gotten to know so well in the past campaign.

"Like meself, I'm sure ye had hoped to be spendin' the next few months in front of a warm fire with a good brew while ye counted yer loot."

The officers laughed as the prince smiled.

"I am sorry to disappoint ye by callin' ye back into battle." He patiently waited as low voices murmured in consternation. Grimilzor had just confirmed the rumor spreading throughout the Empire. He continued. "Aye, the rumors are true. As of yesterday, we learned that Prince Dunrow is retreatin' to Southgard. He estimates the force that drives him back to be at least one hundred thousand strong."

This time Grimilzor had to slam his hand down on the table several times before the room grew quiet again. "Our forces will march to me brother's aid. As of now, we do not know what to expect when we arrive at Southgard. Reinforcements will be piece-meal, and they will be limited and poorly trained. We are on our own until our allies send help. Let's mount up."

His speech over, the room emptied. Prince Grimilzor waited until the troops were ready before leaving the room and heading to the yard of the way station. Dargan held the reins as he mounted his sturdy mountain horse. Then with Dargan at his side, he rode to the front of his army. The Borderers had been sent ahead to scout for danger.

As the prince passed his troops each soldier saluted, and the chant of Grimilzor's name spread through the ranks of the dwarves. There was a bit of shuffling as the sergeants got the soldiers in formation and like a giant snake, the army began to head south.

The dwarvan army consisted of less the 25,000 soldiers. Borderers ranged far ahead, while Parthian Lancers kept a close watch near the main force. If their allies each sent 10,000 troops, and if another 15 to 20,000 dwarves came later, Grimilzor figured he might have enough to challenge the besiegers. Nevertheless, the odds would still be against them. The lone thing in their favor would be the orcs' complete disregard for their own lives and willingness to sacrifice untold numbers to achieve a goal. Then again, that same disregard for life could also win the day for the enemy.

Chapter Fourteen

Taza once more traveled through the Void, trusting the staff to guide him true in the complete darkness. Soon he happened upon a world where evil beckoned him like a beacon. The staff led him down to the ground surface. This was a journey to recruit allies, and the staff had led him to this planet and a small settlement amid rolling hills. His plan was to find out how these creatures would respond to the mission to kill Celedant and Tarquin. If they were successful, he would recruit more to swell his armies further - perhaps even to invade Dragon Isle.

He approached the huge iron gate, calling to those inside in their language, thanks to the staff, which translated his words. Along the parapet, ape-like soldiers appeared, staring at Taza from odd, expressionless faces. Each held a weapon of some sort with many bows aimed at the new arrival.

"Come forth, O leader!" Taza called in an amiable voice. "I offer friendship and a gift."

The staff of Adois had told him that this planet's copper was practically nonexistent. Therefore, he summoned several bars of the metal as a bribe to help them make weapons with the valuable metal.

He held aloft the bars, and using the Staff to mimic their language, Taza called out again, "I bring gifts of friendship that you can put to good use."

The gates to the city opened, and twenty sizable guards ran out on all fours. Their appearance surprised the vampire. They were ape-like creatures with a huge chest encased in near impenetrable leather-like armor, and powerfully muscled arms and legs. Although they ran on all fours, Taza instinctively surmised they would fight upright on two legs. Swords and other weapons were strapped across their backs, and he would later learn that they could spit a stream of acid that would burn through anything, including metal armor.

A large creature advanced, its stance denoting curiosity and caution. "Who comes to offer us a reward," it asked.

Taza squared his shoulders. "I am Taza, Vampire Lord of Muiria. I seek aid from your mighty warriors."

"Throw me the presents that you have brought," the creature replied.

Taza held the two bricks of copper before him and uttered a single spell under his breath. The copper floated upward in midair toward the creatures. He could not tell if the guards were impressed, because he could not read the expression on their faces or their stoic stance. However, the Staff of Adois interpreted the creatures' response as indicating surprise and more accommodation toward Taza. It also told him that the warriors before him were female.

The chieftess caught the copper blocks and weighed them in her hands. "This is a fortune in copper that you willingly hand over."

Taza laughed. "The planet I come from has a surplus of this mineral. I can bring you as much as you desire."

As the leader thought about how her city could grow and prosper if they were to get an unlimited source of this copper, tall, sleek males and children formed in small groups around the edges of the clearing to watch the meeting.

Taza called out. "In exchange, I need some of your soldiers to perform a simple task on my home world."

The chieftess, still weighing the bricks of copper in her hands, asked, "How would we get to your world," she asked.

The Staff of Adois urged Taza on, letting him know blood lust was forming in the leader's mind.

Taza raised his staff. "The Staff of Adois will take you. I will give each warrior a small amulet. With them, my staff can transport your soldiers."

"Give me the amulets, and I will distribute them to our best warriors who will await the staff's call."

Taza bowed to the chieftess. "It should not be long before your soldiers are needed. Should they perform well, I will return for more and transport additional copper for your coffers." He threw a bag containing the amulets to the chieftess, who handed it to one of the males for distribution.

"I look forward to seeing your soldiers at work. I'll let you know how effective they are." *If they are effective, I will give you more copper,* he thought. *If they aren't, you will rue that day.* Taza walked ten steps away from the village and vanished.

The creatures of the city cheered mightily when the chieftess showed them the bricks of copper. She summoned the city's most valorous warriors and handed them the amulets. "Represent us well, and we will receive a steady supply of copper that will make us one of the mightiest of kingdoms."

The dwarvan army marched for days without sighting many other than the local inhabitants. As the army advanced, riders were sent ahead to spread the word to remote villages to flee north. A week later, the army left the snowy landscape behind for the warmer southern climate, where they encountered crowds of fleeing dwarves escaping the coming storm.

Each way station they passed was crowded with refugees, all bearing a similar story of orcs roaming the mountains. Dwarvan guards on high alert paced the small ramparts that surrounded the way stations.

Meanwhile Prince Dunrow's army retreated toward the fortress city of Southgard. Losses in the foothills and at the border forts had been staggering, but the prince made their retreat a fighting withdrawal, successfully slowing the enemies' advance.

Most unnerving were the stories of unknown monsters that attacked the enemy. These creatures were nigh impossible to kill. Messages from the clergy at Southgard flew north with increasing rapidity, requesting more brother and sister clerics to be sent to battle the approaching terrors.

The next day, the leading elements of the army came across the chilling sight of a burned-out way station; its inhabitants had been massacred by the enemy. That night Grimilzor camped near the ruins. Sight and smell of burning timber and dead bodies filled him with rage. The prince was a master at controlling his emotions, but his pent-up wrath was all too clear to Dargan.

The army was still four days' march from the valley that surrounded Southgard. Yet the enemy had ranged further north, not through Hywel's Way, but via seldom used trails. The prince sat in his tent, studying the map of the southern territories for the hundredth time. In reality, Southgard sat on the southern ridge of a valley carved out of the mountains by the River Wye. Forces bent on attacking the empire would have to neutralize the city before launching an attack.

The bridges and fords large enough for an army to cross lay at the foot of Southgard. Any enemy attacking the way station would have to come through one of the smaller fords on the plains to the west. The orcs had picked a known trail that led them there, and the well-planned assault caught the dwarves off guard. Although Grimilzor hated leaving any soldiers behind, he realized that he had to protect the roads, trails, and villages, so he set up small, well-armed garrisons along the way.

As the prince pondered the situation, Dargan entered his tent.

"What news have ye?" Grimilzor asked, looking up and rubbing his tired eyes.

The sergeant, his red hair and beard liberally streaked with white, handed over several small tubes. "We've received messages by carrier pigeon from both Nars and yer brother."

Grimilzor waved his retainer to a chair as he unrolled the missives. The first was a brief note from General Falsoof in Nars.

Prince Grimilzor,

I have received a commitment of troops from the East and West. The West will send word once ye approach Southgard. The Eastern forces will follow ye.

Falsoof

This was good news, and Grimilzor was relieved that they would soon receive aid from the empire's allies. The message meant that the Eastern Confederation or at least some human nations would also send troops. The West meant the Wood Elves. The news filled him with relief. Elven bowmen could whittle the number of enemy soldiers. After hearing this news, Dargan smiled and poured his commander a glass of wine, while Grimilzor bent to read the next message.

Brother,

By the time ye read this note, I will be trapped in Southgard. The enemy has overrun us at every turn, and the city is our last hope of stalling their advance. Hurry if ye can. Nevertheless, do not...I repeat...do not try to join me at Southgard. I suggest that ye hold the northern passages leading out of the valley. They will have to take Southgard to advance their plans. Gods willing, we will stop them here. When they have wasted their strength on the stout walls of the city, we can counterattack and drive them west. I wish ye the luck and blessings of the gods.

Yer loving brother,

Dunrow

The news sparked a rush of frenzied activity in the dwarvan camp. To accomplish this feat, Grimilzor's column would have to occupy and hold the two major passes in the valley, not to mention numerous smaller trails. They would also have to prevent additional enemy forces from slipping in through the main pass where Hywel's Way was located. There was no other way to keep the invading army from advancing into the heart of the Empire. He chose the Parthian Commander Major Rohaus to hold the northeast road, leading to the southern Dwarvan City-States.

Prince Grimilzor hoped these two forces would draw the most attention, since the smaller passes and trails would be sparsely guarded until more troops arrived. For now, those platoons would report enemy advances so that when needed, he could dispatch a larger force. It was a flawed plan, but the best available under the circumstances, at least until reinforcements arrived.

To keep the enemy from gaining a foothold on the passes, Grimilzor sent Dargan to accompany the column that sped ahead of the main army. This unit consisted of mostly Borderers, light infantry, and Parthian lancers. It was a dangerous mission that could extract a huge toll on those fighting to keep the passes open, but if they were successful, the prince would be able to get the main army through when the time was right.

CHAPTER FIFTEEN

Apparently, word of the invasion had reached Southgard, yet the warlock had suspected that would be the case. As he watched the invasion of the border fort, his focus changed, bringing up a mental picture of Southgard with the towering walls of the dwarvan city's battlements that gleamed in the sunlight. Each tower flew large flags depicting the mighty castle and signifying protection the city provided to the eastern settlements. Behind the stout walls rose a mountain with a sheer cliff where the city had been carved out many centuries ago. The master stonecutters had covered it with designs depicting ancient battle scenes that had occurred in the western hills.

As his mind returned to the scene below, he was startled to find that, for the most part, the battle was over and the army was on the move toward its next destination.

"It's time to leave," he told the chimera. "Our work here is finished. Head for Southgard. I have a very important meeting with three orcs to ensure the outcome there is as favorable as it was here. If I leave it up to that stupid giant, the battle will be lost before it has begun."

The chimera rumbled a reply and headed east. By air, the trip lasted several days, but for the massive army marching on foot, it would take far longer. When the warlock arrived, he flew over Southgard's village, where the roads remained clogged with settlers and farmers running from their homesteads in the fertile valley, directed by dwarvan forces sent to aid them. A feeble number of soldiers gathered around the entrance to the gates of Southgard. Borderers on stout horses rode along the south side, facing the hills from which the enemy would attack.

Several days later, the valley was empty and the villagers settled inside Southgard when the first battalions of orcs and giants began pouring over the hills. Despite the orderly withdrawal from the valley, the sight of the massive enemy army caused fear and panic.

Melgor watched with a wry smile as a battalion of Parthian lancers stationed near the entrance of the valley drew up in battle formation and charged the foremost orcs. Arrows rose three times from the orcan lines, arching up and then descending upon the charging ranks of Parthians. Men and horses fell dead or screaming in pain as the arrows found their marks. They collided with the enemy in a crash that was audible even to the wizard as he soared high above them. The fighting was quick and furious as Parthian soldiers fought with all their strength, but the overpowering number of orcs drove them back. Then a horn sounded above the melee, and the horsemen beat a hasty retreat to the walls of Southgard. Sadly, few of that brave battalion returned to ride through the gates.

Later that night after growing bored with the siege, Melgor returned to his tent to rest when he heard a call from his lord echoing through his brain. The warlock answered, "Yes, Lord Taza. I am here."

"Celedant has stopped at Roule's Inn. Do you know of it?" Taza asked.

Melgor indeed knew of the inn. He had stayed there many times. "Yes, my Lord."

"Good," Taza answered. "Go there and deal with the wizard."

No further instructions were forthcoming. Therefore, Melgor left to handle the next step of Taza's plan. He would use one of the hardest necromancy spells he had learned to gain control over the minds of the patrons in Roule's Inn. If he succeeded, he would use the second part of the spell to kill Celedant and his band of troublemakers. Melgor would use a spell from a forbidden book that contained some of the blackest magic in existence to reshape the patron's minds and turn them into ghouls. The spells would be useless against Celedant or his companions because their minds were too strong but would work well with the riffraff that occupied the inn. Besides, Celedant or one of the clerics could disrupt the enchantment before it had a chance to affect anyone in their party. He jumped into the saddle of the chimera and placed the picture of Roule's Inn in the creature's brain. He had little time to reach the inn before dawn, but he had witnessed firsthand how fast his steed could fly. He knew deep in his black heart that they would arrive in time.

Mentally he had already enlisted the aid of a powerful being, but Melgor needed fodder to add a distraction for his new allies. Landing the chimera in the middle of a wide alley, he dismounted and moved close to the inn. His inner sight could count at least twenty minds inside that he could overpower. As the dark warlock readied the spell, the sewer grate next to him slid open, and a dripping wet head and shoulders of a dwarf appeared, pushing a small box before him. Melgor instantly retrieved a scented cloth from a pocket of his robe and covered his nose.

The little dwarf smiled broadly, and when he saw the warlock said, "Carrots a little rotten and mushy with a bit of mold. Care for one?"

Melgor's nose wrinkled in disgust. He signaled with his hand that he did not want any, and the figure walked away, dripping heavens knows what, oblivious to the chimera as he happily chewed his vegetables. When the dwarf was out of earshot, the warlock once more began the spell, and as the minds of those in the building writhed and transformed into zombies and ghouls that were subservient to him, he smiled and ordered them to kill those that were still alive inside.

CHAPTER SIXTEEN

Panting with urgency the story tumbled out of Tarquin like water rushing over a waterfall. Alarmed by his words, Celedant gathered his few belongings and joined the others who waited, donned in their armor, weapons ready in the upstairs common room that interconnected the two other rooms.

Celedant moved to the fire, his back to its crackling warmth. "You've heard what our most observant members have witnessed. Taza appears to be an undead warlock. I am not certain where he came from, since no such creatures have existed on our world before that I know of. However, I recently learned that he is the wielder of the staff of Adois and the driving force against us who will do anything to claim the Staff of Adaman for himself and keep us from recovering the remaining piece. We cannot allow this to happen. The world would be thrust into anarchy with terror and evil its masters. Tarquin, you led us through the underworld. How should we proceed?"

Tarquin had his dwarvan-made magical sword, Dragon Bolt out, running a sharpening stone along its blade. As he was about to speak, his sword's dark blade flared, emitting a searing red light.

Watching the exchange from the corner of the room, Eldahir understood and spoke. "I believe - and Celedant will agree - that Tarquin's blade has answered our question. The enemy is here. Leaving quietly now is out of the question."

Celedant nodded. "As in the past, Tarquin's sword had revealed an approaching danger at an appropriate time. Secure and bar the doors until we can be certain what manner of foe is coming for us."

As the companions barricaded the doors with furniture and shuttered the windows, Hortus and Baldo sat in the middle of the meeting room and began softly chanting, evoking the blessings of Thierry. The clerics remained focused until a scream erupted from one of the lower rooms.

Hortus stood. "The enemy is seizing control of the inn. Aegir, defend this room while Baldo and I guard the others."

"Celedant and I have cast spells that will aid us," Eldahir said, standing. "Beware! A source of great power waits outside, and it probes the wards we have erected around these rooms, looking for weaknesses."

Vannor and Donli guarded the windows, while Botreg and Tarquin stood by the main door, nervously listening and with swords drawn, but instead of more screams, the sounds of doors broken down, or crashing furniture, eerie silence shrouded the inn.

"The warlock has cast a spell of silence to hide the sounds of the attack," Celedant announced.

"It sure is nice to have all these mystical warnings," Botreg said to Tarquin, "but give me an orc to chop or...."

Before he could finish, Botreg's mind grew numb. His speech slowed and then slurred as drowsiness overcame him and his eyes lids drooped. Tarquin felt it, too, and he shook his head, but his eyes closed, and he was almost asleep on his feet. He heard a weapon drop in another room but could do nothing as he helplessly tried to call out a warning. It was as if a distant power had seized his tongue. He could not utter a syllable.

Celedant was about to cast a counter spell when he heard Azimuth shout, "Licentios!" The wave of sleep that had washed over them was pushed back, and as Tarquin's eyes snapped opened, he noticed the door in front of him push inward, nudging back the table they had placed against it. Large hairy fingers appeared along the edges, straining against the door's weight.

"Botreg!" Tarquin shouted, and they threw their shoulders against the table. Despite the added pressure, the door continued to ease open. It was like trying to stop a moving iceberg.

Botreg was nearest the opening. With his shoulder to the door, he pulled out one of his daggers and cut sharply downward across the intruder's fingers, severing two hairy digits that flopped to the floor. No blood oozed from the severed appendages; instead, a thick, viscous liquid dripped from the wounds, accompanied by a bellow of rage. The creature on the other side threw its body against the barrier and shoved the door open another foot. In the firelight, the hideous face of Roule and his bullish shoulder thrust through the ever-widening gap.

The dwarf reversed his dagger and struck the half-minotaur, penetrating Roule's right eye with its eight-inch blade and burying it in his brain. Roule merely laughed and with a shove of his mighty arms, knocked the door off its hinges. The giant filled the opening as both Tarquin and Botreg lay sprawled on the floor in front of him.

Belying his age, an agile Hortus jumped between the two prone figures, holding his war hammer before him as he called on his god. "Thierry - lead this unfortunate one to his grave."

Roule gave a pathetic growl and folded backward, acquiescing to the power summoned by the Theirrian Abbot. More attackers lurked unseen in the hallway. As Tarquin and Botreg regained their feet, a mass of bodies rushed through the door. The two comrades took the defensive as they faced a dozen undead enemies, many of whom bore fresh wounds that had recently condemned them to their semi-living state.

In one of the bedrooms, Ralav and Ronli stood watch next to a barred window while Aegir and Eldahir stood near the room's door, watching the struggle in the common room. Then the window rattled. Someone or something was trying to force its way through. The bar, bracing the inside shutters, jumped in its holders, and Ralav and Ronli added their strength in an attempt to keep the wooden brace in place. Eldahir moved toward the window while motioning for Aegir to guard the door.

As the elf took position, Ralav whispered, "Look at the hinges."

Eldahir watched as the nails pushed out of the wood and fell to the floor, followed by the hinges, as though being pulled by an invisible hand. The bar's holders came next, causing the shutters to drop with a crash, revealing a face of evil staring through the broken windowpane. Deathly pale skin stretched over a bony skull, and bright red light glared from deep within its eye sockets.

Eldahir shoved Ralav aside shouting, "Lich!"

As the elf dove away from the window, he summoned his magic, feeling it respond and well up from within. The energy was a white-hot essence that churned in the pit of his stomach, aching for release, and as Eldahir hit the floor, he sent several streams of energy from his outstretched hand. One bolt blew a flaming hole through the window's seal. The second struck the lich in the shoulder as it crawled through the opening, searing through the creature's leather armor and blackening the undead skin beneath as it propelled the screaming lich backward into the night. At the window, the moonlit sky greeted the defenders as they sprawled on the floor. Great finger gouges scarred through the wood where the Lich had latched onto the framework. As they watched in horror, the flames from the errant blast of energy began spreading along the old, dry timbers of the inn. If they did not get out of the building shortly, the fire would finish what the warlock had started.

In another bedroom, Baldo paced the floor over a threadbare carpet. He sensed the evil advancing down the hallway, as the wards he had cast warned him that something terrible was heading their way. The look of concern on Morganna's face made him even more apprehensive. She seemed afraid, and if the elf was concerned over an attack by undead creatures, her fear might foretell of an onslaught unlike any he had ever witnessed.

Celedant stood near the doorway between the bedroom and the common room, sending fist-sized balls of intense energy toward the melee taking place in the meeting room. As he watched, Azimuth felt a surge of power building beyond the bedroom door – an evil of intense power he had seldom encountered. The protective spells he and Eldahir had laid about the rooms warned that danger was imminent.

Those warnings and his draconic intuition determined his next action. He slipped into the room with Baldo and Morganna moments before the ancient wooden door splintered inward, exploding in a blast that sent splinters flying across the room. Morganna and Azimuth threw up their cloaks, which shielded them from most of the debris, as Baldo rolled along the floor for six feet before coming upright in a battle stance, his ornate war hammer ready for whatever lurked in the hallway.

A smoke screen hovered about the disintegrated door and dissipated, revealing a figure dressed in a shade of black so dark that he appeared to be shrouded in deep shadow. The cruel fanged smile spoke volumes as two of the three companions were about to meet their first vampire. Having recovered from the blast, Azimuth and Morganna assaulted the dark figure.

Morganna sent two daggers flying at it, while the dragon sent an arch of white-hot energy. The daggers met an invisible shield a foot in front of the creature where both weapons briefly hung suspended in midair before clattering to the floor. Meanwhile, it deflected Azimuth's magical bolt of energy upward into the ceiling with a quick counter-spell. As the vampire began the words of his next assault, Morganna and the dragon mouthed incantations, but Baldo knew there might not be enough time for them to finish. Gripping the worn wooden handle of his weapon, the cleric sent a silent prayer to Thierry and threw it at the creature. The hammer rocketed through the air faster than the eye could follow, causing a thunderous clap that echoed around the room as the weapon slammed through the magical shield and into the creature.

The magical shield was no match for the enchanted hammer, and it shattered like glass. The vampire never had a chance to question what the clap of thunder meant. Instead, the last syllable of his spell disappeared from the air as the hammer penetrated the protective barrier and buried itself in the creature's chest. The sound of it striking the target was deafening as the doorframe and a huge section of wall shattered. Morganna decapitated the creature with her sword, disintegrating the vampire. Baldo remained kneeling at the center of the room with the hammer miraculously back in his belt.

In the main meeting room, Vannor and Donli joined Hortus, Botreg, and Tarquin in a confusing melee that raged violently. The patrons of the inn, like its owner, were now undead creatures, and they attacked the living in a maddened frenzy of rage. Tarquin guessed that these formerly living beings had been transformed into ghouls by a powerful warlock who might control them from outside. The ghouls had all the movement and strength of the living without the fear of being injured or killed. The creatures would even impale themselves on the defenders' swords to get closer to their intended target.

It was all Tarquin could do to defend himself from the relentless attacks. Out of the corner of his eye he saw small bolts of energy cast by Celedant, Azimuth, and Morganna impact a few of the undead and blow them into fragments that showered the room. Hortus seemed undeterred and used his enchanted weapon to batter his enemies, first knocking them to the floor, and then crushing their skulls with his hammer.

Tarquin's sword cut into the unarmored attackers, yet no matter how horrible a wound he inflicted, they kept advancing. Botreg moved with fluid grace among the enemy, neatly cutting their legs out from under them before decapitating them while they squirmed on the floor. The dwarf glanced at Tarquin and noticed that his friend faced a ghoul with both of its arms sliced off, but the creature still attacked and had backed the prince into a corner, ramming his head repeatedly into the young man's chest while trying to bite him.

"Tarquin, remember your training and cut off its head!" Botreg shouted.

Hardly hearing him through the din of battle, Tarquin shoved the creature back to give him more room, and with his sword flaring a brilliant red, he swung, severing the ghoul's head from its shoulders. The body jerked twice before collapsing in a heap.

"Thanks!" Tarquin called to Botreg, but the dwarf had already disappeared into the melee of whirling blades and bodies.

At that moment, Hority strode into the room, accompanied by his unmistakable odor. He looked around the crowded war zone, smiled, and then waded into battle, using his branch like a long mace that disintegrated the ghouls on contact. Looking around, another opponent emerged from the massive battle and came at Tarquin. An elderly unarmed woman who had served him ale in the taproom attacked with fists and claws. Tarquin hesitated, not wanting to attack the old woman until she connected with a strong right punch that knocked the helmet from his head.

As stars swirled before his eyes, he struck in a reflexive action with his blazing sword, neatly slicing the ugly, grinning head from her body and causing it to spin through the air with its wiry gray hair fanning out before landing upright in the corner. As the severed head spun to a stop, the hideous grin remained on her face.

Tarquin looked around for more enemies, but the undead were no longer pouring through the door. Vannor and Garth had one pinned against a wall, and the Brae swiftly removed the ghoul's head. Then as quickly as the battle had begun, it was over. The companions had suffered nothing major, just a few minor injuries. They waited for another attack, but none came. Apparently, their attackers were either destroyed or beaten back. Tarquin's sword still glowed, but the intensity had diminished. Hortus closed his eyes and cast a spell.

After a second, the Abbot looked to Celedant. "The danger still lingers around the Inn but we are safe for now," he said, wrinkling his nose as the familiar odor of the Clorian monk reached his nostrils.

"Why did ye let me sleep through all the fun? That's just not right," Hority grumbled, consternation plainly showing on his face, but he received no answer.

"I wounded a lich that tried to gain entry through the window," Eldahir said as he joined the others. "It disappeared into the night but may still be nearby."

Celedant looked about the destroyed rooms to where his friend Roule lay at rest. Fire from Eldahir's magic spread along the dry walls and had reached the hallway. They needed to abandon the structure before it blazed into an inferno.

"The fire will cover what has occurred here," Celedant said, coming to a decision. "Gather your gear and leave now. Botreg, Ralav, and Ronli, check the stable and courtyard. We ride as soon as the horses are ready."

As the company rushed out of the burning Inn, they stood face-to-face with the Lich that had tried to enter their rooms. It stood in the stable yard, shoulder and cape still burning lightly from Azimuth's spell, the white bone under its tattered skin broken and useless. With a mere swipe of its other arm, it threw the company against the stable yard walls.

Tarquin felt a great force hold him in place. He began to gasp for air as if a giant hand was choking him. The only person not affected by the spell was Celedant who stood his ground. Quick as a flash, he countered the spell by raising the cobbles of the stable yard to zip towards the Lich. The stones slammed into the monster and broke its spell, releasing the others from the strangling force. Gasping for breath, they fell to the ground in a cacophony of armor and weapons.

Eldahir and Morganna bombarded the creature with arrows, but they either passed right through the rotted body or struck and hung limply from the Lich's tattered clothes and dried flesh. The dreadful monster turned his gaze on the two elves. As it began an incantation, Eldahir chose one of his own, hoping he chose the right spell to cast a shield of protection around himself and Morganna.

A rolling ball of fire came directly at them, and he knew he had chosen well. When the fireball struck, the protective spell bulged inward. Its blue-hued walls deflected the Lich's attack. The companions looked on as the magical battle raged. The attack gave Celedant time to act, and a silent command to Forestae sent a jagged bolt of lightning hurtling at the Lich.

Giving the monster no time to react, the powerful spell struck the ground right before it. Stones and electricity flew into the Lich's body, throwing it back ten paces. As the beast struggled to its feet, it looked down and realized that the blast had destroyed its left leg. Using its magic, the creature rose from the ground, floating back into the stable yard. It surveyed the area and sent small bolts of energy in a wide ark. Those who were still standing dove for cover. Not wanting to change to dragon form in the city, Azimuth launched a series of spells. A simple dispel magic spell caused the Lich to drop to the cobbled yard, having difficulty standing as it wobbled on one leg. Several energy bolts seared the skeletal body, causing small fires to break out on the cloak it was wearing and the withered skin beneath.

Thinking that Azimuth's attack had weakened the monster, Celedant and the others charged. Another sweep of its useable arm sent them flying again to be pinned against the walls. This time it even threw back Celedant. Although his magical nature kept him from sticking to the wall, it jarred him terribly. He crawled to his hands and knees, and using Forestae, called forth the energy around him to channel a spell.

The other magical members of the band felt their power drawn into the wizard's staff, and when Celedant let lose, the combined energy in the staff emerged as one. The blast blinded everyone, causing many to shake their heads to clear the stars from their eyes. As they regained sight, the destruction was overwhelming. Portions of the gates and walls had deteriorated, and where the Lich once stood, nothing but a smoldering crater remained. The company crawled cautiously from their positions, looking for the Lich, but all they saw was Celedant standing in the middle of the stable yard. All was quiet except for the roaring of the fire as it engulfed the inn and Celedant's urgent call, "Everyone gather your supplies and get the horses we leave this place of demons!"

Fortunately, the stable was a safe distance from the burning inn and the courtyard was empty of enemies. During the battle outdoors, Hority had slinked off to mope and fell fast asleep in one of the empty stalls. Having missed most of the fight, the skinny cleric was upset. Baldo woke him as Tarquin and the others exited the stable, leading their horses. Hority was still grumbling as he pulled his stubborn donkey along.

"From now on, Hority, we won't separate," Baldo said. "You'll have to pray to Clor and sleep in an inn."

A crowd of anxious proprietors rapidly filled the street and began dousing the neighboring buildings with water to keep the flames from spreading further. Watching the scene from the back of his chimera, Melgor realized that he would have to wait for another opportunity to kill Celedant and his comrades. Now that he knew where they would be heading, a plan was already forming in his mind, and this time, he was sure it would work.

CHAPTER SEVENTEEN

The leader of the lancers, Major Rohaus, a tall young human with dark hair pulled back in a ponytail, serious brown eyes, and a scar that ran across his lower jaw, had sent the Borderers ahead, followed by infantry and his lancers. They had twice encountered groups of dwarvan soldiers retreating from the valley who told stories about masses of orcs that overran their positions, sealing off Southgard. Leaderless and without anywhere to go, the soldiers headed north to locate the dwarvan army. Clerics treated the injured, and the mismatched soldiers were integrated with Rohaus' infantry.

As the column neared the valley, the Borderer scouts discovered small parties of orcs holding the northern pass. Considering his options, Rohaus sent two lancers back to inform General Grimilzor that he would seize control of the pass and await the main army.

As night fell, one hundred Borderers spread out in the darkness. They led a company of light infantry to a hidden position near the orc camp. A low wall of stones and packed dirt blocked the trail with guards placed at ten-pace intervals behind the barrier. The Borderers advanced to within twenty paces of the makeshift wall, and waited. As the sun began to lighten the eastern sky, five arrows hissed through air from the dwarves' hidden position, ensuring the silence of the orcish guards. Before the enemy's bodies hit the ground, the Borderers were over the wall, followed by wave after wave of infantry.

The enemy was still asleep in their bedrolls when the dwarves poured into camp and slaughtered most of the hundred orcs still entangled in their bedding. Those who fought back had no armor or weapons at hand and were unable to stop the attack. Ten minutes later, Major Rohaus entered the camp and ordered his troops to begin building their own defenses.

With the pass retaken, Rohaus and a company of curious Borderers climbed one of the small hills to get a better view of the valley. When they reached the rocky summit, a morning haze still lingered but began to burn off as they stood and watched. From their vantage point, the Wye River ran for a third of a league through the valley to the northeast and a full league to the southwest to the main road of Southgard. The orcs had built much stronger defenses where the river met Hywel's Way. The Major watched the flaming red sunrise as it made the valley floor near the city appear to be ablaze. Thousands of burning campfires throughout the massive orc encampment further enhanced the illusion.

Taza stared through one of ten, five-foot wide and seven-foot high crenellations spaced around the outside of his tower room. Unable to tolerate the sun any longer, he drew the draperies and turned, releasing a dry scream of frustration that echoed through the nearby mountains.

As far as he was concerned, the dwarves and Parthians were a symbiotic pair from the seven hells. He distrusted humans and had thought about transforming those living in Dormin to zombies, but that would take too long and the city would evacuate in a hurry. If he decided to proceed with the transformation, however, his vampire captains would anoint those foolish enough to remain within the city walls, including the Warlock's Council.

The Parthians and dwarves had sent ambassadors to every nation, reminding their allies of the accord signed years ago, and persuading them to honor it. The document stated that if the countries in the East were threatened, the races of the accord would give military aid to the dwarves and Parthians. He sat down hard on his onyx throne with a huff of annoyance. Despite his meddling, most of the dwarvan allies were gathering troops to honor the alliance. He would have to step up attacks on those nations.

In the end, it was going to take far more to bring about Southgard's downfall than he had anticipated. Nevertheless, he felt certain that the overwhelming number of orcs he had sent against the city would do the trick. Melgor could be trusted to do that, at least, even though the warlock had sensed discord within the giants' army. Taza smiled. Many would die pushing the towering idiot's forces back into the hills, and in the end, victory would be his.

Two days later in the High Elven city of Melemas, a young boy, walking home after visiting a friend, spotted several strange insects that intermittently glowed with a bright yellowish-red light as they fluttered about. He decided to capture a few and placed them in a small sack he carried attached to his belt. Amazed by the discovery of such unique creatures, the young elf hurried back to the city to show his prize to parents and friends. He was unaware that hundreds of small fireflies were following him until the bag he was carrying burst into flames. Dropping the burning sack, the young elf was horrified as the fireflies that had followed him morphed into clouds of tiny demons that dispatched the youngster before they raced through the city, setting everything ablaze.

When the elven guard saw what was happening, they raised their bows and shot at the bright clouds of fire. Feathered shafts flew accurately into the demon horde, but it was like shooting at air. The insect demons were so small that arrows were incapable of harming them, and as the arrows passed through cloud, they became charred and disintegrated into dust. The panicked elves next drew swords and shields and held them in front, forming a steel barrier as they ineffectively slashed at the horde, but when the elementals encountered the shields, they spread around them and overtook the warriors, who dropped their weapons and raced for the nearest stream.

Elven wizards sent spell after spell toward the small demons, yet the fireflies seemed immune. Even rain spells proved useless, evaporating before they reached the fiery beings. Although a heavy downpour had soaked the forest and city two hours earlier, the remaining moisture did little to stem the onslaught. The surrounding forest and half the elven capital was soon in flames.

A blind elven seer, aged beyond the oldest elf in the city, watched the destruction with her inner eye. Using an ancient walking stick covered with runes, she hurried a bit unsteadily to the fountain in the main square of the capital. For centuries, many elves had come to the fountain to gaze into its depths while pondering an important course of action. Fed by several clear streams that meandered through the city, the fountain was round and surrounded by giant columns carved with illustrations of elven history. Dropping to her knees, the seer bent over the water, gently breaking its cool surface with her hand so that it reflected the inferno around her.

As soon as the seer touched the water, it flared to life with a blue/green brightness that pulsed around the fountain's perimeter to overpower the blaze's reflection and cause those nearby to shield their eyes. When the light dimmed, a beautiful water sprite with shimmering blue hair that fell to her knees and deep sea-green eyes broke the surface. Her form was elven, molded from the same clear water as the fountain, giving her the appearance of a goddess.

"Greetings, ancient friend, what can I do for thee? It hast been many years since thou last contacted me."

"Welcome, Airyella. As you can see, mine capital city and surrounding forest hast been set ablaze by fire demons," the elf replied, honoring her friend by speaking in the sprite's tongue.

"Why dost thine wizards and sorceresses not destroy the demons with healing rain?"

"They have tried, but the rain dissolves upon contact without harm. I fear that thee and thine sisters are our one remaining hope. Will thou come to our aid?"

"The bond between the elves and the water sprites is an ancient one. Mine sisters and I would not like to see thee harmed so."

The water sprite reached into the fountain, bringing forth an orb of clear liquid that swirled with multiple shades of blue and green as it hovered above her hand. Bringing it close to her mouth, she began to whisper. Within seconds, other sprites appeared from the foam, and when they saw the destruction being wrought against the elves, their expressions turned from serenity to anger. They flew down the streams that fed the fountain toward the demons and hovered above the streams on thin strands of water. They attacked the clouds of fire elementals, which sizzled as magical water met fire. From there, the beautiful creatures, who could take any form, exited the streams as giant pelicans and followed the puddles and rain-soaked ground, taking the fight into the trees as they attempted to save the elves' homes and forest.

Many attacked the burning hordes while others tried to put out the fires that freely burned, but it was not a one-sided battle. The youngling elementals fought back. Retaining their cloud-like formation, the demons singled out and overwhelmed individual water sprites, causing the water that was the sprite's lifeline to sizzle, steam, and eventually explode. Yet, as the defenders fell and the battle raged, ancient wisdom and water magic took its toll against the invaders.

Heavy rain, brought on by elven water spells, soon doused the forest and town as the sprites dumped gallon after gallon of water on the attackers. With half their number depleted, the fire elementals decided to cut their losses. Breaking their horde formations, the demons reverted to their firefly forms and disappeared into the forest. The battle had lasted for many turns of the clock, and the devastation left behind stunned the elves and their allies. In thousands of years, never had such an attack been perpetrated against them. Virtually half of the city was destroyed, and the surrounding forest was burned and blackened, becoming disfigured stakes that pointed to the sky like dark skeletal fingers. The number of elves injured or killed from the fires was unknown and would remain so for weeks.

Those uninjured began the arduous task of transforming some remaining buildings into hospitals, which soon filled with the injured awaiting relief from burns and other wounds as a call for healing clerics was magically sent far and wide. Families stunned by the unprecedented attack searched for missing family members, while others set to work finding places for homeless friends and neighbors to stay until their houses could be rebuilt. The seer had remained at the pool with Airyella.

"I do not know how to thank thee and thine sisters. I mourn the losses thou hast suffered in our defense, but without thine intervention, mine city would have been utterly destroyed."

"We have both suffered grievous injuries and will mourn accordingly," Airyella replied sadly. "Our races have shared friendship for centuries; mine sisters and I could do no less. I must leave thee now, my friend. Hopefully, our next meeting will not be so dire."

The water sprite sank into the water, and the seer left the fountain to determine if her home remained intact.

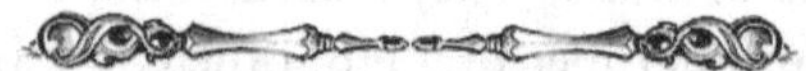

Using the font, Taza had watched the entire battle from his tower room. He was generally pleased with the results, and the undead warlock knew it would take a long time to rebuild the city and replace the burnt trees, even using magic. He hoped that the devastating loss would force the elven warriors headed for Southgard to return home.

Later, he would discover that his desired effect had worked. Once the High Elven army learned about the situation in Melemas, it turned around. The army headed back toward its sacred forest to forestall any further attacks, the treaty with the dwarves forgotten. They sent a lone rider south to the dwarves to inform them of what had happened and that they would receive no help from the High Elves.

In essence, they tore up the treaty that had existed for many years and cared little about the dwarves' reaction. Their forest home was in danger.

Water sprites: how could I have anticipated that? Earth magic, yes, but calling on the aloof and secretive fairies had come close to ruining his plans. He had wanted every High Elf living in Melemas destroyed, along with their city and forest. Their loss would have sent a message to other nations that interference would lead to harsh consequences, although the partial destruction would still cause fear and make some think twice. The face he would present when he next confronted the large fire elemental would be one of anger. Although the powerful creature expected its reward, the warlock intended to let his full rage fall on the useless ally. The fireflies should have stayed and finished the job, even if it had meant their total destruction.

CHAPTER EIGHTEEN

Celedant mounted his horse, and as his steed spun around the cobblestone courtyard of the inn, he shouted above the clamor of the growing crowd. "We ride hard and fast. If you spot anything suspicious, call out. We must assume that we are being watched."

The warning given, Celedant spurred his mount to a canter, and the others followed suit with Hority bringing up the rear on his cantankerous donkey. The thirteen other members of the quest forced their way through the gathering crowd, scattering residents and visitors as they hurried away from Roules' Inn, which had become a towering mass of flame. The night was damp and a little chilly as they rushed through the streets. Once the crowd thinned, the riders picked up speed until they approached the closed and barred gate, the final barrier blocking their escape. A bored, sleepy dwarvan guard paced his route along the wooden palisade above the gate as the company's horses came to a stomping halt.

"Hoy there; what's all the fuss?" the guard called out.

"Open the gates," Celedant responded, raising his voice. "We need to leave immediately."

Seeing how many riders were facing him, the guard blew a quick warning on his signal horn and called back, "The gates aren't opened at night. Ye'll have to wait till mornin.'"

The wizard sighed, "I'm sorry, but I wasn't asking. We cannot wait."

At the guardhouse, located in a small barracks next to the gate, they saw lanterns brighten and heard the sound of the guards hastily donning their armor.

Celedant was about to cast a spell when Botreg yelled at the guard. "Get off the gate if ye value yer life, laddie!"

As the guard scampered from the platform, Celedant completed the incantation, and energy coalesced along the edge of his staff, but before a lightning bolt could sever the large oak beam holding the gates closed, the wizard had a change of heart. Had he completed his spell, the blast would have blown the gates outward a full thirty paces, leaving the small community defenseless against an orc invasion until they could repair the damage. Celedant stopped the incantation and redirected a portion of the energy, temporarily stupefying the approaching guards. He then ensorcelled the guard they had spoken with to open the gate and allow them to pass, directing him to close and lock up tight after they left. The spell would dissipate within five minutes, returning the soldiers to normal, unaware of what had happened and scratching their heads as to why they had left their bunks.

Leaving the town behind, the companions were about to spur their mounts to a faster pace when Baldo caught sight of Hority, who had gotten off his donkey to examine a discarded piece of rotten fruit dropped by one of the soldiers the previous day. The cleric of Thierry spurred his horse over, grabbed the protesting donkey's reins and pulled Hority up and across his own saddle. A moment later they raced off, their presence swallowed by the darkness of the forest, heading east as if all the demons of the seven hells were in pursuit.

At sunrise, Celedant and his party stopped to rest the horses. Reunited with his donkey, Hority proudly placed the offending garbage in a sack and tied it to his belt. Celedant confronted him with a chilling stare.

"I'm placing you in charge of this one, Baldo. I don't care if you have to tie him to his saddle; I'll have no more of his nonsensical delays."

The wizard stalked away, leaving an open-mouthed Baldo and a grinning Hority who cheerfully added, "I will find a suitably dirty rope for ye, Baldo. Have no worries; Clor will lead the way."

After their narrow escape from Hemlit's, the road that led to the coastal city of Bau's Port seemed tame enough. They traveled all day and at night, Azimuth, Eldahir, or Morganna would cast protective spells, setting wards about the camp to warn them of evil's approach. Celedant decided not to add a protective barrier of his own, conserving his strength for battle, and instead posted extra guards. The days passed with nothing troublesome occurring as they made their way eastward to Bau's Port.

So far, Ress had tracked and hunted down eight firedrakes, killing five and amazingly coming through the fights without a scratch. One morning she sat astride her horse in a pretty meadow, her left leg crossed over the saddle horn as she ate an apple and washed it down with a drink from her water skin. She was about to toss the core away when she heard a loud crash. Several trees fell and before she realized what was happening, the beast was upon her. Dropping her snack, Ress jumped to the ground and mentally berated herself for allowing the soft breeze and peaceful meadow grass to lull her into complacency. She grabbed her spear, which had a long shaft to keep firedrakes at bay.

The beast struck with the force of a tidal wave. Its claws missed her but grabbed her horse as she backed away, and she thrust her spear at the creature's chest. Out of nowhere, a galloping wolf raced past, causing the dark red firedrake to take flight and spiral through the air, its attention diverted from Ress.

As Celedant and the others rounded a corner in the lush forest trail, Azimuth dashed back, bringing the scent of the beast with him, causing Tarquin's horse to roll its eyes and neigh as the line of horses skidded to a halt and began sidestepping and backing off the trail. As Azimuth telepathically shouted an alarm to the wizard, a loud screech sounded ahead and for some unknown reason, Tarquin knew he had to follow that cry.

Celedant was all too aware of what kind of beast lay ahead. Standing in his saddle, he called after the prince. "Beware - Firedrake!"

The horse's hooves threw up clods of dark earth as it carried its rider toward the commotion. Tarquin drew his sword and flattened his upper body against the animal's neck. He could hear nothing but the wind and crackling of branches as the horse left the trail and lunged into the underbrush with the others riding hard on his heels in an effort to catch their comrade.

Tarquin's horse broke through the undergrowth and charged into an open field, filled with bright blue wildflowers. He scanned the area and spotted the source of the cry.

When he saw a flash of color pinned under the beast's front legs, he spurred his horse to a galloped and charged. As he neared, Tarquin noticed that the creature carried a blood-covered horse, still fighting for life, grasped between its front claws. Then to his utter shock, he spotted a bit of green cloth and watched as a spear thrust toward the firedrake's head, causing it to flinch and rush toward the charging newcomer. Tarquin spurred his horse harder, riding for the creature's massive head, swinging his sword across the drake's face as he crossed before it. The sword bit deeply with a bright flash of red. As he raced past, Tarquin slowed for another attack, but it took several strides for his horse to slow down enough to turn. Before he could gain control, Tarquin was unseated as his mount screamed and bucked in fear.

Tarquin shook off the spill and jumped to his feet, grabbing his horse's reins in an effort to keep the animal from running off. As he did, he glanced at the firedrake and saw that his sword had sliced through the lower jaw of the monster. Although the agony the wound inflicted was intense, the drake's instincts turned from pain to a new threat approaching in the sky above.

Charging toward the firedrake was a golden beast so monstrous it dwarfed everything in the immediate vicinity. Few in the company had ever seen anything like it and while the drake dropped the horse and the rider who was continually piercing its chest with a spear. The creature swirled its head around to stare upward, as Tarquin realized that the once-fierce drake shook with terror.

"It's all right," Celedant called to the others. "That's Azimuth. He'll dispatch the beast."

The members of the company looked at the wizard as if he was touched in the head.

Hortus yelled out what was on everyone's mind, "What might that be?"

"A dragon, what else?" Celedant chuckled.

Azimuth was about to blast the male drake into oblivion when something made him hesitate. A flash of color carrying an elongated spear appeared from beneath the firedrake. Thankfully, the dragon realized it was a young woman dressed in a mismatched suit of chainmail, and he delayed his fiery blast to avoid roasting her to a crisp along with the drake.

"Get out of the way and let the dragon to finish it off," Celedant yelled to her when he received the dragon's mental warning.

Ress, however, ignored his words. With her red hair flying, she deftly stepped past a flailing claw and rammed her spear into the firedrake's side, finding the beast's heart. She twisted and turned the spear several times until the drake dropped to the ground and lay still.

Ress then scrambled with practiced ease to the top of the head and cracked open the skull with a broad axe she carried on her belt, making sure it was dead. As she stood defiantly on the skull of the drake, the rest of Celedant's party stared open-mouthed at what they had just witnessed, and as Ress turned to see what was happening, she fought to keep her balance as she realized that something much larger than what she had just killed had landed beside her.

Although Eldahir and Morganna joined Tarquin and the wizard, Vannor and the dwarves pulled their protesting horses to a halt in the middle of the field, their hooves tossing dirt and flowers into the air. Celedant could not help smiling at their stunned expressions as they got their first glimpse of a true dragon, but they weren't half as startled as Ress when a warm baritone voice entered her mind and addressed her.

"Nicely done, my lady, but next time, just get out of the way. I nearly roasted you along with the drake."

"Who...what...are you?" she asked, her voice coming out in a squeak.

The voice inside her head said, "A dragon, my dear. The name's Azimuth. Pleased to meet you."

Ress lost her footing, falling from her perch. Before she reached the ground, Azimuth extended a front claw and caught her, gently lowering the shocked young woman to the ground. Getting her bearings, Ress stood up and confronted the dragon.

"Why are you here? I need no help."

Tarquin spoke from a few paces behind her. "I didn't see you at first, but once I did, I agree, you seemed to have the situation under control." He and Celedant moved closer. "I was worried about the horse, but I was too late."

She spun around and locked angry eyes on him.

Hority left the group and called back to the others. "Friends, this monster has a strong odor I have never encountered." He began rubbing his habit against the firedrake, taking deep breaths.

Ress turned, and the movement caused her hair to uncover the hideous scars that marred the side of her face. "What are you doing?"

Hority was too busy to answer at first, but a moment later, he looked up at her visage. "Harrumph, ye had a bad healer not in good graces with the gods. Best see one of ours. Now, might I explore the monster's head? That fluid leaking from its skull needs documenting for Clor's knowledge."

The others put their weapons away and gathered as Celedant approached.

"My name is Celedant, and this dragon is my friend and lifelong companion, Azimuth." He named the others. "We were headed south when we heard the firedrake, and our impetuous leader spurred off like some noble knight of the realm."

Ress planted the butt of her spear against the ground. "Believe me, no one from your company looks noble."

Hority began excitedly hopping from one foot to the other. Ress gave the cleric a questioning look.

"I am Hortus, Abbot of Thierry," one of the dwarfs said. "Yon monk means no harm. It would take too long to explain his actions at the moment, but he seeks out garbage and other foul things in honor of his god, Clor."

"A person can get used to his antics," Tarquin snorted, "but the smell is hard to escape."

Hority scampered up the head and was soon arm deep in the firedrake's skull.

Tarquin moved closer to the head of the creature, coming face to face with Ress. There was no reaction to her appearance as he nodded, stopping a moment to clean his blade with dried grass.

"Your name, lass?" Hortus asked.

"I am Ress Logdan," she answered proudly. "My mission is to avenge my village and wounds against all firedrakes."

Hortus dismounted, standing significantly lower than she did. "Ye fight them yerself? Some would call that heroic, and I do not believe yer deity ignores this. Yet others would call it madness, a willingness to die. Have ye chosen wisely between the two?"

She bent down and whispered her answer. "I have yet to make that choice. In truth, I have never thought of those questions."

Celedant addressed everyone. "Azimuth believes we should put as much distance between us and this carcass as soon as possible before it draws other evil denizens this way. I agree."

Celedant and the others mounted up while Ress scavenged her belongings from her dead horse. Tarquin rode over and extended his hand.

"My horse is the strongest and can carry two riders without difficulty."

She grasped his hand and swung into the saddle behind him. As the party moved off, he whispered, "Once we camp, you might want to speak to Aegir about the scars you bear. He is the best healer I know. If he cannot help, one of the other clerics probably can. Believe me, I have seen miraculous occurrences on this quest." He felt the point of a blade held to his side.

"I would prefer if you did not mention them."

"Trust me," Tarquin said, turning his head to look into her eyes. "As a King's Borderer, I have seen much worse, but heed my advice concerning the clerics. From what Azimuth says, your face troubles you a great deal. There is no reason for you to continue suffering if one of the clerics can heal your scars. Oh, and one final thing, stay upwind of Hority at all times."

The company and its guest were about to leave when Hority shouted down from his perch atop the firedrake's skull. "Prince Tarquin, this is a perfect spot to camp. I have gone to great lengths to hollow out a place to sleep in this skull. It is blessed, according to me tenets."

"Come down, yer idiot," Baldo said, irritation in his voice, "or I'll tie a rope to yer leg and drag ye to the next camp."

Grudgingly, Hority slipped down from the creature's giant horned head and headed for his donkey, passing Azimuth who, still in dragon form, flicked the foul-smelling dwarf with a toe and sent him tumbling toward his donkey. Unperturbed, Hority picked himself up and grabbed his donkey's reins. "But Baldo, this new finding isna dry yet. Me habit would collect many things along the forest floor."

"Me good Clorian," Hortus interjected, "I feel that ye have done enough for yer god this day."

With Hority mounted on his donkey, Azimuth returned to wolf form and backtracked through the undergrowth to their original trail, while Baldo cursed a string of sharp briars entangled in his clothing and his horse's mane.

Turning his horse with a quick pull on the reins, Celedant faced Tarquin and Ress. "Lady Ress, we ride on an errand of great importance. There is a mid-size town within two days' ride along our course. We can leave you there, if you like."

"I have never met individuals who weren't disgusted by my appearance. With your permission, I would like to continue with your company. Besides, I still must consult the clerics about my lack of healing."

Slippery goo from the firedrake caused Hority to slide half off his donkey. "I would, of course, be pleased to look at yer wounds."

She turned to the Abbot Hortus, Aegir, and Baldo. "I would appreciate your help."

Hority nodded sagely. "We will need to consult on such an old wound. If I had been there when ye were first injured, I know of a poultice made from cow dung, beetles, and turtle claws that might have worked."

Ress wrinkled her nose and inwardly thanked the gods the dwarf had not been there. Yet she could not help noticing the seriousness on the cleric's face, while several of his companions unsuccessfully hid their laughs.

"I believe we should wait till we camp for the night before pursuing your healing. Right now, it is most important to vacate the area," Celedant interrupted. "The smell of that carcass will bring the orcs running to dine on it."

Everyone agreed, and the party was soon rapidly moving away from the area, talking about the amazing fact that Azimuth was an elf and a wolf, as well as a mighty dragon, something none of them had ever seen or even known truly existed. They had previously believed that firedrakes were actually dragons.

That night and many miles down the trail, the party stopped as Ronli and Ralav vaulted from their horses and vanished into the undergrowth. They were gone less than ten minutes when Ronli's leaf-covered head reappeared.

"We found a good place to camp," she said, wiping the sweat from her forehead." If ye will dismount and follow me?"

Because of the dimness of the thick undergrowth combined with the fading sun, Tarquin advised everyone to proceed cautiously so as to avoid becoming separated. It was slow moving as they led the horses through the thick growth. And before long, he felt Ress's calloused hand grab his. It was amazing that Ronli and Ralav had come this far. Yet the dense foliage at last opened to a stand of fir trees where the tracker's horses grazed in the verdant grass.

The one complaint was from Hority, who stood looking over the thick carpet of branches and leaves in disgust. "Tarquin, this place reeks of evil. I shall not sleep under those trees."

Tarquin nodded sagely. "In that case, find the largest path and bed down across it."

Hority snapped his fingers and began searching the surrounding area.

Ress placed her bedding in the notch of a tree with plentiful fresh branches covering her nest and laying out a soft fur hide for comfort. She had just gotten comfortable when she noticed the four clerics, including the downcast dwarf with slumped shoulders, speaking together. The Abbot Hortus kissed the downtrodden cleric on the head and sent him on a quest for the perfect place to sleep. A cleric in travel-stained robes that had once been white approached, stopping at a respectful distance.

"Might I approach yer campsite? Me name is Aegir," he began.

She held out a hand, and he shook it. Her interest piqued, Ress said, "With all the commotion, you must know mine."

The dwarf nodded and sat on a log near her bedding. "Some have called me a heretic, but I prefer living as a Borderer over burning. I must admit I had lost me beliefs and wandered with no purpose until I was discovered and chased by fellow members of me monastery." The brown-haired dwarf looked around before continuing. "By any chance, have ye recently been visited by a strange dwarf dressed in immaculate blue robes and sporting a snowy white beard?"

Ress's mind whirled as she wondered how a dwarf she had just met could know about what had happened weeks before. Her bewilderment was all Aegir needed to confirm his suspicions.

"I dreamed several nights ago that I brought a faceless woman in front of Dolgar, the dwarvan god of healin'," Aegir continued. "He is a deity that strives for goodness and balance, and is most assuredly the one ye saw. When Dolgar chooses, ye will dream as ye sleep. When this happens, do not be frightened. I will appear to lead ye to Dolgar, and he will speak with ye. This is important, human. Do not stray, or ye might be forever lost."

Ress laughed nervously. "Why would your god appear to me?"

"He must decide if ye are worthy to join our cause and receive his healing touch."

"You appear to offer no more than dangerous courses from which to choose."

Aegir shrugged. "Ye don't know with whom ye seek to travel. Many have died so we could be sittin' here talkin'. Tarquin has led his soldiers into one hopeless battle after another, and although he won, many close friends were lost. This company rides to what could end with their death to find an ancient artifact in order to stop an evil greater than ye canna imagine that threatens to overtake our world. They have sworn allegiance to the Wizard Celedant, and with Prince Tarquin as our leader, we will succeed. If ye choose to meet Dolgar, he will guide ye." Then he stood, brushed dry leaves and twigs from his robes, and disappeared into the darkness.

CHAPTER NINETEEN

Taza, the greatest warlock living in the primitive world of Muiria, felt like he could not accomplish even the simplest task. He paced back and forth, the staff of Adois ringing hollowly against the stone floor with every step. What was happening? Then he caught the slimmest memory. As ruler of a distant planet exiled for his attempt to enact what he'd considered well-intended changes, Taza's downfall had begun with a single spy.

Could his own people be working against him here as well? Members of the Warlocks' Council were capable of such treachery, but the only two privy to his most important plans were Melgor and Sellis. Sellis was locked away in Taza's dungeon, his magic held tightly in check by the dampening field placed over the cell. On the other hand, Melgor was free, and a valuable lieutenant in carrying out his wishes, and although the vampire believed he had cowed the warlock into subservience, he could never be certain of that one's allegiance. Melgor's hate could push him into acts that would undermine everything he might accomplish for his master...and Taza was certain the warlock hated him with a passion.

Other than his vampire guards, there was no one he could really trust, including the household staff that had been with him for years.

Word must be reaching the enemy, regardless of how fast I work, Taza mused. It was possible for messages to cross any distance in an instant if one used magic.

He concluded that at least one spy must have infiltrated his castle, and it had to be a member of the senior staff or possibly one of the servants. Members of both groups had been in attendance, at one time or another, during every critical decision. The commoners could go about their business, waiting for tidbits of information they could pass on to the enemy. They could be listening even now, using a broom as a ruse. Taza raced to the door, startling his guards, and swung the portal open, hoping to catch the spy nearby, but no one was there. Paranoia ate at his insides like a maggot devouring rotten meat.

He pointed to several guards. "Quick, down the stairs and capture anyone you meet - and send up more guards!"

They sped away while he scanned the exterior tower doors and walls. *I need to post two guards here and at the entrance,* he thought. *Everyone entering and leaving the tower will be stopped and searched.* He rushed back inside and examined the area behind every curtain, throwing them aside. Finding no one, he checked the stonework and every niche and corner, any place where a spy could hide.

Then ever so softly, the staff whispered in his mind, "Roof."

As four guards ran into the chamber, Taza turned and pointed upward. "Two of you, scale the top of this dome. Make sure there is no place for a beast to land or any protected places for a spy to hide."

They found no one, and a smile graced Taza's features when the screams of one of his guards pierced the air as he fell to rocks below. The guard would not die, but he would suffer the agony of broken bones and bruises until his vampire nature healed him.

Taza's mind remembered everything and everyone, storing the information for later use. He called over another guard and ordered pen and parchment. Once equipped, he wrote furiously. When he was finished, he called his Captain over.

"This list contains all the people present or nearby when discussions were being held regarding the takeover of the continent. Round them up and shackle them in line on the tower stairs. Then bring in one at a time for questioning. If need be, draft the mercenaries to help."

Nevertheless, the Staff of Adois continued to plague him with doubts. *What if one of your bodyguards is the spy?*

Taza had personally hired every guard in his employ, and he had never heard of a vampire turning against its sire. One guard would not be a problem. The undead warlock could dispatch him, but if several of his children attacked? He would trust no one but himself. He had reached the pinnacle of his magic by becoming master of the Staff of Adois and believed that the other dark warlocks were jealous and sought that power for themselves. "Bah, this is madness," he said aloud to no one.

Taza ordered his guards to bring a table with funnels running to bowls to slake their thirst while the shackled prisoners ascended the staircase of the high tower in leg and arm irons. The first prisoner was a human woman who cleaned Taza's floors. Two guards held her down on the table during the interrogation. His questions required a simple yes or no answer, and although she denied any knowledge of magic and the goings-on in the tower, Taza remained unconvinced.

"Kill her."

"No, master, please! I swear I never heard a word...."

Her words were cut short as one of the guards slashed her throat, allowing the blood to drain into the collection buckets. Afterward they tossed her body out a back window to the rocks below like the boney remains of a chicken eaten for dinner.

One by one, the prisoners were led to the table, now stained red. The questioning became routine, leading to more blood and more corpses. Then the guards brought Taza's long-time castellan, Culliver, before him. His usually neatly pressed white shirt and tan pants were ruffled and torn. Culliver stood proudly in front of his master as two vampire guards struggled to handle him. Having grown bored with the proceedings, Taza's interest was aroused by his servant's resistance, which was proving very entertaining. Culliver was an elf, captured during a raid on a human village near the Wood Elves' border, and had been with Taza for over a hundred years.

The guards muscled the castellan to the table and bent him over the bloodstained oak.

"Tell me something, Culliver. Being a proud, arrogant elf, you must have hated the years you have been forced to work for me."

"That is so, my lord."

Taza smiled wickedly. As much as he cared for his Illanni children the dark elves, especially once they accepted the mantle of vampirism, he hated the elves of light. During the time that Culliver was his servant, the undead warlock never tired of finding ways to demean him. As he thought about the enjoyment he had received from tormenting his castellan, Taza realized that of all his servants, this one might possess the magic needed to be a spy.

"It's *you*, isn't it? You're the spy...the fly on the wall with hearing sensitive enough to eavesdrop from a distance, and since all elves are born with some degree of magic, no doubt you are capable of sending whatever you hear to my enemies."

"I will not miss you, warlock of darkness."

Taza grew angry at what he believed were the condemned elf's last words.

"Insolent slime! You will not enjoy a swift death like the others. Instead, I will turn you into a vampire and return you to your precious forest, where you can feed upon your own kind until they slay you."

Culliver, however, had other ideas. He struck backward with his elbows, crushing the guard's throats and with a single word, set them ablaze. Another spell shattered the arm and leg chains, sending the links flying in every direction. As Taza stood up and approached the table, Culliver jumped.

Taza laughed, believing that whatever magic the elf possessed could be overpowered, but the leap was unlike that of anyone he had ever witnessed, even for an elf. Culliver flew twenty feet through the air over the table and out the window. Taza raced after him, expecting to see Culliver's body shatter against the rocks below, but instead of falling, the elf's body elongated, two wings sprouted from his back, and a tail formed. The metamorphosis happened in seconds, and a huge, red dragon soared away from the tower and disappeared into the mountains before Taza could utter a single word.

The undead warlock's eyes practically popped out of his head as his inflammable temper raged out of control. He turned to the captain of his vampire guards and shouted, "Why didn't you tell me that dragons can take the form of an elf?"

"I...I did not know, my lord. None of my kind did. Although the dragons supposedly commune with the Wood Elves, High Elves, and wizards, they turned against the Illanni eons ago."

Taza lifted the Staff of Adois high, prepared to destroy the Captain in his anger.

"Please, my lord, you know how secretive the dragons are. I believe the dragon hid this ability from everyone. Culliver, or whatever his name really is, revealed it because it was the only way to save his life."

The Captain's words rang true, even to Taza. Lowering the staff, he pointed to the dust that was all that remained of two dead guards. "Have that mess removed. The rest of the servants can be turned into zombies or ghouls, whatever takes your fancy. Add them to my army. From now on, no one but vampires will attend to my needs. Now leave me!"

Taza returned to his obsidian throne and allowed his anger to cool. Once his mind was calm, he was even able to enjoy the irony. A dragon in elven guise was worthy of admiration. During the great span of his lifetime, many creatures had tried to infiltrate his household, but they were detected so fast that it had become laughable. Turning one of his own tricks against him was genius. Taza had been planting Illanni spies made to look like Wood or High Elves in human and elven cities for centuries. The dragon had probably been a plant in the village where he was captured, waiting for the right opportunity to become a spy. Of course, Taza's was the better plan - a plan centuries in the making with a subtle hand to shape flesh as well as history itself.

He wondered how many dragons disguised as elves had been planted in the various kingdoms and outlying communities. He had never been able to determine the number of dragons living on Muiria, because they revealed themselves to no one but the wizards. As his Captain of the guards had said, dragons were a secretive lot, even worse than elves. Moreover, they were powerful possessors of the old magic. It would be difficult, if not impossible, to find a revealing spell that would work on them. Nevertheless, Taza was determined to find a way to unmask their presence and destroy them.

CHAPTER TWENTY

Two days later as they neared the coast, Celedant and his friends encountered an increasing number of rivers and their tributaries. Hortus asked the wizard if they could stop earlier than usual by one of them. As they made camp, Hority led his donkey a short distance from the others. He had not spoken since the incident with the firedrake. With the wizard's angry words in mind, Clor had led him to a slimy rope used to tether a half-submerged boat to a sturdy bush along the shore. When Hority learned that what Celedant had commanded Botreg to do was simply a threat, the monk had slung the dripping rope about his shoulders and remained silent.

Hortus had spent the past two days mulling over ideas about how to bathe Hority. They would not escape the enemy's notice with the rancid smell their obstinate friend constantly gave off. He settled on an idea, and as the camp settled, Hortus called Botreg and Tarquin over and explained what he had in mind.

"When the time comes, be ready to go swimming," Hortus concluded.

The Abbot ambled around the camp, preparing for the upcoming ordeal. He sat down across from the Clorian monk and watched as Hority stared longingly at the rope. The filthy monk did not glance up at Hortus.

"Me brother, do ye often dream of your patron deity?" Hortus asked.

Hority shook his head no, keeping his eyes downcast.

"I had a remarkable dream last night," Hortus began, "and have been pondering the meaning all day. I dreamed of Thierry and Clor sitting next to each other at the Great Hall where dwarves go when death takes them."

The Abbot finally got the Clorian's attention. He looked away from the rope into Hortus's eyes. "Clor is a forgotten god. How could he sit at the High Table of the worshipped?"

Now came the hard part.

"In my dream, I stood among the privileged Abbots behind my lord and master, and called out. To my amazement, Thierry spoke to me. This rarely happens. He introduced me to Clor, who wore shimmering white robes. In me mind, both deities agreed that in order for this special mission to succeed, ye will need to bathe. Putting aside yer beliefs to accomplish somethin' for the greater good is the ultimate sacrifice one can make for his god."

"Blasphemy!" Hority screeched. "Away from me, oh demon of temptation."

The Abbot had expected this reaction. "Me son, I must tell ye that the dream was all that I experienced last night. When I awoke, I found this folded in me prayer book."

Hortus held out an immaculately clean square of cloth with the sign of the Clorians stitched in the center. It had been difficult to stitch it in secret while riding, but the Abbot was determined to clean up the little monk.

He handed the cloth to Hority, who recognized the flaming bird emerging from a heap of rubbish. He stared in disbelief at the pure symbol of his faith. Tears formed in the corners of his eyes, leaving clean runnels as they flowed down his grimy cheeks. He looked up at Hortus.

"Clor led me from the valley to become a part of this company. Now he speaks louder as he presents our order with a relic to be worshiped by all Clorians."

Thus, the Abbot got Hority to agree to a bath. It took a full hour, using a thick bar of lye soap and heavy-duty scrubbing to wash the accumulated dirt away. Unfortunately, Hority's robes were beyond redemption. They were so threadbare and badly encrusted with filth that they fell apart during the washing. Hortus retrieved a spare robe from his own pack for Hority. Once the grime was removed, Botreg, Tarquin, and the Abbot were astonished at the number of scars marking the monk's body.

"By the looks of those scars," Baldo called from the riverbank where he sat watching the proceedings, "ye have fought more than just firedrakes."

"They matter little as long as I am doing Clor's good work," Hority laughed.

Now that he was clean, they warned Hority not to foul himself with any kind of filth, and the Abbot made him discard the slimy rope, the piece of brain he had taken from the firedrake's remains, and all the other debris he had collected along the way. This bothered the little monk more than the bath had, but he agreed with the Abbot that it would do little good for him to bathe if his belongings still reeked.

"The orcs have an enhanced sense of smell," the Abbot explained. "They would scent ye a mile off."

"Ye would think that would make them a cleaner lot," Botreg added.

"One person's garbage is another's perfume," Hority said with a sigh.

That night the party slept peacefully with the sweet smell of grass and the fresh night air in their nostrils. It was the first time since the Clorian monk had joined their ranks.

Early the next morning as the company continued their journey, Celedant and Botreg described Bau's Port, constantly interrupting each other until Celedant stopped talking. Botreg had won round one of their little war of words. When the dwarf finished his narrative, the wizard described the darker side of the city.

"Bau's Port is a coastal city, and like most coastal cities in the Confederation, it is very prosperous, but the place is far from typical. Unlike most coastal cities after the downfall of the Zeiglon Empire, it thrived after the great quakes that had changed the land so drastically. Yet its leaders unwisely drew attention to their prosperity by being boastful and too greedy for their own good. As a result, the neighboring cities banded together against them, and Bau's Port was repeatedly burned and beaten into submission by uneasy neighbors."

"In the end, the city remained small, while its neighbors grew larger and more powerful. Bau's Port survived by becoming a city of secrets and turned to piracy as its primary trade. Most of the piracy was overlooked since they never preyed upon the larger ships. The City-States accepted the losses suffered by smaller boats, telling their owners that their security was not the government's problem. Ever mindful of the harm their boastfulness had caused in the past, Bau's Port became a prosperous haven for adventurers and developed a lucrative trade in illicit goods."

"Although the city's past actions had brought about its downfall, thievery now brought safety. The pirates were a vicious lot, feared by captains and sailors alike, partly because the strong Thieves Guild had agents operating in every city of the Confederation. The port was also the stronghold of the Assassins Guild. Crossing one of these feared groups was bad for the health. Even the combined might of the Confederation could not bolster the confidence of anyone foolish enough to contemplate attacking Bau's Port."

"The thieves and assassins provided the power and mystique that kept the Confederation's attention turned away from the small coastal city. Pirates controlled everyday activities, and although their leaders were known as traders, they were nothing more than pirate lords. Each trader operated a fleet of fast ships that sailed on every waterway of the world. They honored a contract that ensured peace between the traders while anchored in the city's port, but once the ships were out of sight of the city, each trading vessel became fair game."

It was toward this metropolis and ever-shifting den of iniquity that Celedant and his party now rode. They were within a day of their destination when they stopped in a small patch of moss-covered oak trees to camp. Tarquin had realized that the closer they came to Bau's Port, the more withdrawn Botreg became. That night as they set up camp, the prince called him over for a chat. The two friends sat on a fallen log and stretched the muscles of their tired legs.

"What's bothering you, Botreg?"

The dark dwarf looked even more morose than normal and with a shake of his head, he replied, "Its Bau's Port. I'll bring us nothing but trouble if I enter the city."

Tarquin laughed. "Nonsense, we're always one step ahead of trouble. What more could you possibly add?"

The dwarf lowered his head into his hands. "There's a wee problem that Celedant seems to have overlooked."

"What could Celedant possibly have missed?" Tarquin asked, concerned over Botreg's demeanor.

Botreg looked at his friend with intense dark eyes. "Bau's Port is the headquarters for the Assassin's Guild. Every man jack of them will be trying to collect on my death warrant the moment I step inside the city. Everyone with me will also be marked for death."

Tarquin understood his friend's dilemma. Botreg had run away many years ago, tired of the control and manipulation the guild held over its agents. The Assassins Guild jealously guarded its secrets and never allowed any of its members to leave without a specific mission. Their agents knew too much. If that information became known to non-members, it would cause untold problems. Deciding it was time to get out, Botreg had journeyed across the continent and joined the Borderers, hoping to find safety in the dwarvan empire. Yet here he was, headed into the very heart of a city controlled, in part, by the assassins. His presence would endanger his friends and the mission.

Tarquin never claimed to have all the answers to their problems, and he hated to see his friend leave. He believed that the dwarf's participation was vital to the success of the mission.

"My advice is to keep your hood up. I'll speak with Celedant tonight."

Nodding, the dwarf got to his feet, stomped over to where he had set down his gear, and spread his bedroll across a thick patch of grass.

Later that night after the company had shared a tasty meal of roast rabbit, courtesy of Ralav and Ronli's hunting skills, Tarquin took a seat next to the wizard and his constant companion Azimuth.

Unsure of how to begin, he picked at his fingernails until Celedant lost his patience.

"Out with it," he growled.

Startled, Tarquin hesitated a moment longer before the story tumbled out.

"Botreg is correct," Celedant agreed. "His being a former assassin had slipped my mind, but the Sergeant's presence should not be a problem. Our stay in Bau's Port will be short. I have a friend in the city that will put us up for a few days. Botreg can keep to the rooms until we are ready to leave. With caution we should be able to keep his presence a secret."

Celedant's firm belief was enough to persuade the young man. Tarquin went to Botreg and passed along the wizard's words. The good news eased Botreg's fear. At least for now, the former assassin could cease worrying about leaving his companions.

Later that night, Ress Logdan bedded down after eating her fill of the evening meal. For some reason she felt anxious, and it took a long time to fall asleep. Once she did, her eyes popped opened and a startled expression crossed her face when she felt cold stone under her back instead of her comfortable bedroll.

"Awake, Ress. Dolgar awaits us," Aegir whispered as he stood next to the bench on which she now lay. Although fearless when facing firedrakes, Ress found herself shivering with anticipation. She had never met a god before. Aegir placed a comforting hand on her forearm, removing fear and anxiety, and led her through several empty halls to a massive chamber that opened before them. Dolgar stood by the door, wearing sapphire blue robes that matched his twinkling eyes. His waist-length beard and hair were as white as new-fallen snow, his features kindly, reminding her of a much beloved grandfather, and the laugh lines next to his eyes were proof that he frequently smiled. He motioned them over to a white marble bench with beautiful swirls of gold embedded within the stone.

"I apologize for not helping ye sooner," Dolgar said. "Even a deity must be careful. I needed time to judge ye and yer nature."

"Did I pass?" Ress asked with a nervous grin.

"Why, of course," Dolgar replied, enjoying her playful nature.

He led her to a room with a bench similar to the one on which she had awakened. Sitting down, he patted the seat beside him while Aegir wandered far enough away to give them privacy, but not so far that he could not hear Dolgar's summons.

The dwarvan god stared deep into the young woman's eyes and did something she allowed no one else to do. He brushed back her hair and closely examined her scars.

"Ye have had to bear these hideous marks far too long. I can feel the pain ye have suffered from mockery and fear. I wish I could erase those emotional scars from yer soul, but that is beyond me power."

Dolgar stood and took her head in both of his hands. Ress felt pressure on her scars followed by pain caused by the stretching of her skin. Then a bright blue light flashed, stunning her, and she lost her equilibrium. Ress would have fallen off the bench but for Dolgar. Once she was stable, he sat down. Ress's hand flew to her face, but as her fingers explored the damaged cheek, the irregular creases and scarred flesh were now soft and smooth.

Dolgar snapped his fingers and a mirror appeared, floating in front of Ress. At first, she dropped her eyes to the floor, afraid to look, denying what her questing fingers had already revealed. She had avoided her reflection for so long, her response was an unconscious one.

"Go ahead, lass. Take a look," Dolgar kindly encouraged her.

Swallowing the lump in her throat, Ress raised her eyes and risked a peek. The reflection that stared at her in the mirror was the face of a flawlessly beautiful young woman – one she had not seen since the firedrake attack five years ago. She was speechless as tears ran down her cheeks.

Dolgar hugged her. "Lass, yer once again to the eyes the lovely young woman ye are at heart. All I ask is that ye watch over Celedant and the rest of his party. In some ways, ye are a better fighter than the others. They have survived countless battles, but ye alone have single-handedly taken on firedrakes. The wizard and his friends travel to a place of evil beyond description. I need ye to watch over Tarquin. Aside from Celedant, he is one of the most crucial members of the expedition, and he would gladly lay down his life for any member of the group. This unfortunate habit developed when he became a Borderer, and we must do our best to curb it. Ask Aegir to tell ye of the prophecy. Although every member of this quest is vital to success, the wizard and the prince are the two who must fight the final battle against Taza."

Speechless, she nodded, and Aegir led her back to the bench where he had found her. "Go back to sleep."

"But..."

"Ye did not travel here physically, but spiritually," Aegir told her.

"Does that mean that when I awake, my face will be scarred again?"

"No, lass, ye are healed in body, but a journey such as this is usually accomplished in the spiritual realm."

"I don't understand."

Aegir smiled. "Ye will...in time." As she lay back on the cold bench, the dwarf touched her forehead with his warm hand, and she fell into a deep sleep. In the morning, she would awaken in her bedroll – healed, and ready to begin her new journey.

Chapter Twenty-One

General Grimilzor's army arrived a few days after Major Rohaus' detachment seized the pass. The general wasted no time moving his army into the surrounding hills and trails as he waited for reinforcements.

In the meantime, orcs continued to set up defenses along the river. Unable to help the besieged city until more troops arrived, the dwarves had no choice but to sit by idly as the enemy's army swelled and spread across the valley floor. In the northern foothills and passes, the defenders began building their own defensives, hoping to swell their numbers sufficiently to launch a successful attack. Meanwhile, word of the orcs' attack spread through the mountains of the Dwarvan Nation and the Eastern City-States. Yet support for Grimilzor and his army remained slow in coming.

Small groups of dwarves from distant villages filtered into the growing camp, bringing tales of well-timed raids throughout the Empire that cut into the number of soldiers sent south. The wood elves were the first to arrive. Even though raids from the great swamp had increased, two thousand elven soldiers marched into camp from the west. Arriving in good spirits, they joined the defenses near the dam that helped to form a large lake. Lake Mirowmir served as a water source for the farms that dotted the landscape.

The Eastern Nations and City-States sent small detachments of men-at-arms and foot soldiers, comprised mostly of younger sons out to prove their courage. Heroic deeds in such a grand adventure certainly would enhance their prospects later in life. Often, these forces bore ill will toward many of their neighbors, and as they headed toward the growing army, their leaders had their hands full as they tried to prevent conflict from breaking out. This forced Grimilzor and his staff members to separate the various groups and intermingle them with his own troops.

One of the forces from the City-States to ally themselves with the dwarvan army was under the command of Prince Thomas Gildahar, a noble human mercenary from of the lost city of Carline. Tall and handsome with blond hair and serious brown eyes, the thirty-five-year- old had been an Earl in a thriving city until wild elves, remnants from the Illanni that had chosen not to go underground, raided and burned his region. Badly wounded during the battle, two retainers had helped him escape by carrying him out of the city on a makeshift stretcher along with a small chest of gold.

Before long, Prince Thomas' despair turned to a thirst for revenge. The fact that he had survived as he defended his lands still raised his ire. In the following years, he raised a band of warriors to make the wild elven tribes rue the day they had destroyed his homeland. Being the last of the Carline dynasty had riddled him with overwhelming anguish and rage.

Over the following ten years, Prince Thomas fought the wild elves along the border in countless small conflicts within the Eastern Confederation of City-states. In the past, he had been a drunkard and a slouch as an Earl, but he soon discovered that he had a knack for war.

It had been three weeks since the dwarvan army had taken the passes when Thomas arrived at Hywel's Way with two hundred soldiers. Tired of the constant border struggles, he saw the dwarves' troubles as something of a mystery and ordered his small army to break camp after sending a brief message to his most recent employer that he and his men were leaving.

Thomas wore simple mail armor with a steel breastplate and iron helm, and his shield bore the Gildahar Crest featuring a scarlet rose clutched in the talons of a falcon. His followers wore an assortment of armor purchased or looted from a dozen different territories. Fifty archers were High Elves more eager to see the world than most of their secluded race. Years ago, Thomas had put aside his anger toward the elves. Although the High Elves had not been involved in destroying his city, he had hated them all, regardless of their clan. However, as he fought against their wild cousins, Thomas learned to respect their way of life. He had never forgiven the tribes that had attacked his city, but he was not naïve, and soon enlisted some of the more outgoing High Elves to join his band.

These elves were mostly half-elves with one elven parent and the other human. They enjoyed a good fight, and Thomas formed a close bond with them. An elf named Durian was his second in command, and Thomas's human soldiers had adopted the habit of painting their faces before battle, a trait used mostly by wild elves.

Durian once explained to Thomas, "We do it to scare away demons and frighten the enemy."

Thomas' troops received relatively comfortable positions in the defenses, camping on several mossy outcroppings created by frequent rain over the years. Some of his men found flat dry spots for their tents, while others chose ledges carved out of the natural limestone walls caused by flooding. The dwarves had constructed a rough wall with a ramp formed from the dirt of the moat they had dug. As they settled into position, they waited for the coming battle.

CHAPTER TWENTY-TWO

It was Tarquin and Morganna's turn to stand first watch. The sorceress had been especially quiet these past few days as they traveled across the Confederation's wide forested lands. During supper that night, Ronli asked her about it, and the Illanni confessed that although she was becoming acclimated to living above ground and the wondrous beauty it offered, travelling in such vast spaces was still a little discomforting for her as she was used to teleporting through the confines of the underworld tunnels.

Morganna had fled above ground many months ago when her father ordered her death and placed a bounty on her head because she would not accept the vampire nature her family, as a leading Illanni clan, had adopted to honor Taza. She moved into a woodland cottage deep within dwarvan territory. Later, her best friend, Kalsti, along with two hundred rebel Illanni, joined her to further her fight against the vampires.

As Morganna spent more time above ground, she began to revert to the elven nature of her ancestors, and when she made the decision to save Tarquin's life and join him in the fight against Taza and the Staff of Adois, Dolgar blessed her with a gift. Now she no longer simply looked like her wood elf ancestors; their very nature had reasserted itself so dramatically that anyone unfamiliar with her origins would never realize she had been born an Illanni.

Growing up in the underground caverns of the dwarvan cities, Ronli understood the problem.

"The one difference between us is that dwarves frequently go above ground for trade and travel, especially when yer a soldier or a Borderer. Centuries ago, the dwarves had similar concerns when they first ventured above ground. Both our races were born to live a lifetime confined to the enclosed finite spaces of an underworld filled with caverns and tunnels. A sudden switch to the limitless expanse above ground would bewilder anyone."

The land stretched endlessly around her, and although Morganna felt comfortable in the woodlands, she was still somewhat overwhelmed by its vastness.

That night, Tarquin and Morganna began what they hoped would be their last night of guard duty, at least for the next few days. The air was heavy and rather warm, and perspiration soaked their clothing. The cool breeze that earlier had blown off the ocean tailed off, and as the sun sank into the horizon, biting insects emerged.

The two sentries took up positions on opposite sides of camp, staring into the darkness as their companions drifted off to asleep. Guard duty had always been tedious for Tarquin and less than an hour into it, he began to pace. The salt from his perspiration attracted mosquitoes, and he felt as though they were eating him alive. At least walking might take his mind off their unwanted attention. As he paced, he fought a losing battle, trying to keep a clear mind and stay wake. At one point during the boredom of guarding the camp, Tarquin leaned against a tree. A moment later, he thought he heard a distant sound. It was faint and might have been a dead branch hitting the ground. As his head began to nod, he pushed off the tree and began pacing once more, knowing that if he did not, he would soon be asleep.

The prince had just completed his circuit and turned to make another when he heard the noise again. Tarquin drew his sword halfway from its sheath, but Dragon Bolt's red metal blade remained cold with nothing more than the soft glow of the moon reflecting off its polished surface. The telltale glow of danger was not there. He shoved his sword back into its sheath and sighed as he continued his rounds. Then he heard it again, a slight rustle this time. He had the distinctive feeling that something was watching him, and as he picked up his foot, Tarquin paused - not setting it down. A light footfall in the forest copied his exact steps. Putting aside his trepidation, he continued to a tree, the hair on the nape of his neck prickling.

As he grasped a thick vine that grew up the tree's bole, Morganna's hushed voice called out to him from the low branches. "Beware, Tarquin. Something prowls the area around our camp. I woke Celedant and Eldahir as I crossed to this tree. Be ready to stand and fight if they charge. I will join you."

The Borderer steadied his back against the tree trunk. Tarquin could just hear the adversaries making their way through the woods, but then he had not seen or heard the Illanni as she crossed the camp and climbed a tree within ten paces of him. Self-doubt clouded his mind, and Tarquin tried to control a nervous shiver that shot through his body. Was he ready for what was coming?

Morganna's calm voice whispered down to him. "They're fifty paces away and advancing steadily. They move on all fours. It shouldn't be long now." The last thing he heard from her was a soft, "Be ready."

Moments later, wild yells erupted from the darkened woods and the sudden rush of feet sounded as if an army were charging through the forest. Tarquin drew his sword and it flared brightly, proclaiming that an enemy was near as it illuminated the area around him.

Morganna dropped silently from the tree to stand beside him and smiled. "At last, we're going to fight. Guard duty was miserable."

Tarquin never had a chance to reply as an enemy charged him, fangs gleaming in the moonlight. In the flash of a second, he realized that he was fighting an unknown creature. They were from the tribe Taza had purchased for a quantity of copper. Clad in coarse leather armor, the bear-like creature wielded a boar spear that it tried to drive through the human. Tarquin sidestepped his opponent's thrust and as the weapon flashed past, he swung Dragon Bolt down from over his head at his attacker. The blade bit deep, slicing into the creature's right shoulder and continuing down into its chest cavity - parting the chest plate that it wore and delivering a shock to the prince that these assassins were female. As his assailant died, the monster's momentum carried its body past him, but instead of lodging against the rib bones, the magic sword slid free of its own accord. The assassins attacked using a variety of weapons, many holding spears, bows, and swords and filling the air with an assortment of grunts, yowls, growls, and roars.

All around him, other members of the quest were involved in a desperate battle for their lives. Morganna fought two at the same time as a third came from behind to attack Tarquin. Swords, axes, and hammers swirled in defense as the creatures attacked the camp's occupants, but the tide soon turned. The enemy had expected to encounter a sleeping camp. Instead, they found themselves facing armed and deadly foes that had come out from their bedrolls with weapons drawn. This was not the easy prey they had been promised.

A bear-like creature that now came at Tarquin approaching cautiously. She was an older, more experienced fighter. One of her yellowed fangs had been broken in a long-ago forgotten battle and one of her eyes was milky white from a sword stroke. There was a wild gleam in her eye as she came at him with a curved scimitar in her right hand, a short sword in her left. She recognized him as one of the main targets they were required to kill to receive the copper.

What happened next startled him. The expression on her face changed to one that struck him as maternal. Then she cooed; her voice was soft and pleasant. She cocked her head, and Tarquin would have sworn that she was talking to him as she beckoned. She was speaking, but if he had been able to understand her words, his guard would have never slipped. Instead, the sound of her voice almost wooed him into trusting her. He took a step toward her as if to better hear her words when like a snake, the short sword leapt toward the young man's thigh, cutting him, and the scimitar headed for his throat, causing him to step backward. As he did, his heel caught a hidden root, making him lose his balance and fall.

Tarquin rolled backward until he could return to an upright position. Shaking his head to dislodge the near trance he had fallen under, he held his sword in front him so that he could block a quick thrust. She pressed her attack while following the rolling human. As they exchanged sword thrusts, the beastie smiled and spat a long stream of brown juice at him. Tarquin felt a wet stickiness hit his left shoulder that sizzled and burned right through his mythril mail armor like acid. He glanced away from his opponent when he felt the burning pain and dark stain of blood soaking through the shoulder. He wanted to rip his armor from his chest, but doing so would have exposed him to even greater danger.

Tarquin staggered to the tree, his right hand clamped to his bleeding shoulder and his left to his thigh as he tried to stem the flood of blood. The prince's frantic retreat had foiled a deadly blow from her scimitar, aimed at his exposed neck, when he tumbled over a tree root. Instead of severing the Borderer's head from his body, her swing went wide, so she had used her acid spit to deliver the deadly blow, opening his shoulder to the bone.

Time seemed suspended as he sat down hard with his back to the tree, pain clouding his mind as he surveyed the battle. Only seven of the creatures remained. He watched as Celedant struck three of his attackers down with magic. Morganna took out the final four who were attempting to kill the wizard from the rear as she moved through the shadows like a cat. The rigid training, she had put herself through for the past one hundred years had made her an efficient killing machine.

His eyes now turned to his opponent, who smiled cruelly as she admired the blood that seeped down Tarquin's shoulder. In the many battles he had fought, he had never faced an adversary with natural weapons such as she possessed. The monster's gloating brought him back to the present, and as she leaned out to deliver the final blow, he went on the offensive. His glowing sword lashed out, striking out and blocked the scimitar, but his injuries prevented him from rising to his feet and effectively fighting back. Blood loss began to take its toll, clouding his vision and slowing his response. Soon he would be incapable of stopping her from ending his life.

Then an angel appeared next to him. At least, that's what she seemed like to Tarquin. As the creature's blade bypassed his she entered the fray, knocking aside the short sword that would have finished him.

Remembering her promise to Dolgar, Ress had gone looking for Tarquin shortly after the battle started. Engaged in her own skirmishes with the enemy along the way, she had almost found him too late. She had but a moment to assess his critical condition before stepping in to fend off his attacker. Face-to-face with the bear-like creature, she snarled at her opponent, who did not take this slender female as a threat. The creature exposed long, sharp canines, capable of tearing her smooth flesh to shreds. As the beast pursed its lips to spit a stream of deadly juice, Tarquin barely had enough strength to warn Ress.

"Look out for her spit - it's acid!"

Ress jumped aside just in time, spun around, and came up with her sword to meet the blade of the deadly scimitar. The two females fought viciously. The memory of old scars gone from her newly healed face had her comparing firedrake's fire to the acid spit. Fury and strength rushed through her from an adrenalin rush, and she drove her opponent backward, forcing it to give ground foot by precious foot. Changing from backhanded blows to thrusts, she had the alien beast flailing with both scimitar and short sword as it tried to deflect the human's lightning-fast attacks. To its amazement, it found itself fighting for its life. The creature over-extended its left claw and Ress' blade struck, slicing through the thick-boned wrist.

The creature screamed and stared wide-eyed at its left arm. It spit at Ress again. She flung up her arm to protect her face and the acidy moisture hit the sleeve of her leather coat. Relieved that it had missed her newly healed face, she drew back her sword to end to the creature's life, but before she could strike, blood began to seep from its mouth. The creature dropped its swords and staggered several feet before falling, exposing a grinning Botreg standing behind it.

Then she felt the substance penetrating from her sleeve to her skin and Ress screamed aloud as she ripped off her coat and threw it to the ground. With the battle over, Hortus ran to her side and began chanting words of healing over her arm.

"No, you have to help Tarquin," she told him. "His wounds are severe."

Botreg overheard her and called to Aegir as he rushed to his fallen comrade. Aegir slid to a halt at Tarquin's side while Botreg took up a guarded stance, facing into the dark forest.

"Rest easy and let me heal you," Hortus told Ress as he examined her blistered and bleeding skin. I will join Aegir as soon as I get ye fixed up. He continued chanting and the skin soon returned to normal. "I'm glad ye took Dolgar's words to heart."

"I promised to look after Tarquin."

"And so ye have. Now I must help my fellow cleric."

As he joined Aegir, Hortus saw that the injury to Tarquin's neck was too severe to heal without additional measures. "I'll take over the wound on his thigh while ye assess the greater injury," he said.

Aegir got a close look as he tried to stem the flow of blood, causing Tarquin to grit his teeth. "Deeper than I thought. I can heal ye, but ye will need to rest and keep bandaged for several days."

The cleric began a short chant, calling upon his newly returned powers to heal the wound in the prince's shoulder. As his large hands cupped the human's injury, Tarquin felt warmth spread from the dwarf's fingers to his body. Several minutes passed before Hortus released his grip and rocked back on his heels, drained as he surveyed his handy work. "Ah, tis stopped bleeding. There'll be no more worries for ye over that wee scratch," he joked as he made a quick sling.

The company suffered no injuries that were beyond the ability of the dwarvan clerics to heal, and as Celedant examined the dead creatures, he noted their unknown appearance and the odd tribal markings.

"I have never seen or heard of beings like this on Muiria. This reeks of creatures from the Void. No doubt it was yet another assassination party sent by Taza. The attack was deliberate and well planned."

"We must be even more vigilant," Azimuth agreed.

They settled down for an uneasy rest as Eldahir and Vannor took over guard duty.

The next morning dawned chilly with a light fog blanketing the area. The quest party mounted their steeds and rode east, knowing that they would reach Bau's

Port within a day. After assuming his wolf form, Azimuth led the way back to the small rutted road they had taken the previous day. They traveled at an easy pace that morning, dodging jagged ruts and deep holes in the well-worn path. Two hours later the company left the moss-covered woodlands and entered the marshlands of the coast. Numerous small and large bridges spanned a myriad of waterways that crisscrossed the area.

The company had traveled but a few miles when Hority, who traveled at the rear of the column, called out, "Celedant - we're being followed."

The company turned as one and spotted a long line of riders exiting the forest, and as they entered the open country, spurred their horses to a gallop, heading directly for them. With two miles separating them, it was difficult, at first, to gauge the approaching riders' numbers, but as Eldahir stood in his stirrups, his superior elven eyesight allowed him to get an accurate count.

"There are forty well-armed men and orcs headed this way."

"Ride hard!" Celedant yelled to the others. "There's an outpost a few leagues from the city. If we can make it there, we'll seek refuge within its walls."

The company spurred their mounts and a chase through the marshlands began, but as they rushed toward safety, the riders continued to gain on them. Hority's donkey was having difficulty keeping pace with the faster, more agile horses, and he refused to whip the poor beast to make it run faster.

Meanwhile, Ralav and Ronli had galloped ahead to spy out the land and reached the river bank. At low tide, its muddy course was crawling with fiddler crabs. Celedant and the others had just crossed a small wooden bridge over a narrow channel when Ralav and Azimuth came charging back and joined Celedant.

"We're headed for a trap," Azimuth said in a panting voice as he changed to his elven form. "There's a wagon drawn across the beginning of a long stone bridge up ahead with several armed men guarding it."

Celedant looked ahead as though trying to see across the miles. "The outpost is still some distance away. Those that hold the bridge hope to delay us long enough for their friends to trap us and attack."

Tarquin who had been riding alongside the wizard asked, "What should we do?"

"My magic will take care of the barrier," Celedant replied. "You and the others must cut your way through the defenders to the other side."

"I believe I should change into dragon form," Azimuth whispered.

"Good idea. If we're lucky, the sight of dragon barreling down upon them might be enough to scare away those waiting on the bridge." Turning his attention to his companions, Celedant called, "Grab your horses' reins firmly, Azimuth is going to change into dragon form and see if he can scare off the attackers on the bridge."

As he finished speaking, his life-long friend once more became the golden wolf and sped out ahead of the lead horses. As he ran, he began the marvelous transformation from sleek lupine to massive golden dragon, taking flight as soon as the change was complete. Having a dragon this close startled the horses, causing them to scream and roll their eyes as they tried to buck off their riders, but they weren't the only startled ones. As Tarquin and the others struggled to control their steeds, shouts and the sound of frightened horses assaulted their ears from behind. Celedant turned his head for a peek back at their pursuers and smiled at the total chaos Azimuth's appearance had caused, noting that several riders had been thrown to the ground as their mounts bolted in the opposite directions.

Regaining control of their horses, Tarquin and the others rounded a small strand of scrubby trees where they found Ronli patiently watching and waiting. The company came to a halt beside her as she reported.

"They're staying behind their wagons and not doing a thing. I did ride closer, but they shot a few arrows to chase me away. Was that Azimuth I just saw?"

"Yes, indeed," Celedant chuckled. "With any luck, he'll have them on the run before we arrive at the bridge."

"Then we had better get going," Tarquin said.

When the bridge was a little over a hundred paces away, Celedant reined to a stop and dismounted. The others slowed and gathered around him, and as they studied the scene before them, several members of the group started grinning. Azimuth's appearance had indeed caused panic and confusion among the attackers. Several armed men took off in fright, fleeing from the scene as fast as their horses could carry them. Others began firing arrows at the dragon, most of which either missed or bounced off his impenetrable scales. One of the remaining attackers spotted the approaching party and fired off an arrow, which arched toward Botreg but landed short and twenty paces to the left.

"Fortunately for both Azimuth and us, their bowmanship doesn't seem to be very accurate. After I cast my spell, ride fast and clear them away. Eldahir and I will do our best to slow our pursuers before catching up with you."

The two wizards stood in front of the mounted company, ignoring the arrows as more and more of the armed men at the bridge noticed their approach and began shooting at them. Although he did not feel threatened by the projectiles so carelessly aimed at him, Azimuth did not take foolish chances. He made careful sweeping dives, spewing fire and scattering those brave enough to stand and fight while setting several ablaze.

Eldahir faced their disorganized pursuers and began chanting his own spell.

"Vulgus expolsun!"

The spell blasted across the open grassland like an invisible wave, knocking horses and riders to the ground and slowing their advance.

Celedant raised Forestae and concentrated. *"Fly clear,"* the wizard mentally warned his friend. *"I'm about to blow the bridge."* Azimuth took heed and chased some of the enemy soldiers who were fleeing away from the bridge as Celedant thrust his staff toward the wagon blocking their way and shouted, "Electriskt Kastasig!"

A loud clap of thunder rent the air as a brilliantly white bolt of lightning shot forth, blowing through the wagon and striking the end of the bridge. Their horses shied from the noise when a distinct backlash of wind buffeted them. Tarquin spurred his horse onward as the explosion shook the ground and blew a foot-wide hole through the stone of the bridge. The wagon disintegrated and wooden shards flew through the ranks of their enemies like jagged spears. Tarquin, Morganna, and the dwarves charged three abreast, their swords ready to strike down any remaining enemies.

They reached the beginning of the bridge as the remaining defenders were just recovering. Several men and orcs lay dead near the remains of the wagon. Another dozen bodies dead by either the blast or the dragon fire lay scattered upon the bridge, water, and surrounding land. The remaining fifteen orcs and men valiantly formed a solid line to stop the onrushing riders. Tarquin and Morganna were the first to jump the blackened, jagged hole that the spell had punched through the bridge, followed by their dwarvan companions, reaching their foes before they could complete their shield wall.

In desperation, the enemy thrust swords and spears over their upraised shields in an effort to take down the horsemen, but the foot soldiers soon fell to their blades. Tarquin's sword rose and fell as his steed drove through the disorganized enemy. Bodies dropped like sacks of grain, slaughtered or trampled by the horse's hooves.

Before he knew it, Tarquin was through the enemy with nothing but open bridge remaining. He spun his horse around, finding it difficult to control after the intense charge and the battle that followed. The others joined him, leaving nothing but dead and wounded in their wake. Vannor held his side and grimaced in pain as Celedant and Eldahir reined their horses in beside them.

"Can you ride, Vannor?" Tarquin asked the Brae, concerned.

"I can ride," Vannor replied, smiling grimly.

Maneuvering his horse through the milling company, Celedant called a warning. "The riders are approaching fast."

His voice died as everyone turned to see that the pursuers had regained their feet and were closing the distance between them. Spurring their horses into action, the company rode hard for the other side of the bridge, while Azimuth attacked them with sweeping dives, blasting several with his flaming breath.

Celedant and Eldahir rode ahead of the others, and as Tarquin closed the distance and drew abreast, the wizard yelled, "The outpost is at the end of the next bridge. If we can reach it in time, we can count on the guards' help."

Twenty minutes later, they reached the bridge, which spanned a wide stretch of open water. Azimuth broke off his attacks when a well-aimed spear missed his left eye, and he realized that the men and orcs chasing them were better trained than the ones on the first bridge had been. As his companions reached the second bridge and began the lengthy trip across, the dragon soared ahead so he would not spook their horses. Before long, he spotted the welcoming sign of spiraling smoke from Bau's Port.

"It's not much further to the city," Azimuth told Celedant, his warm baritone voice entering the wizard's mind. *"I'll fly ahead and change back to a wolf to approach the city. Then I'll return to my elf form so as not to frighten the citizens."*

"Good," Celedant responded. *"I'll see you shortly."*

As they spoke, their pursuers reached the bridge. Tarquin and the others had arrived at the midpoint across the wooden expanse, which connected to a small islet before arching over to the bank of one of the marshy rivers. Celedant held up his hand calling for a halt when he spotted the small fortification on the other side where the guards hurried to man the walls.

"Use your bows and slow them down. Otherwise, the guards may not realize what is happening. We don't want them to shoot us and worry about the consequences later."

When Tarquin and the others had left Nars, everyone had been equipped with either a bow or crossbow in addition to their other weapons. The party now retrieved and aimed their deadly arrows down the narrow bridge as the enemy charged across, riding three abreast. Thirty horsemen jammed the narrow bridge, offering an easy target for the waiting archers. On Tarquin's command, their arrows fired as one, speeding across the expanse at the charging riders, while Tarquin and the others notched their arrows for a second volley.

The missiles lanced down the bridge's path and slammed into the front two ranks of the enemy, plucking riders from horses and pitching them over the railing where they drowned in the deep chilly water. Others were knocked to the wooden floor and trampled by their comrades' horses. A few arrows hit the galloping horses, driving deep into unprotected chests and necks. Two front horses screamed and stumbled, causing the animals behind to careen into them and fall. The first volley started a grisly pile-up as horses, and their riders dropped to their knees - to be ridden over or crushed by those behind. As confusion reigned, a second flight of arrows struck home.

Only two horsemen made it through the tangle of warriors and beasts, and they collapsed as the missiles thundered into the packed mass atop the bridge. As they fell, a wall of dead and dying enemies piled across the roadway of the bridge and stalled the charge. Riders bringing up the rear slowed enough to keep from becoming entangled in the pile-up, but a third volley soon took them out of the battle. They trapped their pursuers, much as the enemy had hoped to trap their prey, and the enemy's courage broke as first one and then another turned and headed for the opposite bank of the river, leaving behind dead and broken comrades.

Tarquin had seen enough carnage and ordered his men to put away their weapons. They turned their horses toward Bau's Port, with Celedant leading the way to a small outpost located at the end of the bridge. The guards had watched the battle with interest and as the riders neared the fort, a soldier in a plumed helmet hailed them. He leaned through a wooden parapet and called,

"What's this business all about?"

Celedant reined his horse near the wall and replied, "Robbers, Captain, orcs and brigands' intent on separating our necks from our bodies and taking our gold."

"Most of Bau's Port is made up of brigands," the Captain laughed. "I hope you don't end up killing half the population there as well."

The wizard chuckled and motioned to the smoke that betrayed the city's presence. "We'll try to stay out of trouble. We sail in a few days."

At that, the wizard waved farewell and led his party toward the safety of the town. As they rode out of the fort's sight, the Captain turned from the wall and called to another soldier, a pockmarked man who ran up the stairs and saluted before standing and waiting. The captain took out a small parchment and scrawled a few words.

He handed it to the soldier and asked, "Do you know the location of Darnigan's Tavern?"

The pockmarked soldier smiled. "Aye, sir there's a fine serving wench...."

The captain shouted him down. "If I needed a woman, I would not ask your advice. Mind your horse and head there. When you arrive, hand this to the innkeeper. Tell him I sent it and return with his answer in one hour."

The guard listened intently to his orders, his slow mind calculating that it would take more than an hour to deliver the message and return. The messenger shuffled his feet before hastily grabbing the note and running for the stables. The captain turned and watched as his soldiers headed across the bridge to finish off the wounded and relieve them from their valuables before tossing the remains to the alligators that prowled the marsh.

The captain smiled. He was certain he had recognized one of the riders, and he knew a man who had posted a handsome reward for information leading to the rider's whereabouts. He then slapped his hands together and in a quiet voice said, "Botreg has returned. I'll be paid well for that information."

CHAPTER TWENTY-THREE

Taza was delighted with the results of the elementals' attack against the elven capital. He would have been happier if the pointy-eared near-immortals had suffered a staggering loss of life as well, but he had to admit that killing an immortal was almost impossible. The destruction of so much of their city would shock the elven nation to the core, and they would now understand what it meant to defy him. As the vampire lord stood at the edge of his font, a mere thought along with the aid of his Staff called to the fire elemental. It appeared in the dark viscous fluid that filled the stone receptacle. Taza stared into its swirling depths, smiling at the flaming mystical creature.

"You have fulfilled my request. The elves are in disarray."

"The battle, however, has cost me, killing many of my kind," the elemental replied gravely.

"That's unfortunate, but not my concern. Who would have thought the water sprites would come to the elves' defense?"

The elemental flared in rage. "Curse those haughty sprites! They take unmitigated pride in destroying my kind. What of our bargain?"

Taza smiled. "As I promised, I have created a new volcano home for you and your ilk, and I will transport you to your new habitat when you are ready."

The elemental's visage showed no expression. "Show me."

Taza drew intricate flaming designs in the air. The lines of the spell shone so brightly that it blinded him until he appeared on a snow-covered peak, deep within the Calderan Mountains, directly south of the Dragon's Teeth. Moments later the huge fire elemental appeared. It did not touch the ground. Instead, the flames seemed to hover mere inches above the rocky surface, melting the snow for hundreds of feet in all directions.

"Where is the promised volcano for my children?"

The undead warlock laughed. "You should know better than I that there hasn't been an active volcano in this area for eons."

The fire elemental raged, but its size shrank. "You lied. I have been drawn into a trap."

Taza nodded breezily and as the elemental raged, he magically lifted a huge mound of snow and ice from a surrounding peak and dropped it atop the beast, forcing it from the air to the ground. The freezing powder and chunks melted its shell and it flowed away, revealing a much-diminished being. Uttering the words of another spell, the warlock harnessed the clouds above, collecting all the moisture within the diaphanous effects of the sky. The fire elemental was just able to spit out a final summoning spell to its children before a wave of water poured down on it.

Taza strolled over to the blackened crisp of the creature and sneered. "You bargained with death when you should have given aid without expecting compensation."

He drove the butt of the Staff of Adois into the fire elemental, draining its remaining power. What was left of the monster's essence surged up to replenish the warlock, but as it did, an unusual buzzing sound came from the South, growing louder as a dark mass of tiny fire elementals rushed to their master's aid. Taza called forth several spells, killing many creatures, but as they fell, more arrived to take their place. When they were almost upon him, he realized that the elementals were the small fireflies that had attacked the elven lands. As he found himself in the midst of the swarm, he grasped his cloak about his body for protection. Yet he could still feel the sharp burning strikes of their attacks. The burning bites penetrated the cloak, singeing his skin as his cloak caught fire.

Taza swung the Staff of Adois about his head, and the small elementals backed away. Then a spell placed in his mind by the staff formed in his head. Chanting in a language unknown to him, the area turned pitch dark and a blast issued from the depths of the ancient artifact. As the smoking air dissipated, Taza peered about. The elementals had been destroyed, and the mountaintop on which he stood had disappeared, leaving him standing on a two-foot wide column in the center of an immense circular blast zone a thousand feet in diameter.

The column that held him began to sway and its foundation peeled away. Taza cast a spell and hovered over the gap as the column collapsed into the depths of the mountain range. Satisfied, he traveled home. He had a relatively difficult meeting to prepare for as he strode up the stairs to his chamber. Sitting on his throne, he commanded the Staff of Adois:

"Divine the location of the last piece of the Staff of Adaman and its location."

Quivering to life, the staff showed him the formerly great metropolis of Zeiglon, the capital city of a once-vast empire before the great upheaval of the earth had destroyed it. The variant city teemed with races from around the world, and its towers were double the size of anything now in existence. Amazingly, the crumbling towers, buildings, and walls still retained the bright hues they had been painted centuries earlier.

"Knowing its location is one thing," he sighed. "Retrieving it will be the difficult part."

The task Taza now faced was to secure the aid of the Shadow Lords, the ghostly remains of the city's former powerful rulers, who over the millennia remained the protectors of the ruins. After their defeat, a powerful curse had solidified their hold on the city and created a magical shield that kept prying eyes away, including the Staff of Adois.

In little under an hour, he would meet with the Shadow Lords' leader, Zoxian. He cared little for their politics but needed help. One must tread lightly when dealing with these wraiths. Over the years, many of those who had tried to communicate with them had lost their minds, but Taza was sure the Staff of Adois would protect him, and he had a few bargaining points he was certain the Shadow Lords would appreciate. While preparing for the meeting, he learned that the city was rife with armies of undead that constantly fought over small pieces of the town. What they needed was more land, which would keep the constant bickering to a minimum.

Thanks to his staff, Taza could assist in that regard. It would require the release of the Shadow Lords from the binding spell that held them prisoner during the day and would allow their minions to spread across the continent, searching for living beings to destroy and add to their army.

Later, as Taza sat upon his throne gathering power, a floating humanoid shape appeared. It had no substantive body as it materialized before him. Its darkness swayed and shifted before the warlock, but with the aid of the staff, Taza's eyes focused on a gaunt figure lurking in the shifting shadows.

A wispy hiss issued from the Shadow Lord in a voice that seemed to come from the Void. "Why have you disturbed us?"

"Are you the leader of the Shadow Lords?" Taza asked.

"I am Zoxian, their spokesman. We no longer have a leader."

Welcome, Zoxian," Taza greeted the foul creature. "I need your help in a matter that is critical."

"Why would we help you? What could you offer the powerful Shadow Lords that would be of any interest?"

Taza was incensed by its conceit. Nevertheless, he decided to overlook it for now. "How long has it been since your kind left Zeiglon?"

"You will address us as Lord," Zoxian growled. "Your question is moronic. We are the protectors of the city, where we are destined to remain for eternity. We venture forth at night and by the stipulations of the spell must return by daylight or descend into oblivion. That is our curse. Does the self-titled Lord Taza have no knowledge of this world and its histories?"

Taza's control disintegrated. Firmly grasping his staff, he stood and shouted the words of a spell.

"Investris genuas! On your knees before me, you pompous idiot."

The shadowy form surrounding the Wraith Lords' spokesperson vanished, and the corruption that had once been a man fell to the floor. Although thousands of miles separated Taza and the Shadow Lord's projection, the magic he had used to contact them was infinitesimal compared to the true power of the Staff of Adois. Yet, he felt an even greater power within the staff trying to gain control as the creature writhed in agony on the stone floor.

"This is a mere pittance of my magic, Zoxian. The glorious and powerful goddess Adois has placed me above all others to rule this world in her stead. She bestowed my title. Now that you have experienced my supremacy, might we now converse in a more civilized manner?"

Screaming in agony, the Shadow Lord wailed, "Yes!"

Taza smiled and released the spell that held the creature within its grasp. As it straightened, the insubstantial shadow essence formed around it once more.

"Do I understand correctly that you speak for all the Shadow Lords?"

"Yes, I speak for all."

"Good. I want the Shadow Lords to keep watch for a group of adventurers. They have wronged me and are heading for Zeiglon to seek your treasures."

The creature hesitated before responding. "That can be accomplished with no trouble, but I believe you require something else?"

Taza stood on his dais, twice as tall as the Shadow Lord.

"How perceptive you are. Yes indeed, I also need a sizable force to assist in overcoming the dwarvan city of Southgard."

The Shadow Lord was mentally shown a map of the area, which it studied for several moments. "How can we help when the curse holds us captive in Zeiglon?"

"This is the Staff of Adois," Taza exclaimed, holding the powerful rod so that the wraith could see it. "By combining my magic with its power, I can dispel the curse that keeps you locked within Zeiglon's borders."

Zoxian was stunned into silence. He decided to proceed cautiously.

"When will we be released from this curse, and for how long?"

Impressed for the first time, Taza smiled wickedly. "I will release you within the hour and provide you with flying steeds. The curse will not return...unless of course, you would be so foolish as to defy me. Should that happen, I can reinstate it and let me reassure you, the new curse will be much worse than the one you suffer now."

Zoxian did not comment. Having gotten a small taste of the vampire's power, he knew that he and his fellow Wraith Lords would have to do as they were told, at least for now. He cocked his head as though listening to someone speak – the other Shadow Lords. They were eager for Taza's words, but first they had two questions.

"Will we have to continue performing tasks for you? Freeing us will mean little if you bind us to you for all time."

"No," Taza assured it. "In order to be set free, I require just these two tasks."

Zoxian scanned the hidden figures seated around him. "The Council has given me the power to negotiate our freedom. They voice no objections to your offer. We give our oath of alliance for this battle. Once we are free, several of my brethren will remain in Zeiglon. When the adventurers enter the city, we will deal with them as you have said."

"Just so you understand. Should this oath be broken, the curse that the Shadow Lords have been under will seem like a walk in the woods compared to the retribution I will extract."

"We are aware of the penalty."

Taza smiled. With the right words and treasure, allies would flock to him like fish to bait, ignorant of the hook.

Zoxian bowed low. "It has been an honor to meet you, Lord Taza. The Shadow Lords are pleased with this accord. When you need us, we will be ready. May you fare well in your endeavors."

His good humor restored, Taza decided to be generous. "I knew we would reach an amicable accord. When the time comes, I will free you from the curse that has held you bound for two thousand years. May you have good hunting in the South."

The dark warlock broke the spelling holding the Shadow Lord, and sat down. It disappeared.

"Stupid, self-important dolts," Taza said to no one in particular. "I will use you now and anytime I have need of your services, and there is nothing you can do to stop me."

He still felt the hint of the power behind the Staff of Adois seeking a way to gain control. Although Adois had warned him that no one but she could control it, he wondered if the continuous power struggle was something accidentally instilled within the staff by the warlock who had created it, or if it was the goddess's clandestine way of gaining control over him. The answer was elusive. The one thing the vampire was certain of was that each time he used the staff, he could feel more of his own energy waning. It was a disturbing problem; one he would have to eliminate before it was too late.

CHAPTER TWENTY-FOUR

Lord Grimilzor set up camp on the first hill that jutted out further than its neighbors and was the strongest portion of the expanding allied defense. His main concern now was not Southgard but his massive army. Adventurers, soldiers, and the curious flocked to camp, along with regiments from the north, bands of eastern dwarves, and a staggering array of human soldiers from the Eastern City-states. Other than the regular dwarvan regiments - the Parthians and the elves - most volunteers had little or no experience in the preparation of war.

The elves were the easiest to position. Companies of these veterans from Ravenhall and the northern territories were responsible for setting up defensives near the dam that had fallen to the orcs. Dwarvan engineers worked on a road that wound behind their defenses with small wood or stone towers placed at regular intervals. Sloping downward, dry moats riddled with sharpened stakes that would kill or cripple any who tried to cross the wide spaces between hills.

Meanwhile, the orcs were set up for a siege, hoping that as the dwarves' food, water, and supplies ran out, it would force them to leave their protective walls and fight. Once that happened, the enemy felt confident that their superior numbers would soon overwhelm the defenders and grind them into the dust. The fords and bridges across the Wye were well guarded as enemy soldiers built earthen works along the river's eastern side.

As the dwarves and their allies scrambled to build their defenses, Lord Grimilzor and his staff mapped their next move. They met in the dwarves' strongest fort, located where Hywel's Way emerged from the hills. Here the General set up his command post on a rocky crag that jutted out several hundred paces into the valley, offering a splendid view both east and west. The commanders consisted of five dwarves, two elves each from the Wood Elves, two Parthians, including Tarquin's eldest brother, Prince Kaleb, heir to the Parthian throne, and representatives from the Dwarvan Confederation and Eastern City-states.

The council members sat around the table saying little, while Grimilzor spoke in hushed tones with Nestarion, the leader of the wood elves' forces. Nodding, the general, his plate mail soiled from relentless work during the first few weeks, stood to address those assembled.

"I would like to take this opportunity to thank ye for comin'. Me father King Braveslayer is grateful and proud that our respective races are willin' to set aside personal interests to come together and fight at this time of great peril." He scanned the table and those standing on the sidelines. "I'm sorry we didna have a large enough table to accommodate ye all, but we're kinda limited on space."

There were some laughs at that statement and General Grimilzor waved them to silence. "As ye likely know, we are still vastly outnumbered. The landholders that did not reach the safety of Southgard have painted a grim picture, confirmin' our suspicions. Orcish raiders roam this side of the river, screenin' the approaches to the bridges."

There were nods around the room as he continued.

"Our scouts have confirmed that the bridges are fortified on this side of the river, and even if we move under the cover of darkness, the difficulties to such a move would never allow us enough time to form a coherent attack. The orcish army can pour across the bridges and overwhelm us in no time, forcing us back to our defensive positions with an unacceptable cost of lives. Needless to say, that plan canna be considered at present."

The expressions on the quiet faces gathered around told him they were as much at a loss about how to attack the opposing army as he was.

A man from the City-states asked, "Could we not lure them to attack our positions?"

The dwarvan commander nodded. "I have considered and rejected that idea. The commander of that horde can send battalion after battalion to storm our defenses, regardless of how many orcish lives it costs. Our army, however, is so thinly spread out, they would defeat us without difficulty, thereby weakening our forces. But we should not despair," the general said as he laid a heavy hand on the shoulder of the elf seated next to him.

"Lord Nestarion has a bold proposition." He looked down at the elf. "Please outline the plan for the others."

The elf nodded, his face displaying a serious expression.

"It has been years since many of our nations joined together in such a grievous endeavor. When I first arrived, General Grimilzor handed me a detailed map of the valley and asked how I might manage the situation." He spread a rolled map of the valley across the table, securing the corners with fist-sized stones. "The Orcan commander is no fool." Using a silver rod covered in runes, the elf pointed to specific areas of the map as he spoke. "He realizes that rescue will come from the north and has positioned his forces accordingly, using the river as a natural barrier. He has also fortified all viable crossing points while doubling his defenses around Southgard. Advanced scouts have confirmed that siege engines surround the city as well as trenches to cover any attack from the valley."

Nestarion looked to Grimilzor who motioned for the elf to continue. "General Grimilzor and I sought a way to use the enemy's numbers to our advantage. I believe that we have a suitable plan that will give us the edge we desperately need." He pointed to specific areas on the map. "See how the valley slopes from north to south? The most productive farms are located across the river where a water table lies near the surface."

Nestarion looked around the room, noticing the blank stares on several faces. The elf chuckled before continuing. "Our forces will ambush the orc patrols on this side of the river for the next several nights in an attempt to lure them into thinking that our goal is the eastern road. Then several battalions of foot soldiers will fortify that belief by attempting to seize the eastern road. Our foes will send a larger force to dispel this move. Foot soldiers will guard fords and bridges, while a thousand Parthians on horseback make it seem as though we are marshalling our forces in the eastern valley, focusing the enemy's' attention on that area."

"As our forces keep them occupied in the East," General Grimilzor added, "a large force will attack the dam. This will be a risky move."

Lord Nestarion tapped the top of the dam on the map and continued. "Our troops must cross four hundred paces to the top of the dam. A small structure that houses the dam's machinery is located near the midpoint, and we must take control of it before we can cross to the opposite side. The top of the dam is in the open, except for a low wall that keeps workers from falling, leaving our troops vulnerable to their bowmen. If that happens, the casualties will be high, but if stealth is used, our losses might be kept to a minimum."

"Then what happens?" one of the assembled asked.

Nestarion pointed to the far side of the dam. "We'll need to add fortifications on the southern portion of the bridge so that when the counterattack comes, we'll be ready."

"If you will allow me," Grimilzor said to the elf, "I will take up the narrative."

Nestarion nodded his consent.

"Our next objective, lads, will be to close off the flow of water, causing the southern side of the valley to become waterlogged and let lake Mirowmir overflow its banks. This will force the orcs further east. As the water rises, the orcs will have to use boats to attack the top of the dam. We aren't sure how high the water will rise, but it will give us an advantage. We will then be able to bring our joined forces against a smaller front at the foot of Southgard."

He cleared his throat and drank from a mug. "The narrower front will be to our advantage, even though the orcs will attack in mass, breaking against our well-positioned army. Make no mistake. It will be a fierce and costly battle, but we expect aid from the defenders of Southgard, who can attack the enemy in the flank and break them. I'm sure me brother Dunrow will be chompin' at the bit to get revenge."

"I cannot predict the outcome," Grimilzor added, "but if we win the day, our reserves should be ready to follow the retreating orcs and set up defensible positions several miles into the hills."

Sober nods and low murmuring filled the room as Grimilzor signaled to Dargan. His old retainer stepped up and bent his ear to his seated prince.

"Go, me friend," Grimilzor whispered, "and luck be with ye."

Chapter Twenty-Five

As Celedant and the others exited the sparse cover of woods, Bau's Port came into view. Situated on the banks of the Snake River where it emptied into the ocean with three wide bridges connecting its northern and southern portions, the city was small compared to other coastal cities of the Confederation.

Celedant led them to a small gate near the landward side. The gate, like the surrounding walls, was equipped with well-armed guards patrolling between strong granite towers. The company passed through the gate without being questioned, and as they entered the city, Botreg kept his face hidden within his hood as they traveled narrow streets with tall buildings that arched out and over, creating a tunnel-like atmosphere. An open ditch ran along the sides of the street that served as the city's sewer, which its citizens nonchalantly stepped over, hardly noticing the intense sludge or the odor.

"This smell is intolerable," Eldahir said, wrinkling his fine elven nose.

"This is low tide," Celedant warned. "Wait till high tide; then you'll know stench."

"Really?" Hority asked, perking up. "Then I can't wait for high tide. Clor has sent me on a wonderful adventure...such sights and smells."

Hortus slowed his horse to ride beside Hority, who peered into the sewage.

"Remember, Hority, these might be wonderful sights and smells, but Clor has made it clear that although you can look and smell, you cannot not touch or collect."

Sighing, the disheartened cleric nodded. "Of course, venerable Abbot."

As they rode through the streets, artisans plied their trades on the first floor of the buildings. Yet for each honest-looking citizen, two dubious looking men or women stalked the streets. Bau's Port was a haven for adventurers; it offered the dangers and riches of the southern Mordolwyn Mountains while promising bountiful employment for pirate princes. The traders, going by the title they preferred, were always in need of a strong back or skilled sword. As Celedant and the others made their way through town, Tarquin counted a number of goblins and a handful of orcs bringing in gold and silver from the southern mountains. He also saw a giant ogre towering above the pedestrian traffic with a huge mound of pelts balanced on his broad shoulders. Tarquin later learned that in Bau's Port, everyone was welcome as long as his or her presence benefited the city.

Celedant took no notice of the sights. Using his horse to plow through the crowded roadways, he maneuvered his steed down a wide street, halting in front of a monstrous mansion constructed of grey stone that covered an entire city block.

Stone turrets rose from the corners of the house and in those lofty perches, mail-clad guards were stationed. Celedant dismounted and approached the entryway that was wide enough for two carts. The gateway had an iron portcullis that could be closed at a moment's notice. As they entered the yard beyond the gate, a guard approached, wearing dented chainmail and carrying a spear.

Celedant spoke with him and a moment later, the man smiled and called for the stablemen. Rough looking men, wearing dirty homespun clothing, came and took charge of their horses. Tarquin was certain that these so-called stable hands would become formidable foes when armed. His gear thrown over his shoulder, Celedant mounted a broad stone stair that led to the stout door of the mansion. When he reached the door, he turned to address the company.

"We'll be staying here at the home of Sir Nicolas Thornsby, an old acquaintance. While I arrange passage on one of his ships, you can relax in the lap of luxury for the next few days, or at least until the ship sails."

They entered the pirate's mansion through tall double doors made from expensive mahogany. The surface of the doors were polished to such a high sheen that it reflected the company's images as they passed into the residence. The foyer beyond was large enough to house a whole family; its marble floor was laid out like a checkerboard with white and pink-hued stones. Along the walls were pegs to hang cloaks, and thirty feet into the foyer was a wide staircase covered in heavy red carpeting that led to the second floor.

Coming down the stairs was a man who radiated authority. He was tall, well over six feet, tanned from years at sea, with black hair that was beginning to gray at the temples. His bearing indicated that he could be either a sincere friend or an intense enemy.

"Nicolas, it's been awhile," Celedant said as the suave man moved with long, easy strides toward him to clasp hands.

"Celedant, it's good to see you again. What brings you and your friends to my humble abode?"

The wizard gave him a sly smile. "It's best that you don't know the reason. Suffice it to say, we need a fast ship sailing south."

"Come, I'll show you to your rooms where we can talk over business in private."

The trader took them up the main stairs and down a short hall to another staircase, which led to the third floor and another long hallway. After showing them to their rooms, Nicolas asked Celedant to join him in his private office. Nodding, the wizard motioned Tarquin and Hortus to follow.

Nicolas and Celedant spoke of mutual friends as they strolled back to the foyer and turned left into the main and more opulent portions of the house. The many hallways and rooms seemed to have been built at different times and put together piecemeal, forming a maze. Noticing Tarquin and Hortus' bewildered looks, Nicolas laughed.

"There's a reason to my home's peculiarities. Over the years, my family consolidated this entire city block. As we took over the neighboring buildings, we built partitions to connect them. My family figured that if we were ever attacked, the maze-like qualities of the house would confuse our attackers, while allowing our own retainers to run circles around them."

Tarquin agreed to a point. "I was trained in the dark, twisting halls of Nars, but I believe this maze of yours is more complex. I doubt I could find my way back to the main hall."

Nicolas approached a solid mahogany door and held it open for the others. The trader's private chamber was a library that made even the Abbot Hortus jealous. At the center of the room sat a huge walnut desk with antique walnut chairs arrayed in front and along the walls. Floor-to-ceiling bookshelves held a king's ransom in manuscripts and tomes. Nicolas preceded them, taking his seat behind the desk and motioning to the others to make themselves comfortable. A crystal wine decanter filled with a deep red wine sat on the corner of the desk, and their host promptly filled four matching goblets and passed them around to his guests.

"So my friend, what problems follow on your coat tails this time?" Nicolas asked with interest.

Celedant sipped his wine and leaned back in his chair. "Before I say, you might want to take a drink of your wine."

The trader obliged him, set down his goblet, and steepled his fingers, patiently waiting for the wizard to continue.

Celedant paused before continuing. "We need a ship to land us near the escarpment near Zeiglon. It's as simple as that."

Nicolas' smile vanished. "You never cease to astound me. If you had said you wanted to sail to the lost continents of the east, I would have laughed and grudgingly lent you a ship. Yet...."

The wizard interrupted. "Then you won't aid our mission?"

The trader waved his hand in dismissal. "That's not what I meant. Please, allow me to continue."

Celedant nodded apologetically.

"Ships have not sailed to the rugged islands that lay off that escarpment in years," Nicolas began. "The last one to do so returned to port with tales so farfetched, we feared the crew had drunk sea water and become crazed."

Everyone sat quietly, absorbing this information. The trader looked first at Tarquin and then Hortus, and seemed to like what he saw. "What more could I request than Celedant's word?" he asked with a reassuring smile. "I will lend you a ship and my finest crew." Nicolas refilled their goblets before continuing. "I will need a few days to prepare the ship, after which you can sail. Let us toast your coming adventure."

The next few days passed slowly for the companions. They stayed hidden in the vastness of Nicolas' mansion, knowing they would make easy targets in the wild streets of Bau's Port. Their host left the following day, stating that he had business to attend up the coast. He assured them that the ship would be ready in three days and that Captain Weir would alert them when it was time to leave.

CHAPTER TWENTY-SIX

Spotlessly dressed in clean red robes, Melgor stood in a side alley that smelled worse than a dead body. He had been waiting for an hour, but that was how the Assassin Guild did business. Disgusted, he muttered to himself.

"Why do they always insist on meeting in a nasty alley? Why couldn't this business be carried out at a pub or somewhere cleaner and more civilized?"

Inwardly, he knew the answer. No one ever carried out meetings involving cloak and dagger work in the public eye. To do so would seriously jeopardize an assassin's excuse of plausible deniability. As long as no one saw the actual murder, the criminal did not want his connection to be unearthed simply because someone saw him talking to the person who had ordered the assassination.

Melgor could care less who commanded the Guild, or how they carried out the contract. As long as his enemies ended up dead, he would be satisfied. Nevertheless, he had to admit that Bau's Port was perfect. People disappeared there all the time. Many were conscripted into ships' crews and often died during raids, while others were murdered and disappeared forever. The city guards did their fair share, as well. They took bribes, turned their heads, and for a small fee, arrested people who subsequently disappeared. Could there be a better location for exploits like these?

A dark shape caught his eye as it dropped and landed with a splash and loud thud. His back to the warlock, the small figure stood and shook his head.

Ah, I'm afraid that I was too greedy, and now me lord will punish me, the figure thought as he turned and blinked at Melgor in surprise.

"I have been adventuring for birds' nests and eggs," Hority explained. "Might ye like one? I am sorry the rotten ones broke when I fell."

The dwarf held a small egg with the yolk of another clinging to it.

Melgor stared down at the dwarf as a brief memory came and went.

"No, my friend, I have already eaten," the warlock replied before wrinkling his nose as he watched the simple little dwarf wander aimlessly down the alley, splashing in every puddle he could find.

His attention returned to his surroundings, and Melgor felt the assassins' presence when the men were half a block away. He was alert to their approach for no other reason than his own safety. The warlock carried a small fortune for the pending endeavor, and he would not put it past unsavory men to try to kill him for the money.

A silent spell spoken by the warlock incapacitated all but the lead assassin. Although his shadow cast the image of a much larger man, when the leader, a cowl-covered individual of medium height and build stepped into the ally, his foot faltered. None of his compatriots was where they were supposed to be. Melgor called out:

"Your friends are fine. Just a precaution if you will."

The assassin had greasy blond hair and a well-kept suit of leather armor hidden by a heavy cloak. When the assassin was within ten feet, Melgor tossed a heavy leather bag to the man.

"I have met your master's requirements, and I expect him to do the same."

The warlock abruptly turned, walking fast to escape the miasma and stench of the confined alley. When he reached the fountain located in the center of the city, his mind raced, and Melgor stopped in his tracks. The thought that had been gently niggling at his mind took root. Apparently, a Clorian monk had joined the company he was chasing. Then the warlock hit the side of his head with his hand. The small fellow falling off the roof...that had to be him! Had he not been among the crowded central portion of the city, Melgor would have been out of his mind with anger. It seemed as if the gods of good were interfering, which puzzled him as generally they were content to sit back and watch.

Don't I have enough to deal with without having a forgotten dwarvan god adding one of his monks to the mix?

He calmed, thinking Lord Taza need know nothing of this as he entered the posh hotel in which he was staying. Passing through the main room, a servant boy caught his attention and hurried over with a scroll made of the best vellum. He did not recognize the symbol on the wax seal. Melgor broke the seal and opened the scroll. Written in neat block lettering were the simple words, "We never fail."

The warlock turned to ask a question, but lad had disappeared. Melgor appreciated the efficiency of the Guild. Although he had left the alley a mere ten minutes ago, the missive was already here awaiting his arrival. Even if it was nothing more than a grand gesture and prearranged, Melgor did not care. The show impressed him.

Five minutes later when he reached his room, the magical wards he had placed around the door and window were still in place. After releasing them, he entered the room and lit several candles with a word. Then he placed the scroll on the mound of hot coals within the fireplace, watching the paper flair and burn brightly until nothing but ash remained. Melgor tossed another log on the fire and reached for the bell cord, giving it a pull as he mulled over what to order for dinner. Later when his meal arrived, he relaxed and enjoyed every bite of the steak and kidney pie, fresh baked bread, and hot blueberry pasties, which he washed down with a bottle of the finest vintage of elven red wine.

Unlike the worthless warlock Sellis, whom he had relied on in the past, the Assassins Guild was a vast and far-reaching society. Melgor felt reassured that this time there would be no more failures. If one assassin failed, another and another would try until the job was finished.

Chapter Twenty-Seven

Their stay in the grand house of the trader was neither tedious nor wasted. Besides giving them time to rest and recover from the bumps and bruises of their journey, the house offered a huge library and several training rooms. Everyone except Celedant and Hortus, who lost themselves in fascinating books and scrolls, took advantage of the training rooms. Botreg and Morganna particularly enjoyed testing their skills against each other, and even Eldahir, considered by many to be a master swordsman, was impressed. Tarquin had never seen two combatants move as fast as the dwarf and Illanni when they sparred.

After crossing swords with Morganna in a vigorous sparring match, Tarquin was glad he would never have to face her in real combat. She had started by probing his guard for weaknesses, while allowing Tarquin to mount an increasing attack. For a split second, he thought that he might have a chance, but then she pressed back. In a lighting series of thrusts and hacks, she placed him on the defensive. Inch by inch, he gave ground across the training room until his back was against the wall. Morganna's wooden sword landed multiple blows as he vainly tried to counter. She smilingly stepped aside, leaving the overwhelmed prince shaking his head as he offered his hand in congratulations.

Word came later that night that a ship called the Rapier would sail the next day with the tide. This news set the company into a frenzy of activity, gathering their gear and seeing what special equipment, if any, they would need for the coming mission. Nicolas' aide, Westcott, a thin man of average height with features easily forgotten, was on hand to take down the growing list of supplies. He assured Celedant that his men would have the items delivered to the Rapier before the sailing. As the trader's guards began their evening patrols, the companions settled in for the last night of peaceful sleep they would have in a comfortable bed for some time.

Because the house contained the trader's most valuable items, the mansion maintained a large number of guards consisting of Nicolas' most trusted retainers. Bau's Port was a city where pirates continually vied for power, and sometimes those power plays included open fighting. The night was cloudy, obscuring the moon's brightness as it soared high above the clouds.

In the pitch darkness of an alley, a grappling hook twirled in a tight circle before sailing over a balcony at the rear of the mansion. When it bit into the stone railing, the rope was drawn tight, and dark shapes scampered upward. As soon as all six figures reached the balcony, one of them pulled the rope up and hid it in the shadows. Soon the killing would commence.

One person knelt and using a lock pick forced the balcony door's lock. All six entered the mansion. The intruders found themselves in a dark corridor that a guard, making his nightly rounds, had just passed. A prowler slipped behind the unaware guard, dispatched the unfortunate man, and concealed the body on the balcony as the remaining trespassers spread out in search of prey.

Donli shared a bedroom with Aegir. The cleric had prayed long into the night for a safe voyage before lying down to sleep. Pleased with his prayer, Aegir fell asleep, but his loud snoring soon awoke his roommate. Donli was excited about heading out to sea. It was something he had dreamed of doing since a young lad. He tossed and turned but could not sleep and gave up trying.

Instead, he decided to take a walk through the hallways of the mansion. Donli slipped from his room, a shadow in the darkened corridors, and as he turned two corners and was nearing the stair that led down to the kitchen, his bare foot slid across a wet spot on the floor. Looking down, the dwarf spotted what was unmistakably a pool of blood - and froze. He had left the bedroom unarmed. With evidence that their enemies had found them, Donli turned to rush back to his companions.

As he neared their rooms, a dark figure materialized in the doorway of a side room not three paces in front of him. Donli never hesitated. Letting his training take over, the dwarf silently moved on bare feet, coming up behind a figure that was tall like a human and dressed in pitch-black clothes with a hood, a bloody dagger held tightly at the assassin's side. Donli drove his fist into the man's kidney and kicked the back of his knees. The figure did not utter a sound as he collapsed to his knees. The dwarf stepped between the man's legs and grasping his head, gave a quick twist, breaking the intruder's neck.

As the body slid to the floor, Donli felt a strange pain. Glancing down he saw that even as he had dispatched the invader, the man had struck with his dagger, burying it in Donley's stomach, and causing unbelievable waves of pain as the dwarf stumbled down the hallway. He had almost arrived at his room when he heard a soft step behind him. Pausing and holding onto the wall for support, the stricken dwarf looked back and saw five more shadowy figures. He was about to break into a run when a dagger slammed into his shoulder, and then another struck him in the thigh. Gathering his last reserves of strength and using all the willpower he possessed, Donli tried to flee his attackers.

But his body was going numb, and the dwarf found that he could no longer control his muscles. As the dwarf fell to the floor, he knew that the intruders' blades were poisoned. He watched helplessly as a dark figure bent over him with a blade in his hand that picked up the flickering light of the hallway candles. Donli knew that his life was about to end, but then a hurtling dwarf hit the man standing over him. Hority bounced off the killer and slid across the marble floor until his head met a stone pedestal.

With mere seconds of life remaining, Donli summoned what force he still possessed and called out a warning to his mates. In the darkened corridor, his shout, a garbled and guttural yell, rang out. In the comfortable rooms, men and women with instincts forged in bloody confrontations awoke at the shouted alarm, grabbed their weapons, and poured into the hallway.

Vannor stumbled from his bed with sword in hand and ran toward the door of his room just as it was shoved open. Two dark figures burst in from the doorway. The Brae attacked at once, howling a fierce northern war cry as his sword swept toward his attackers. The assassins had entered the mansion, intending to find their prey as they slept in their beds. They were not prepared for the armed warriors that now spilled into the corridor.

Vannor struck one attacker down, his sword cleaving the black shrouded head from its shoulders. As the assassin fell, the second attacker closed with him, holding a dagger in each hand, but as the intruder jumped at the Brae, Vannor's sword struck the leaping man, slicing through his stomach. As the attacker died, both daggers clattered to the floor next to his body.

In the hallway, the remaining assassins moved up the passage, but they were surrounded as Tarquin, Botreg, and the others rushed from their rooms. Tarquin stepped into the hall almost bowling over one of the intruders. He never got the chance to attack. Morganna ran at him, pinning the intruder to the floor with her sword. Eldahir sprinted down the hall, his elven sword bright in the semi-darkness as he engaged a dark figure and thrust his blade deep into his opponent's chest. As the dark figure slumped to the floor, Botreg disarmed and cornered the remaining attacker.

Celedant waited in the doorway of his room to see if they would need assistance. He soon joined them, the crystal on his staff emitting a bright magical light. Seeing Donli lying in a spreading pool of blood, the clerics ran to aid their injured companion, but it was too late. His hood ripped off by Botreg, the last living murderer stood defiantly staring at those he had been hired to kill. He had a youthful appearance, and his fair hair was plastered to his head with sweat.

The dark dwarf spat in disgust. "Assassins."

That brought a smile from his prisoner and in a mocking voice he said, "Welcome home, Botreg. This was to be a present from Orthas."

Before the dwarf could respond, Baldo shouted.

"Donli is dead."

"Ye will die slowly for this, ye mangy dog," Botreg growled.

The mocking assassin shook his head. "I don't think so." Then with a wink, he opened his mouth displaying a small capsule, and before anyone could intervene, he bit into it. Seconds later, the assassin convulsed, slamming his head backward into the wall and sliding down to sit upright on the floor, his unseeing eyes staring into nothingness.

Unaware that the fight was over, Hority regained consciousness and sat up, blood streaming from a gash in his scalp.

"By all that's holy, is the killing over?"

He slumped over and Aegir hurried over to treat the head wound.

His eyes tightly closed, Botreg looked heavenward. His friend and former Captain was dead, all because he had accompanied them into Bau's Port. In desperate anger, he thrust his sword into the dead form of the assassin and made a vow.

"Ye will pay for this, Orthas!"

Celedant joined the grieving dwarf and placed a gentle hand on his shoulder.

"Leave it for now. Revenge will not soothe the loss of our comrade. Our mission must take precedence. Tomorrow we sail, and you will make things worse if you challenge him."

The remorseful dwarf stared down the hallway to where Donli lay, and grimaced.

"Don't worry. I'll be at the ship on time."

The dark dwarf stormed to his room, slamming the door behind him.

Celedant swore. "Damned impetuous dwarf! I can see he will not let this go. Tarquin, try to stop him from doing something stupid."

The wizard went down the hall to alert the remaining guards of the intrusion and that a mess needed cleaning. Baldo and Aegir carried the unconscious Hority to his bed before helping the others take Donli to a room Hortus had prepared to receive the body. They would inter his remains in the sandy soil of the coast and send word back to Nars, detailing his deeds before meeting his death. Tarquin left the others to their duties to find Botreg and speak to him. They shared a room, and the door was unlocked, although the door handle was now loose from the dwarf's frustrated slam. Botreg stood beside his bed as his friend entered. His body racked with sobs, the dwarf blew his nose into a handkerchief. Taking several deep breaths, he grew calmer.

"Of all the men and women I or my actions have killed, this night's deeds have struck me the hardest. In me past life, I had no friends. It was easier that way. Now I revel in friendship, yet I have led me friend to his death."

Tarquin sat on his bed. "We knew that we would face death many times in this quest. It was a chance we took. Donli was unlucky...nothing more. He was in the wrong place at the wrong time. His death is no more your fault than if a lightning bolt had shot from the sky and struck him."

Botreg turned. His dark, cold eyes stared at Tarquin.

"Yes, I can accept that. And I know who to pay a visit to avenge me mate's death."

The dwarf turned back to his bed where he had laid out his weapons, and he began to arm himself. Tarquin opened his mouth to say more, but he realized that there would be no reasoning with Botreg. He was determined to kill Orthas. In doing so, he would even a score with the assassins. Before joining the Borderers, the dwarf had carried a fearsome burden. Now he was going to repay that fear and frustration at the point of his sword.

Tarquin, his human friend...his best friend if truth be told, stood and began gathering his gear.

"You'll not be going alone. Donli was my mate as well."

Botreg growled and ran the sleeve of his tunic across his face.

"Thanks, me friend." His gruff voice hid the emotion he felt.

Leaving their packed gear on their beds, the two Borderers dressed for combat, armed with their weapons. A turn of the clock later, they slipped noiselessly from their room and padded down the silent hallway that had already been cleaned by the servants. When they came to a small stair that led to an alley behind the mansion, a dark form waited for them, leaning casually against the wall. As they neared, Eldahir stepped forth.

"Celedant wants us to use reason," Eldahir said with a thoughtful expression. "But I knew that you would not be satisfied to let this matter drop and thought you might want some help."

Tarquin smiled gratefully as Botreg replied, "We'll need all the help we can get to go after Orthas, the Assassin Guild's leader."

Eldahir nodded. "I thought as much. By the way, Morganna is watching the alley. Naturally, Ralav and Ronli wanted to come, but I persuaded them to stand guard over the rest of the company."

Tarquin was thankful for the help and equally glad the others would be staying behind.

"If we're going to make it back to board the ship in the morning, we had better get moving. It's time to take some revenge."

The stairs were dark and narrow, ending at a small hallway that ran from the kitchen to a service entrance. Three figures made quick time, avoiding the guards as they unlatched the door and slipped into the night air. The alley was pitch dark and smelled of rotting garbage. The mansion's servants apparently dumped any old food into wooden bins, which later would be collected and removed. The smell reminded them of their friend Hority as they moved down the alley. Their eyes picked out Morganna as she approached and motioned the direction they needed to go.

"The streets beyond are clear of watchers, and traffic is light."

Tarquin smiled and gave her arm a squeeze of thanks. Morganna grinned, a smile that penetrated even the darkness of the alley. Moving on, Botreg took them through the sleeping city of Bau's Port, using back roads and alleyways. Unfamiliar with the city, Tarquin, Morganna, and Eldahir became disoriented in the many twists and turns of the dark streets in no time, but Botreg led them through the maze as though he had a map permanently ingrained in his brain. After several minutes, the dwarf signaled for a halt, and the four figures gathered in the gloom of a sheltered doorway.

"At the end of this street," Botreg said, pointing the way, "we'll turn right into an alley that dead-ends at an old warehouse and the back entrance of Orthas' stronghold. The way is closely watched." Pointing upward, he continued. "We'll head to the rooftops and make our way to the warehouse that way."

He looked at the Illanni while pointing at Tarquin. "Morganna, watch this one." He is human after all, and might find the high footing treacherous. According to the prophecy, he is critical to the success of our quest."

Tarquin was about to protest when Morganna spoke up.

"Don't worry. I'll keep an eye on our young prince." She smiled and playfully slapped the dumbfounded human on the back.

"All right then. Up we go, lads and lass."

The doorway in which they stood was boarded up, but a few hardy tugs opened the way into the interior. The building had once been an apartment flat and over the years, it had fallen into disrepair and was abandoned and boarded up. From the apartment, the four companions made their way up a narrow staircase of timeworn steps, past open doors that led to empty rooms choked with dust. After climbing two more flights of stairs, Botreg led them out onto the roof of the building, emerging from a small trap door. They clambered onto a high pitched, slate-covered roof with several brick chimneys that dotted its surface. Some of the tiles were missing, and rotted beams were visible below. Botreg again took the lead with Eldahir next, followed by Tarquin, with Morganna bringing up the rear.

The dwarf climbed to the apex of the roof and walked across. Eldahir and Morganna appeared to have no trouble, but Tarquin's booted foot slipped on the old slate as he climbed. Twice Morganna was there to steady him as the human began to fall. Eventually, Tarquin was aloft and following Botreg. The buildings of this section of town shared a wall so that the roofs were evenly connected. Occasionally, a few were slightly higher or lower. Tarquin found his balance and discovered that he could move rather fast in the wake of Eldahir and Botreg. As the four companions neared the warehouse that served as the assassin's lair, they came to an alley with a space of seven feet separating the buildings.

Tarquin had jumped wider crevasses in the underworld, but the possibility of falling through the roof of a three-story building bothered him. He looked across the gap at the waiting Eldahir. Steeling his determination, Tarquin backed up, took a running start, and vaulted to the next roof. Night air whooshed past as he sailed across the opening. When his feet touched the other roof, the elf reached out to steady him. Morganna made the jump and joined the others as they moved across the roof with the warehouse in sight.

As they neared their goal, Botreg motioned them to a crouching position, and they crab-walked to the peak of the roof, which shielded them from watchful eyes. The dwarf stopped, and the others gathered around him.

"There should be a guard post ahead," Botreg said softly, pointing toward the area separating the building they now stood on from their final destination. "Two guards are positioned in the attic with twine strung along the roof that, if tripped, will start several alarm bells to clangin'. We should be able to avoid the traps, but if we sound the alarm, follow me lead. We will silence the guards and see what happens next. Once we reach the warehouse roof, there will be more guards."

"Ye should be able to take them out with yer bow," Botreg said to Eldahir. "Once we reach the warehouse, just follow me lead."

As they cautiously made their way across the roof, Tarquin spotted a dormer window ahead that proved to be the guard post the dwarf had mentioned. Botreg slowed to a snail's pace, pausing every few feet to scan ahead. Twice they came upon twine that ran down the slate roof. The dwarf pointed them out to his companions and they gingerly stepped over them to avoid alerting the guards. Light streamed from the dormer window as they crept past, and Tarquin risked a peek over the windowsill where he saw a short, thin man reading by the flickering flames of several fat white candles. Once past the window, Botreg motioned them to a halt and pointed to a patch of slate ahead. On closer inspection, they realized that the section was new, since the tile did not match the others.

"Trap," Botreg whispered.

He led them up and around the suspect portion to the roof's apex. Once clear, the four companions climbed to the top of the roof and peered at the warehouse, studying its shape and the position of the guards without being seen. The building was long with a gently sloping roof. Two small, evenly spaced rooftop enclosures housed the stairs leading to the lower levels. Two guards patrolled the edge of the roof, continually scanning the streets as well as the tops of the surrounding buildings.

Botreg pointed as the guards walked along the front and rear of the building.

"Ye should take them out as soon as they are in position. Try to keep their bodies from falling into the street."

Eldahir considered the task. "I can take the one along the rear. We are at a right angle from his position, but the other shot will be difficult."

"If the roof doesn't have any traps, I can use my magic and reach the other guard undetected," Morganna said.

Botreg pondered a moment.

"I wonder if they changed their security. The roof was never rigged with traps before." He sighed. "Just rejoin us after ye get the guard. The stairs leading into the building are decoys. I'll take us in another way."

They waited as the guards made a leisurely circuit around the warehouse. Eldahir had his bow ready, testing the string for flaws, while Morganna readied herself. She waited for the guard to pass their hiding place before casting her spell. It was a simple incantation, learned by all Illanni children almost as soon as they could walk, but it was useful. She moved away from her companions and spoke a single word.

"Recedo."

She disappeared without a trace, even though she was but a foot from the others. As soon as the spell took effect, Morganna was on the move. Although no one could see her, the Illanni could see perfectly well within the obscuring spell. She moved to the edge of the warehouse and when she reached the gentle sloping roof, she hurried toward her intended victim.

Soft leather boots made no sound as she approached the balding human, whose attention was fixed on the street below. He never suspected or felt her approach, but her ears picked up the audible twang of Eldahir's bow and the distant impact of an arrow. The guard ahead of her remained unaware of what was happening. The Illanni drew her dagger and slipping up behind the unsuspecting man, cut his throat. With his vocal cords destroyed, the guard could not cry out. Morganna grabbed his collapsing body and eased it down to the roof. Within fifteen seconds, the man was dead.

Morganna turned and whispered the counter to her spell. "Apparreo," and the illusion of darkness fell away.

The others headed for the center of the roof where she joined them a moment later. There, Botreg stopped and intently studied a section before peering up at the elves.

"Can ye sense anything about this door?"

Eldahir closed his eyes and focused his inner eye on the spot.

"I sense no traps."

Satisfied, Botreg reached down and opened the trap door with a jerk, revealing stairs that curled down into the darkness. The dwarf led the way into the unlighted space below. Twelve steps later, they found themselves in front of a stout wooden door. He paused and listened before turning to his companions and whispering,

"There may be people in the passages beyond. Do not attack unless they are on to us. They will believe we are supposed to be here if we act like it."

Once his instructions sank in, the dwarf sheathed his sword and opened the door. The warehouse had changed over the years; the wide-open space once used for storage was now sectioned off with a stronghold built in its place. They entered a corridor brightly lit with torches, and turned right. As the four invaders made their way down the hall, a door to their left opened and a dark man exited, heading in the opposite direction. He glanced at them. Tarquin's heart pounded. He squeezed his hands so tight that his knuckles were white against his sword hilt. Botreg led them to a stair that took them down to a large landing with three doors, and as a man came up the stairs, he nodded a welcome.

Once the man was out of sight, the dwarf took the center door, and as they continued, he whispered over his shoulder. "If we're lucky we'll find Orthas in the meeting hall."

The hallway ended at a set of heavy double doors made of brightly polished copper set into a pine frame. The door reflected the companion's images as Botreg pushed them open. Tarquin stopped in his tracks at the sight before him. The hall overflowed with people, with well over forty men and women standing about murmuring to each other. As the dwarf led the three into the meeting hall, a loud voice called the room to order.

CHAPTER TWENTY-EIGHT

Lord Taza was furious. Thus far, an old wizard and a boy who had just entered manhood had spoiled every one of his underlings' traps. This was unacceptable, and he placed the blame at Melgor's feet. So what should he do with the red warlock? All of his underlings had misjudged Celedant, and the feeble attempts made against his enemy smacked of ineptitude. Taza stared out at the dark night. As he studied the distant stars and their constellations, he admitted to himself that Melgor was a formidable warlock in his own right. *I could never entrap him as I did Sellis. He is also my most valuable asset in this endeavor, my eyes and ears in the world of light.* Unlike Sellis, he could be trusted to tell the truth and face the consequences of his failures.

He turned his back to the window. "What to do? What to do?" he muttered to no one in particular.

The news that Melgor had recently ferreted out was an important accomplishment. Yet he did not want the warlock to grow conceited. The warlock had learned that the orb would be travelling south on a ship called the Rapier. This news confirmed Taza's thoughts that the staff rested somewhere within the wasteland of Zeiglon and its ruins.

If the Rapier survived to disembark its travelers on shore, his enemies would face the relentless harshness of the desert. Scorching heat and dry winds would drain their bodies of energy and precious fluids as they searched for a way to reach the top of the escarpment, weakening them when they faced the wrath of the

Shadow Lords and their undead minions.

He was reasonably certain that Zeiglon and the jungles surrounding it would swallow the adventurers as it had so many others. Taza envisioned his scheme as if on a giant chessboard. He would have his chief enemies tightly blocked into an inescapable corner while Melgor located the final piece of the Staff of Adaman. Once in his possession, Taza hoped that by using it and the Staff of Adois, he would be able to call the powerful amber crystal to him so that he could reunite Adaman's staff for ultimate, universal power.

To accomplish his goal, the two staffs had to be together in the designated place at the allotted time as foretold by the prophecy. Otherwise, his plans for world domination would fail.

Leaving the window, he walked over to the black onyx font and waved his hand over the dark water in its basin, causing the Southern Ocean to appear within its murky depths.

At first, the vampire was unaware that the staff was taking advantage of his distraction and used the extension to launch an attack of its own. The farther its power spread, the more creatures it touched and brought under control. As Taza bent over the font, a stream of cloudy energy flowed from him. That was when the staff pounced.

The passage from the font to Taza's tower snapped shut. The warlock screamed in agony, dropping the staff while grasping the edges of the font. The staff's power washed against the warlock's will like a massive tidal wave, and as the battle of wills turned, Taza lost control. His fingers turned white against the edge of the font, and the skin started cracking and pulling away from bones and muscle.

Somehow, he had to break the font's blockage to regain power. Thinking fast, he recalled a possible solution he had briefly studied. Using all the force he could, the vampire slammed his face into the water of the font, which instantly responded to its master's presence. The blockage fell apart, and he regained his lost energy, causing the staff to withdraw its attack until it lay unresponsive on the cold granite floor.

The undead warlock raised his head, which amazingly remained dry even though his face had been fully immersed. Spinning around, he stomped on the staff's slender length.

"When will you accept my dominance?" he shouted angrily. "I have overcome your attacks time after time, and still you test my powers."

Taza did not know if he was shouting at his goddess Adois, or her staff, but clearly, he had had all he could take.

"This constant struggle will take vital energy away from our shared goal," he continued as he turned his face skyward. "I cannot be the effective leader you want me to be if you don't stop testing me!"

By now, he realized that he did indeed blame the goddess for the staff's resistance. He knew that if she would just issue the command, it would become compliant to his wishes. Moreover, even though she had taken him to task over the amount of time it was taking to claim his dominion, she would not lift a finger to help. He believed that through her staff, she purposely threw obstacles in his way, forcing him to overcome them as though his battle to make the world his own were not hard enough.

Kicking the staff and sending it skittering across the room, he collapsed into his throne chair. He allowed his anger to cool, turning it into dogged determination. He *would* rule the world, even if he had to empty the seven hells of its demons and bring all evil creatures from the Void to accomplish it. If Melgor or the Shadow Lords could not destroy Celedant and the boy, he would do it personally. As long as the wizard did not have the reformed Staff of Adaman, Celedant would not stand a chance against him.

CHAPTER TWENTY-NINE

Sellis thought about escape as he paced the length of his cell. There was nothing else he could do in his predicament. The warlock knew that not all magic was pure good or pure evil. There was always a flaw. A wizard or warlock might call upon his powers to perfect a lightning bolt spell, and no matter how well he performed, it could still be off by a hair's breath. It was a fact of magic that his old teachers had drummed into his head as they studied the nature and use of spells on Dragon Isle.

What he currently needed was to find that chink in the spell that ensnared him. Once he did, he could siphon off its magic to recharge his ring. If he could gain enough power, Sellis could teleport from his cell into the surrounding hills, using even the tiniest opening. Once there, he could rest and regain his power. Hiding would not be a problem. There were so many refugees that it would not be difficult to blend into the masses.

Sellis went to the worn granite steps hewn into bedrock and sat with his back to the wall. He decided to focus his concentration on the spell's construction, positive that he would find that chink. It was time for his dinner, so he studied the place where his food appeared each day, believing that the opening he was looking for would appear there. The food would penetrate the spell at that point, creating a brief opening.

As he stared at the spot, the slime that coated his robe dripped on his bare leg, making it itch. At that instant, his meal appeared beside him and his mind, so attuned to the room, fastened on the opening. He projected his mind, seeking an escape route. His magic snaked toward it like small tendrils extending across the room. Before he could widen the rift, it was gone. Each time a meal came, he was able to get closer. Now that he knew where the chink was, he could move his starting point closer. Two days later, he found what he needed.

The chink was well hidden, but persistence paid off. Sellis could feel the small stream of magic. It would take weeks to drain enough power from it to act, so he sat directly under it, providing instant access. Moving only to eat and eliminate, Sellis placed himself in a trance, allowing tiny bits of power to enter his body before channeling it into his ring Nashmeol. Soon his mind felt refreshed and invigorated. The ring had regained enough of a charge for a single teleport.

He fingered the ring, pictured a small clearing in the woods to the west of the city. Power surged within, and in a blink, he was there in ankle-deep grass, surrounded by the sound of birds chirruping in the lush trees. The warlock took a deep breath of fresh air, filling his lungs with a sweet essence he had not felt in months. Then he exhaled - the feeling so delightful after the stale stench of his prison cell. The wind stirred the trees, and swaying branches and leaves were like music to his ears. His elation was indescribable.

He would have to wait a day for Nashmeol to recharge with enough energy to teleport as far as possible. Sellis looked around and found a suitable tree with a huge hollow made by giant roots, providing a perfect place to rest and conceal himself. He longed for a hot bath to wash away the accumulated stench of confinement, but feared being discovered if he bathed in a nearby stream or lake. Spotting a small growth of jasmine, he picked some and hurried toward the shelter, hoping its sweet scent would disguise his body odor.

Stepping into the hollow, he was just settling in when his body hit a solid object. Sellis' feet slipped and with his arms propelling to try to stay upright, he fell back into cold, foul-smelling muck. In place of the serene meadow, the grimy stone wall of his prison once again surrounded him.

He looked about, mumbling, "The cell? But how?"

At that moment, a cutting voice echoed through the chamber.

"How did you like your brief taste of the outside world? Have you missed it? I thought it especially kind to allow you a breath of freedom you will never have. There is no reason to thank me for my largess. The look on your face is payment enough."

Dark silence cloaked the room, and a tear ran down his face as he once more sat in the sole dry spot on the cold stone steps that he had occupied for so long.

CHAPTER THIRTY

"Do you not realize the trouble your actions will bring, Orthas?" a smooth, deep voice called out. "Our guild attacked a trader's mansion. It will ruin the peace that reigns in Bau's Port. Your heavy-handed measures may work in other cities, but not in our town. You have overstepped your authority."

Many supporting voices shouted in agreement.

A strained, cough-wracked voice answered. "You say I have overstepped my authority, Wessel. Yet I think it is you who now oversteps yours."

"So what if Botreg the turncoat has returned," the smooth voice responded. "Has he done anything to jeopardize us in all the years since he disappeared? You have placed our guild at risk for your own senseless purpose, simply because you hate the dwarf. Yours is a personal vendetta that will not benefit our order."

They shouted the speaker down as Orthas ranted from the front of the hall.

"What do you know, Wessel? You were the turncoat's friend. For all we know, you may be planning to follow in his treacherous footsteps. Besides, this was a job ordered and paid for by a red cloaked warlock."

"And even at that, you failed to fulfill your mission," the speaker added. "So not only have you brought trouble to our door, you have besmirched the Guild's reputation."

At that point, Botreg pushed through the crowd and called out in his deep booming voice.

"Enough of this dissension! I am here."

The crowded hall went deathly silent, and the members parted to allow the dwarf access to Orthas, giving Tarquin his first look at the leader of the Assassins Guild. The man had a slight build, pale blond hair, and weak blue eyes. He wore bright blue clothing with tufts of white shirt fashionably peeking through slits in the sleeves of his doublet. Old scars that twisted his features into that of a grotesque monster ringed his face.

Orthas had a scar that ran from forehead to the center of his cheek. As Tarquin and the others inched closer, he realized that the eye patch the assassin leader wore probably covered an empty socket. The lower right portion of his bottom lip was so damaged that it was drawn downward in a perpetual sneer, leaving his mouth half-open through which the blackened and broken stumps of lower teeth were displayed.

When he saw Botreg's approach, Orthas shouted, spraying spittle as he spoke, "Seize him."

Before anyone could react, Wessel stepped up beside the dwarf and called out a warning. "If anyone moves, I'll kill them on the spot. Let Botreg speak. He has returned of his own free will, risking life and limb. We owe it to him to listen to what he has to say."

Tarquin and the two elves remained in the shadows, watching as events unfolded among the assassins. The gathering was divided, showing support to either Wessel or Orthas, but they waited to see which side would win out before openly committing to either.

The dark dwarf addressed Orthas but turned to capture the gathered members in his steady glare.

"What was done tonight was against the principles set forth by this brotherhood since its beginning. Orthas has started ye down an impossible path this night. He has attacked a trader lord and killed not just the trader's guards but a friend of mine as well."

A few members shouted "turncoat" and "traitor," while others nodded in agreement. Most remained silent, listening.

"There is no denying that I broke from the Assassins Guild," Botreg continued. "Yet in the years that I have been in hiding, I have kept me vow of silence and never betrayed ye. I left because I didna like the direction the guild was takin' when Orthas assumed leadership. Yet I was not the only one to leave. Even now, I look about and see fewer brothers and sisters gathered in this hall. His policies have cut yer force by a third. Tonight six of your number were dispatched to find me. They are all dead. I'll wager Orthas and his lieutenants did not tell them that I traveled with Celedant, a wizard from Dragon Isle."

Surprised murmurs rippled through the crowd with a few openly hostile remarks shouted at their leader.

"You lie, dwarf..." Orthas laughed. "You would say anything to spare your mangy hide."

"Botreg speaks the truth," Tarquin shouted.

Everyone in the room turned to see an unknown human, accompanied by two elves.

"He travels with other magic users besides Celedant," Eldahir added. "We are on a vital mission to save this world from domination by a most foul creature...a vampire."

"A vampire," Morganna explained, "is an undead creature that lives by draining the life blood from its victims. It is impervious to death except by fire or beheading."

This news brought the assembly around. Whatever their feelings about Botreg had been, they now had a new admiration for what he was up against.

"It is ye who have lied to everyone here," Botreg shouted. "Ye have violated the assassins' neutrality in Bau's Port. It is ye who shall pay, and I challenge ye for leadership."

Once more the gathering of assassins broke into a chorus of shouts until Wessel quieted them as he walked about the room to bring order.

"Botreg is right about several things that occurred tonight," Wessel said once he had settled everyone down. "And the fact that Orthas' actions could have endangered such a vital quest should make every one of us angry. Assassin or no, I do not want some undead creature telling me what I can or cannot do. Nevertheless, Botreg is a turncoat and as such, cannot challenge for the master's seat. Therefore, I will."

The hall again erupted with a chorus of shouts for several minutes. Orthas did his best to appear amused, but found it difficult to hide a growing fear. Botreg tried to gain the crowd's attention. Once they had quieted, the dwarf addressed them again.

"Wessel is right. I have overstepped me bounds. Still, me friend died this night, and I claim the right of retribution. If I fight Orthas and win, I can tell Sir Nicolas that this night's attack was not the action of the guild, but a few rogue members, and their leader has been dealt with. It may go a long way in appeasin' him and preventin' further bloodshed."

The mere mention of Nicolas' name sent the gathering into frenzy. Botreg had purposely withheld the information until this moment, suspecting that Orthas had not informed the guild which trader would be the target. The news of an attack against the home of the most powerful pirate lord in the city was sure to cause an uprising. Angry voices called for Orthas' head, and a few took threatening steps toward the master's chair. Some of his more loyal supporters formed a living barrier between him and the enraged assassins. Orthas drew his sword and stood in front of his chair. Brushing his retainers aside, he motioned for quiet.

As the hall fell silent, he pointed his sword at Botreg. "I'll skewer you like the pig you are."

Botreg's sword and short sword appeared almost magically in his hands as he advanced toward Orthas, but Wessel got between them.

"This is for retribution, not the chair," he told his fellow assassins. "If Orthas is killed, the mastership will be decided once Nicolas has been compensated for this slight."

As soon as he stepped back into the crowd, Orthas attacked. The lithe figure vaulted toward Botreg, his sword flashing in the torch light, wielding a long rapier that struck like a snake at his shorter opponent. Botreg ducked the first attack and deflected the next series of blows with his blades. Then he went on attack, driving the lighter and less muscular Orthas back toward his chair. The master was quick on his feet, and he managed to be a step ahead of each attack that Botreg launched.

Tarquin had always admired watching how the cool-headed dwarf made fools of anyone he fought, but in the dark fortress of the assassins, he realized that Botreg had met his equal. Orthas spun, dropping to the floor with his sword held like a scythe to cut Botreg's legs from beneath him. The dwarf reacted by diving away from the blade. He rolled and skidded into the noisy crowd of spectators that shoved him back into the open combat area of the room. The watchers acted like a moving wall, keeping the combatants hemmed in. There would be no cowardly escape for either of the duelists.

The hall was brightly lit and crammed with people, making the room warm and causing the warriors to sweat profusely as they circled one another. Orthas' hellish face nervously twitched as they maneuvered around the hall, while Botreg's expression was the picture of concentration as he calculated his opponent's next move. While they fought, Orthas seemed to thrive on the noise of his fellow assassins and would occasionally look into the crowd as though drawing energy from it. During one of those moments, Botreg chose to strike, aiming his long sword high and straight at Orthas' head. The master struck the dwarf's blade aside at the last moment, but when Botreg's short sword opened a deep wound across his left bicep, it wiped the smile from his face.

As the spectators applauded the dwarf's attack, Orthas grew enraged, drooling from his distorted mouth as he launched a desperate series of attacks. His sword flashed faster than the eye could follow as he pressed the dwarf's defenses. Tired from his frenzied attacks, the old master stepped back, leaving Botreg noticeably panting and bearing a small cut on his left cheek. The dwarf absently wiped at the dripping blood with the back of his left hand. In a burst of motion and power, he sent his short sword flying through the air toward the grotesque assassin leader.

The human had a split second to block the spinning weapon. Orthas intercepted the dwarf's sword in time and the steel blades clashed in midair, their impact ringing through the hall. Although Botreg's short sword was deflected from the assassin's heart, it provided a distraction for the razor sharp edge of his long sword that pierced Orthas' lower stomach, cutting his spinal cord and leaving three inches of blade protruding from his buttocks. The pain was unbearable, and Orthas screamed a high-pitched wail as he collapsed to the floor, paralyzed. Botreg cautiously approached his opponent and pulled the bloodstained blade from his body.

Those who had gathered to watch the duel fell silent; Orthas had met his match in the dark-haired dwarf. Only the master's deranged and pain-wracked will kept him conscious. As Botreg stood over the still figure, the master gazed at him in disbelief until Orthas' good eye rolled back into his head. Botreg had never been a superstitious dwarf, but what happened afterward made him recall a childhood prayer. Suddenly, the lights in the hall dimmed and flickered wildly.

Orthas' head snapped, and an unearthly hiss issued from between the blackened stumps of his teeth, holding the dwarf in its inhuman stare. Spittle bubbled out of the assassin's mouth as a voice that seemed to come from the depths of hell spoke through tortured lips.

"I am Lord Taza. It is regrettable that you defeated Orthas. He was a valuable pawn. Give Celedant my regards. Tell him that he will be dead before the year is out. The Staff of Adaman will be mine to..."

Lifting his sword, Botreg severed the grotesque head from its shoulders. As the head spun to a stop on the floor, the mouth opened one last time and said, "Pity. You're not much of a conversationalist, dwarf."

Wessel approached the dead body. "Who was that?" he asked Botreg and his companions who had moved to stand beside him.

"Taza is the vampire we spoke of," Eldahir replied.

"If you had any doubts about the seriousness of the quest that Botreg and the others have undertaken, the vampire has just proven their words," Wessel said to the assembled crowd. "The master has fallen. We shall elect a successor within the week. But first we must determine Lord Nicolas' response to what has occurred this night and offer compensation for his losses."

Breathing hard, Botreg interrupted. "Master, Celedant and I will try and persuade Lord Nicolas that the attack on his property was a rogue action, instigated by the evil that is trying to overrun our world. I suggest that ye send word to the trader and ask what sum would appease him."

Wessel nodded and slapped the dwarf on the back.

"We owe this turncoat a great deal of thanks for preventing serious repercussions against us, and for warning us about what is happening across the continent. I am not sure what we can do about the vampire. But we will do whatever is necessary to prevent him from taking over and disrupting the balance of power. Now, I think it is time for you to leave and allow the Guild to go about its business."

Their futures uncertain, two members of the assassins escorted Botreg and the others to one of the street-level doors in the alley behind the warehouse. When the four companions reached the night air, the portal slammed shut. They breathed a sigh of relief. Botreg led them out of the warren of alleys that surrounded the assassin's lair toward Sir Nicholas' mansion.

As they walked, Tarquin let loose with a nervous laugh.

"That was easier than I expected. I thought we were going to die."

Botreg nodded. "The gods have something more important planned for us. That was a sideshow." He turned and walked backward, so he could face his friends. "Ye see, I didna need yer help after all. I could have done it alone."

Tarquin was skeptical and Morganna sneered.

"Sure, dwarf, and who would have taken out the guards on the roof? You're either the craziest person I ever met or the bravest."

"Courage is often confused with insanity," Eldahir added. "Anyway, I would not have missed that fight for all the trees in Ravenhall."

CHAPTER THIRTY-ONE

Melgor had returned to the scene of the battle for Southgard to check on the giants' progress. It was dark. It had been a long day, and he rested in his tent, drinking a full-bodied red wine before venturing out to observe the battlefield. He had just emptied his cup when he heard the sound of galloping horses come to a sudden stop outside his tent.

"Now what has that idiot of a giant done?"

Grabbing his sword and staff, he brushed aside the canvas opening to the tent and stopped, surprised, although his face showed no sign as he counted twenty Illanni horsemen. Melgor watched as what he assumed was the leader dismounted and handed the reins of his horse to one of the others. The warlock had had few dealings with this evil race, and he was unfamiliar with their signs of rank.

The normally pale elf was warmly dressed, but his face and hands were exposed, reddened from sun exposure. Three fingers from his left hand were missing along with a pointed ear, as evidence of prior battles. Coming to a stop before the warlock, he bowed curtly and handed Melgor a scroll with Taza's seal.

Melgor was puzzled as to why his lord had not contacted him magically in the usual manner.

The elf stood stoically waiting as the warlock broke the seal and unrolled the parchment that somehow felt odd to the touch. He knew these elves were never to be trusted. They killed dispassionately and without remorse. The scroll read:

These Illanni are our allies. I want them to observe the battle in order to judge the fighting ability of both sides.

Taza

Melgor snorted, sticking the scroll into his belt. "Come, I have an excellent place to watch from where you can observe for yourselves the ineptness of the giant leader."

The dark elves secured their horses near the tent and followed Melgor up a steep path to an outcropping that offered a view of the entire valley. He pointed to Southgard.

"The dwarves stubbornly command the walls. The orcs seldom reach the top. The wall is immensely thick as you can see by the holes left by the trebuchets. Now turn your attention to the west. See Lake Mirowmir and the dam? The orcs seized it as soon as they arrived, building a decent defense on the far shore. Since they cannot take possession of the entire bridge, they built a strong point at the dam's operations house."

The dark elves remained silent, looking where Melgor pointed and intently listening to the account. The warlock continued. "Several nights ago the elves arrived."

One of the Illanni stopped him.

"The elves of light fight here?"

Knowing about the long-standing hatred between the Illanni and the wood and high elves, he said as little as possible.

"Yes. A contingent of wood elves is bolstering the dwarvan army."

He heard angry mumblings behind him but dared not look back. The warlock continued.

"Will the dwarves lose?" the Illanni leader asked.

"At the beginning of the campaign, I would have said that we had a good chance. But after scouting the escape routes and watching the dwarves slaughter the orcs that assault the walls, I am doubtful."

"We will camp here and observe. If the battle goes ill, we'll meet you to escape the slaughter."

Melgor descended the path to the ground below.

He spent the following day in frustration. The warlock had ridden the lines now spreading out across the river to the north nearer the dwarvan-fortified camps and away from the orcish bases built at each bridge that crossed the river. He discovered the eastern portions of the valley were sparsely patrolled and a prime site to launch an attack.

He was determined to push the giant king into motion and reined the chimera at the entrance to the series of tents that housed the king and his generals, not to mention serving wenches. As he approached the tent, two giants stood.

"I must see the king."

"The king is busy. He will see you in the morning."

Melgor was speechless. "I am here on Lord Taza's behalf. I must see the king and his generals."

The guard remained unmoving.

"At least tell him that the dwarves will attack soon, and he'd better get a grip on his army."

With that, he jumped into the saddle and flew toward the hills and sparse comforts of tent and wine.

Melgor dismissed the chimera to go hunt. Pausing in the tent's doorway, he looked toward the rock shelf where the Illanni were camped and caught the slightest movement as a head ducked beneath a boulder. He trusted little, and after whispering a spell that turned the flap into a one-way mirror, he continued scanning the outcropping.

When nothing appeared, he turned and headed for his small makeshift desk, pulling over the cot to act as a seat. Melgor spent an hour writing what he had seen – the disposition of troops and the outrageous attitude of the giants. Then he cast a spell - the parchment disappeared into air. Taza would soon be aware of what was occurring at Southgard. Melgor usually felt uneasy, but the presence of the Illanni intensified his wariness. Just before he was ready to bed down for the night, he sat cross-legged on his cot, weaving protection and warning spells to cover the area surrounding his tent.

It was late at night as twenty Illanni sat on the granite outcropping in a circle. They had used colored sand that they had brought with them and made various ominous signs within a circle. The dark elves all bowed their heads and concentrated, calling with their minds to summon a beast from hell.

In the middle of the circle, a dark shape began to take form, and the Illanni doubled their efforts. When it was over, the elves looked up to find a vile demon from the underworld standing in the circle. It was grayish in color with elongated head curving toward its back and two boney, skeletal arms tipped with razor-sharp blackened talons. It stood on four stout legs with a long bone-white tail. When released, the beast acknowledged his summoners as it strode purposely down the trail toward Melgor's tent.

The warlock need not have placed protection and warning spells about his tent. Once the demon was summoned, his protective spells were set off. Something powerful was nearby and closing on him. Melgor stood holding a small lantern, waiting. A single gesture from the demon lifted the tent from the ground and blew it away in a hurricane force wind.

Melgor had no idea what he faced, but he reacted instantly, throwing the lantern to the ground. Earlier, the warlock had emptied all the oil he had and then lit the lantern shading the flame. As it struck the ground, the oil caught fire, lighting the area. Caught off guard, the demon tried to shade its eyes from the bright light.

The warlock now knew that he was facing a demon from the lowest reaches of the underworld. Melgor advanced several side steps while uttering a spell. The hell spawn did not see the warlock cast the spell, but it felt the energy as it toppled over and was sent rolling across the ground. As the creature regained its feet, a ray of deep red energy struck it on the left shoulder. Its arm hung loosely, but given time, it would heal. Regaining its feet, the demon cast a spell. Because of the light, it was unsure of exactly where the warlock was, so it sent a rolling firewall that traversed the area like an incoming wave.

"Partum defensiva!" Melgor shouted. As a protective barrier sprang up around him, he dropped behind a boulder for additional security. The fire swept over him, and while he was safe, it severely weakened his shield and he felt intense heat. He crouched to the side of the boulder, his staff pointed at the demon. The warlock saw the creature advancing on him stood tall and arrogant. Leveling his staff, he called on a little-used spell that shot out fingers of ice at the figure. "Gelidus digitorum."

At the same time, the demon sent a bolt of red-hot energy. The two spells struck each combatant at the same time. Hellfire burned through his shield, destroying it, and Melgor was hurled backward, pain shooting through his right side where the flame burned through his robe, leaving a channel of bleeding flesh from front to back.

The creature had just cast its spell when the darts of ice were hurled at it. It took another step, faltering as it dropped to its front knees. The demon looked down to see an icy bolt sticking out of its heart, its body fighting the pain where the frozen projectile had lodged. Reaching up, it grabbed hold of the melting projectile and agonizingly pulled it from heart and chest.

Hearing a wild yell, the creature looked up and caught sight of Melgor rushing by as the warlock's sword slammed into the demon's neck. The creature leered as the sword bounced off, jarring Melgor's arm and sending him tumbling. Jumping to his feet, the warlock sent a red lightning bolt that struck the hellish creature with a powerful blow and sent it spinning head over hooves some thirty feet. Wobbling from the assault, it managed to lance out a torrent of molten lava. The warlock threw up a blocking spell that sent the lava cascading like a waterfall to each side of him. It was time to end this. Melgor had not cast his next spell and hoped its toll would not be great. His staff flared, and a crack in the earth began to open beneath the demon. The hell spawn fought to stay upright, but the warlock's magic pulled it downward, and it screamed an ear-wrenching wail until the fissure closed.

Melgor had little time to watch what his spell had accomplished. Pointing his staff at the camp of the Illanni, the warlock called on every ounce of energy he still retained, tapping even into the earth and air energy that surrounded him. Then he pointed his staff toward the camp of the dark elves, shooting a powerful beam that struck the ground beneath them. A tremendous grinding split the air as the rock shelf exploded, raining stones and Illanni body parts down the mountain and across the entire area.

Chapter Thirty-Two

Transportation out of the city comprised two covered wagons used to haul goods along the Confederation roads. Nicolas's aide, Westcott, ordered a tarp placed over the opening to prevent prying eyes from seeing the occupants. When Celedant and his companions were aboard, the drivers cracked their whips and moved out, lurching once before smoothing out on the cobblestone street that led to the docks.

Street noises reached the passengers' ears as they sat in the confining darkness. The trip seemed to take forever as the heavy wagons negotiated busy streets, and the passengers bounced around under cover. Although the clear, crisp morning was bitterly cold, the sun's rays were hot, promising a much-needed increase in temperature later in the day. When the wagons came to jolting halt, the drivers jumped to the street and made their way to the rear of the wagons, drawing the flaps aside to reveal the harbor. Ships of every kind were moored along the docks. Many more traversed the harbor, their sails filling the sky with a sea of canvas. As the passengers climbed down from the wagon bed, several leathery-skinned sailors came to unload the crates and barrels that Nicolas had provided.

As the group headed for their ship, Vannor laid a gentle hand on Celedant's shoulder.

"This is where I leave you, Celedant. Nicolas was kind enough to get me a berth on a ship headed for Braenaughtan. My father will not be pleased when I tell him what happened to my ship and crew, but I believe he will forgive me when I give him the crown."

Vannor was referring to an intricate silver crown with a single black pearl mounted on the front that Celedant had discovered among the hidden treasures at Brackus. Centuries past, the dwarves had created it as a gift for the Selacian King, but when the Brae reneged on a treaty, they stole it back in retribution. This had happened so long ago, the lost crown of Braenaught had become a myth of great importance to the Brae.

"I wish I could accompany you on the remainder of this quest," Vannor said, turning to watch the others ascend the gangplank.

"And there is no one I'd rather have along," Celedant assured him. "But you can be of greater service in Braenaught. You must convince your father to prepare his people for war. Taza has been spreading attacks against more and more nations. Since he has sent either armies or monstrous creatures against the dwarves, the elves, and several human cities, I believe it is just a matter of time before your people come under attack."

"And for that reason alone, I will abide by your wishes and return home. I must make sure my father understands the gravity of the situation. We don't want to be caught unaware."

"Please deliver this missive to your father," Celedant said, handing him a sealed parchment. "This explains the valuable service you have given us and should help convince him of both your words and your worth."

Having overheard Vannor, Tarquin, who was walking behind the wizard, stopped and joined the conversation.

"We will miss your sword and your companionship," he said, shaking Vannor's hand. "But you will be a valuable asset to your father, King Trebau. I recommend that he contact my father, King Benton. Thousands of Parthian soldiers are helping the dwarves, including my older brother, Crown Prince Kaleb. Father should be able to answer any questions he may have."

"Thanks, Tarquin. That will help much, as will your missive, Celedant."

Vannor bid goodbye to each of the others, shaking hands with the men and hugging the women. He would miss them all. Together, they had fought well during the battle for Brackus. Nevertheless, the prince knew his duty, and as he headed toward the ship that would take him home, his lips parted in a lop-sided grin. When he had left Braenaughtan on his own ship many months ago, he had been a brash, irresponsible young man with a bevy of illegitimate offspring.

His father had been tired of his youngest son's wild ways and sent him off to sea to become a man, unaware of the horrors his son would face. Vannor knew his father would be amazed when he discovered that the irresponsible youth no longer existed. Moreover, although he would never have willingly suffered the hardships and torture he had faced, he had to admit that they, along with the battles he had fought, had indeed molded him into a mature, responsible human being.

With a final wave, the others headed for the Rapier, a sleek ship fit for smuggling and raiding coastline communities. The ship had a small forecastle at the bow and a wide poop deck atop the stern. A single mast rose mid-ship, its sail furled tight to its boom with a smaller sail located at the forecastle. The rigging looked to be in excellent shape, and the polished wood of its deck gleamed in the morning sunlight. They would later learn that the ship had three decks. The first was where the crew and passengers slept and ate. The second was for cargo, and the third had a low ceiling and was inaccessible to everyone but crew who knew the secret to getting inside. This was where the Rapier hid illicit goods.

A dashing middle-aged man strode confidently down the gangplank to meet the ship's new passengers. Captain Weir introduced himself with a flourish.

"Gentlemen and ladies, this is the Rapier. She is the finest ship afloat, faster than a dolphin and sturdy as a whale. She is crewed by the best sailors, although they look like the worst sort of bilge waste that ever sailed the seas."

Several sailors laughed, and Tarquin could see the pride the captain held for his ship and crew. Captain Weir had tanned, weather-beaten skin like the other sailors. His dark brown hair was peppered with gray, and his hands were callused from years spent at sea. He wore black, long loose pants and a flowing scarlet shirt with a scarf wrapped about his waist where a long rapier hung in a leather scabbard.

Celedant followed the captain up the gangplank as he commented on the fine ship, leaving the others to help the sailors gather their gear. Aboard, Weir escorted the company to the raised aft deck where the ship's wheel stood.

"The Rapier is a stout vessel. There isn't much space for luxuries, mind you, but you will grow used to her. Your quarters are here below the wheel."

"How many crew do you have?" Celedant asked.

"At this point, I've twenty," the Captain said with a shrug. "I'd like to carry more, but I put some ashore at Nicolas' request to make room for you. That reminds me. The supplies Westcott sent are stowed in your cabins. I wish I could offer grander accommodations, but as you can see, space is limited. The deck is filled to capacity with cargo to last us through the voyage."

Indeed, Tarquin thought.

Every available surface was stacked with crates and barrels, all tightly lashed to the deck. High above them in the rigging, sailors scampered about on tarred and callused feet to check and recheck the lines that would carry the ship's sails. Tarquin's military mind appreciated and envied a crew so well trained that they did not need an officer standing around shouting orders. Each of the Rapier's crew had the look of a professional, both sailor and soldier. Although safely moored in the harbor, each man openly wore a weapon. The favorite of the sailors seemed to be a short sword that Tarquin guessed would be advantageous in close quarter fighting along the packed deck of the ship.

The captain broke into his musings when he called out across the deck. "Hoy Varnas."

From the bow, a one-armed man named Varnas came running. He was immaculately dressed in black, with the sleeve of his missing arm cut off and sewn together at the end. His hair was as black as his clothing, and he had a neatly trimmed mustache that stuck out like pike points.

As he approached, Weir said, "Let me introduce my first mate, Mr. Varnas."

The one-armed pirate gave a mock bow and in a surprisingly aristocratic voice said, "It is a pleasure to sail with a distinguished group such as yourselves." Turning toward Celedant, a bit of awe entered his voice. "And it is truly a thrill to meet the famous Wizard Celedant of Dragon Isle."

The wizard visually examined the thirty-year-old man for a moment until his eyes lit with recognition.

"Ah yes. You must be related to Varnas of Galasgas. Last I heard, your kin were wiped out when the city fell. Such news saddened my heart."

"You're right," Varnas replied gravely. "They were murdered in cold blood...everyone but a forgotten young novice in a hidden monastery. When I heard what had happened, I left the order to seek revenge. I have lost my family, my kingdom, and my arm. Ten years later, I am still doling out my revenge. And to think that my father believed that I was only fit to be a cleric."

"Revenge is a hard road for one so young," the wizard replied.

"But Varnas is my best fighter," Captain Weir said. "I would have him no other way. Come Varnas; show our guests to their cabins. We'll be sailing with the tide."

The first mate escorted Celedant and the others down a ladder to a narrow hallway with doors that opened into tiny cramped rooms. With most of their gear already placed inside, it made their accommodations appear even smaller.

Varnas saw their downcast looks and laughed.

"You will sleep in comfort on feather-stuffed mattresses with blankets to keep you warm, while I am forced to sleep below deck in a hammock with the rest of the crew. Don't worry about me though; when the water gets rough, I'll be swinging in my sleep while you roll out of your beds."

He laughed so hard, a passing sailor grinned at the jest.

"A word to the wise," the first mate continued. "Put away your gear so it won't roll about in rough weather. When you are finished and once we get underway, come up on deck. The captain thinks it best for you to stay hidden below until we sail." Having said his piece, the dashing one-armed man disappeared, leaving them to sort through their gear.

The cabins had two tiny bunks and a rolled-up hammock with only enough space for three people to stand comfortably. There was storage space beneath the beds and drawers that could be latched shut along the walls. Sturdy rope netting hung from the walls to stow things up and out of the way. Tarquin and Botreg again shared a small room and much to Tarquin's' surprise, the dwarf said he would follow Varnas' advice and sleep in the hammock.

The company spent a seemingly endless day sorting through gear that Westcott had gathered and dividing it among their surviving members. The cramped ship had very little ventilation and soon became stuffy. They could not wait to be finished and looked forward to fresh air above deck.

Although docked, the ship rocked softly, bumping against its moorings. Ralav noticed Aegir and Ronli's faces turning a sickly shade of green and could not help teasing them.

"Better get used to it. It's gonna get a lot worse once we're out to sea."

Shortly before nightfall as the sky turned a soft umber, a short, grizzled sailor came and knocked on their doors.

He spoke with a slight accent, common to those living in the southern portion of the Confederation. "We'll be shoving off soon. The Cap'n says you can come above decks now."

He disappeared up the dark hallway with Tarquin and the others on his heels. Their cramped quarters were already wearing on them, and they desperately wanted some air.

"It's a good thing we don't have to spend the whole voyage below deck," Ress said to Tarquin. "I would go stir-crazy."

"You and me both; I hope I don't get seasick," Tarquin replied. "Maybe we can get to know one another a little better."

"I'd like that," Ress said with shy smile.

Outside, night soon fell, and a cool breeze off the ocean dissipated the last vestiges of warmth the sun had provided. Tarquin followed Celedant to the wheel deck where Captain Weir stood watching his crew prepare to cast off. A couple sailors stood on the dock, unwinding the thick mooring lines, which they threw onboard before vaulting over the ever-widening gap as the ship backed away from the dock. Varnas ordered the smaller sails unfurled. These ran from the forward mast to the bowsprit and stuck out ten to fifteen feet from the bow of the ship. The evening breeze caused them to billow as the ship pivoted away from the shore and headed into the harbor.

CHAPTER THIRTY-THREE

Tarquin was surprised how easily the ship maneuvered in such tight quarters with little more than a light breeze. Seagulls flew in and out of the rigging as the vessel made its way into deeper water. Many ships were anchored in the harbor, and Weir wove the ship through a small obstacle course of anchored vessels. Soon the Rapier was beyond the harbor mouth and had entered the river's slow current. The water was choppy where fresh water met the salt water of the ocean and the ship surged into it.

A shout from one of his men drew Captain Weir's attention.

"Three long boats trying to cut us off!" the young sailor called.

"Do you think they're after us?" Celedant asked, concerned.

"Anything is possible, but I'll warrant it's the cargo they're after. "I got my start the same way," Weir said with a shrug.

"Master-at-arms, bring about the bows," Varnas called.

Tarquin and several others retrieved their bows and approached Varnas.

"May we be of service?" Tarquin asked.

"Always glad for an extra bow," the first mate replied, "especially with some of my crew land-bound. It'll be a turkey shoot. Aim for the men at the rudder. They'll soon be going in all directions."

Eldahir, Tarquin, Morganna, Ress, and the dwarves joined the crew, launching arrows toward the approaching boats. For most, it was tricky to judge the pitch of the ship and the smaller boats. Eldahir and Morganna, however, had no problem, thanks to their elven heritage. While several arrows shot by the others fell into the water or struck unintended targets, the elves calmly sent arrow after arrow toward the boats, hitting their targets with exact precision.

Soon the helmsmen of the boats lay dead, forcing members of their crew to take over the rudders. Those that remained alive did not have the experience to intercept the Rapier, and the smaller boats took off, heading back to shore. Instead of valuable goods from the ship, their boats were littered with dead and wounded pirates.

Varnas and Weir were in fine spirits as they watched their attackers scurry away.

"An extra ration of grog tonight," Captain Weir called good-naturedly.

The sailors cheered the captain three times before continuing their work.

Aegir, fascinated at being afloat, turned a pale color, ran to the side of the ship, and with heaving shoulders, doubled over.

The sailors around the retching dwarf nodded and winked knowingly. Tarquin and the others gathered at the opposite rail to watch the coast grow smaller in the setting sun. The main sail was unfurled, making a loud snap as it caught the wind, propelling the Rapier out to sea. Once they were far enough from the shoreline, Captain Weir turned the wheel hard, bearing to starboard on a more southerly course. The captain called the first mate over to take the wheel.

Glancing at Aegir and Ronli, who had joined the other sick dwarf at the rail, he said, "Your sickness will calm as you get used to the roll and pitch of the ship." He joined the others and motioned to the scene before them. "What do you think?"

"It's wonderful, truly wonderful," Morganna replied, bubbling with enthusiasm. During her long life, the only boat she had ever been on was a small rowboat miles beneath the earth on small subterranean lakes or rivers.

"It is that," Weir said, looking lovingly at the ocean. "A person really understands how small we are in the scheme of life when one sails the sea." Throwing a wicked grin toward Ronli and Aegir, he added, "The galley will have food ready within the hour. We can dine in my cabin."

"Excellent, we'll go over some of our maps after dinner," Celedant replied, rubbing his hands together as the sick dwarves moaned and retched again.

Tarquin turned to Botreg and asked, "Where is Hority?"

"He's set up a hammock close to where the bilge collects in the ship," the dark dwarf laughed. "Says it will help him sleep, and the rats will remind him of his childhood."

That brought a chorus of laughter while the others returned to admiring the scene before them.

Once the ship settled into a steady pace, the companions broke into groups and meandered around the deck as the sailors lolled about keeping watch on the rigging and sky. Tarquin and Ress walked hand-in-hand, talking and sharing stories of their lives. This was the first chance the prince had had to thank her for saving his life, and now that her face no longer bore the horrible scars of burn marks, he could admire her beauty without offending her. Hortus took Aegir and Ronli below deck and settled them into their bunks, each with a chamber pot nearby. He made sure they were as comfortable as possible and gave them a sleeping draught before joining the other dwarves touring the ship.

Standing alone at the railing, Morganna breathed deeply, enjoying the salt air and brisk breeze.

"This must be quite an experience for you," Eldahir said as he joined her at the rail.

"All my life I lived below ground, never knowing the joys the surface could offer."

"What brought you to live above ground?"

"The vampires," Morganna replied, her brow darkening. "You cannot imagine what it was like in Illan. As more and more of my people accepted the mantle of vampirism, life became a living nightmare for the rest of us. Families that sent their servants outdoors on errands never knew if they would return or end up a meal for the bloodsuckers. When my father became the clan head after he killed my uncle, he turned my entire family. I barely escaped, and when I did, he put a price on my head and ordered my death. Fortunately, I had suspected this might happen and had prepared a cottage in the lands between Nars and Korvanna as a safe haven."

Her words hit the wood elf hard. "I cannot imagine a father doing something so...."

"Vile? Evil?"

"Both. I'm sorry you had to endure such horror."

Morganna turned and smiled, her features softening to such tenderness, it strengthened her elven beauty, taking Eldahir's breath. "My father never loved me because I looked more like our ancestors than an Illanni. He used to call me a mongrel throwback. If he could see me now that Dolgar has completed my transformation, I dare say he would be tempted to ignore Taza's orders to keep me alive and kill me himself."

"I'm still mystified why a dwarvan god took interest in an Illanni...or any of us for that matter. Gods usually don't like to interfere with the races."

"That's true. However, since Adois has already interfered and continues to do so, upsetting the natural order, Dolgar decided he could no longer sit back and do nothing. As for why he saved my life and helped complete my transformation to wood elf…. He believes I have an important part to play in the fight against Taza and bringing my people back to the light. After all," she grinned, "I did save Tarquin's life. My cousin would have murdered him had Dolgar not sent me to the prince's aid, and that would have destroyed the prophecy along with any chance of stopping this madness."

"That vampire was your cousin?" Eldahir asked, aghast.

"My uncle's eldest son. I'm surprised he hasn't gone after my father, but it would seem that vampires…or maybe it's just my cousin…have little love for anyone but themselves. I suppose I should be grateful. If he hadn't brought me to the brink of death, Dolgar would never have come to my rescue."

"Was it difficult getting used to the light?"

"At first, but the longer I live above ground, the more I love all the sights and sounds it can offer. Now, I cannot imagine living a day without the smell of flowers and spices or hearing birdsong and the wind rustling through leaves. I have a deep respect for the woodlands and the creatures that live within. I have developed a friendship with some of the animals – a female deer and her fawn, a family of rabbits, half a dozen squirrels, and the birds nesting near my home, or so it seems. It makes it difficult to kill others of their kind for food," she said.

"I imagine so," Eldahir said, smiling.

As their discussion continued, Eldahir realized he was becoming more and more attracted to Morganna. He loved her laugh, her courage, and her strength of conviction. His next thoughts shook him to the core. *I believe I am falling in love with an Illanni; I wonder what Father will think about that.*

The company was happy to be on the move again. Varnas ordered a crewman to the crows' nest, a small platform high up the mast, to keep a lookout for raiders. Two more sailors, who were obviously guards, made regular rounds about the ship, ever alert for danger. Having finished their private walk around the deck, Tarquin and Ress were leaning against the rail listening to Ralav tell a story about the last time he had sailed.

They gathered in Captain Weir's cabin a short while later. The cabin was large in comparison to the others aboard the Rapier. It encompassed the entire width of the stern and was twenty feet long. The cabin also had the luxury of several small portholes, affording a view of the ocean during daylight hours. Varnas, Celedant, and the others joined Weir, while Aegir and Ronli took the Captain's advice and ate their meal on deck. They were feeling better after the medicine Hortus had given them, and their nap. Two crewmembers brought out a large table and assembled it in the center of the room. The galley's cook had prepared a feast for their first night at sea that included fish stew, fresh baked bread that had been purchased before they left port, and a roast that was too well done for most of the diners' tastes, washed down with either elven wine or a fine dwarvan brew, depending on the individuals' tastes. Overall, the cook had done a passing job.

Days passed and the Rapier made good time with southwesterly winds blowing fresh off the Mordolwyn Mountains. Ronli and Aegir had gained their sea legs and wiled away the hours with their fellow travelers. Captain Weir's ship ran smoothly. The crew knew their tasks, and when Vargas shouted an order, the men went about their duties efficiently and in good humor. The sea flowed fast under the keel, tossing up great gushes of froth as it plowed through the waves.

Celedant thought it best not to inform the crew of Morganna's true heritage. *No sense in creating problems in case anyone had ever had a bad experience with an Illanni,* he thought. The Captain and crew believed Morganna was just another wood elf, as it was now impossible to tell the difference, thanks to Dolgar's blessing.

Having lived most of their lives underground, she and the dwarves were awed by the endless expanse of ocean. Morganna spent most of her time on deck in the company of Eldahir, and their budding romance soon became common knowledge to everyone aboard. When the passengers asked about the large grey monsters that frolicked in the churning water at the bow, the crew laughingly informed them that they were dolphins, not monsters. Tarquin and the others spent hours watching the creatures with rapt fascination.

The crew, along with Tarquin, Ress, and occasionally even Celedant, spent time catching fish to supplement their bland meals. The dwarves examined the catch as they were hauled aboard, amazed at their size. They even tried their hand at deep-sea fishing. Once after catching a ten-foot shark and hauling it aboard, everyone marveled at its ferocity and rows of sharp teeth.

Morganna pointed at it. "These creatures are similar to a type of fish that swims the streams where I come from. They have rows of teeth that grow back when broken or lost. Yet, I did not know that this type of predator existed in the distant seas."

"There are many dangerous things that walk the ground or swim the waters, many of which we have yet to discover," Celedant said.

"I think I have already seen too many," Tarquin said with a laugh. "If I never come across another new monster, I will be content."

Chapter Thirty-Four

The journey passed swiftly for the Rapier, and a storm blew them at an even quicker pace. Afterward, the wind shifted to the south, and the ship was tacking back and forth, plowing through the open water. The crew let out all her sails, keeping them up until a sailor in the crow's nest called, "Land ho." This puzzled everyone, as they weren't near any islands or the mainland. Instead, giant jagged fingers of rock reached from the depths to prodigious heights.

Celedant and the company joined the sailors at the railing to watch as they sailed past the first of the jagged rocks. The captain ordered the sails taken in as the Rapier entered the dangerous-looking sea. Standing anchored in place at the ship's wheel, Captain Weir never took his eyes off the water that crashed against the rocks and ever-changing currents.

A moment later, Celedant came and stood by him. "These are the remains of Zeiglon, are they not?"

Clutching his pipe between his teeth, the captain replied, "Aye. We have turned west in hopes of finding the escarpment or the desert shore. Dangerous currents are these. We must be careful not to hit the underlying rock hidden by waves."

A quiet came over the two as the wizard marveled at Weir's calm demeanor. The only sign he showed of the danger that threatened the ship was by how hard he clutched his pipe with his teeth. He navigated the rocky pinnacles as the ship zigzagged in the choppy sea. This sent several dwarves to the railing, the motion getting the better of their stomachs.

They passed a large pinnacle of rock - and there before them was the seaward side of the escarpment. The captain whirled the wheel and the Rapier cut north.

"We have reached our destination, Master Celedant. That is, if we don't get pushed by the current into the escarpment."

The wizard glanced at him, noticing the beads of sweat running down the captain's forehead. Celedant fell silent, closely watching the rock slide past. He swore that he could touch the escarpment if he reached out and extended Forestae. After several hours of navigating the treacherous waters, battling the currents and the ever-shifting winds, Captain Weir called out to the wizard.

"See there, Celedant," he shouted and pointed northwest. "The escarpment ends."

The wizard looked on with relief as the last of the escarpment slid by, and the rolling dunes of the desert began.

The Rapier cleared the escarpment and the captain sounded excited as he laughingly called to Celedant. "There! Do you see that arm of rock? It looks to form a natural harbor – if we don't run aground on hidden rocks or a sand bar."

Several sailors gathered at the bow of the ship and threw depth lines into the water even though no one had issued any orders. They called back the depth to the captain as he made his final approach into the harbor. The line showed deeper water than expected, and the Rapier sailed through the breakwater and into the harbor, where the ship slowed to a standstill. Weir ordered them to lower the anchor.

The crew filled the boats with cargo, lowered them to the calm water, and began rowing to shore. The captain and Celedant shared a laugh as Tarquin and the others joined the sailors and hurried over to the rails. There they grappled with the ropes, straining to keep a strong hold of the rope netting.

Celedant turned and made his way along the deck to the railing and waiting sailors, leaving Weir standing on the wheel deck of his ship.

"I wish you good luck and good fortune, Captain. May your journey home be a calmer one."

The sailors rowed the boats and their passengers to shore, and Celedant and his party stepped on land for the first time in several weeks. They gathered their belongings and headed for the escarpment and their first night's sleep on solid ground.

From the camp, Tarquin and Morganna stared at the sheer rock face that rose from the sandy desert, extending into the sky for half a mile. Years of wind erosion had left the surface nearly smooth. It reflected the rays of the bright sun at the watchers while hot, arid air blew sagebrush and tumbleweed across the seemingly endless horizon. A ridge of rock stretched out to sea, undermined by the ocean's current. Without a sturdy ship, it would be impossible to conquer. It seemed that the way to the top would have to be accomplished by magic...or a miracle.

Chapter Thirty-Five

Melgor had one last throw of the dice to kill Celedant and Tarquin. He put down a book of demonology, his favorite that never left his person, and exited his tent overlooking the valley of Southgard and the siege. He went to a large flat granite surface and using the blood of an orc he had killed earlier, drew two large circles, and in the center of the rings, several ruins. Early in his life as a wizard, he had attempted to kill the bothersome Celedant but had failed. This act turned him from wizard to warlock and cost him the bond with his dragon. This time, however, would be different. He would summon one of the most powerful demons he had ever dealt with.

Melgor began chanting the summoning spell in a language forgotten by all but the elders of Dragon Isle. He had to get it right the first time or the demon would turn on him. As the words poured forth from his lips, a reddish glow began to fill the enchanted circle. It was so bright that Melgor had to shield his eyes to complete the spell. Once the glow subsided, he carefully looked up and in the circle of power stood a humanoid-shaped demon. It was as tall as a man with flames that danced along the surface of its skin.

"Why have you summoned me?" it asked in a harsh, guttural voice.

Melgor hid his fear that it might break out of the circle, and replied, "I have need of you. There is a company of travelers that I would have you deal with."

The demon walked toward Melgor and touched the barrier wall of the circle. "You have constructed a remarkable cage to tether me in."

The demon showed much more tact and manners than the demons Melgor had summoned years ago. He wondered if he could control it.

The demon spoke in a calm voice. "What do I get for killing these adventurers?"

Melgor stood as tall as he could and stated, "I will release you from your bond that you may roam this world as you like."

"Hmm," the creature mused. "What guarantee do you offer that my bond to you will be nullified at the end of this venture?"

The warlock shivered inside. This was a key point of the contract, one he did not like making, but if he were to rid the world of Celedant and Tarquin, it was a chance he had to take. "In that case, you may track me down or have others kill me. It would be easy for one such as you to gather an army and seek me out."

The demon laughed, and the inside of its mouth was like looking into a furnace. "You believe it would take an army to kill you?" It studied the warlock standing before him. "If you were simply human...but no, you are a creature of black magic, so maybe you are right. I will kill these people for my release. This planet intrigues me, and I would explore it."

Melgor spoke a few words, and a map of the area appeared before the demon. He began to explain it, but the demon abruptly interrupted him. "I can read a map, wizard. Set me free, and I'll do your bidding."

"One last caveat," the wizard said, hoping he had not gone too far. "When this is finished, we part company and never see each other again. Those are my terms for your freedom."

The demon laughed, fire shooting out of its mouth. "Done."

Melgor stepped to the edge of the circle and brushed away a small section of salt with his foot. The demon strolled out of its cage, heat causing the wizard's robes to smolder, and without a word, the walking furnace headed down the trail to the southern rolling dunes of the desert.

Eldahir, Ronli and Ralav returned to the company from what they called a little scouting trip along the base of the cliff as Celedant and the others relaxed against some boulders beneath the escarpment.

The wizard looked at the dust-covered trackers and asked, "What did you find?"

"This tumble of rock forms a shelf along the edge of the cliff for about a mile into the desert," Eldahir replied, wiping gritty sweat from his brow. "It is there the soft sand begins. We should be able to make good time, but the escarpment seems un-scalable. It is oddly shaped and high along the rim. Clouds and lightning linger about the peaks, acting like a warning beacon to stay way."

"No one said this mission would be easy," the wizard sighed. "I hope we can discover a suitable place to climb up. My magic is limited in what I can transport over vast distances. It will be easier and safer if we can find a natural track to the top of the plateau."

"Why don't I just transport everyone up?" Azimuth asked. "It would be a simple matter if I change into dragon form."

Celedant let out his breath and stamped his staff on the boulder. "Good idea. I knew there was a valid reason for asking you along."

Azimuth snorted and moved away from the others to a space large enough to hold his immense size, but before he could change into dragon form, he saw a bright light casting a shadow onto the cliff face. He alerted the others. Their weapons were ready when the shadow neared their camp. Then from over a great boulder stepped a flaming man.

Celedant instantly recognized it. "Fire Demon!" he yelled.

The defenders loosed a volley of arrows and crossbow bolts, but reaching the demon, they turned to cinder on impact.

The demon spoke to his prey. "None of your weapons will hurt me. Surrender now and I will grant you an easy death." He then jumped down onto the sand that melted in less than a moment, turning into glass. Ronli and Ralav charged the demon, but with a flick of its hand, they were slammed into a boulder. Celedant cast a water spell, and it began raining on the creature, creating the sound of sizzling as it struck. The demon ran from under the rain, approaching the group. Then Azimuth morphed into dragon form and attacked the creature.

The dragon struck with gleaming white teeth, but the demon grabbed Azimuth's front leg and flung him into the desert a great distance. Botreg threw knives as fast as he could, to good effect. As each dagger struck the creature, it stumbled. Tiring of the daggers, the demon raised its hand and hurled a bolt of energy that struck the ground in front of the dwarf, sending him flying backwards. Baldo ran ahead, his mythril armor and magical facemask hardly heating up, and struck with his hammer.

Celedant, Eldahir, and Morganna called forth every water and ice spell they could remember, attacking the enemy unceasingly. As water and ice pellets found its target, the glow of the demon's skin diminished. Ress went to throw her spear, but Tarquin held her back, saying, "Your spear is useless against it."

During this onslaught Baldo kept hammering the demon, hurting it as it had never been hurt before. Raising its arm, it slammed into the dwarf with a powerful punch, knocking him down. As Baldo fell, he connected with the demon's leg, sending it flailing to the ground. Tarquin advanced to strike with Dragon Bolt but the heat was too intense. Stepping back, he raised his magical sword and threw it at the demon, causing an earsplitting clap of thunder when it struck. The demon toppled over, rolling on the ground until it struck a boulder. Raising its head, it screamed in pain, with flames from its mouth shooting ten feet into the air.

Baldo got up and advanced on the creature that still being pelted by the water and ice spells. It was no coward. It stood, using a rock for support. It leapt upward to the top of the boulder, and pulling Tarquin's blade from its midsection, the demon dropped the red-hot sword onto the ground, raising its hands in surrender: "Stop! I have never been so sorely wounded."

Ronli and Ralav returned from where the creature had thrown them, their leather armor smoking. Azimuth also recovered from the blow and flew to land next to Celedant, his mind still whirling over what had happened. Baldo, his mythril armor not showing any damage from the demon's fire, stood at the bottom of the boulder swinging his hammer by its strap, ready to let it loose at the first sign of trouble. The demon dropped to sit on the stone.

"Hold your weapons," it pleaded. "I was sent to kill you, but you are too strong for a single demon. That cursed magical sword has defeated me. I have nothing left. Now I must report to my master and admit defeat, and he will return me to the hell that has been my home."

"Who sent you to waylay us in this miserable place?" Celedant asked.

"I'll tell you," the demon said, "if you break the bond the wizard holds on me."

"Why would we do that?" Azimuth asked.

"Because there is nothing to keep my master from summoning me again and again to bother you," the demon replied.

"That's not a problem," Tarquin said. "I can defeat you with my sword again and again."

"That's true," Celedant interjected. "However, his interference could come at a time that is inconvenient. Have you a name?"

"I am called, Feurig. Please grant me this boon. I have no desire to be sent against you in battle." When no one spoke, he continued. "My word is my bond," the demon swore. "There are mindless demons aplenty, but my kind is intelligent and can reason."

"Once freed, where will you go?" Hority asked.

"I live in fire," the demon replied. "I shall find a volcano and make my home there. As long as I'm not disturbed, there will be no trouble."

"Who sent you?" Celedant demanded again.

"I do not know his name, but he was a powerful warlock."

"And where were you summoned to?" Celedant asked.

The hell spawn shook its head. "I know not the name of the place, but we were high in the mountains, and my senses felt a place of great death nearby."

"The battle of Southgard," Tarquin said. "It has to be."

"Yes," Celedant agreed. "And the nearest wizard powerful enough to summon such a creature would be Melgor. He was well versed in demonology at Edain. How do we set you free, demon?"

"A lightning bolt to my neck will break the bond," it replied joyfully.

"If I do this, you must swear an oath never to attack or interfere with the members of this quest again."

"I so swear."

"Electriskt Kastasig," Celedant chanted.

There was a tremendous crack of thunder, and a massive lightning bolt struck the demon's neck, picking it up and throwing it backwards off the boulder.

The company ran around the rock and found a blackened husk of a man struggling to stand up. When it saw the others it said, "You see. I'm as defenseless as a newborn baby. If you wish to back out of our agreement, do it now. It will take some time for me to return to normal."

Celedant harshly stated "No, leave here. My word is likewise my bond, but if I hear even a rumor that you are causing havoc, I will find you and destroy you."

The demon complied. "You have my word. I will not stir up trouble." That said, it turned its back on them and walked into the desert.

"Are you sure about this, Celedant?" Azimuth asked. This was a foe he was not eager to tackle again.

"I have studied the library in Edain and when such a demon's word is given, it will stand," Celedant explained. "Now if we can, let's get a good night's sleep. I fear the dangers we face on the morrow and hereafter will be serious."

Azimuth flew the members of the company to the top of the cliff in threes, starting with the dwarves. Lightning shot at them, stopped by the protective spell the dragon had woven around himself and his passengers. Celedant went up with Tarquin behind, and Botreg braced between the dragon's neck and arms so the dwarf would not fall off. While waiting for Tarquin to climb down from Azimuth's back, Ralav and Ronli got a good look at the top of the escarpment. In stark contrast to the desert below, the plateau was lush with jungle growth. When the entire group was safely above, the clouds and lightning moved away from the cliff and hovered over the sea. The storm would return when anyone arrived to try and climb the cliff.

"It's a good thing we had you along to fly us up," Celedant told Azimuth. "Had we tried to climb to the top, the lightning would have made quick work of us."

As they began the trek toward Zeiglon, they spotted the dilapidated ruins of a city that lay hidden in this part of the jungle. Hardly a wall remained standing. After the fall of Zeiglon, the earthquakes had dropped a portion of the continent into the sea and raised the land upward, forming the escarpment and destroying every city and village from there to Zeiglon. As Azimuth returned to human form, Ralav and Ronli scouted the jungle ahead, returning a short while later to report that the immediate area was safe, and that they had heard river sounds to the south.

Celedant had spread out an old map on the ground and was conferring with Eldahir. He called the others to gather near him.

"This city must be the remains of Troyn, a small provincial town off the main trade route. If we head southeast, we should reach the remains of Zeiglon in a week or so."

Uneasy, Tarquin and Ress continued to scan the dense foliage that surrounded them.

"Aegir, see if you can detect any immediate danger," Tarquin said.

Celedant smiled. "Are you worried?"

Tarquin returned the smile and nodded. "Always. I find that it helps keep me alive."

The wizard turned to look down at the dwarvan cleric.

"Go ahead. I have to agree with him."

The cleric solemnly closed his eyes and chanted a prayer to his deity Dolgar. As he finished, he held out his arms and did a complete circle, encompassing the entire area. When he finished, his eyes snapped open, and he looked pale. Seeing the disturbed look on his fellow cleric's face, Hortus likewise called on Thierry's aid. The Abbot's senses screamed at him as he saw the vision that Aegir had seen.

When Hortus opened his eyes, he turned to Celedant with a grim expression.

"Me spell gives no direct information," the Abbot said as he motioned toward the forest, "but there is danger all about us. The evil chiefly emanates from the southeast. Yet all of these woods are in the shadow of dark forces. This land is in the grip of a most powerful evil. We must be wary."

"Morganna, Eldahir, and I will cast a spell of protection about us," Celedant said. "It will aid and alert us should danger approach."

As the wizard and two elves began the spell, the sudden appearance of the most beautiful bird they had ever seen broke their concentration. Had the spell been completed, they would have realized that its beauty hid an evil heart, festering with cruelty and malevolence so devious that most of its prey never realized their danger until it was too late.

Chapter Thirty-Six

Dargan was sent west by Grimilzor, and he now stood at one of the boulders that overlooked the stone dam. Behind a small hill, 500 elves and 1000 dwarves waited to flood across the dam and take the other side. Still more soldiers waited if needed.

Fifty elves entered the lake that the Mirowmir dam had created and floated on the quiet water toward the structure that raised and lowered the flow of water through the dam. It was a small building, hardly defensible. The orcs seeing that same weakness had constructed a haphazard wall some thirty feet further down the dam towards the Dwarvan lines.

Dargan watched as the elves floated to the wall of the dam that was rough from years of the rise and fall of water. The elven soldiers found ample purchase and climbed the upward until all soldiers were at the crenulated top of the dam.

Dargan hadn't seen a signal to move, but the elves were over the wall on top of the dam in an instant, taking the small control house without any noise. When one of the elves vaulted the wall and landed on a sleeping orc's foot, alerting the enemy of their presence, a brisk fight broke out. There were twenty orcs bedded down on the bridge, and as the fifty elves attacked, swords clashed and battle cries echoed off the surface of the lake.

As the fight began, a column of dwarves rushed up to the bridge, running pell-mell towards the battle. They pushed through the wall and were soon fighting alongside the elves.

Eager to join the fray, Dargan didn't consciously consider his actions, but he soon found himself jumping from his vantage point to join the second company of dwarves. As he pushed ahead, sweat-soaked cursing dwarves crushed against him. There was hardly enough room on the dam for four people to walk abreast. At last, the pushing slowed as he stepped through the remaining pieces of the orcan defenses. Their pace increased to a run.

The first wave of dwarves darted across the dam while elven archers followed. The result was brutal. The orcs released a wave of arrows that shot out of the night and embedded in the dwarves in the front of the charge, cutting them down. Several died outright, but many more were wounded. It was their mission to reach the other end so those behind continued at a run with their shields held before them. A second massive arrow attack rained down, bouncing off the shields, forcing the orcs to concentrate on individuals. Still, the lead company of dwarves suffered from the orcs' arrows. Their rush slowed as more fell to the side wounded or toppled dead from the dam's wall.

The second wave of dwarves, including Dargan, caught up with them and as planned if the first wave did not make it across the bridge, they now passed through, offering the orcs an excellent target, but the elven bowmen were now in position, and they unleashed their arrows. Their excellent eyesight could see the orcs on the far side, and their arrows reached for every bowman they saw, ending the dwarvan slaughter. For every orc that shot an arrow, the unerring elvish archers struck down five more.

On the dam, the dwarves had both sections intermingled with a third section of men behind, reaching the end of the dam. Dargan realized he was just a few dwarves from the front row. The defenders had expected most attacks to come from the landward sides or possibly rafts. At the dam's entrance was a half-moon dirt embankment. Dwarves and men flowed around it into the midst of the orcish camp.

Dargan made a quick decision when he saw the attackers sprinting around the redoubt and enemy archers that were shooting into the masses. He didn't know or care if any dwarves followed as he ran straight up the dirt fortification. An orc notched an arrow, aiming it straight at his chest, but he kept on. He laughed at the archer's surprised look as an elven arrow entered the orc's right eye. The orc fell backwards off a platform filled with archers unwilling to give up. Dargan sensed there were dwarves behind him, which gave him heart as he reached the top.

He kicked dirt in the face of the first orc to challenge him and then jumped into the mass of orcan defenders. His body twirled with an axe in his right hand

and a sword in his left. Unknown to him, several enemies died as his weapons cleared a space for him to land, where he found himself surrounded by the foul-smelling orcs. His axe chopped arms and legs while its pointed top pierced armor and faces. Covered in blood, the sword rose and fell like a well-oiled machine. Then the orcs that had been watching the contest turned and tried to jump for safety.

Dargan looked around at the dead and wounded orcs and seven dwarves that remained standing, and nodded approval. He pulled a large flask and offered it to his cohorts. Unexpectedly, he struck backwards, finishing a wounded orc that was about to strike at them.

Smiling pleasantly as the flask returned to him, he said, "Well fought, me friends."

With that, he and the seven dwarves jumped into the melee that the center grounds of the fortress had become. The whole of the dam's walkway was crammed with dwarves, elves, and men rushing to aid their comrades engaged with the enemy. Among these attackers came clerics wearing armor who saw to the needs of the wounded. Inside the fortifications, a swarm of fighting mingled all groups. More dwarves from the reserves crossed the dam. Soon, major fighting inside the camp slowed, but along the battlements, it continued with wild ferocity. The orcs had nowhere to go, and relief was miles to the east.

Of necessity, the orcs began jumping off the walls, and those that could run headed for the safety of the forest. Dargan stood on the battlement shaking his head. The orcs had dropped most of their weapons and armor as they fled west. It was a complete rout.

With the area cleared, the attacking forces sent their engineers to survey the orcan defenses. Accordingly, they reported to Dargan that all the defenses needed repairing.

Several companies of dwarves ran in single file to begin fortifying the south end of the dam, while a line of stretchers headed north to a small compound where the differing sects of clerics had gathered to tend the wounded. The elves ordered to hold the dam took control of the southern end and protected those working on a proper defensive fortress that covered all approaches to the dam.

After rendering the farther side defensibly sound, one thousand elves crossed the dam to patrol the land near and around the new fortification. Their job was to spot and waylay any columns of enemies coming to retake the dam and dispatch any wounded they might find. By the next day, Dargan saw that the defenses were much improved and enlarged. He was pleased that the new fort could hold several thousand soldiers with reinforcements.

Dargan wrote a precise recount of the battle along with the improvements made. The fact that the elves were patrolling unhindered was a promising sign. He also asked when General Grimilzor wanted to start the next phase of the plan.

The messenger had just departed when the first of the giants' boats and barges arrived from the banks of Lake Mirowmir. Their construction was shoddy, and two of the boats almost capsized from the weight of the four giants paddling them. The ten barges were faring little better. The orcs on the barges stood in two feet of water.

Dargan had just reached the roof of the small house that held the dam's machines when he heard the loud twangs of the ballista. Two four-foot-long metal shafts sped out. The first struck a giant through the shoulder. His huge right hand grabbed the gunnels, spilling the giants and their paddlers out of the boat. The other shaft overshot the second boat but cut a bloody swath through the middle of an overcrowded barge. The motion of the orcs on that barge rocked back and forth before tipping upright.

The dwarves rewound the ballista tight while the engineers operating the weapons calculated two more shots at range, hoping to get a good angle once the boat and barges were against the dam. The loud twang was like a shock wave as the huge bolts shot outward. Dargan watched one bolt strike a giant through the thigh, pinning the behemoth to the wooden seat. Another barge took the impact of the ballista, striking the rear, spilling its occupants over the end as their weight upset the raft.

Elven bowmen stood fast, unleashing countless arrows into the boats and barges. The first boat grappled near the dam's housing as a giant used a hand to pull himself up and over the crenellation. Then a ballista bolt struck his head and exploded. The headless corpse tumbled into the small lake. The other giant dragged his body over the collapsing wall, grasping his leg. He waved a white handkerchief as large as a flag, which brought a cleric running to his side.

From every direction, the enemy threw grappling hooks to attach to the dam. The dwarves were impressed that the hooks were made of chain. There was no cutting through those, and soon the first orc appeared. An arrow dispatched it, sending the creature screaming over the edge of the wall. Dwarves and men exchanged places with the elves and waited for the remaining orcs.

The enemy continued to attack the dam because they did not think their barges would make it back to shore. Quick as possible, they climbed up the grappling line. Arrows peppered the first to reach the top, throwing them back into the lake. Yet they kept coming, and soon most orcs were at the top, screaming war cries as they were speared or shot by the remaining elves that had not joined the fray.

The vast numbers of enemy fell, jumped, or were pushed into the boiling mass of fighting men, dwarves, and elves that manned the parapet of the dam. No quarter was given to the combatants as they were shoved over both sides of the dam. Within the fighting, the defenders used shields to block swords and axes, leaving the attackers open to a frontal killing blow.

It was chaos, enemies fighting back-to-back without realizing it. Weapons and shields were broken, and the splintered wood used to bloody effect on the attacker. Some orcs dropped dead as the remaining elves picked out officers or the most dangerous foes. Elven bowmen suffered tremendously as they stood openly on the back of the dam. Although some would not die, their wounds were grievous, and they would suffer quite a bit until healed.

Before long, so many dead and wounded crowded the dam's small top that the warriors had trouble attacking each other. The lucky ones dragged themselves to the sides. There were small pockets of orcs all along the bridge, and still more came. Starting at the western side, bowmen marched forth and struck down each island of resistance. When they reached the watershed, the wounded giant sat with splinted leg, several spears, and bloody bandaged wounds in deep conversation with a dwarf.

The giant waved the ally leader over, but Dargan was hesitant until he saw that someone had tied the giant's hands.

The giant spoke quietly. "Master Dargan, if you will offer me sanctuary, I will order the orcs to stop fighting."

To prevent further death and injury, Dargan said, "Granted."

Humans and dwarves covered their ears when the giant shouted at the top of his lungs.

"Listen, my orcan warriors. Battle is lost; certain death awaits you. Dwarvan leader give us freedom." There were snarls among some orcan captains, but he continued. "Keep one weapon and go down western trail. Kill one defender and ten orcs die. Go now! Those that stay, let mates pass in peace."

The giant's speech must have made sense to the doomed orcs as the clang of weapons sounded along the top of the dam. A solemn line of their kind marched away from the dam. Clerics attended to those that needed medical attention, including the dam's defenders.

Piling the dead to one side and arranging the wounded along the other side created a lane in the center of the dam. Archers and the troops of clerics carrying stretchers rushed through this opening.

An hour and a half later, a panting page trotted across the dam, doing his best to avoid the pools of blood that caused bile to rise in his throat as he looked for Dargan. When he reached the newly conquered fortress, he stopped a dwarf busily chiseling a stone.

"Where is Lord Dargan?"

The dwarf pointed to the tallest tower. "Last I saw; the red-bearded devil was pacing that tower."

The mason lowered his head and began reshaping the stone. The page rounded the redoubt and with a look, everything he had eaten came spewing from his mouth. Several dwarves called to him, but one veteran yelled above the other, "Don't worry, lad. Ye'll get used to it."

Before him was a ten-foot high mound of dead orcs in a hastily dug hole. Several dwarves poured oil over the bodies and set it alight. Looking away, the lad noticed an endless line of covered stretchers that bore the bodies of dwarves, elves, and men. Young novices of various dwarvan gods carried the injured back across the dam to areas where healers worked their magic.

Then the courier sighted Dargan sitting on the wall staring out at the forest and valley. The new arrival made his way past struggling dwarves and men carting cut stone to shore up the walls. He climbed the stairs and made his way to the side of the famous attendant to Lord Grimilzor.

The dwarf had red-rimmed eyes with a deep sense of loss etched in his face. He stretched out his hand, but said nothing.

Handing him the scroll, the runner waited as Dargan read the missive. When Dargan looked up, he tentatively asked, "Do you need to reply, sir?"

"Tell his lordship it will begin soon."

As Dargan watched the improvements being made to the defenses of the dam, he reflected on the fact that Lord Grimilzor's plan had failed.

The entire plan was based on the idea that the orcs would attack eastward, leaving the dam isolated. In actuality, the orcs had shifted some battalions to face west and moved more units between the river and the mountains, believing the dwarves would use the eastern position to launch their attack.

Never one to let opportunity slip, Lord Grimilzor had his forces build fortifications near the fords and bridges. The one real interest the enemy showed was in moving a large contingent of horse-borne troops and sending battalions of orcs to block the dwarves should they attempt an attack that way.

The general's aid followed the courier to the spillway house that controlled water levels. Five grease- and oil-covered dwarvan engineers worked on the controls, ensuring proper function. Dargan looked over the levers, dials, and chains that disappeared through holes in the stone building.

Glancing at the head engineer, the cleanest of the five, Dargan asked, "Will it work?"

"It's suffered from years of non-use," the engineer replied. "So the lads and I went over it top to bottom. We've added fresh oil and grease, and examined the dials and levers, and all appear to work. The true test will be when we use it."

Dargan placed his axe and sword against the stone wall. "Let's give her a try. Lower it five feet." He asked, "Do any dials show how far the blocking stone moves or how much water flows through?"

The head engineer shrugged, "We can watch."

He and three dwarves went to a windless and removed the wood block holding it. They soon felt the immense pressure the windless held, and Dargan and the other dwarf joined to help. As they pushed, the chain played out, and one of the dials inched downward. At about ten feet, they chocked it again, sweating profusely.

The head engineer and Dargan examined the dials. One showed how low the block had descended, but the meaning of several other dials mystified them.

Dargan caught the attention of an elf scanning the area with his bow. "Noble elf," he asked kindly, "we will need this section well-guarded. I will send a company of dwarves to guard this area."

The elf nodded and raced off to the south side of the dam to fetch his brethren. He also asked one of the engineers to go to the east side to find a company of men. Dargan knew that this would yet be another key to saving Southgard. A moment later, he spotted a signal from the highest tower of the reconstructed orcish forts. He sprinted, red beard flapping behind as he pushed his legs ever faster. As he ran, he realized that he was breathing a bit heavier after climbing the stairs than he would have as a youth.

An elf motioned him to the parapet of the tower, saying, "The orcs grow impatient."

Dargan looked over the devastated forest that had once grown up around the fort. The orcs had used timber for fortifications, cutting down every usable tree within three hundred paces around the fort.

Dargan glanced at the elf. "Their plan failed. Instead of attacking from the south, we came by way of the dam."

With a haughty look, the elf looked down at the dwarf. "Watch and see what happens to incompetents."

Dargan wasn't sure if the elf was including the dwarves in that statement. He could see the orcs lining up in the forest for an attack. Then it happened: hundreds of horns sounded from the woods and the battle cries of the orcs roared between the blasts.

The first wave, numbering over a thousand orcs, charged and fell to the arrows of elven archers. The lives of fifty comrades paid for every foot gained. The second wave poured out carrying ladders, and again, a hail of arrows fell on them. Soon, human archers joined in the slaughter.

The orc commander had enough. He ordered two thousand of his best fighters to charge into the hailstorm of death. The first two lines faltered close to a small stream that cut the field in half near the fort. The fresh troops dragged their cowering comrades out of the way and continued attacking. When several ladders made it to the wall, an elven horn was blown, and a round of fire arrows covered in tar and oil shot into the stream where they flared to life, trapping most of the orcs between the wall and stream.

The arrows did not stop, and in fact, several loads of extra arrows arrived just then. The enemy forgot the ladders as more and more fell. Many orcs threw away their arms, but age-old hatred did not spare them. Dargan had seen many battles, but never one so one-sided. Orcs were heaped atop one another, the wounded killed where they lay. Archers dispatched those lucky enough to jump the creek.

The better part of ten thousand orcs lay dead or dying. Dargan turned his back to the sight as the defenders jumped from the wall to finish off the wounded. He eased down the steps in a daze, thinking of the slaughter. When he reached the dam's control house, he found the same five dwarvan engineers still fussing over the mechanics of the machine.

They looked up expectantly when he ordered, "Block the spillway to the top."

The dwarves went to work with the gears, and a second stone slab slid into place. A third followed, and the water began to rise.

The dam rose high above the valley floor to trap the seasonal snowmelt in a lake for the rich farms that dotted the landscape. Most of those beautiful farms now lay in ruins, many burned to ashes. The dam would stop the annual melt, and according to the amount of water, could be raised and lowered by the spillway's stone gates.

Now, Dargan ordered the stone blocks placed at the highest level. Water from streams and river rushed to the dam, hitting the immovable wall. With nowhere to go, it began flowing backwards into the valley. The lake was rising steadily. Since the ground on the northern side of the valley was higher, the water spread through the churned earth in the south where most of the best farms were located.

As he watched, Melgor grew frustrated. King Jordic would listen to his reports and wave him away haltingly, saying, "Dwarvan city fall, then we deal with others."

Having flown so much over the past several days on his mount, Melgor had grown a little fond of the chimera. He looked over the valley, absently stroking one of the beast's ribs, drawn to the eastern valley that led to Southgard's plains. In order for the campaign to work, the area had to be captured. Otherwise, Parthian lancers and men from the eastern city-states would charge down the valley and wreak havoc with the unorganized besieging forces. Grimilzor could also seize lands north of the river, separating Jordic's army. Melgor was no fool. The besieging host was huge. Nevertheless, most were ill trained and unprepared for the battle-hardened dwarves Grimilzor had at his command.

The dwarves would have to overcome two deep rivers and several streams, though the larger human horses could wade through them. Grimilzor could mount an attack across the river, while the orcs positioned along the banks would do their best to stymie any invasion. Melgor had placed these notions into the orc chieftains' plans, and they were already in motion along the river when battle horns sounded up and down the dwarvan defensive lines. When word reached Melgor that the dam had fallen to the dwarvan army, he was furious. The report also confirmed that a sizable force of elves had accompanied them. The giant's King shrugged it off and ordered one of his followers to gather a force and dislodge the enemy from the dam.

Melgor struggled with different thoughts. The army was huge and the siege was going well, but the dwarves now occupied a sizable amount of land in the east and west, almost surrounding the besiegers. It would come down to how prudently the King used his forces, and that did not bode well. The King drunkenly ordered a counterattack.

Melgor predicted from the start that it would fail. The King ordered the orc commanders out without any purpose other than to face the enemy. The lieutenants liked the flowing wine and showed little in the way of logical judgment.

Jordic's military strategy was brute force, keeping his own people in reserve. Now the warlock's misgivings were unfolding in the valley of Southgard. There was one last option Melgor could try, but if it failed, he would leave for good, getting as far away from Taza as he could. Sellis had been a novice when he tried to escape Taza. He had used magic, leaving a trail that the vampire could easily follow. Melgor's escape would be by horseback, using small spells and great patience. If he planned it right, Taza would think he had died during the attack and forget him forever.

It was pitch black in the subterranean cavern. A small fire kept him warm as he waited. Three huge orc captains appeared out of the darkness and settled around the fire. The giants' army had just secured the valley to the east and west, so Melgor's plan just might work. If it went well, he would be a genius. If it failed, his involvement would be unknown, with the orcs taking the blame. Vakar, Ouhgan, and Dudagog were the orc captains he had weeded out from a limited number of potential candidates. They were actually sane, keeping their minds on the battlefield and showing some concern for their soldiers. This was unique for an orcish army and just what Melgor needed.

The orcs wore an assortment of armor scavenged from countless battles, and as they settled around the campfire, Melgor passed around some of his best wine, along with three heavy pouches that jingled. He looked each orc in the eye as he spoke.

"When they have sufficient numbers, the dwarves will use the dam to flood the valley floor and attack. Holding the dam gives them the upper hand, which Jordic does not understand. The dwarvan city guarding the south has never fallen. They will rush from the eastern fortifications and push Jordic back across the river. Joined by additional city defenders, the giants' army will be driven from the valley."

Melgor reasoned that the battle would be bloody, but the dwarves had shown that they would do whatever necessary when they had taken back Brackus. He could not imagine what they would do to protect their southernmost city.

The warlock handed out maps to each of the commanders, the best that orcdom could offer. He had spent more gold on these three and their soldiers than on any others of the smelly, lice-ridden race. They and their soldiers wore the best armor and weapons that either money could buy or they could steal.

The plan was difficult. Three groups of orcs would have to be in place at the exact moment. To facilitate this, Melgor provided three small discs. He explained they acted like an hourglass powered by gravity and sand. The discs would move backward, showing how much time they had to get into position.

One of the orcs nodded. "We follow what you say. Three bands attack the bearded ones at same time. This can be done, or I kill slow ones."

The others agreed. Melgor spread open a larger map of the area and went over what would transpire in the coming days. He pointed to the dam. "This is critical. The dwarves hold both the large southern fortress and the smaller northern fort that surround and protect the dam and its approaches. Timing is everything. Your soldiers must be in position as soon as the battle is fully engaged in the valley. Wait while the battle rages before springing your trap. "

Melgor trusted their battle shrewdness, but the small timepieces were not durable and could be broken, and in the rough hands of an orc, who could be certain how well they would hold up. He pointed to the smaller northern fort guarding that side of the dam.

"Vakar's thousand soldiers will attack the northern fort near the dam. The dwarves and elves built it in a hurry. Dwarves have seized the dam and its southern fortress, and they still hold them. Once the battle becomes a rout, many defeated dwarves will try to reach the safety of the eastern fort. That is why it is critical for you to seize the smaller northern fortress. Don't worry about dwarves. If they get close enough, pepper them with arrows, but under no circumstance are your forces to leave the fort once you have control of it. The dam is your responsibility. Hold that side, and you will block the larger garrison from the southern fortress from linking with the main dwarvan attack. Your lads will have enough bodies to loot afterward."

The warlock looked at the second orc, Ouhgan, who was squinty-eyed and did not have much of a chin. Melgor watched in disgust as two fleas crisscrossed the orc's forehead.

"Ouhgan, you are the commander of the main force of ten thousand. Your army will come through a hidden path near the western end of the dwarvan defensive wall. After the dwarves commit to the attack, you will fall on the dwarves from behind." Melgor looked closely at the captain. "Attack hard and they will break. Taza has dark allies to assure this. After that, herd them toward Southgard."

He pointed to the last orc. "Dudagog, you will come from the direction of

Hywel's Way down the mountain and hill paths. When you reach their camp, divide your forces, half going west and half, east. Kill anyone left behind from the attack. Remember, the fall of the northern fort will be the signal for Ouhgan's mass attack into the dwarvan rearguard and should come as a complete surprise to most of your enemies. While this is going on, the attack from Hywel's Way will take place. Do you understand?"

The orc captains smiled ruthlessly, nodding with pleasure at the plan.

Melgor's intent was to drive the dwarves to Southgard. The dwarves would have no other safe route except for the valley on the south side of the city. Once surrounded, the dwarves would swarm to the safety of the city, where they could be trapped and destroyed.

Chapter Thirty-Seven

Ress and Morganna had never seen such a beautiful bird. As they moved closer, their hands outstretched, the animal did not flinch. It came to them, craning its neck for attention. The women reached out, stroking it, and the bird cooed in pleasure, its feathers rippling like water across its body to create a mesmerizing effect. The bird attached itself to the company, weaving in and out of their legs, pausing often to let each member reach down and pat its silky coat.

Cutting through the dense tropical forest, Botreg sweated profusely as he swung his blade, chopping through the underbrush.

I should have remained an assassin. Joining the Borderers was the worst mistake of my life.

He did not know where these thoughts were coming from and tried to reason them through, but whenever he did, the negative feelings rose higher and stronger, driving back the voice of reason.

The stuffiness and heat of the forest was stifling, and his mood suffered. Tarquin had volunteered him for every dangerous mission they had undertaken, and now this fiasco. His face flushed red, and he shouted at his friend. "This is what I get for joining you on this crazed adventure." He stomped to the rear of the company, practically shoving Ralav over.

Tarquin was feeling irritable, and when Botreg yelled at him, he almost exploded. In fact, his head was hurting so much he was afraid it might explode. He rolled his eyes, muttering, "Useless dwarf," under his breath as he took the front position and began hacking at the undergrowth.

Celedant looked suspiciously at Hortus and Baldo who traded barbs, and he wondered what was manipulating his friends. The monk's spells had shown them intense evil lurking all around the dense jungle, and the wizard knew that somewhere, hidden in the tangle of vines and ferns, lurked an unknown presence bent on driving the party apart and creating discord.

The jovial monk Hority started rubbing at his robes. "These plants are soiling me clothes."

This brought an uneasy laugh from most of the group. Their response angered him, and the sinewy dwarf turned on the first person he saw, which was Ress.

"Ye should have sought out better healers," he snapped.

He whipped around, disappearing toward the front of the company. Having observed this scene, Celedant moved next to Ress and laid a hand on her arm to keep her spear from following the dwarf. She jerked around and stared at him, her angry expression troubling.

"Something is amiss," Celedant told her, keeping his voice low. "Think about what just happened. Did it deserve such an exaggerated response?"

Ress all but snapped back a reply, but his words entered her psyche like a soothing balm, and she blushed with embarrassment. "You're right. I am not the only one affected."

"Something in this forest is causing it. I have to find out and stop it before we're all at each other's throats."

As he spoke, Morganna and Eldahir were walking together. Stepping aside to avoid tripping over a root, Eldahir brushed against her. She spun, her sword half-drawn.

"I warn you not to touch me again."

Eldahir stared at her. "As if I would sully myself by touching a dark one," he replied.

It took both Celedant and Hortus's intervention to prevent an all-out duel in the stifling forest. After separating the two elves, Celedant extended his senses in search of the cause.

Ronli and her Uncle Ralav marched in silence behind Tarquin as he cut a path for the company. Ralav ranted on about how it was his job to lead the company through the forest, not some zeffan just out of the cradle.

Ronli looked over at her uncle and snarled, "Ye think him young? What about me? Am I not just out of the cradle and a child that ye can control? I'll have ye know that this is the last time I will take orders from ye, ye senile old orc."

The older dwarf swatted her on the back of the head, sending her to her knees. She kicked out, tripping her uncle. This time, Tarquin stepped between the angry dwarves until they simmered down and with grim faces resumed the march.

"What the matter with you two?" he asked angrily. "For that matter, what is wrong with all of you? You're snapping at each other for no reason with anger in your eyes and murder in your hearts!"

Celedant called the company to a halt and uttered a spell. Evil blanketed the forest like a bank of clouds. More importantly, a red glowing aura emanated from the beautiful bird, and as he focused on it, he sensed malice and evil flowing from it in waves. Instead of beautiful plumage, the wizard saw through its illusion to the darkness that covered its feathers. Trying not to startle the beast, he cautiously raised his staff and in an instant of understanding, the wizard locked eyes with the bird.

In that moment, the bird knew that feeding off the fears and doubts of the group was over. It spread its wings and pushed off the ground, going airborne. Celedant was quicker. A green bolt of energy lashed from his staff, Forestae, hitting the bird in mid-flight and sending it into a tailspin that propelled its body through the tree limbs, slamming it into the massive tree trunk. Colorful feathers floated downward, turning oily black along with those still clinging to the once-beautiful bird, revealing its true nature.

As the others watched what had happened, they turned in anger to Celedant and raised their weapons, but as soon as the bird died, anger, despair, and gloom lifted from them, and their eyes opened wide with shock over what they had been about to do.

Tarquin called to his dwarvan trackers. "Ralav, Ronli - find us a path to the southeast."

The dwarves smiled before plunging into the jungle. The rest formed a single line and followed, with Morganna and Eldahir bringing up the rear. The scouts had to cut their way through most of the undergrowth. They found no game trails, but later reached a shallow stream that looped out of the jungle and flowed in the direction they needed to go. Ralav waded into the water, and the others followed. The water was dark, but after performing a cleansing spell, Celedant pronounced it fit to drink.

They made quick time for a while. Small animal noises and chirping insects filled their ears until the constant droning began to wear on everyone's nerves. As nightfall came, the stream took a westerly turn. Celedant called a halt, and they set about hacking out a campsite beside the water.

For the dwarves and Tarquin, the jungle was far different from the cold rocky Mordolwyn Mountains. On the escarpment, the land was damp and teeming with strange insect life that crawled and flitted about on tiny wings.

"What are these strange insects that look like they have a torch in their exterior?" Ronli asked.

"Lightning bugs," Celedant grinned. "They thrive in the warm, temperate climate of the jungle. Most of the time, they're harmless." Seeing his companions' questioning gazes, he added, "Just don't try to trap them."

"Why would anyone want to do that?" Ress asked.

"A long time ago, a human boy captured several and imprisoned them in a sack," Celedant said.

Azimuth picked up the story. "Celedant and I were off on our own youthful adventures and were visiting Troyn at the time. The boy was fascinated by the way the bugs flashed their lights on and off, and he wanted to see if they could stay lit longer. I think he wanted to use them as a light source."

"Did they attack the lad when he tried to trap them?" Ralav asked.

"Not at first," Azimuth replied. "But once he had several in his sack, they began buzzing loudly. He opened the sack to peek inside, without letting any escape, and before anyone realized what was happening, the bugs emitted tiny electrical shocks. The boy might not have noticed the tiny jolt from one or two bugs, but he had captured twenty. Their combined power was enough to shock the boy pretty badly. He squealed like a pig and dropped the sack, allowing the angry insects to escape into the jungle."

"Serves him right," Ronli said.

"I don't believe he ever bothered the lightning bugs again," Azimuth chuckled.

Ralav and Aegir fretted over the campfire until they had a smoky blaze going. Botreg stayed near the edge of the campsite exercising, trying to work out the aches and pains from the long hike. After dining on rabbit stew, Celedant and Eldahir circled the camp with protective enchantments, and everyone settled in for a night's rest.

Chapter Thirty-Eight

The first enemy to notice the rising water was an orc, sent to fill water skins. It squatted down at the edge of Lake Mirowmir and lowered the first into the water. As it slowly filled, he realized that the water was now flowing around his boots and leaking into them. Startled, he slipped in the thick, muddy soil as he looked around and saw the water rising at an alarming rate. He spotted the dam and realized what the dwarves had done. Dropping the water skins in panic, the orc ran back to camp, yelling the news. Several hours later, word of the dwarvan dam reached King Jordic's council and Melgor.

"Good! Water rise high. Orcs smell better now!" the King laughed.

The other members of the council joined in his merriment, but Melgor shook his head.

Stupid oafs have no idea what this will do to their campaign. He slipped out of the massive tent, found his mount, and headed to the battlefield. The giants' forces had not organized their camps. Instead, they were spread helter-skelter about the area. As he crested a small hill, what he saw made him bring his chimera to a sudden stop.

Thousands of orcs that had been camped close to the dam were streaming toward him. Melgor was awed. The once serene river had crested its bank and was now a vast lake that submerged nearby trees halfway up their trunks. Several orcs precariously hung onto the topmost branches, bending them closer to the rising water. Turning, Melgor saw a sight that made his stomach lurch. The large southern bridge was almost totally under water, and the valley was still filling. Some 10,000 orcs and giants had died during the assault against the dam's fortifications. Their sacrifice had been in vain.

The orcish commanders acted without word from the giant's King, marching troops across the bridges to the north where the ground was higher. Still more orcs were sent up the eastern valley. It was then that Melgor sensed rather than felt that his steed was standing in mud.

He looked down to see the plowed field turning into a morass of slime. Melgor urged the chimera into the air and using the amulet he had received from Lord Taza, he called to him across the miles of mountains and seas. "My Lord Taza, hear me."

Taza answered Melgor's plea. "I see the dire problems that have befallen you. Find able-minded orcs and set up a defense along the river. Remember - I have a surprise for General Grimilzor."

The next day after he broke his fast, Prince Grimilzor looked out across the land and noticed something odd. The trees to the south had water lapping at their roots, and the largest bridge had water up to the roadway. As he watched, it overflowed the road, creating a muddy pool.

He surmised the dam had caused the expanding lake. The first bridge was under water, and the rising lake threatened the next bridge. Even better, he noted with a laugh, was the massive retreat of the orcs from the southern lands near the bridge. The sheer number of the orcan army was proving to be its downfall. The orcs were in complete disarray.

Meanwhile, Dargan watched as Lake Mirowmir continued spreading from the dam. Orcs were bunched together in groups on the east, north, and south side of the river near Southgard. A proper siege had turned into utter turmoil. As the sun rose, Grimilzor began the attack. His portion of the army drove down from the walls of the valley. Alongside the lake, the northern army attacked. Dargan led the force as it headed east into the forest where flooding was minimal.

Horns blew from the north to the walls of the dam. Men, dwarves, and elves, tired of the long wait, gleefully donned weapons and armor, and lined up on the wall, ladders already in place. This was pleasing to their commander, Prince Thomas of the City States. When the company was ready, they descended the ladders and reformed on the ground. The attack was ready to begin. Almost without command, the army was at the entrance of the small valley, marching on the softer plowed ground, making their footing treacherous.

The lads behind him let out a huzzah as they continued their slow advance. Some units in the allied army charged where their commanders were supposed to hold an even line. Prince Thomas knew they would be too weary after that long run to fight properly when they reached the enemy. Luckily, the two companies to his right and left, one a human contingent and the other dwarves, continued marching, keeping a straight line with Prince Thomas' men.

They covered the distance to the orcish battle line and then fighting erupted. The orcs howled as they attacked Prince Thomas' soldiers. He had been to the beaches three times in his life. This charge reminded him of a rumbling surf charging the shore. The orcs slammed into the advancing allies. Prince Thomas cut through two of the faster orcs, and then came the onslaught.

The attack was like a wave on the ocean sweeping down from the east. In addition, the allied army spilled forth from the defensive works, charging south toward the disorganized orcish army. Dargan's troops met little resistance other than the mud for a few hundred paces until an orcan arrow struck one of them down. The orcs gathered in front of their defensive works that was filling with water. Dwarves loosed a barrage of arrows in response and charged the position with shields held high.

All along the line, the allies struck in force, trapping many orcs without their commanders. The enemy retreated south, further mixing the orcish lines. Behind the orcs, an assortment of dwarves and men crashed in a cacophony of steel on amour or weapons. In places, the line gave with little effort, but where a strong orcan leader held his soldiers together, the orcs put up a fight. They were trained warriors, thanks to the constant fighting in the west. Their war horns blew, and the enemy counterattacked.

CHAPTER THIRTY-NINE

Tarquin, Hortus, Azimuth, and Celedant were closeted together out of hearing by the others.

"As night has fallen, the spell I cast is warning that our danger is growing," the Abbot said, indicating the area around them. "Whatever haunts these regions must do so by the light of the moon."

"I have increased the wards around our camp as we head toward Zeiglon," Celedant said. "Even though we do not know what we will face there, I sense great evil lurking within its boundaries. The closer we get to Zeiglon, the stronger the feeling grows."

"If we come to a decent-sized clearing," Azimuth said, "I'll scout the area between here and Zeiglon. Unfortunately, as long as we are in dense growth, there is no room to change to my dragon form. I can range ahead faster as a wolf than our trackers to give us a little more warning, but that's about it."

"Any idea of what might be out there?" Tarquin asked the Abbot.

The dwarf shook his head. "The spell warns of danger. If we are attacked, I can cast another to gain information on the nature of the creature, but by then, the battle will be joined."

"I'll set two guards on watch within the perimeter of Celedant's wards," Tarquin said. "Aside from that, we'll have to wait and see."

That night after a tasteless dinner amid the humidity and condensation of the jungle, the company gathered close to the campfire, hoping that its circle of light would chase away the dark gloom that had descended on them with the coming of night. Most settled down with weapons near at hand on their bedrolls, while Hortus and Celedant sat smoking their pipes. Hority lay on his blanket, occasionally swatting at flying insects.

Just when the two smokers thought all were asleep, Morganna raised up on her elbows.

"Celedant, how does a rainforest sit above a desert?"

The wizard pondered the question before replying. "It seems that when the quakes hit, after the struggle over the staff of Adaman, this portion of the continent was lifted upward a mile or so, while the desert dropped almost the same distance. The ground here slopes to the south, and so far, the stream that we have traveled heads in that direction. For some reason, the escarpment retains most of the moisture, keeping rain from dropping over the desert. Why it happens that way remains a mystery."

Hority was about to add something when a shrill wail sounded to the south of camp. As one, the company jumped to their feet, hands going to their weapons. The scream ended abruptly, answered a moment later by another wail further west. The night air continued to echo each new wail, but whatever was making those eerie sounds did not appear to be coming closer to the camp. At some point, the companions dropped off into an uneasy sleep as Eldahir and Aegir took their turn standing guard.

Although few of the company enjoyed uninterrupted sleep, the night passed without further incident. Most were awakened at least once as the strange wails continued periodically. The band started their journey shortly after sunup. Azimuth became a wolf and scouted ahead, while Ralav and Ronli led the rest, picking their way through dense brush and trees with trunks so thick that three grown men could have hidden behind one. At times, Ronli and Ralav happened upon small game trails and made good time, but as the trails petered out, they needed to cut a path once more through thicker foliage. At noon, they came upon a small stream. Ronli drew abreast of it, and what she saw made her draw up short.

Hair plastered to her head from the humidity, she stopped as the undergrowth parted, revealing the end of the stream. The water did not cause her to stop, but the odd footprint near the bank did. She motioned the others to a halt and called to Tarquin. He studied the print from the opposite bank. It was three-toed and larger than a human footprint, with taloned claws on each toe and a dewclaw in back. It looked like the print of a giant lizard.

Tarquin scanned the area and touched Ronli on the shoulder. "Take Ralav and follow the tracks to determine their direction."

She and the old tracker moved and over the stream into the woods beyond. The others soon joined Tarquin and studied the tracks. Whatever they belonged to, the creature had come from upstream before entering the jungle. As Celedant examined the footprints, Ralav returned to report that the tracks continued southeast.

Eldahir squatted beside the wizard and pointed to the footprints, saying, "I've seen similar tracks in the great swamp. Yet, these are a bit different."

Hortus overheard and arched an eyebrow. "Lizard men would find this environment pleasant."

"These tracks are similar to the creatures called the Aloi," Morganna agreed. "My people call them the Echlairias, which translates to something similar to snake men. I have battled their kind in the deep tunnels that run to the swamp."

Tarquin shrugged. "We can't be afraid of a set of tracks. Let's get moving."

They made good time as they progressed further east. The lizard man had left the stream and was following a larger game trail, which made traveling easy for a change. As evening approached, Ronli found a small clearing off the path, and they camped for the night. Celedant once more set wards about the camp, and they roasted several rabbits that Eldahir had shot during the day's journey. They could not find any fresh vegetables and had to make do with the dried ones they carried with them.

As the moon rose and midnight approached, Botreg paced back and forth, trying to keep awake, while Ralav sat with his back against a tree, sewing the newest rent in his pant leg until a loud crash startled everyone awake. Ralav fumbled about, trying to pull on his leather britches as several more sounds tore through the air.

Celedant glanced at Eldahir. "Someone is using sorcery."

He disabled the wards and led the others toward the noise now mixed with cries that sounded like screams for help. Moving fast, they arrived on the outskirts of a small village. What they saw was unbelievable.

Tarquin knelt next to Celedant. "The Aloi seem hard pressed to defend themselves against the sorcery of whatever is riding that flying creature. What should we do?"

"That creature is a draven," Celedant replied. "Azimuth and I battled a few a while back. They resemble a black and white manta ray with wings and are covered in rocky scales, have a long tail spiked with thick protrusions like a mace, and a head that looks like a neckless extension of its body."

At that moment the draven dove again and this time the creature riding its back sent a stream of hot purple liquid that struck a wall of the village, obliterating a ten-foot portion in its blast and setting three buildings ablaze. Celedant decided to act, but before he could step into the clearing, Azimuth moved up beside him.

"Allow me," he said with a grin.

Running into the clearing, Azimuth transformed as he moved, and the mighty dragon was soon airborne. The sight of his golden body should have further frightened the Aloi, but as he soared upward, light from the blazing fires reflected off the scales of his massive body, and the lizard people cheered. As far as they knew, a golden being of light had come to chase away the dark terror that threatened them.

With two mighty downward strokes of his powerful wings, Azimuth closed the distance between himself and the beast of darkness. The dragon's mouth opened wide, shooting forth a blast of fire that seared the side of the monstrosity. The draven screamed and flew higher before turning, allowing its rider to respond with a purplish blast at the attacker. Azimuth evaded the attack. He dropped under the stream and shot ahead, spewing fire over the creature's right wing. The wing withered and collapsed, folding in mid-air. As the draven plummeted downward screaming in agony, Azimuth swung around and sent the next bout of fire at the animal's head. Its screams died just before crashing in the center of the village. Its rider jumped free as several more draven and their riders entered the battle. Azimuth was surrounded as he sent more flame bursts toward the nearest creature. He shot upward like a speeding arrow, leaving the enemy behind. Two followed, but the rest turned to the village and those below.

Celedant stepped from the trees and summoned his power, allowing it to build within his staff. Then, raising Forestae high, he directed it into the wake of another dark creature and a long, thin bolt of lightning soared skyward, ripping through its belly. Eldahir and Morganna moved up beside him, sending fire and lightning at the remaining beasts. As their mounts died, riders floated to the ground unharmed.

"What are those things?" the wizard asked as he got a good look at the wispy form.

"Shadow Lords," an unfamiliar voice replied.

Eldahir and the others joined Celedant, and they turned almost as one to look upon the tall green Aloi standing before them.

"Shadow Lords?" Celedant asked.

"They are the cursed remains of the Lords of Zeiglon," the Aloi replied. "Most of the time, they are as you see them, wispy skeletal forms in black robes, impossible to harm or kill, except with the most powerful magic. Whenever they fight or do anything that requires substance, their bodies solidify into the forms they wore in life. Their robes become armor, and their skeletal forms take on flesh grey, wrinkled with evil. In this form, they are vulnerable and can be destroyed, sending their spirits to the seven hells from which they were begotten."

"No wonder no one has ever returned from this accursed place," Eldahir said.

Celedant looked up and watched the dragon battle the remaining two draven and their shadow riders. He wanted to help, but he dared not interfere from the ground for fear of hitting Azimuth. Purple and reddish-yellow flames shot through the sky, creating a light show that might have been fascinating if his friend wasn't fighting for his life.

Celedant sent his thoughts skyward. *Azimuth! Drop lower, and I will meet you. Those are Shadow Lords on the dravens' backs. Let's even the odds.*

On my way! Azimuth thought back as he dove toward the ground. Since he was faster than his two pursuers, he covered the distance in relative safety, but combatants now filled the clearing in the village, so he could not land. He paused a moment, hovering eight feet above the ground. That was all the time Celedant needed to boost himself magically into the air and land on the dragon's back. As Azimuth shot upward, the wizard whispered a spell. A saddle appeared beneath him, and he securely lashed himself in place.

Tarquin pulled out his sword and charged across the open area toward the blazing wall. The others followed, while Eldahir grabbed his bow and sent a series of arrows flying at the enemy in rapid succession. He stood for a second and watched the first two strike home. One arrow hit the Shadow Lord in the head, but instead of falling, it turned to look at Tarquin who had outdistanced the dwarves. As the prince approached, he saw the face of the figure coming at him with the feathers of an elven arrow sticking out just above the left eye. He had never seen such evil in anyone's face, and he shuddered.

"It's time to return to the hell you came from!" Tarquin shouted.

In answer, the creature let out an ear-splitting screech and ran toward him.

"You must behead them," the Aloi shouted as he joined the fray.

Seeing that his arrow had little effect, Eldahir returned his bow to its place on his back and drew his sword. Morganna did the same and before long, they were busy fighting off Shadow Lords.

Tarquin and the Shadow Lord rapidly closed the gap. When he was within reach, the human dropped to one knee and struck out with his sword, neatly severing the left leg at the middle thigh. The creature's armor would have stopped most swords, but it was no match for Dragon Bolt. The sword flared bright red with dragon fire, burning and cutting through metal like a knife cutting through cheese. As the shadow toppled past Tarquin, the prince changed the arc of his sword and struck the creature's head from its shoulders before the body hit the ground. The body crumpled to dust and bone, sending its wailing spirit to the netherworld.

By this time, close to thirty shadows, alerted by the death cry of one of their own, headed for Tarquin, intent on killing those who had interrupted their nightly activities. They were deadly enemies to the Aloi, who hid to avoid capture and slavery for the Shadow Lords. Worse yet, the Aloi who died during imprisonment were turned into undead creatures, locked in slavery for eternity.

Baldo put on a burst of speed, sliding to a halt beside Tarquin. The dwarf warrior-priest held out his order's holy symbol and knelt before the onrushing horde, calling on Thierry for aid. The symbol emitted a bright light, and the front rank of attackers exploded in dusty fury, filling the air with unearthly screams that ripped through their psyche like sharp daggers. Still, this action dissolved ten of the beings. The rest slammed into Tarquin and the others.

Above, Azimuth and Celedant were embroiled in a fierce battle with the last two draven and their shadow riders. Since the draven were non-magical, relying on physical attacks to take down their foes, they had to be held in check so their riders could battle using magic. The dragon had to concentrate on flying to keep out of the paths of the liquid purple fire aimed at him. Whenever he made a pass near one of the draven, Azimuth shot flame at the shadow, which promptly lost its physical form so that the flames passed harmless through its body.

Whenever this happened, the shadow was incapable of using magic until it solidified again. Celedant took advantage of these brief respites, using Forestae to send powerful balls of earthen green energy at the draven. However, they could only attack one enemy at a time. During one such attack, the Shadow Lord on the other draven's back sent a blast of liquid fire, hitting Azimuth in the thigh of his left rear leg. The dragon roared with pain, and turning his head, he blasted the shadow before it could lose its solid form. As it exploded into dust, its draven, which was already suffering from several injuries, realized that it was free of constraints. It turned from the fight and flew away, evening up the odds.

"Forget the shadow and go for the draven," Celedant shouted to his friend. "Once the beast is dead, the shadow will be forced to the ground where he'll have to remain solid to continue the fight."

Azimuth nodded his great horned head. He and Celedant sent blasts of blazing energy at the remaining draven, severely damaging both wings and sending it plummeting to the earth.

On the ground in near darkness with the fire of the burning buildings providing light, the two groups clashed. Botreg moved through the dark with ease, dodging the swinging swords of the shadows and striking off their heads with a quick flip of his wrist. When their adversaries' numbers had dwindled, he stopped and looked around at Tarquin's progress. He was amazed to see both Baldo and Hortus in a killing frenzy, attacking the shadows with abandon, their enchanted war hammers destroying the creatures on contact.

When a few shadows remained, the enemy returned to wispy forms and fled, leaving Tarquin and the others breathless with exhaustion in the clearing. Unfortunately, their attackers had been but a tiny, weaker portion of the Shadow Lords that occupied Zeiglon. When Celedant's band arrived in the city, the battle for the last portion of the Staff of Adaman would prove to be far more difficult.

Lowering their weapons, the group realized that they had an audience. Sometime during the fight, the defenders of the village had exited their homes and surrounded the fighting band, their spear points flickering in the dying firelight. Tarquin gave Botreg a nervous glance and half raised his weapon. Even though they had saved the Aloi from the Shadow Lords, would he and the others now have to fight the lizard people?

CHAPTER FORTY

Out of the circle of waiting lizard men, a bent figure, accompanied by a smaller one bearing a torch, approached. The torchbearer was a short, adolescent reptilian creature wearing a loincloth. His muscles had not yet filled out, giving a youthful gangliness to his body. Bent with age, the older lizard's teeth were yellow and dull in his green-scaled snout. He was clad in loose-fitting clothing with colorful feathers and beads strung about his body. The creature had a cudgel in his right hand, and in his left, he bore a crooked staff adorned with the bones of small creatures that rattled in the night air.

He advanced to within a few feet of Celedant, staring at the wizard with one intense black eye. A coarse woolen patch covered the other. Celedant recognized the elder as a shaman, as near to a wizard as the lizard man could become.

The creature grunted at Celedant and then began shaking his staff, rattling the bones menacingly before saying, "Slur uf tar ne?"

It was said in a way that Celedant took to be a question though he could not recollect the language.

Azimuth landed, changed his appearance, and approached the elder, who bowed low. The rest of his people dropped to their knees and bowed, speaking words of adoration that the dragon had no difficulty understanding.

"Tarnos dorno. Tarnos heli cor Aloi," Azimuth replied.

The shaman let out a racking cough and bared his dull teeth.

Tarquin was amazed at the adoration the Aloi showed the dragon. Most people were terrified until they realized that Azimuth had no intention of eating or roasting them.

In a thickly accented and slurred voice, the shaman said, "Me not talk too good in human tongue."

He rested the staff against his shoulder and grabbed the youth by the upper arm, pulling him to his feet.

The youth spoke to Azimuth. "Great leader of the mighty dragons, my people welcome you and your brave friends. I am called Adder, and this is my master, Wilcor."

His voice was thick with the difficulties of speaking the common tongue of the north, but Celedant could understand him well enough. He motioned to the other lizard men, and they retired to the village. Then he and Celedant followed in their wake, walking on either side of the youth.

"How is it that you speak our tongue?" Celedant asked.

Adder bared his teeth in a manner that they would later learn was similar to a smile. "My people keep in contact with our kin to the north. We know that they war with your kind, but you have destroyed many Dark Lords. Therefore, you are accepted as friends."

The shaman, walking a pace behind Azimuth, spoke, and Adder translated.

"A common enemy often sets aside many grievances," the lad continued, showing more experience than a normal youth his age. "We are too few to battle the Shadow Lords and their undead armies, but then fate brought you in our midst. Our enemies are now our saviors. As you know, great dragon, we honor our distant cousins the dragons of Dragon Isle," he finished, looking at Azimuth.

"I'm surprised you weren't shocked by Azimuth's appearance," Celedant said.

The lad smiled. "Even if he had approached us in his present form, we would have known who he is. My people can see his draconic aura."

Azimuth chuckled over his friend's amazement as they picked their way through the ashes of the undead that lay strewn about the base of the gate. The guards carried long spears with foot-long blades mounted on both ends. Adder led the company to the center of town. There was a blackened area where one of the draven had struck the ground. Its body still twitched. The company ringed it as Celedant, Azimuth, Tarquin, and Adder advanced to the blackened circle of earth. The rider was still alive, pinned beneath the draven.

Adder motioned to it. "There was little time to dispatch the monster. But the fall wounded it enough that we could wait and destroy it later."

Tarquin saw the remains of a broken man with burns over most of his body

244

and obvious broken bones. The thing tried to move, bringing moans of agony as they studied him. Hortus joined the others and drew their attention to the Dark Lord's right arm. It was broken and stuck out at an odd angle, but even as they watched, it moved back in place, healing itself. The fingers flexed.

"This is not a Shadow Lord but a vampire," Hortus said.

"What was a vampire doing with the Shadow Lords?" Celedant asked.

The vampire looked at him and hissed.

"No reply? I sense Taza's hand in this," Celedant said. "Speak, and I will relieve your misery."

The vampire remained silent. If enough time passed, he would be able to heal himself. He knew that the wizard offered an easier death. Yet if he spoke and revealed Taza's plans, the agony his master would put him through would make death a welcome relief. Therefore, he remained silent except for his moans, which grew less and less as his body continued healing.

With practiced ease, the Abbot knelt next to the vampire and brought forth his holy symbol gripped in both hands. The creature, seeing the small bejeweled hammer held before its eyes, brought up the newly-set arm to stop the cleric. Tarquin's booted foot stomped, keeping the creature's arm pinned.

The vampire struggled, but its body could not heal fast enough to save him. Calling on strength from Thierry, Hortus brought the holy symbol of his order down to touch the vampire's chest. The body convulsed as it strained away from the touch of the relic, but the dwarf kept the pressure steady. The undead creature shook its head back and forth, and the convulsions slowed until the vampire's flesh exploded to dust and blew away in the night air. Only a faint outline remained. The lizard people who had witnessed the banishing yelped with joy.

Wilcor sat at a fire while other Aloi hastily prepared a meal of thanksgiving consisting of roasted venison and fish, along with fresh vegetables. Everyone ate with relish. As they had finished, the shaman spoke, using Adder as his translator.

"We wish to thank you for killing the dark one. They feed on travelers waylaid in the Deep South along the edges of the forest, and if that isn't enough, they have resorted to feeding on our cold-blooded bodies. An escaped prisoner said our blood is unpleasant to the taste, but when hungered, they have no choice." He stopped and poignantly asked, "You are a strange company of mixed races. Why do you travel the land of the Shadow Lords?"

Celedant cleared his throat, unwilling at first to talk about their mission and wondering how much he could trust these people. "It is better that you do not know our mission, but the ruins of Zeiglon are our ultimate goal."

"It is folly to enter that dark realm," Wilcor said, shaking his head. "They say the sun does not rise on those ruins. Your quest must be dire to require a journey into a land of death and horror."

Hortus leaned from his place beside Adder and said, "Our quest is that important, not just for ourselves but for the welfare of all who dwell on Muiria."

"The jungle is a dangerous place. I will lend you two of our bravest warriors and my own Adder to lead your company to the undead realm of the Shadow Lords."

Celedant was about to refuse his offer, but Wilcor waved him off and continued. The shaman's apprentice was beside himself, teeth flashing in the firelight and a colorful frill opened up and expanded around his head. Tarquin could sense the excitement that ran through the gathered villagers. One bold lizard man stepped up, waiting for Wilcor to recognize him. Wearing a worn suit of leather armor, he was thickly muscled, standing well over six feet in height with a powerful tail. He bore many scars, attesting to his prowess in battle. Adder introduced him.

"This is Tallon. He is battle chief of our village. He wishes to ask the newcomers if their journey to the Shadow Lord's lands might bring peace to our forest."

Celedant thought before answering. "There is no way to know for certain, but while we are in the ruins of Zeiglon, we will do our best to destroy the evil power that now holds domain over your forest."

Tallon gave the smile that is particular to lizard men and moved to the edge of the fire, slamming a clawed fist against his armor. "My lord dragon, my spear and sword will accompany you, along with two of my best trackers."

Soon everyone retired for the night. The Aloi offered their guests huts, but it would have displaced several families. Celedant thanked them, but said they preferred sleeping around the campfire.

The following morning after breakfast, Wilcor sent Adder to bring the companions to the shaman's hut. The old shaman sat cross-legged with his tail wrapped over his thighs. Tallon was also present as well as two other Aloi. They were dressed in leather armor but had a slighter build than the war leader. One tracker had lost an arm.

Wilcor gave a hacking cough and through the translations of Adder said, "My people will leave for a new home by mid-morning, but you must depart without delay. I hope you will be successful in your quest and in so doing, you will aid our cause as well. Tallon is a brave warrior. He has picked two of our best trackers to guide you. One Arm has been all the way to Zeiglon and should be able to get you deep within the city without incident. Zornet is a capable tracker, as well."

Celedant thanked the old shaman for his knowledge, and One Arm motioned for them to follow. They left the jungle village of the lizard people. The Aloi scouts found paths that even Ralav grudgingly admitted he would never have seen. Following the trails, the company made good time. As darkness began to fall, they searched for a campsite twenty miles further to the southeast.

One Arm led them to a small clearing and a cache of dry wood hidden in the hollow of a tree. The lizard men started a fire. Ralav fussed over the company's dinner, while the Aloi prepare a stew that smelled like rotten eggs, making Celedant and the others glad they had their own meat with them.

When Morganna asked Tallon the nature of the concoction, the lizard man offered her some. "Molic free sacrens."

She looked at Adder who with the typical smile said, "It is the Molic worm mashed into a paste and stewed with stagnant water. It is considered a delicacy among our people."

Morganna graciously shook her head to the offer and reminded herself never to criticize her companions' cooking again.

After the meal, Tallon addressed the group while Adder tried to keep up with the translation. The tall lizard paced in front of them, his giant tail swishing back and forth as he addressed them.

"This night we will post a single guard. I will be first, followed by one of your party. The Shadow Lords prowl the skies on the backs of their flying beasts while their minions search the ground beneath them. Stay still, and we will be safe. The wails of the undead should cause no alarm. If they draw close and the night become quiet, then it is time to worry." That said, he paced over to a tree and wrapping himself in a blanket, sat against the trunk and was silent.

Throughout the night, Celedant and the others were awakened by the wails of the hunting undead, but their camp was not discovered. At one point when the cries seemed to envelope the camp, Tarquin looked up at the sky and saw the dark shape of a draven. When the sun rose, ground fog limited their visibility as they continued the journey. Zornet and One Arm took the lead down a small beaten game trail as the others followed.

Traveling southeast, the swampy ground gave way to slightly elevated terrain, and the undergrowth lessened as they climbed. Tallon, through the able translation of the apprentice shaman, spoke to Celedant. The tall lizard man spread his arms, indicating the surrounding forest of hardwoods.

"The ground between here and the accursed city is much like this. There is little cover to hide from hunting parties. The city is but a day's journey from here. Zeiglon must have been an important city, because its ruins are immense."

"Yes, Tallon, the city was large. Its lords ruled over a vast kingdom stretching hundreds of miles in all directions," Celedant responded. "Ultimately, their craving for power was their undoing. They tried to conquer the entire continent, and the gods made them pay. The fury unleashed by their king's use of a forbidden relic doomed their city and caused great movements of the earth that created the plateau."

Tallon grunted. "The city is still evil. The king, his nobles, and his army were cursed to become Shadow Lords and rule over the ruins for eternity, and we became their slave labor. We were unable to keep up with their demands, so they started hunting our people."

The wizard felt for the plight of the Aloi. "The curse of immortality is great. The Shadow Lords need blood and souls to sustain them, and the pain of hunger plagues them unmercifully."

"Great wizard, vampire hunting parties go south where humans flourish. So why do they still pursue us?" Adder asked.

Tallon surprised everyone by answering. "They must keep their minions occupied. That is what I think. I have been in the city and seen the ghouls, zombies, and skeletons clash against one another. The Shadow Lords war among themselves, pitting their personal followers against one another as they strive for dominance over the ruins."

The Aloi's insight impressed the wizard. "So the immortals are a kingdom unto themselves. They seek dominance over each other to gain just rewards, whether access to warm-blooded thralls or treasure."

As the sun began its descent, the travelers came to steep rise where a massive, ominous cloud was visible through the treetops. They paused as One Arm and Zornet headed back down the sloping ground. The two Aloi came to a stop in front of Tallon, their green skin moist with perspiration, breathing hard.

"We scouted a few miles into the shadow lands," Zornet said, pointing. "Nothing is stirring."

Tallon roughly slapped the scout on his shoulder. "Good job."

He turned to Celedant. "Those clouds mark the beginning of the shadow lands and extend a day's journey outward. The city is perpetually shrouded in a dark cloud. This is the work of sorcery. It allows the Shadow Lords to move about while the sun is high."

248

"That doesn't make our job any easier," Tarquin remarked.

"No, but we have ventured into the shadows many times," the Aloi leader said. "The land and ruins are large, so we can stay hidden from their eyes. We will camp here tonight and enter the darkness at first light. The Shadow Lords prefer true night and tend to rest during the day to conserve strength. However, their underlings are alert and protect their masters."

They settled down in a small camp, eating dried fruit and meat, fearing a campfire might draw unwanted attention. The travelers, old and new, sat talking about past lives and experiences as darkness fell on the lands above the escarpment. Tarquin and Morganna took the first watch, and almost immediately, the wails of the undead and their masters rose into the night, echoing from over the rise.

Tarquin sat next to Morganna. "How do you feel about fighting the undead and their masters?"

Morganna cocked an eyebrow. "In the underworld, their kind is abundant with vampires. My people have had an uneasy truce with them for centuries. As long as none trespasses our lands, we do not hunt them. Yet, we remain prepared for battle." She shook her head. "It was more like an alliance. True friendship is not a vampire attribute. Once a person is transformed into a vampire, they still possess original feelings and morals. However, they find themselves needing to kill and must adjust their thinking or perish. Yet, if they can adjust, they will retain most of what made them what they once were."

A dark look came over Morganna. "What I said was true in years past, but now darkness clouds the underworld, taking hold of my people. Taza's promises seduce many, and more of my race embraces vampirism. This is why I joined your quest. I have to do whatever I can to stop this abomination."

She was quiet after that, and Tarquin sat in silence, contemplating her words, as the eerie wails grew stronger. With their backs to a tree, Morganna reached over and touched her friend, pointing to the ridge above. There in the half-light of the shadow lands, they saw figures moving through the trees and descending the ridge a few paces from the camp. Tarquin's night vision, developed within the depths of the dwarvan capital city of Nars, still had difficulty picking out the skeletal bodies or pale faces of actual ghouls and zombies. It was a large party, and overhead, three dark figures sped westward above the treetops. Undead creatures crept down the hill in a noisy scramble. By the time they reached the bottom, the entire camp was awake and holding their collective breath as the horde disappeared into the woods at a fast run.

At the bottom of the rise, a creature paused, allowing the others to move ahead. Tarquin could make out very little in the darkness, but it had stopped and was testing the air with its nose, sniffing for some time. Then it cocked its head toward the hidden company and limped toward the camp.

Tarquin looked to his right and saw that Morganna was up and moving to intersect the creature. She melted into the darkness, reappearing behind the creature. Her sword scraped against its scabbard, and the creature had but a second to turn before her weapon struck the inquisitive ghoul's head from its shoulders, spinning from the body to land several feet away. Morganna caught the headless body before it crashed to the ground.

Tallon was up and whispering quick instructions. "We must hurry. They might miss this one."

Hortus gathered the undead creature's head and silently prayed over the body. Tarquin approached for a better look at their foe. It was a pale man with limp black hair, sunken eyes, and ropy muscles. Rotten teeth filled its mouth. No blood flowed from the body, but a greenish viscous liquid that smelled horrible.

As Hortus finished his prayer, Tarquin asked, "What did you do for him?"

"Only what I could," the Abbot replied solemnly. "I sent what was left of his soul beyond this world, severing its ties with this abused body."

Then Tarquin heard Tallon's harsh words. The two Aloi scouts were already at the top of the ridge, urging the others upward. It would have been an easy climb in the shadowy daylight, but cloud cover blocked out even the stars, and Tarquin slipped several times before he reached the top.

Once everyone had assembled on top of the ridge, Tallon motioned everyone to silence. "We need to move fast."

He headed out after the Aloi scouts. The shadow lands lay in total darkness, and a sense of deep despair settled on everyone as they pushed closer to Zeiglon's ruins. The trees in this region were dark and shriveled from countless years of inadequate light. The one thing that seemed to thrive was a dark moss that covered the ground. Hour after hour, Celedant and the others moved deeper into the woods without sighting any of the land's denizens. Every so often, odd wails drifted through the wind but never threatened to draw near their path. As their legs muscles began to tire after endless miles of hiking with little sleep, the clouds above took on a brighter luminescence.

Tallon called a halt and pointed upward. "The sun rises. We must find shelter and rest."

It wasn't long before they happened on an old, decrepit farmhouse, and as they approached, the trees opened to display the badly damaged building. Zornet was poised at the structure's wall when One Arm appeared over the wall and waved them on. The company found a devastated building of three rooms in which none of the ruined walls stood over five feet in height. They spread out in the central room with guards at the two doors, and after a cold meal, gathered in the main room where Celedant brought out an old faded map drawn on an ancient roll of parchment.

The wizard called the Aloi leader to him and motioned to the map. "Tallon, you and the others have traveled into the ruins of Zeiglon. Can you make out any of the features of this map?"

The Aloi looked over the map and began a heated debate among themselves, arms waving, tails whipping back and forth, their crests fully extended.

Adder, who was standing by Celedant, said, "They are arguing over what the ruined buildings might represent on the map's layout."

Tallon turned to the wizard. "We have been through the ruins on many occasions but haven't paid much attention to the remaining buildings. We were more intent on avoiding capture. Yet, Zornet swears that he has hidden in a structure similar to this one." He pointed a clawed finger at a great coliseum. "He says that the flooring has fallen in, but there are rows of seats still intact."

Celedant pondered this a few seconds. "The coliseum is still a long way from the palace, which is here. The old sewers marked on the map run along the four points of the compass." He pointed to a large building about a mile to the east. "But it gives us a good idea which direction we need to travel."

"We must go, or all might be for naught," Tallon interrupted. "The city is situated along the sea with a mile-high cliff. That building must have fallen into the sea."

"Hopefully not," Hortus interjected. "Most of the text I have read indicates that the portion of the palace we need to find did not collapse into the sea. It maybe perched at the edge of the cliff, but it is there. I'm sure of it."

Tallon looked skyward and said, "It is difficult to judge, but we may have enough daylight to make it to the coliseum if we hurry."

"Right, lads, let's go. Be ready for anything," Tarquin said.

CHAPTER FORTY-ONE

The company came to the old outer wall of Zeiglon. In the past, it had been a plastered wall gleaming white, but now it was a crumbled ruin with decayed skulls set on pikes along the top. Tarquin saw that many of the skulls were Aloi, a warning to keep out of the city. Celedant and the others made their way to the tumble of masonry that littered the base of the once-great wall. Zornet led the way, and soon they were slipping unnoticed though the streets. Tarquin took a second to glance around before continuing. The city looked like a mass of fallen buildings. At one time, mighty trees had grown in the rubble, but now they were mere shadows, stunted by the never-ending darkness.

It was into this maze of ruins that they encroached. Zornet took them on a circuitous path that wound among the collapsed buildings. At times, they had to dodge into ruins to hide from undead creatures also using the paths of Zeiglon. After an hour of playing cat-and-mouse, they spotted the tall structure of the coliseum in the distance. Zornet led the way through the ruins, pushing aside a small boulder, and they climbed into the interior of the building.

The travelers stared across the large floor of the old arena. It was tremendous, fully half a mile in circumference, with thousands of seats. As they stood taking in the sight and wondering what titanic events had taken place here, a dark shape appeared, jerking them back to the present danger they were in as the eerie wail of the undead sounded directly behind them. The message was clear: The creature was calling its brethren to attack.

Tallon reacted with lightning speed as he threw his spear. It transfixed the creature and was embedded into the stone that rose behind the undead monster. Botreg dashed into the ruins and with a quick slash of his sword ended the wail. Yet, Tallon and Botreg's actions were too late. Already undead cries echoed outside the coliseum.

They were trapped.

Zornet spoke in rapid fire Aloi to Tallon who in turn went to Adder.

"Follow Zornet to a defensible place in the bowels of the building," the apprentice shaman said. "Tallon has volunteered to hold these rooms until you accomplish your mission."

The wizard motioned to the scaled scout. "Lead on."

The Aloi took them across the floor of the building through a maze of pillars that had once supported the roof of the coliseum. Then he led them through a doorway into the pitch-black darkness of the interior. Dwarves and elves could see fine in the darkness, but Tallon took out a small torch from his pack and set it ablaze.

Zornet took the torch, and they advanced deeper into the building. They soon reached a large doorway with an ancient iron portcullis recessed into the ceiling.

Zornet said, "We can hold them here and in the many rooms beyond for a long while."

Tarquin ordered the dwarves to see about lowering the portcullis while Morganna and Botreg slipped out the way they had come to slow any pursuit. Celedant followed Zornet to a small trap door fashioned in the floor in the last of the rooms. It was through here into the sewers that they could escape and find their way to the Palace. Once they were sure it was secure, they went back to the first room. Having lowered the Iron Gate to where it almost touched the ground, there remained barely enough room for the rear guards to escape.

Celedant and Hortus talked as they made their way back to the first room where they came up with a plan. The Wizard spoke slowly so that Adder could translate.

"Tallon, you are brave to offer yourself for this delaying action, but you and your kindred would be overwhelmed by the undead creatures. Assuredly, the Shadow Lords will soon enter the fray. While you draw their attention here, a few of us may slip unnoticed into the palace. However, not everyone needs to go. Hortus has agreed to remain with the dwarves to aid you. Baldo will accompany me, along with Azimuth, Tarquin, Eldahir, Morganna, and Ress.

The Aloi agreed as the wizard continued. "Adder should come as well. All the races should be represented if we are to accomplish our mission."

"My Lord Clor feels it is important for him to be represented in this final clash," Hority insisted.

Hortus understood. "That is true. His god sent him with us, and his presence is called for."

Morganna and Botreg sprinted down the corridor and rolled under the gate. Ralav shut it the rest of the way, as Tarquin joined his friends and explained the situation.

"The undead tracked us to the entrance, and a large force has gathered," he told them. The two stout warriors had ambushed them at several places, but they were unable to stop the advance.

As the warriors tested their weapons, Tarquin spoke to Botreg. "I'm leaving you in charge of the lads; see to their safety. I'll be back as soon as I can."

The dark dwarf smiled. "Don't ye worry, Tarquin. I will do me best. I just wish I could accompany ye, zeffan."

Tarquin nodded solemnly and rested his hand on the dwarf's shoulder. "You'll be with me in spirit, my friend."

From the corner of his eye, Botreg saw Hority climb into the old sewer. "Get in the sewer, quick, before Hority does something wrong," he urged.

While the others barricaded the doorways nearby, Tallon and Hortus stood at the gate staring into the dark corridor. The wooden door collapsed into a pile of rubble when they tried to shut it.

Hortus sighed and spoke to Botreg. "I can use me powers to destroy the undead but a few times within each given hour. Therefore, I will save me power for the Shadow Lords. Ye must dispense with the undead on yer own for the time being."

When Celedant and the others reached the trap door, Zornet, who had followed them, said he would seal and hide it after they descended.

Celedant looked at those accompanying him. "There is little to say, but remember the sacrifice our comrades are making. We must succeed and return."

He motioned to the former Illanni to lead, and Morganna disappeared down a ladder built into the tunnel's floor. At the bottom, they found Hority with two hands full of dirt.

"This isn't a proper sewer at all."

The others grinned, and Tarquin pushed him ahead. The tunnel was so small that even Baldo had to duck to keep his helm from scraping the ceiling. The other crawled on hands and knees through the sand.

Celedant surmised that this had once been part of the city's sewer system, but luckily, the tunnel was dry and unused. Zornet told them they needed to travel a hundred paces and past two tunnels heading up before taking a right-hand passage that would become large enough for them to stand. From there, they would climb the first ladder they saw, which would deliver them into the cellar of a building.

Zornet was true to his word, and the remaining members of the company crawled with their weapons drawn into a cluttered basement. Morganna took the lead, and soon they stood in the doorway looking out on a darkened street. Several blocks away, the coliseum rose out of the ruins, and the wailing cries of the undead echoed from its bowl shape. It sounded as though the entire city had assembled to fight the intruders as Shadow Lords flew about the sky. Tarquin noticed that a few of the winged flyers fought among themselves.

Celedant smiled grimly. "Our friends have attracted attention. We'd better hurry."

Morganna and Eldahir sprinted down the street in the direction of the palace. The streets were indeed empty, and they soon found themselves near what had once been the walls of the palace, but a mass of rubble that had leveled nearby houses was all that remained. Beyond the rubble, barren ground was all that was left of the palace. Centuries ago when the cataclysm had struck, the explosion spread out from the throne room, miraculously leaving the immediate rooms standing but destroying the rest. These stout walls had deflected the blast's main impedance upward but still wreaked havoc on the city.

The company stood in awe at the palace's standing portions. The windows, their colorful glass blown out by the release of magical forces, stared blankly at a desolate world. Meanwhile, the remaining building, which was poised on the edge of the cliff, was silhouetted by sudden blinding flashes of lighting from a storm off the coast with nothing but dark clouds and a wind-torn sea as its backdrop.

The surrounding area was surpassingly empty as they hurried toward the remaining buildings of the complex. Its stonework had eroded over time, and the gargoyles that had stood sentry for centuries were nothing more than indistinct bulges of rock. Equally worn stone steps led them to the door's portal and into the chamber beyond. It was barren with rusted iron brackets that had once held glorious tapestries clanking dully in the wind against the stone walls. Celedant studied the layout of the palace before leading them to a doorway on the right.

In the darkness, their way appeared clear. Then a flash of lightning illuminated the room better, and they spotted a cluster of undead blocking the door. Unlike the usual shuffling zombie or skeleton they had encountered before, these wore antique armor and wielded swords, spears, and maces. Tarquin slid to a halt on the smooth marble floor. The rest did likewise a few paces from the undead, but the enemy did not attack. Their dull eyes stared hollowly at the companions, daring them to advance.

Deep beneath the coliseum, the remainder of the company prepared to hold the underground corridors as long as possible. They hoped to give Celedant and the others time to recover the staff. With the portcullis dropped into place, they wedged pieces of stone into its grooves to make it difficult to open. The dwarves readied their crossbows, while the Aloi stood close by the Iron Gate with spears poised.

Within minutes, the first of the undead entered the corridor. They rushed the portcullis, using force to try to lift it while Ronli fought to lock it down. Arrows thudded in the first rank while the lizard men thrust their spears through the bars. The defender's pointed weapons had little effect on the attackers. They thudded into their bodies briefly, driving them back a few steps. However, the undead shrugged off the blows and grappled at the gate. The defenders' swords and axes sliced off fingers and hands with little effect as the portcullis began to rattle gradually upward under pressure.

Aegir stood before the portal, calling on his deity's aid by using his holy symbol to destroy six of the attackers, but even as they folded into dust, still more undead took their place. A spear blade was thrust deep into One Arm's thigh. He ignored the pain, wrapped a bandage around his leg, and fought on. Half an hour passed as the undead relentlessly attacked. Then they mysteriously retreated a few steps down the corridor, affording a brief rest for the harried defenders who retreated from the battered portcullis, leaving Ralav to watch the dark corridor for any sign of the enemy.

Botreg sat with his back against a dirt-encrusted wall. "When will the Shadow Lords attack?"

The Abbot shrugged. "Soon, I should think."

In answer to the assassin's question, Ralav approached on the run from the entrance, shouting, "Get down! Get down!"

Following the dwarf's warning, they heard a crackle of magical energy from the corridor, followed by a roaring blast that thundered into the iron portcullis. The Shadow Lords had arrived. The spell ripped into the barrier, melting a four-foot hole in the centuries-old iron. Before the companions could recover and regain their feet, the horde of undead fearlessly plunged through the breach, ignoring the white-hot ends of melted iron.

Botreg and Tallon were the first to react to the danger as they charged into the attackers, their swords a blur of flashing steel as they hacked their way through the lunging assailants. The attack slowed, giving other members of the company a chance to join in the fray without the whole room being overrun. Swords, axes, and spears rang against an odd assortment of antique weapons and armor worn by the undead warriors. Yet, as they fell to the defender's blades, more climbed through the breached gate.

The never-ending attackers firmly pushed back the defenders. Zornet and Ronli had already fallen back to the second barrier, leaving a trail of blood from their grievous wounds. Nevertheless, the companions fought on, desperately trying to buy time for Celedant and the warriors.

Hortus's war hammer, imbibed with the power of Thierry, destroyed his undead foes with a touch, but he could tell their numbers weighed on the company. With a mighty swing of his weapon that sent three skeletal foes to their final resting place he called out, "Aegir, fall back and see to the wounded!"

He shouldered his way closer to the portcullis and using the sheer strength of his broad shoulders and war hammer, Hortus beat aside the undead. Once he was in a clear space, he called on Thierry's aid and evoked a spell that he hoped would buy some time to regroup. The Abbot wove a complicated enchantment, intermingling several components that he hoped would ward off the Shadow Lords' magic.

From the corner of his eye, the dwarf saw a decaying Aloi zombie approach, swinging a heavy club. At that instant, the Abbot knew he did not have time to complete his incantation. Then Tallon stepped in front of the attacker. Both Aloi and undead struck at the same time; while Tallon's sword lopped off the other's head, the undead's club slammed into the Aloi's left shoulder with a crushing blow. Tallon dropped to his knees, but the dwarf could not take time to go to the Aloi's aid. The Abbot had to complete the spell, which placed a wall of energy in the doorway of the breached portcullis to act as a framework. Intricately woven into the spell's barrier was another component, giving the wall the properties to repel other magical attacks and reflecting them at the attackers.

Hortus hoped he had created it subtly enough to catch the Shadow Lords by surprise. Once his spell was complete, the dwarf stooped to help the Aloi up. The undead in the corridor were already hammering at the invisible barrier. In the chamber, the companions had almost eliminated the ones that had come through the breach. Hortus helped the lizard man to the next defensive barrier as Botreg stalked the last of their foes cowering in a dark corner.

At the same time, Celedant decided the company's course of action as he lowered his staff and spoke the words of a spell. In the distance, Tarquin could hear the crash of the sea and the sound of thunder as it leapt from the wizard's staff, deafening them all. The bolt spanned the few paces in a split second, blowing three of the undead to oblivion, while arms of the electrical charge danced around the rest, throwing them backward as the company attacked.

Reverting to his dragon form, Azimuth stood next to Celedant and held the remaining undead at bay, breathing blasts of fire so fierce it seemed like hellfire.

The front rank of the undead had fallen, but others waited in the throne room, and they swarmed toward them to attack. Morganna danced around the armored undead, her sword, magically imbued by a powerful spell, was a blur of motion as arms, legs, and heads fell. Tarquin engaged two dull-faced ghouls wearing rusted plate mail; their swords rang on his as they clashed. He parried and thrust at them both and then caught one of the creature's swords and landed a direct blow on the flat of the blade, shattering the ghoul's sword. Tarquin followed with a swing that decapitated the undead creature. He turned and attacked the remaining creature with renewed energy.

Hority attacked with vigor of a true berserker, fearless and deadly. He wielded his branch, and whatever it touched dissolved into ash. He also had a sharpened piece of metal that he put to good use, severing necks as he jumped from stone to stone.

Meanwhile, Baldo strode into the midst of the ghouls, his thick dwarvan plate mail turning aside their blows. Helmet visor closed, he looked at the world through magical eyepieces built to withstand the hottest dragon fire. The jeweled pieces were ruby red and highlighted the carved faceplate that covered the dwarf's face. The stout cleric dealt massive blows with his magical hammer. Few of the undead could withstand more than one mighty blow. When struck, most of his foes crumpled to the ground and lay still, released from the misery of their undead lives.

Celedant and Azimuth stood in the doorway casting balls of energy and blasts of fire that engulfed the undead in flames and added to the macabre atmosphere.

Eldahir stood on the other side of the wizard, adding his own special spells as tiny darts of energy lanced from his fingertips and shot into their foes, causing the undead to fall to the ground, writhing in agony.

In the flashing light of the storm and flames of spent magic, the company dispatched the remaining guards, and the hall was theirs. Celedant looked about the chamber. Across from them, the floor led to a flight of stairs that ended at the cliff's edge. The wizard sprinted up the steps to where the throne had once stood as Azimuth back in elvan form and the others guarded his back. When he reached the edge across from him, a sheer finger of rock remarkably remained, holding what was left of the marble flooring on top.

The companions retreated to the third chamber where they had built a small chest-high wall with fallen stones. Botreg stayed in the second room no larger than ten feet square to watch the barrier and give word when the breach occurred. The others gathered by the wall, while Hortus and Aegir saw to the wounds of Tallon, Ronli, One Arm, and Zornet. The latter Aloi had a serious injury with a spear thrust deep into his chest. The harried clerics stabilized the lizard man as best they could by using spells to stop the bleeding, but they knew that only bed rest would save the tracker. Against the Aloi's will, Tallon carried him to the last chamber, placing him by the trap door that would be their last chance for escape.

In the outer chamber of the makeshift fortress, the undead attacked the barrier ferociously, filled with blood lust and hatred for the living. They beat at the spell that Hortus had cast, their claws causing sparks of blue and green to erupt along its surface. All this Botreg observed in the darkness of the small room. Then a commanding voice called to the undead, and the attack ceased. They disappeared where a second before they had been angrily howling as they tore at the fabric of the spell.

Through the shimmer of the Abbot's spell, Botreg saw two dark shapes approach. The assassin knew these were the undead masters. The Shadow Lords studied the barrier a few seconds before striking. One cast a spell, and the barrier flared bright blue, repelling the attack. The other Dark Lord raised its hand and sent a jagged bolt of energy flying at the offending wall. The cleric's spell reacted differently than Botreg expected. It absorbed the bolt and reversed its path, sending the bolt back at its creator. An explosion told Botreg that it had struck. Afterward, all that remained in the hallway was smoke, but Botreg expected the spell casters had paid dearly for their attack.

Then a muted light affected the barrier, and the explosion of the conflicting spells forced the dwarf to turn away briefly. When he looked back, he saw the two spells vying for dominance. Hortus's barrier flared deep blue as it fought to hold off the attack of the Shadow Lord's magic. Nevertheless, Botreg could see it was a losing battle. The barrier began to balloon outward at the center as the Shadow Lord poured more power into his spell. Then the dwarf saw dark lines appear in the blue of the force field like a pane of glass cracking, and he knew the barrier would be gone in seconds.

Turning, he took a few quick steps and vaulted the low stone wall, landing in the midst of his friends as a large explosion echoed through the outer chamber, heralding the destruction of the barrier. There was space enough for two attackers to come through the doorway at a time, so Tallon, his shoulder bruised and swollen, and Botreg positioned themselves at the wall, their well-used weapons poised for the attack. The others gathered behind, ready to help where they could or shoot arrows at the attacking undead – anything to slow them down.

The wizard motioned the others to draw closer. "This chasm is where the staff was thrown. Tie the ropes we brought together and bring them here."

As they set about linking the ropes, Celedant reached into his robe and brought forth an object wrapped in a dark cloth. He leaned down and grasped Tarquin's shoulder, and as the young man looked up, the wizard said, "I think you are meant to fulfill this quest."

There in his palm was the stone of Adaman, a fist-sized crystal of gold rhodium that picked up all available light and sparkled in a multitude of colors. Rainbow hues danced across the chamber.

The wizard handed Tarquin the gem. "This will draw you to the staff by its light, but be very cautious. You must resist the temptation to join them together, for anyone without the power to control the staff will have his life force drained into it, leaving a hollow husk. Do you understand?"

Tarquin sucked in a breath and nodded. As they were about to lower him down the cliff face, a bright lightning flash exposed them on the edge of the abyss, and they heard ominous laughter. Tarquin, his concentration intent on the fearful task before him, looked up as he leaned over the cliff. His friends hung tightly to the rope but behind them, the room was filling with dark figures. Tarquin pulled sharply on the rope, gaining his balance on the lip of the abyss while fumbling to draw his sword. Having heard the laughter and seeing Tarquin's reaction, the others turned to face the creatures filling the throne room.

CHAPTER FORTY-TWO

The undead shuffled forward, wary of the empty room, but when their night-sensitive eyes spied the small wall and its defenders, their hatred of the living echoed in shrill cries as they charged. It was a nightmarish battle as one monster after another tried to climb the wall, oblivious to the blows dealt them by the defenders. Partially decayed undead fought their way through their brethren to be the first to claim a living being, while the defenders mechanically hacked away. Botreg and Tallon used the cutting edges of their swords to lop off heads and arms as the attackers tried to surmount the wall, and the bodies began to pile up.

An extremely tall skeletal warrior placed its left hand atop the wall and vaulted the barrier, slamming a booted foot in Botreg's chest and knocking him backward to lay helpless at the monster's mercy. Ronli and Ralav stepped up to protect the hapless dwarf, striking the skeleton's legs from under it and then decapitating it. As the head fell to the floor, the other bones lost cohesion and collapsed in a pile. Ralav hurried to take his winded comrade's place at the wall in time to toss another ghoulish warrior back into its pressing companions.

For the defenders, time stood still as they fought, their arms growing numb from constant effort. When the fighting became less intense, one companion would step back and let another take his or her place. Soon the pile of bones and armor of the attackers reached the top of the wall, and the defenders found themselves facing undead that were standing over them. Botreg dragged Ralav away from the wall, unconscious from a blow to the head. One Arm staggered backward, blood spurting from his neck like a gushing fountain. He was dead before either Hortus or Aegir could attend him.

As the attackers gained the upper hand on the weary defenders, the numbness of battle left Botreg's mind, and he saw a way to save them. He had just carried Ralav back and laid the unconscious dwarf with the wounded Zornet by the trap door. As he leaned his head against the wall beside a flickering torch, Botreg watched Tallon frantically fight off two undead before Hortus could add his strength to the buckling defensive line. One of the undead kicked a pile of its brethren's bones, sending a dusty mass of splintered fragments at the cleric. Hortus almost carelessly brushed his eyes before slamming his war hammer into the creature's bony pelvis, sending it reeling off the wall.

Somewhere in that instant, Botreg reacted without thinking. He grabbed the torch from its wall bracket and advanced. The dwarf called to his astonished companions to stand back and then hurled the flaming brand into the other room. The torch glanced off the undead climbing the mound of their own dead and fell into the dried mass of bones, clothing, and armor.

When a skeleton stepped on the flames, its booted foot sent sparks flying about the mound. It took but a moment for the flames to ignite and spread into a wall of fire, trapping many of the undead as they advanced on the defenders. Soon the entire room in front of the companions was ablaze, while the undead ran about blinded by the searing flames.

In the desolate thrown room Adder gasped as he saw what used to be his kindred, now gaunt undead creatures, filling the area. The dead Aloi separated their ranks, and an abomination scurried toward them. Eight giant hairy legs held a bulbous spider body four feet off the floor, but that was where the creature's semblance to a spider ended. Where eyes and mandibles should have been, a human torso rose. If the creature had been human once, it was hard to tell with skin blackened and hanging from its body. Rivulets of thick secretions leaked from the tortured body, and from its charred head large, red glowing eyes stared malevolently at the company.

The undead Aloi, their normally green-scaled skin turned a dull Shadow Lord's gray, gathered behind the creature as its many legs brought it closer to the companions gathered at the edge of the abyss.

It looked them over and in a hissing voice asked, "Why do you disturb my peace?"

Adder trembled with hatred over what had been done to his kindred.

Celedant spoke up. "We search for something that was lost years ago in this place."

As he spoke, the others prepared for battle. Baldo knelt to call on Thierry's help. The creature caught sight of the gem in Tarquin's hand - a gem that was beginning to glow brighter as the creature drew closer.

The monster's eyes flared a bright red, and it shouted in maddened glee. "The gem of Adaman - you have returned with it."

It pulled an unadorned five-foot length of mythril from a leather thong behind its back, arming the creature with both staff and sword. The wizard shuddered because in the beast's hand was the missing piece of the staff of Adaman.

"The staff can be remade," the hissing voice said joyfully. "Now I can be reborn!"

As the creature took a step closer, Celedant stepped up and addressed it in a loud, stern voice. "Stop where you are. Who are you to lay claim to the staff?"

The creature folded its legs beneath, causing the bulbous body to spread out, covering most of the floor. "I am, or rather was, Zachary, the Emperor of Zeiglon. The joining of the staff transformed me into what you see before you. I became a living nightmare to spend eternity in unending pain. The staff caused my wounds that never heal. Only your precious mortal blood can allow me comfort."

Celedant was stalling, hoping to figure a tactic that might work against such a creature.

"Then I am afraid I disappoint you, for I am not mortal," Celedant replied with a small smile.

"Maybe not, wizard, but your companions are, and any of them will do."

"I find myself mystified as to how a thing of such goodness could create such misery."

The emperor laughed. "I was never considered a good ruler by any means, and as the accursed Aedith and I struggled, the staff accidentally reassembled, revealing what it was. It overwhelmed the putrid little elf prince with the desire to rescue it from my clutches. However, I was more powerful. Aedith had languished too long under my throne, and as we fought, I seized control of the staff."

Celedant understood. "Then it wasn't the actual struggle and the rejoining of the staff that caused the destruction. It was you exerting your will on it."

The creature that had been a man smiled, showing pointed teeth. "It is such a pleasure to talk with an enlightened soul. I will dislike killing you. However, your assumption is correct. I felt the power and took control. The staff blazed in defiance, resulting in the destruction that took place, and leaving me burned as you see me now, but I saw a chance to save myself. Using the staff's power, I forced open a portal to another world and sought safety there. The staff fought against my will and drew me back, bringing along some creatures from that world by accident. When I awoke at the bottom of the cliff, I was as you see me now. It was years later that my minions discovered the staff."

"If you attempt to use it again, what will you gain?" Celedant inquired.

"I hope it will release me from the pain," the emperor answered.

"What makes you think it won't inflict an even worse fate on you?"

"That's a chance I am willing to take."

"It will doom this world if you do."

Zachary's maniacal laugh echoed. "I would gladly destroy this world to end my pain. Then I will escape to the Void and the rich worlds that lie therein."

"I might be able to help," Celedant said as he lowered his staff, unleashing its power.

A bright green burst of energy flew from the wizard's staff, enveloping what used to be the emperor of Zeiglon. The creature howled in agony as the energy washed over him, but holding the staff like a shield, Zachary parted the energy, and it flowed around him. The wizard's fire incinerated the undead Aloi behind him, but even more crowded into the room. Azimuth added his own fiery power, but it, too, flowed harmlessly around the evil emperor, destroying more of his undead minions.

Morganna tapped Baldo on the shoulder where he knelt. "Why don't you try your clerical magic?"

"Certainly."

Holding his magical hammer before him, the dwarf called on his deity. "Thierry, deliver us from these creatures."

The hammer began radiating a vibrant light, and the creature that had been Zachary recoiled in pain, while the remaining undead in the room disintegrated. They fell screaming into small mounds of dust blown over the cliff by the storm-driven winds, but were soon replaced by even more.

The spidery beast recovered from the cleric's attack and scuttled back, one arm wielding a crooked sword while the other held the mythril staff of Adaman. Adder and Eldahir ran to meet the monster's charge. The apprentice shaman shot several magical darts at it before the monster was upon them. Eldahir struck out with his sword, severing one of the long hairy legs. The creature struck with the speed of lightning. Drawing back its sword over its left shoulder, it struck out at Adder, forcing the lithe lizard man to skip backward out of the sword's path, but Adder was too slow. The blade landed a powerful blow to his shoulder, driving him to the ground.

Still more undead filled the room. Celedant climbed upon two fallen stone blocks, keeping the enemy at bay with his sword as he cast spell after spell into the mass of undead creatures. His sword lopped off heads as they attempted to scale the stones, while flames and energy rays blasted from the wizard's staff, burning his adversaries. An undead Aloi climbed the stone from behind and slashed at the wizard's leg. Luckily, Celedant's robe took the impact of the dulled blade that swept the wizard off his feet to crash down on the dusty stone. His leg bruised by the blow, he was slow to get up, but the undead used the time to their advantage and gained the top of the stone. Celedant felt them clawing at him and several weak blows. Azimuth rushed to his side, and the two of them used swords and staff to clear the area.

The blow stunned Adder, and his entire right side lost all feeling. He looked at his arm to find it hanging from his body by a thin strip of tissue. Instinct took over as he felt more than saw the spider rise and attempt to trample him underfoot. Ignoring excruciating pain, the apprentice shaman rolled away from the spider before fading into unconsciousness. Meanwhile, Eldahir struck at another leg, severing it. When he saw the staff held high and poised to strike, Eldahir raised his sword to parry the overhead blow, and as the two weapons met, there was a small explosion. The elf watched in horror as the blast blew apart his ancient blade. Shards of the sword flew in every direction, many directly into the monster. One struck the elf in the chest with enough force to drive the warrior to his knees, and a backhand blow from the monster's staff sent him siding across the floor into the base of a crumbled wall.

Separated from her friends by the undead creatures, Ress knew her spear would be useless against them. She dropped it and drew her sword and broad axe. Entering the fray, she angled toward Tarquin, balanced on the edge of the precipice. She hacked and slashed at the undead, driving them away, watching the monstrous spider skirt her comrades in a desperate attempt to reach Tarquin.

Seeing their comrades rush to meet the oncoming spider, Baldo and Morganna launched themselves at its undead allies. Morganna wove her way through their ranks, dodging the slower blows of the undead Aloi still pouring into the room and using the keen edge of her sword, severing arms, heads, and legs

266

from her foes. While the former dark elf looked like a dancer dealing long-awaited death to the Aloi, Baldo was more akin to a bull. The dwarvan cleric lowered his shoulder and barged through the ranks of the undead, his magical hammer destroying foes left and right. Sometimes he engaged his enemy singly, or he would let fly his hammer to soar across the room, slamming into entire lines of the undead as they advanced. His weapon would leave a body-strewn path of destruction wherever it flew before returning to his hand.

Throughout the confrontation, Hority continued his attacks on the undead. Once he neared Zachary and dealt the monster a blow with his branch. The impact caused the former emperor enough pain to look back to see the danger, but by then Hority was back amid undead, laughing as he fought.

Into this maelstrom of battle, the spider creature summoned his undead followers, who, seeing the destruction in the chamber, fought to overcome the control that Zachary, last Emperor of Zeiglon, had on them. These undead slipped away from battle, leaving their master and those still tied to him to the deadly magical forces being flung about the room.

At the cliff's edge, the former emperor cornered Celedant. Ress had run to grab onto the rope that secured her friend. It was all she could do to keep Tarquin from falling into the abyss. Tarquin was beginning to give up at untying the rope from around his waist when the wizard launched another magical attack. Calling on his abilities, Celedant cast a series of spells, arranging it so that one would strike after the other. He hoped that if the being could counter the first or second, the following spell would catch it off guard. With his first spell, he directed a beam of energy at Zachary. The air shimmered as the energy reached the monster and struck its midsection. Spittle flew from the creature's maw, its foul breath driven from its lungs. However, its clawed legs dug into the marble floor, screeching louder than howling wind as it slid backwards.

The creature sneered at the wizard's attempt and took another step before a cold wind swept in from behind to engulf the creature. A ten-foot square of billowing cold encircled it, and Celedant watched as ice formed over Zachary's deformed body. The spell lasted ten seconds before the storm's wind dissipated the swirling cold. What remained was a frozen statue of the monster. Celedant was about to call off the third spell when he noticed one leg move and an inch-thick covering of ice fall to the marble floor. The creature flexed its legs, releasing itself from the ice and shrugged its burned shoulders, freeing itself.

The third spell struck, engulfing the creature in a wall of fire, bathing it in flames. The wizard could see its body writhing in pain. Yet, it gathered itself, holding the staff aloft; the former emperor absorbed the fire with the staff of Adaman and counterattacked, forcing Celedant to throw up a hastily made defensive shield. Zachary lowered the staff and turned the fire of Celedant's spell against its maker. The blast of flames slammed into the shield, but it hit with such intensity that it threw the wizard into Tarquin. Celedant lay dazed and singed by the blast as Tarquin tipped backward off the edge of the cliff.

It was difficult to hold onto the gem and his sword as he tried to cut himself free of the rope. At last, he sheathed the sword and took out his dagger, but then the wizard slammed into him. Tarquin fell for what seemed like an eternity before the rope caught, and he jerked to a halt. Battered against the cliff face and trying to catch his breath, he swung suspended a hundred feet below the cliff edge. Fifteen feet across from him was the finger-thin spire of rock where the throne had once stood; below was the sound of crashing waves. He got his bearings and braced his feet against the wall. Shaking his head, he noticed that he had dropped his dagger but luckily held onto the gem. Then he looked up.

At the edge of the cliff stood Zachary, last emperor of Zeiglon, in his spidery form. Tarquin looked about, but there was no place to hide. The cliff face was smooth and unbroken down to the waves that smashed at the deadly base of rocks. The creature skittered over the edge, its claw-tipped legs finding purchase even on the slippery rock face. Tarquin could do nothing but wait. Holding the gem in his left hand, he drew Dragon Bolt.

In the defenders' chamber several undead cleared the wall before the fire took hold, and these fought to the end. The heat of the flames drove the defenders back to the next chamber. It was the last but for the sewers that lay behind the trap door. They were exhausted and lay on the floor while the fire burned out in the next room. Feeling his age, Hortus leaned against the doorjamb, watching the fire, but something told him the Shadow Lords had had enough. They would come themselves the next time. Worn down, the party did not have much fight left in them. Yet, they knew that they must hold for as long as they could to ensure that Celedant and Tarquin could complete their mission.

Chapter Forty-Three

The spider glided down the cliff face angling toward its prey's until it was under the dangling human. Tantalizingly, Zachary could see the object that he imagined would end his pain. Likewise, Tarquin could feel the power as the two parts of the staff of Adaman drew closer. The call of the gem made the creature unwary, and it moved too close to the human, who struck out with his sword. The ancient blade flared with power as it arched at the monster, cutting a deep wound into the human torso. The spider creature danced back and roared in fury, the sound louder than crashing thunder.

It came at Tarquin again. This time it led with its sword, and the two blades clashed, sizzling and sparking as the prince slammed into the cliff wall, knocking the wind out of him. Then the spider was upon him. Huge claws struck, but Tarquin managed to fend them off, severing two of the claws and sending them hurtling into the sea. The monster was reeling; already half his legs had been hacked from its body, and now desperation and the ever-increasing lure of the gem kept it clinging to the wall. A disgusting fluid seeped from his wounds, burning Tarquin's skin whenever it splashed on him.

Keen to retrieve the gem and unite the staff, the monster still attacked. As the battle continued, both combatants knew this was a fight to the death. Tarquin, the rope attached to his waist, was pinned to the wall with Zachary practically straddling him. They parried and thrust with swords until the creature struck with the staff. The five-foot mythril staff came at Tarquin as he held off the other's sword with his own.

He had no option but to throw up his left arm to block the downward blow he never felt. As the staff neared the gem, there was a flash of light, and for the two combatants, it felt as though time stood still. The space they occupied became a bubble of quiet with the rain and wind no longer buffeting them. The monster's downward swing slowed, and the staff wrenched free of his grip and floated between them as the gem left Tarquin's hand to join with its ancient partner.

The silence was deafening as two mortal enemies who had been trying to kill each other now stared transfixed at the transformation taking place before their eyes. The gem gently rotated, shining with light from within, reflecting its many facets across the cliff wall. When it touched the end of the staff, there was a brilliant flash of light as the two became whole once more, and the Staff of Adaman, the staff of a god, floated between the former emperor of Zeiglon and the young man of the prophecy.

Both were mesmerized. Tarquin shook himself from his trance and acted first. He thrust out his left arm and caught hold of the staff, feeling its power surge through his body. Being mortal, it was almost too much. Seeing the human grasp the staff, Zachery screamed and latched onto it with his charred hand. A brief struggle ensued before both combatants realized that the real fight would be waged within their souls. The essence of both ebbed and flowed in a battle of wills within the invisible void created by the Staff of Adaman as each tried to control the staff.

In his mind's eye, Tarquin saw himself depicted as a white warrior and the emperor as the dark loathsome warlock he had been centuries ago. In a realm beyond thought, he saw their representations battle as the two wills strove for control. In that battle, Tarquin's sword, Dragon Bolt, blazed like dragon fire. Acting of its own will to protect its master, it struck the emperor, who struck back using a wickedly curved sword that he had not wielded since that epic battle long ago. They fought for what seemed like hours in that unknown realm, while their bodies remained suspended on the side of the cliff without any time truly passing. Azimuth and the others stood by and watched helplessly. Only Azimuth and Celedant saw the battle taking place in that other realm, and the wizard prayed to all the gods that he knew that Tarquin's human soul would win the struggle.

The voice of the Dragon's Tear entered Celedant's mind.

Now is the time to act, Celedant. Infuse the boy with your power and strength. For as pure of heart and soul as he is, alone, he is not strong enough to defeat the evil he battles. It is why the two of you were joined for this quest. If Zachary takes control of the staff once more, it will bring about the total destruction of your world.

Having also heard the warning, Azimuth turned his head sharply and gazed into Celedant's eyes, his expression one of amazement and shock.

Tarquin could sense that the emperor was far more evil than he expected and had more strength and power than he had ever fought against. As the battle of wills raged, he knew that what had once been Zachary was inevitably winning the contest.

It was then that he felt such an overwhelming influx of power, it made him dizzy, but instead of losing his grip, he felt it strengthening him, and Celedant's words filled his mind.

Fear not, young Tarquin. I am with you. My strength is yours. My will binds us together, and together, we will win this battle over evil.

As the mental message sounded in Tarquin's mind, the gem flared so bright, it blinded almost everyone looking at it, and it brought Tarquin back for a brief second to the material world. He looked at his foe and saw the smirk of success on the monster's face, but he also noticed that they both had let down their guard as their wills battled. Both swords hung limply at their sides while their left hands remained locked on the staff. Using newfound strength, the wizard had infused him with, Tarquin struck with his sword. The blade flared bright red as it bit into the emperor's flesh and through the bones in its elbow, severing the limb.

For a moment, he returned to the other dimension where the battle of their wills had begun. As in the real world, the creature had lost contact with the staff, and its mind was pulling back to reality. Tarquin now felt his and Celedant's combined will taking control of the artifact and becoming one with it.

The creature stared in horror at its severed arm and at the claw that still gripped the staff. Then as Tarquin raised the staff in triumph, Zachary's hand began smoking and burst into flames. Although he and Celedant were joined in will, the prince was not a wizard, and he was unable to use the staff and its power. Therefore, he struck the monster with his sword.

Above the titanic struggle between good and evil, Celedant stood precariously on the edge, waiting for the moment when he must recall his power before it overwhelmed Tarquin. Once more he called to him telepathically. *Throw the staff straight up in the air. It will come to me, and we can conclude our mission.*

Tarquin heard the call through the battle haze that gripped him. He struck at the monster while pushing away from the wall to throw the staff like a javelin toward Celedant. When the Emperor realized what the young man was about to do, he howled and slammed the prince into the cliff wall. Dazed, Tarquin saw nothing but stars, but thanks to the wizard, he retained enough presence of mind to throw the staff as instructed.

What happened next was like a perfectly choreographed dance. Celedant released Tarquin from his will and drew all his power back into himself. Sensing this and knowing that its new master awaited it, the staff took on a life of its own and flew straight into the wizard's outstretched hand, practically jolting Celedant off the edge of the cliff. The rush of power was so fierce that it made him feel like a god. Once more, the voice of the Dragon's Tear entered his mind.

Choose, great wizard! Will thou be a god? Or will thou retain thy immortality as a wizard?

The question warred within Celedant's mind. The thought of becoming a god was overwhelming. Under normal circumstances, it was a choice he would decline without much thought, but now? The added power of the staff was a temptation almost too great to refuse. He might have become lost within it, but using their lifelong bond, Azimuth remained connected to his friend, knowing that the Dragon's Tear could sway the wizard in the wrong direction. He must intercede. Only a dragon of immense power and magic could overpower the Dragon's Tear.

Remember the choices you made when you were within the Dragon's Tear, my friend? You must continue to be true to your soul, Azimuth told him.

As a god, however, I could drive this evil from our world, Celedant replied as the voice of the Tear continued to tempt him.

That may be so, Celedant. Kill the emperor now, destroy Taza, and annihilate the vampire elves. Then what? Go after the orcs, the giants, and every race that does not agree with the races of light? After all that, would you still be satisfied to return to what would now seem to be a mundane life of a wizard? Would you then become this world's ruler? Or would you enter the Void and seek other worlds to destroy their evil? Would you unwittingly upset the balance of power?

Azimuth's words rang true, bringing Celedant back to reality. He did not want to become a god. That was never his intention. Too many times in the past, he had felt that there were too many gods already. Taking a deep breath, the wizard knew what he had to do.

Azimuth silenced the voice of the Dragon's Tear. *Away with your vile temptations! This wizard has passed your test. His true nature as a being of light has won. You no longer have the right to try to sway him.*

I do! the Dragon's Tear shouted back.

No, you do not. I, Azimuth, the King of all Dragonkind, order you to be silent. If you refuse to comply, I will lead a legion of my dragons to your domain and destroy you. We created you, and thus we can destroy you.

Then who will test the worthiness of the wizards? the Tear asked in arrogance.

We can always make another. One who will be more obedient to its masters.

Beaten into submission, the Dragon's Tear receded to its tower.

His mind clear and his goal firmly set, Celedant called upon his power as a wizard and pointed the bejeweled headpiece at the former emperor. The gem glowed a blinding golden yellow that became a solid pulsing beam of light. It reached out and struck Zachary in the chest. The blast of energy released by the staff hurled the monster backward, slamming him against the rock wall and dislodging a slim pinnacle of several tons of rock that fell into the ocean.

Tarquin, his head recovered from the impact of the cliff, scrambled to keep his position, while the former emperor held desperately with one claw dug into the stone. The light from the staff had torn a huge hole in its chest, and white rib bones were clearly visible. Yet, it was not dead. Indeed, earlier it had claimed immortality.

It reared up on its last legs in an effort to bring its grotesque bulk down on the human to crush him. Recognizing its intentions, Tarquin, with the climbing rope still clinched about his waist, could not move. He was trapped. Holding his glowing sword out as a last defense, he prepared to meet the monster's attack one final time. When the dark bulk came hurtling toward him, his sword penetrated deep into the monster's grotesque head.

A dark shadow fell over both combatants. Giant wings buffeted the cliff wall, and for a second, Tarquin thought that a draven had come. What he saw, however, was a dragon's golden head, jaws wide open and white teeth sparkling in the magical light of the staff. The dragon took the monster in its mouth and soared out to sea. Azimuth released his hold on the leader of the shadow lords, and Tarquin saw a bright gush of dragon fire. With a final wail, Zachary, the last Emperor of Zeiglon met his eternal end, leaving nothing but foul ash to float down to the surface of the ocean.

As Tarquin stared at the pyrotechnics, Azimuth's peaceful voice entered his head. *Would you like a ride?*

"Yes, please," Tarquin replied with relief.

Hold on. I am coming, Azimuth said as he flew across the expanse of sea he had traveled.

As Tarquin reached up to pull himself to a better position, his eyes widened. Sometime during the desperate battle, the rope had frayed or been cut. He reached up, clawing desperately for the end of the rope above the part unraveling far too fast, but before he could reach, it snapped, and he plummeted through the air toward the water below.

"Tarquin!" His name was screamed by everyone as they watched their friend fall toward death on the jagged rocks below.

Celedant! Azimuth's yell entered the wizard's head. *I cannot reach him in time!*

The wizard reached out with his own power, but his first use of the Staff of Adaman had drained him. The most he could do was to push Tarquin away from the cliff wall and further out over the ocean. He would not hit the rocks below, but could he survive the fall and tread water long enough for Azimuth to rescue him?

That question would never be answered as a dark mist descended over the area, paralyzing everyone, including Azimuth. Within the mist, a terrifying creature appeared with a warlock on its back. It was Melgor aboard his chimera. Just as Tarquin was about to enter the water, the warlock reached out and plucked him from the air. Throwing the unconscious prince across the front of his saddle, the chimera flew off and disappeared. Only then did the mist dissipate, freeing everyone from paralysis.

Shall I go after them? Azimuth asked Celedant.

"No. It is too late. You'll never catch up with them," Celedant replied. "We have too many things that must be done first. The fate of all Muiria is in the balance."

"But Celedant, we can't let Taza get hold of him," Ress argued as she fought back tears.

By the looks on their faces, Azimuth, Eldahir, Morganna, and the others thought the same thing.

"Oh, I see," Botreg grumbled. "Now that Tarquin has done his part in reuniting the staff of Adaman, he's no longer important to this quest." His hand and emotions gripped his sword so fiercely that had it been magical, it would have hummed with power.

Celedant wanted to strike the dwarf dead for suggesting such a thing, but compassion overruled the anger fueled by the Staff of Adaman. "That's untrue. Tarquin is just as important to this quest as ever. Shall I remind you of the prophecy's words? His voice changed to sound exactly like that of the crazed human woman who, with her dying words, bespoke the fate of Muiria to come:

"Know ye creatures of light that an evil greater than that of the Zeiglon Empire shall arise to overrun the world and turn it to darkness. To combat this evil, the gods shall bring forth a child of royal Parthian blood who, with the help of a powerful wizard, shall bring about the downfall of this threat, but only if the two can reunite

the Staff of Adaman and use it for good."

The wizard's voice returned to its deeper timbre. "Tarquin is as dear to me as he is to all of you. I promise, as soon as we are able, we'll mount a search and pray we can rescue him before Taza either kills him or turns him into a vampire minion."

CHAPTER FORTY-FOUR

There was no order to the battle. Prince Thomas' frontline tried to lock their shields, but the orcs satisfied their battle lust by jumping at the lines and breaking down the shield wall. Humans and dwarves intermingled as the orcs engulfed them. Yet, they were gaining ground. The orcs, after their thwarted first charge, fell back as arrows showered their reserves. As they fought their way to the orcish defenses, Thomas stepped into a slick patch of mud formed by the rising river. To keep the orcs from firing arrows into his company, he ordered everyone to follow the orcs up the embankment.

Not all of the defenders made it up the earthen hillock, but once over the top, the massacre began along the firing platform. These orcs were for the most part archers, wearing little or no armor. Dwarves and men cut them down like wheat. The orcs they had followed into the defenses jumped into the bands of orcs sent to reinforce them. The disorganized reinforcements had trouble getting all their troops across the bridge. Thus the orc leaders beat them into lines when the routed solders vaulted into their midst.

Prince Thomas' target was the bridge, so he jumped into the packed horde of orcs. He and those that followed found themselves surrounded. He swung his sword back and forth. When he had room to fight, his sword point picked out exposed flesh, and more orcs fell. The enemy began moving for the bridge, backing away from the attacking allies. He looked where the melee had taken place and saw too many of his men down. Surrounding them, the orcs had been able to slip in from behind, felling much larger men.

He looked about for the elven soldiers, signaling them to concentrate on the bridge. Thomas did not wait to see who followed, but charged the retreating orcs onto the stone bridge. His body worked of its own accord - his sword slashing, hacking, and ramming through bodies. Standing his ground at the middle of the bridge, a wave of the deepest despair washed over him. He staggered backward, one hand clutching his forehead. The pain and forlorn was worse than when he had lost his village of Carline. The orcs began pushing his soldiers backward as they fell into a darkness of despair. One of the elves physically dragged him off the bridge and back to the courtyard of the orcan defensive wall.

There, Prince Thomas' mind cleared.

"We can hold off the spell," the elf said, "but we must remain together."

Thomas looked around the courtyard filled with dead and dying from the earlier attack. Sadly, he saw what remained of his company mixed in a defensive wall with some men and dwarves with whom they had fought together. The orcs were right on his heels as he slipped into the allies' line of shields. The fighters spanned the courtyard, facing the charging orcs as they crossed the bridge. The elves fired arrow after arrow. When they ran out, they were sent scrambling for orcan arrows abandoned by the dead.

The prince saw his company shrinking as the surging orcs pushed them back. The elves had to climb down into the courtyard; so many defenders lay dead atop the defensive wall. At one point, a Shadow Lord swooped by, firing off two arrows that struck two elves, causing them to disintegrate into dust. As Thomas gave ground, intense anger over the loss of the men, dwarves, and elves dying before his eyes replaced his fear.

His back was to the side of the stairs leading up to the ramparts; there was no more retreating. A pile of orc bodies surrounded him, and he suffered from more wounds than he could count, but he fought on as his life's blood flowed from a dozen gashes. Looking about the courtyard, the prince realized he was the only man still standing. He was beyond tired, but he pushed off the wall and charged into the orcs, intent on killing as many as he could.

High above, a Shadow Lord flew, looking for a victim. He watched as a nameless soldier pushed off a wall to hack down three orcs. For a moment, the undead flier admired the man's courage, wishing he had soldiers with such power. Then the Shadow Lord summoned an eight-foot solid metal spear and cast it down toward the man.

Thomas could not catch his breath or swing his blade anymore when a hammer-like blow struck his chest, causing a great wave of pain to lance his body. He began to topple backwards but stopped, and he realized a huge spear held him standing upright. He coughed a huge amount of blood on his chest plate, and his head lolled back. The last thing he saw was a dark figure above. Confused as to what it was, he watched as flames engulfed the Shadow Lord and a green dragon turned to spray the bridge, killing everything as the flames swept across the structure. Closing his eyes, Prince Thomas, the last of the Carline line, died.

Vakar, one of the orc captains privately tasked by Melgor, had his soldiers spread out in a deep field of grass that led right up to the dwarvan defensives. He spied what looked like dirt piled in a circle, but it was the handy work of the dwarves. There were stone blocks at several key places and a watchtower within the wall. The main defenses were centered toward the dam. Vakar reasoned that the dwarves on the Southside would retreat this way. Now the mission was clear in his head. The maps and the way the warlock spoke proved little for the orc captain. He looked down at his little disc, which had broken, and shrugged. This would be easy. He stood motioning to his soldiers. They were twenty paces from the wall that appeared to be eight feet at its highest when the dwarves, standing guard on the watch tower, looked from the battle to their rear. Vakar's soldiers were already climbing the wall.

Most of the defenders fought in the main battle. Those remaining turned to see hundreds of orcs climbing the wall with more behind. Dwarves bravely charged into the attackers but were overwhelmed. Dwarvan weapons cut and sliced into orcan flesh, but they were too few. Soon all were dead.

The most casualties happened during the taking of the watchtower. Two dwarves used their crossbows efficiently until the orcs forced the trap door open. Orcan axes rose and fell, and they tossed the two guards over the side, badly wounded. The fort now belonged to the attackers. Vakar posted his soldiers, and following Melgor's orders, he waited.

Chapter Forty-Five

As the fires died down, Hortus felt rather than heard the approach of the Shadow Lords. A sense of dread overwhelmed him, and he knew that battle would soon be joined. He raised his shield by instinct and called to the others to get ready. Then, the wall that they had defended exploded in a fury, sending a shower of rocks and charred undead body parts flying everywhere. Dark bolts of magical energy cast by the Shadow Lords arced into the room, slamming into the far walls and causing the building's foundation to shudder with dust. Small bits of rock rained down on the defenders. One energy bolt landed in their midst. Its explosion threw them about like ragdolls, stunning them all. Hortus lay not fifteen feet from the demolished wall.

The smoke from the fire made it difficult even for a dwarf to see into the chamber, and the cries of his wounded companions settled ill within the healer's chest. Though his ears rang with the blast of the explosions, he heard the ominous crunching of bones coming toward him from the other chamber. The Abbot tried to get up, but then his mind focused on a nagging pain in his leg. Hortus turned his head a bit to see that his right leg ended in a bloody stump just below the knee. Shock kept the pain bearable as he looked up to see five dark shapes dart into the room. Cloaked in darkness, their bodies appeared ethereal, magically contained by the black armor they wore. Hortus dragged himself up on his knees. His efforts brought a grunt of pain from the dwarf and merciless laughter from the dark shapes.

One advanced and in a cruel voice from the depths of the abyss said, "So you thought you could hold against the Lords of Zeiglon. Rash mortals, our time is approaching, and our power grows."

Thunder echoed from outside the chamber, and even in the basement rooms of the coliseum, they heard the high-pitched squeals of the Dark Lord's monstrous mounts. There the sounds of a titanic struggle reached them, and Hortus could feel an enormous amount of magic crackling in the conflict taking place above them. The Shadow Lords he faced were clearly at a loss as to what to do or what was happening in the coliseum. They stood undecided whether to attack or withdraw. Seeing this, the Abbot drew forth his holy symbol, a small war hammer made of mythril, hung on a silver chain about his neck.

Holding it out, he called on his deity. "Thierry, aid me."

The building rocked on its foundation from the battle raging above. Meanwhile, Hortus waited patiently while the small symbol shimmered in cold blue. Meanwhile, the Shadow Lords in front of him felt the presence of Thierry's power as it coalesced in the chamber. Four turned to race to their screaming mounts, while the fifth chanted a quick spell of protection.

Once the Abbot saw them turn and run, he commanded, "Thierry - send this evil corruption of the spirit back to the abyss from whence they were summoned."

Cold blue light emanated from the mythril hammer, bathing the entire chamber in its comforting softness. Hortus's leg ceased its throbbing pain. Yet where the light brought healing to the Abbot and the companions behind him, the Shadow Lords screamed in agony. The ones that had not put up a magical defense howled in pain as the light of Thierry's power enveloped their dark visages. Their black shrouds were peeled away layer by layer, baring warped souls, and in the culmination of the spell what remained of the misshapen Shadow Lords vanished in a final scream of anguish.

Two things were left in the chamber, Hortus and the remains of the Dark Lord that had sought to protect itself by magical means. Its spell had fought off the attack but at great injury to the creature. The Abbot crawled over to the fallen Dark Lord and knelt beside what was left of the creature's face. It was a blackened and twisted parody of a human visage.

Through charred lips it rasped, "Why do you taunt me, cleric?"

Hortus laid his battle-weary hand on the creature's chest. It was nothing more than bones held together by stringy cords of flesh.

"I pity ye. I would never taunt ye."

A rough laugh escaped the creature's maw. "So righteous, little dwarf; when my kind rules here, you'll sing a different tune."

The Abbot sighed. "Before I end yer life, tell me who ye serve?"

The remains gave a choked, garbled cough. "The thing that was Zachary thought his nobles still served him. But it was not him we follow; it is the master of the staff of Adois, the Lord Taza that commands us."

At the spoken name of Taza, the Abbot could sense a power coalescing in the charred body of the Dark Lord. With lightning speed, Hortus placed the small symbol of his order over where the creature's heart had once lain and asked one more favor from his deity. Instantly the body under his hand convulsed and folded upon itself until there was nothing left but a dark stain on the chamber floor.

The power of Thierry ebbed from the talisman while pain coursed through his body. Then before him stood Thierry, shimmering in the smoke-filled room. "Me dear son, ye have served well, and it is time for ye to pass on. Yer time on this planet is over. There are other adventures awaiting ye beyond."

Thierry held out his hand and grasped the old Abbot's, bringing Hortus to stand on two whole legs, and the Abbot followed Thierry into the light. Glancing back, he saw his physical body settle gently to the floor.

Outside, a battle still raged, its echoes reaching the companions deep within the lower chambers. However, Thierry's presence had healed them all of the injuries done to their bodies. Hortus, however, had succumbed to his wounds before the deity's appearance, and tears ran down Aegir's face as he dragged the Abbot's remains back to the others.

CHAPTER FORTY-SIX

As the portion of the company withstood the attacks below the coliseum, enormous shapes made their way silently through the dark skies over Zeiglon. The dragons, Azimuth's kindred, which he had called from their faraway aeries, soared into the ruined city. Over the city, the flight split into two groups. Azimuth called one toward the cliff's edge, while the others flew to the center of the former metropolis, heading for the ruined bowl of the coliseum where they could feel an ancient and foreign power.

As they flew, they ranged out in a V-shape led by a battle-scarred brown dragon named Olrayni the Strong. They could sense as well as see the evil abominations that circled the ruined coliseum. Their minds knew that these creatures were from another dimension, called upon to despoil the planet they loved, and that they were evil.

With the sound of air whipping over their wings, the dragons attacked. Flames shot from their mouths as they passed the winged monsters. Their attack was a complete surprise to the Shadow Lords and their unearthly steeds. Three fell from the sky, leaving a flaming trail all the way to the ground, but still more rose from the ruins, ready for combat.

As the dragon flight turned, the Shadow Lords cast a variety of spells at the dragons. Many of the dragons deflected them or cast counter spells, but some struck home. Magical energy burned through the steel-like dragon scales to gash out huge wounds. Yet, the dragons did not falter. Instead, they renewed their attack, adding different spells to their dragon breath as the battle swirled in the air over the fallen city of Zeiglon.

Dragons darted into the swarm of Shadow Lords, taking hold of and grappling with their mounts as they tumbled through the air. Teeth and claws bit and scraped as each tried to kill the other. Shadow Lords cast their spells at the dragons, while in turn the dragons breathed death upon their enemies.

Dragon fire incinerated the Shadow Lords and their mounts, but the dragons suffered great wounds from energies unleashed by the Shadow Lords. Here and there about the ruins, huge bulks would plummet to the earth, trailing fire or magical energy through the air, causing the mighty dragons to crash into ruined buildings to lay dead or wounded.

It was an equal fight as monstrous forms soared and battled in the dark skies, but from the cliff, more dragons came to the aid of their brethren, and these bore riders. In the forefront came Azimuth with Celedant astride and the Staff of Adaman flaming in his hand. Lighting flashed from the staff that the wizard wielded, and a Dark Lord fell from the sky. The staff glowed with a golden hue as it approached the assembled Shadow Lords. The beast that had been Zachary had used the mythril staff to call them to its service, and now the remade Staff of Adaman had come to put an end to these fearsome beings.

Celedant knew little of the staff's true power, but he allowed his body's energy to flow through the relic and strike down the Shadow Lords. Azimuth went into a glide, and the wizard and his mount veered to engage yet another enemy. Celedant controlled himself, focusing his mind and then releasing the energy of the staff. Rays like that of the sun spun from the staff of Adaman's multi-faceted gem and sought out the abominations that Zachary had brought forth. Each lance of energy darted out to follow its prey until it struck home. At the point of contact, pure energy in the power of the staff engulfed the Shadow Lords. Both rider and steed would blink from existence, banished back to the abyss.

No longer bound by Zachary, many Shadow Lords escaped the battle, fleeing as fast as their winged steeds could carry them or hiding deep in the ruins away from the searching dragons and the wielder of the staff of Adaman. As the sun crested the eastern ocean, the dragons and the staff of Adaman ruled the skies over Zeiglon.

Meanwhile, the wounded and dead were brought to the arena where the clerics could care for them. Five dragons remained as guards.

From his black onyx throne, Taza stiffened and jerked to his feet. The gem on the Staff of Adois was so bright it came close to blinding him. Power blasted from it, engulfing the undead warlock, and for a second time, he found himself ripped from reality and propelled into the presence of his goddess. This time she did not bother with the disguise of beauty. She stood towering over him in all of her hideous blonde furred, clawed, and fanged rage.

As Taza's mind cleared, his hands slammed over his ears as Adois screamed in fury. He sank to his knees and shivered like never before.

The goddess sank her teeth into his neck, and he felt the energy of his latest feeding dissolve, leaving him weak and helpless.

"You incompetent, dim-witted, worthless fool!" she screeched. "You have lost it, and now your task will be insufferably more difficult."

The vampire dared to look up. "I...I don't understand, my queen. Your staff is still mine. Why are you angry?" He dropped his head so that his nose touched the marble floor beneath him.

"Not my staff, you imbecile! My brother's!"

That brought Taza upright. "The Staff of Adaman? But...how? I sent...."

"You sent that narcissistic despot Zachary and his incompetent band of wraiths to prevent its capture. They failed! That upstart, Prince Tarquin from my brother's prophecy, has joined the staff's two parts, and as impossible as it may seem, has survived it, thanks to the wizard. As we speak, the wizard Celedant has taken control of the staff and wields it to destroy Zackary and his minions!"

Her words were like a deathblow to Taza's black, shriveled heart.

"No!" His hands clutched his chest and once more, he fell, howling with all of the pent-up frustration that had plagued him since the beginning of his attempts to take over Muiria.

"I tried, my queen," the vampire pleaded. "I have tried everything I can think of: sent countless assassins against those two, numerous creatures of every evil manifestation to destroy them and their quest." He rocked back and forth, wailing. "Nevertheless - they failed! It's not my fault!"

Amazingly, Adois calmed herself, and after a few moments, spoke in a softer voice. When Taza looked up at her, she had assumed the beautiful countenance he had seen when they first met.

"What you say is true. Your failure isn't due to your lack of trying."

Her words eased his fear somewhat.

"Despite the incompetence of the giants, the battle for Southgard is still going in your favor, thanks in part to the warlock Melgor."

This disclosure brought a look of surprise to Taza's face. "Melgor?"

"Yes. His direct intervention with key orc commanders has turned the tide of the battle." She smiled. "In addition, he managed to be in the right place at the right time to snatch up a prize for you."

"A prize?" Taza asked, mystified. "What prize is that, my queen?"

"One that may yet turn the outcome of this war to your favor. However, I will not disclose this gift. It will be interesting to see just how and when Melgor decides to present it to you." What Adois did not tell him was that she suspected the warlock's hatred of his vampire master, and she wondered how long he would continue to serve Taza. *He is far too clever to accept the yolk you wish to bury him under,* she thought. *I will watch him closely. If he wins out over you, I may grant him my favor and make him the ruler of Muiria instead.*

CHAPTER FORTY-SEVEN

King Jordic of the giants heard the commotion despite his drunken stupor, and stumbled out of his tent. At that moment from within Southgard, a trebuchet launched a large boulder. Jordic called to his counselors, many who had secretly left the night before. Jordic's blood sprayed the ones that stayed when the 500-pound stone struck him squarely in the back.

Dargan's troops faced stiffer defenses because the orcs had no other place to go. Blood covered them as he and his fellow fighters waded into the orcish masses. In a lull, he turned to see his bugler dead with a wicked slash from neck to sternum.

At that point, the 20,000 reserves, who had hidden some ways down Hywel's Way, heard the distant blowing of war horns. These dwarves had been itching for a fight, and they jumped from their positions, racing to aid their comrades on the southern flank. They had gone a hundred paces when Dudagog's soldiers poured out of a small ravine. Both groups stared at each other for several seconds, and the orcs charged. The lead battalion of dwarves held in reserve were ambushed. There was nothing most could do but stand on the road, waiting while the battle took place on the narrow roadway ahead.

At the front of the column, the orcs gained the upper hand as they poured from the ravine. Dudagog had no idea he was facing the entire dwarvan reserve.

His soldiers tore into the dwarves, driving them in both directions. There was fierce hand-to-hand combat in the tight quarters of the road and its steep sides. Dwarves gave way in front, while the rear pushed onward. Every conceivable weapon was in use on that bloody road. Shields were broken. Wounded orcs and dwarves fell and were crushed by the surging battle. The dwarves had better armor, but the orcs canceled that advantage with speed. Dudagog lost sight of the ravine. He had ordered it held, yet still the dwarves pushed from the north. The bearded ones had formed a shield wall that ground his soldiers down. He made the decision, calling to his orcan comrades, "South, go Sou...." In the middle of his command, a well-thrown dwarvan spear brought him down.

The orcs nearest him had heard the order and fought to carry them out, killing or being killed by dwarves that had fallen back earlier. By the time the remnants of Dudagog's soldiers cleared the road, the allies that had stayed behind to man the dwarvan defenses clashed into them. Between the dwarves moving down the road and the other allies, few orcs escaped, and these ran for the small fort, hoping that their kindred tasked with the job to seize defenses were successful. The dwarvan reserve was astonished as they watched the enemy head for the northern defensive walls. Wisely, their commander ordered the reserves to take up positions until new orders came through.

Melgor's wishes had been granted. Taza had sent exactly the help he needed. The fear the Shadow Lords provoked gave the orcs time to reorganize. The orcs rallied, and even though the reserves came to aid the dwarves, the entire allied army started giving ground. The elves, however, seemed immune to this fear. Their arrows were the one effective weapon that could topple the masters of the Shadow Lands.

The battle that had once been a rout had turned. The orcs, led by their own generals instead of the brainless giants, pushed back across the river in a counter attack. The allies could do little more than put up a token defense as more and more fell to the renewed assault. Dargan watched in horror as the Shadow Lords swooped down, disintegrating the allied forces. The fear that clutched at his heart and soul made him want to escape and find a safe hiding place. The soldiers with him all had the same expressions of fright, and it was his job to lead them. He yelled, kicked them, and even struck them with the flat of his weapon. This had some effect. When the orcs came, the dwarves did not turn and run but stood their ground.

Ouhgan had watched the small dial in fascination as it clicked down to when he was to attack the dwarvan rear forces. There were ten thousand orcs getting a last minute's rest or food. Ouhgan stood up in front of his soldiers, motioning to them. His command had been for complete silence until the enemy spotted them. Ten thousand spread out as their jog broke into a run, and they neared the battle line. An odd fate of war happened when Ouhgan's soldiers reached the line. Many dwarves thought they were part of the reinforcements, and hundreds died as a result.

The orcs fought a bloody battle, felling many humans and dwarves. Even when small bands of defenders made a stand, the orcs mowed them down. This attack forced the shaken allies to break and run. Shadows flew hither and yon, taking lives with glee. The allies were being herded ever southwest toward Southgard.

The city would be the salvation for a broken army overwhelmed and broken by evil magic. Dwarves from Southgard were about to sally forth to attack the besieging army when Grimilzor's army broke. Lord Darrow reversed his orders to his troops to make a stand on the small plateau that extended from the mountain gates of the city. He would leave the orcs in the ruins of the outer wall. They took up strong positions, fighting not the orcs but more commonly the Shadows that swooped down on the fleeing army and the dwarves of Southgard. The defenders watched in horror as their kin and allies raced between their lines to reach the safety of the city. Many had thrown down their weapons while the visage on their faces spoke of horrendous deeds inflicted on them and complete fear of the Shadows.

A sense of foreboding spread across the allied army in a growing wave of fear. The allied army that had been pushing the orcs back suddenly stopped in its tracks. Some soldiers turned, running for the dwarvan walls, while others stopped in their tracks as if in a trance and struck down by their enemies. There was no doubt that these flying creatures were responsible for stalling the allied army.

Dwarves and humans regained some of their cohesion and began backing up from the strange, all- encompassing terror that these flying creatures emanated. The orcs pressured the allied army, pushing them backward, and that path became littered with dwarves and men. Dark arrows were conjured by these new terrors. Where they struck flesh, it disintegrated the soldier, who turned to ash and fell into a pile on the ground, blown away by a gust of wind.

Stationed up the southern route to the mountain were Parthian Prince Kaleb and a thousand of his lancers. Their command had been to wait until the orcan line broke, and then charge into the chaotic masses of their foes.

Kaleb addressed his captains. "See what forces we can bring to safety. We will need to fight another day."

They looked grim as several hundred headed south, sending wary dwarves, humans, elves, and Parthian foot soldiers back to the waiting safety. Kaleb had his map out, charting the best way to leave the killing fields. There was one path large enough for the horses and a small path that wound through the foothills to the safety of the east.

He gathered the remaining commanders of the foot soldiers and gave them a map. "Go. We'll round up who we can and follow."

Kaleb pointed to his aide to sound the retreat again. It was time to leave. As he turned his horse to ride off, the hissing sound of arrows filled the air, and his aide along with his horse fell dead.

The Parthian King's son felt the impact of the arrows; one pierced his boot deep into the horse. As his steed succumbed to the pain, it lurched and fell on its side, throwing the rider. With Kaleb's foot pinned to the horse, he fell at an awkward angle, snapping his leg bones. The others had raced ahead to the trail, unaware that their prince was barely alive.

He partially passed out when a jab to his ribs brought his eyes open. Standing atop Kaleb's horse stood an unimpressive orc.

"This one's alive."

In the distance, Kaleb heard the reply. The orc drew back his bow and sent an arrow through his right eye, killing the Parthian heir to the throne.

The evil shadow creatures did not forget the soldiers defending the dam with its adjoining fortress. Two dark figures plunged toward the dam and fortress, eager to spread death and destruction. As they neared the spot, the elves, who seemed impervious to the terror, stood up with bows drawn. Two flights of arrows flew through the sky, striking the Shadow Lords in midair. They fell, winked out of existence. This brought two more black figures and their hideous-looking giant dravens. Elven arrows also brought them down to slam into the lake and disappear under its placid surface.

The shadow lords did not give up. Another attacked from the west, casting large flaming bolts not at the forts but at the dam. The balls slammed into the dam with tremendous force, bending it inwards. As the dam straightened, the displaced water surged back, exposing visible cracks in the structure's stones. Hearing the stones grinding together, the allies recovered their footing and began running north toward the fort, becoming victims to a hail of arrows that flew upward and dropped amidst their ranks. When the dam broke, it bowed backwards with the massive amount of force placed on it from the expanded lake. The rush of water spelled doom for the hard-won stronghold. The men and dwarves that had run toward the larger fortress never reached the ground. They toppled with the dam, their screams diminishing as they sank below the churning water.

At that point, the Shadow Lords took care of attacking the dam and fortresses, even though the elven arrows could topple the dark creatures. One elf took aim at a vile creature, but relaxed his bow when the dark figure erupted into flames. The elf looked in surprise as twenty dragons descended like streaks of lightning from high in the sky, swooping to attack the dark shapes. The dragons flew into the dark riders that until then had ruled the skies. Soon the two groups were engaged in a titanic struggle in the heavens. Sometimes the Shadow Lords fell from the sky, and other times it was the dragons. The battle was fierce, and dark lines marked the flights of the Shadow Lords, with bright flame or blasting magic from the dragons.

The dragons knew instinctively that the evil they faced emanated from powerful foes. Maneuvering through the air in quick strikes was possibly the one chance they had against so many Shadow Lords.

In one such battle, fire shot out at a Shadow Lord, but it dodged beneath the dragon to avoid the flames. That same Shadow Lord conjured a metal spear, which it punched upward to penetrate the dragon's scales, bursting its heart. The dragon rolled and fell onto a milling mass of orcs.

In other battles, a Shadow Lord's magic encountered a blocking spell that caused a translucent circle of protection as dragon fire erupted around it. Some dragons would slam into a Shadow Lord, and then use its talons and razor-sharp teeth to slice the enemy to pieces.

Those soldiers of either side not currently involved in the battle found their eyes drawn upward to see the spectacular engagement taking place. The sun glinted off beautifully colored scales darting and weaving in the sky. The Shadow Lords slipped through the air looking more like windows into hell.

Explosions or eruptions of darkness tossed blackened and bloodied dragons downward. When a dragon mortally struck a Shadow Lord, it blinked from existence in an explosion of darkness. Badly wounded dragons, unable to keep aloft, circled downward in search of a safe place to tend their wounds.

Celedant rode Azimuth, and other dragons carried the remaining members of the quest as they raced across the parched desert that had once been Partha, flying hard to reach Southgard in time. The sun set as they sped north with the heat of the day dissipating but little. Sunrise found them in the southern mountains and foothills, and soon they crested the mountain fortress. Before them, the valley opened.

Unfortunately, they arrived too late. The valley was scorched from fire, and the dead lay where they fell. The finest dwarvan soldiers of the Empire, veterans of the fall of Brackus, lay vanquished. Spread throughout the valley were men from the Confederation. The bodies lay singularly or in heaps where fighting was most intense. Intermingled were the bodies of orcs, giants, and their kin.

As the dragons appeared, Celedant could see how the battle had gone by the positions of the dead. The army had broken and retreated in panic to the ruins of the city, many struck down from behind, leaving a trail of discarded weapons that led to the ruins of the outer town of Southgard. The outer city, defended by a smaller wall, had fallen to the enemy and lay in smoking ruins. The mountain doors remained closed tight, and he hoped that refugees from the battle had made it there safely. The once-fertile valley and farms that had dotted the land were nothing more than piles of charred ruins.

Southgard stood. The stronghold of the dwarves was now a bastion surrounded by a sea of death. The guards walking the battlements of the mountain city froze with fear when they spotted the dragons, until they realized who was riding them. They flew low over the valley, scattering small groups of orcs looting the dead. One of the dragons told Azimuth of the great battle that had taken place between them and the Shadow Lords. Azimuth relayed the message to the Celedant, who informed the others, gesturing to the North to show where the dwarves held the passes.

With no leadership after the battle, many orcs had gone into the Mordolwyn Mountains. However, most fell back to the west to return to their homes. The dam that had once held the small beautiful Lake Mirowmir was destroyed. Now the river formed a waterfall from the broken masonry of the dam to the depths below. Azimuth ordered the dragons to sweep the valley, ridding it of the vile orcs.

As they approached, dwarves and their allies rushed from the gates of Southgard, cheering as the dragons circled. Celedant, Azimuth, and other dragons carrying the members of the quest settled down in the courtyard outside the mountain's gates. Grimilzor hurried to greet Celedant as he dismounted from Azimuth. The two met and embraced, both looking the worse for wear following the battles they had fought.

Grimilzor motioned toward the valley and asked, "Could this have been avoided?"

"No," Celedant replied sadly. "But now we have the key." He motioned to the Staff of Adaman. "With this, we can hopefully ward off further evil."

Gazing into his font, Taza watched as each side limped away to regroup and lick their wounds.

"So, the dragons have joined the battle. I knew that they would, sooner or later." He thought a moment before removing the scene before him and returning to his throne.

"Melgor should be contacting me soon about his 'surprise.' Whatever that is. When he does, I will give him his new instructions. It is time to take the fight to Dragon Isle. Once I destroy the dragons, wizards, and sorceresses there, the others will have no choice but to concede to my rule, or die."